THE BISHOP'S BROOD

THE BISHOP'S BROOD

Simon Beaufort

This first world edition published in Great Britain 2003 by
SEVERN HOUSE PUBLISHERS LTD of
9–15 High Street, Sutton, Surrey SM1 1DF.
This first world edition published in the USA 2003 by
SEVERN HOUSE PUBLISHERS INC of
595 Madison Avenue, New York, N.Y. 10022.

British Library Cataloguing in Publication Data

Beaufort, Simon
   The Bishop's brood
   1.   Mappestone, Geoffrey, Sir (Fictitious character) - Fiction
   2.   Great Britain - History - William I, 1066-1087 - Fiction
   3.   Detective and mystery stories
   I.   Title
   823.9'14 [F]

   ISBN 0-7278-5983-8

For Gill Cooper

Except where actual historical events and characters are being
described for the storyline of this novel, all situations in this
publication are fictitious and any resemblance to living persons
is purely coincidental.

Typeset by Palimpsest Book Production Ltd.,
Polmont, Stirlingshire, Scotland.
Printed and bound in Great Britain by
MPG Books Ltd., Bodmin, Cornwall.

Prologue

It was often said that if a wicked man had the temerity to touch the sacred relics of one of God's saints, he would be consumed by holy fire and doomed to suffer the torments of Hell for eternity. Brother Wulfkill did not know whether that was true, but he did not intend to find out. When he handled the bones of long-dead martyrs, he wore gloves and always fortified himself with prayers and incantations.

The reliquary containing the remains of St Balthere lay in front of him, and he used a stick to undo the clasp and flip back the lid. He had expected to see bones, perhaps wrapped in fragments of rotting silk, and gaped in surprise when he saw the withered remnants of a large coiled snake. He crossed himself, wondering whether the very act of opening the casket had caused the saint to express his anger by turning himself into the hideous object that now occupied it. With mounting fear, he quickly slammed the lid closed.

After a few prayers, during which there was no indication that he was about to be seized by the Devil, Wulfkill summoned enough courage to look inside the casket again. Taking a deep breath, he pushed the lid open a second time, cringing in anticipation of thunder and fury from an enraged God. But nothing happened. The snake was still there, as dead and dry as leaves in winter. Wulfkill sat back on his heels, and pondered what to do next.

He had been paid – handsomely – to steal the bones and leave them in a predetermined spot for someone else to collect. Now Balthere was unavailable, Wulfkill was in trouble. He had already spent some of the payment he had received on a new roof for his sister's house and to buy

1

medicine for the poor. But he doubted whether the men who had paid him would care that these were worthy causes: they would demand Balthere or they would want their money back. And it appeared as though Wulfkill would be able to provide neither.

A crafty look came over his face as a solution occurred to him. The claim that instant death was the fate of those who touched the bones of a saint might be his protection: he would wrap the snake in the sack he had brought and say, quite truthfully, that he had removed the contents of the reliquary. He was a monk, and no one would doubt his word when he declared that he had not inspected what was inside the sack because he feared for his immortal soul. Everyone knew religious men paid heed to the kind of stories that promised eternal damnation, and Wulfkill might yet escape blame when the men who paid him realized he did not have what they wanted.

Quickly, he swallowed his revulsion, reached inside the casket and grabbed the withered corpse. It gave a papery crackle as he touched it, and white bone gleamed through parts where the skin had rotted away. Wulfkill stuffed it inside his sack and secured it with a piece of twine.

Aware that time was passing, Wulfkill closed the lid and eased the reliquary back into its niche in the high altar. With a dusty hand he rubbed away evidence that it had been moved, then walked towards the door. Of the whole venture, the most risky part was where he might be spotted by a parishioner, leaving his church in the depths of the night with a bulging sack over his shoulder.

But it was very late, and the city was silent in sleep. Even in winter, there was work to be done in the fields, and the folk who lived in the seedy shacks nearby were too weary to spend their nights watching the comings and goings of others at the witching hour. Wulfkill left the church unseen, and hurried towards the river to begin the long walk to the agreed hiding place.

It was nearly dawn by the time he approached the spot where the men had ordered him to leave Balthere. He began to relax, knowing the ordeal was almost over, and that he would soon be able to retrace his steps and spend the rest of the day dreaming about how he would use the remainder of his wages. He had just imagined himself buying a position as house priest to some undemanding widow, when he became aware that he was not alone. He spun around in alarm, trying to see whether he had been followed.

There was nothing to see. But when he resumed walking again there was a sharp crack followed by a thud, and he felt something strike him in the chest. It was not a hard punch, and it did not even make him stagger. Yet, when he glanced down, there was a crossbow bolt protruding from his ribs. He was just berating himself for not realizing sooner that he would never be allowed to live after what he had done, when he hit the ground. He died where he fell, and shadowy figures emerged from the nearby trees to take possession of the bundle he carried.

3 February 1101, London

Odard waited at the foot of the White Tower in the fortress that stood on the banks of the River Thames. It was a cold night, and a bitter wind sliced across the cobbled courtyard, bringing with it flurries of snow. But Odard remained motionless, and only the faint gleam of his eyes indicated he was alert and watchful.

It was very late, although dull yellow lights glowed dimly from the prisoner's chamber high above. Occasionally, there was a raised voice and laughter, suggesting the prisoner was not sitting in weary solitude in a dismal cell, but enjoying a butt of good malmsey with his guards. It was not often that the White Tower held a man as important and powerful as Ranulf Flambard, Bishop of Durham, and the castellan had been told to treat him with courtesy. Compared to most folk, Flambard's prison was a palace. It was sumptuously decorated and there was always a fire blazing to ward off the chill of a long winter. He also had fine food delivered daily and wore the rich, warm robes that befitted a man of his wealth and status.

Outside, Odard continued to wait. Eventually, the lights in

3

Flambard's cell were doused, and the sounds of merriment faded away. A dog barked from the sewage-impregnated alleys that comprised much of England's largest city, and then even that was stilled. Clouds obscured the moon, so Odard was all but invisible as he continued his patient vigil in the shadows.

Because it was an icy night, the Tower guards were loath to leave the watch room for their patrols. When their sergeant insisted, they moved in resentful pairs along the wall-walk, glancing into the darkened bailey below, and at the shiny black waters of river and moat on the other side. There was nothing to see, and they hurried inside again gratefully. The King was away, so the garrison left to defend the Tower was small. But no one anticipated trouble, and everyone knew that escape was impossible for the bishop or any other prisoner locked inside.

A cat slunk across courtyard cobbles that were beginning to sparkle with frost. Odard readied himself. It was almost time. He left his hiding place and walked quickly to the barbican gate. It was closed, but the wicket door had been left unbarred, as arranged. Just outside, he heard the soft snicker of a horse, nervous at being saddled up and made to wait so late at night. Not far away was the watch room, where deep, gruff voices rumbled within. Odard edged closer, until he was able to peer through a gap in one of the window shutters. He counted the guards, and saw they were all inside, vying for space near the flickering fire.

He walked back to the Tower and glanced up. Flambard's window was open, and he could see the dark outline of a head as it leaned out. Then there was a soft hiss, and something dropped. It was a thin rope, which uncoiled as it fell and swung this way and that like a pendulum. Odard frowned. It was not long enough, and dangled at least the height of three men from the ground. He tried to gesticulate, to tell Flambard to abandon his escape until more rope could be smuggled in another barrel of wine that he would share with his friendly guards.

But it was too late: the bishop was already climbing out of the window. Odard tensed, all the cool detachment he

4

had displayed during his earlier wait vanished. Flambard's feet scrabbled against the wall, so loudly that Odard was certain the guards would hear and come to investigate. Then one of the waiting horses whinnied, long and piercing, and he closed his eyes in despair at the racket.

And, as if that were not enough, the bishop began to curse and swear as he climbed. Odard gazed upward, willing him to be quiet. King Henry would not be pleased to learn that his most auspicious prisoner had managed to extricate himself from the most secure fortress in the country, and if Flambard were caught, then Henry would exact revenge in a way that only a son of the Conqueror could, and the bishop would be lucky if he ever saw the light of day again. And Odard would fare worse: it was treason to help a prisoner escape, and punishment would be severe and inevitably fatal.

Flambard's curses grew even more profane when he came to the end of the rope and realized it did not reach the ground. Odard could see him hanging there, eyes wide with horror when he saw the hard cobbles were still far below him. And then he slipped. Odard darted forward to try to break his fall, but he landed hard and awkwardly nevertheless. Flambard's cursing became gasps of pain, and, when he tried to stand, he found he could not walk.

'This is a disaster!' he hissed, his face a twisted mask of agony. He held out his hands. 'You did not provide me with gloves, and the rope has ripped the skin from my palms.'

'We must hurry,' whispered Odard, refraining from pointing out that Flambard could have remembered the gloves himself. It did not take a genius to anticipate that rough rope would be hard on hands that had never done a day's honest work.

'I cannot walk,' declared Flambard imperiously. 'My ankle twisted when I fell, because the rope *you* sent was too short.'

Odard was beginning to wish that the ungrateful prelate had broken his neck, not merely hurt a foot. But he kept his thoughts to himself, and took Flambard's arm to help him to the gate. He found he was obliged virtually to carry him across the courtyard, and his breath came in short, agonized gasps

5

– years of good living had turned Flambard's once athletic frame to the contented flabbiness of middle age, and he was heavy. The bishop was in the very act of grabbing the handle on the wicket gate to open it, when the watch-room door was flung open and four soldiers spilled out.

'You told me they would relax their patrols after midnight,' whispered Flambard accusingly. 'Do you not realize what will happen to me if I am caught trying to escape?'

Odard said nothing, but pulled him deeper into the shadows as the guards came nearer. They chatted in low voices for a moment, before splitting into pairs to begin their rounds. One walked directly to where Flambard and Odard hid, evidently intent on checking whether the wicket gate was locked. Odard's heart thumped so loudly he was certain the watchmen would hear, and it was almost painful. He was tempted to abandon the bishop and make a dash for the gate, to leap on to one of the horses and escape while he could. But he did not. He was a Knight Hospitaller and under orders from the Grand Master himself to serve Flambard. Hospitallers were not men who broke oaths of obedience just because they were frightened. He watched the soldier walk to the gate, glance up at the bar that secured it, then go to join his comrade on the wall-walk.

Odard almost swooned with relief, and was moving towards the wicket gate almost before the guard had turned the corner and was out of sight. Outside were four horses. He helped Flambard on to one and mounted another himself. The remaining pair already carried two other stalwart Hospitallers, who would escort the bishop to a ship bound for Normandy. The White Tower was still, silent and brooding when they galloped away from it, heading for the coast.

One

E ven on a cold February afternoon, when the sun had slipped behind a bank of clouds that threatened more snow and the wind sliced from the north as keenly as a Saracen's scimitar, the wharves at Southampton hummed with activity. Merchants strode along the narrow streets that ran between the waterfront and their warehouses, apprentices scurrying in their wake. Soldiers marched this way and that, some going to relieve the guards on the town walls, others returning from patrols into the surrounding countryside, and sailors gathered in noisy, crowded inns where fights broke out. And above it all, gulls screamed, soared and squabbled over the remnants of the day's catch that had been tossed into the refuse-littered water.

Sir Geoffrey Mappestone noticed with distaste that even a hard winter frost could not lessen the rank stench he always associated with ports. Not only was there the gagging odour of rotting fish, crushed and trodden into the churned mud that formed most of the streets, and the ever-present reek of sewage, but there was also the pungent stink of the hot pitch that was used to seal ships' timbers. And there were other smells, too, lurking under the foulness: spices and exotic herbs from southern France, the heady scent of an accidentally punctured barrel of wine, and the damp earthiness of wool waiting to be exported to the Low Countries.

Riding next to Geoffrey, Sir Roger of Durham hummed to himself. He was pleased to be leaving England for the sun and dust-scented air of the Holy Land. Four years before, the two knights had been part of the Crusade to wrest Christianity's most sacred places from the infidel, where they had survived

7

hunger, thirst, searing heat, freezing cold, disease, flies, and even the occasional battle. When the Crusade was over, and the Western princes had established their own little kingdoms in the desert, Geoffrey and Roger had returned to England. Geoffrey had gone to pay his respects to his dying father, while Roger had used his Holy Land loot to enjoy the taverns of London. Geoffrey's father had died, and Roger found that he pined for the adventure and excitement of Jerusalem, and so both were in Southampton to find a ship to take them back.

'Look at that!' Roger exclaimed suddenly.

Geoffrey glanced to where he pointed, and saw two men engaged in a skirmish on the roof of a merchant's house. In the dull light he could see the glint of metal as knives flashed and swiped. Roger was not the only one to have noticed the action: a crowd of onlookers gaped in ghoulish fascination at the two combatants. Their excited chattering encouraged more people, and Geoffrey was forced to rein in his warhorse or risk having it trample someone. Roger muttered blackly at the delay, although his eyes were fixed with interest on the ducking, weaving figures on the roof.

'Who are they?' Roger asked of a man who wore a bloodstained fishmonger's apron, shiny with silver scales. 'What led them to this?'

'They are a couple of sailors, I should imagine,' said the fishmonger, wiping hands that were red-raw with cold on his tunic as he gazed upward. 'Seamen always spoil for a fight when they get paid.'

'It will be a fatal one unless they call a truce,' observed Geoffrey, wincing as one combatant lost his footing and started to roll down the thatching. 'What a ridiculous situation to have put themselves in.'

The fighter's downward progress was arrested when he used his knife to stab at the roof. He had barely regained his balance before his assailant was on him again. His attacker was older than he, and less agile, but the younger man seemed to have hurt himself in his tumble, and one arm was held at an awkward angle. Assessing the two with a professional eye,

Geoffrey saw that while the younger had the stance of a man who had been taught to fight, his injury would impede him, and that the older man's grim but undisciplined determination would probably see him the victor.

'Look out behind you!' roared Roger, siding with the injured man.

His warning came just in time. The youngster twisted to his left, and the lethal sweep that had been aimed at his unprotected back whipped harmlessly past. His opponent advanced, wielding the knife purposefully. Even from a distance, Geoffrey could see murderous intent written in his every move.

'Come on, Roger,' he said, tugging on the reins to ease his horse away. 'I see no pleasure in watching a pair of drunkards trying to kill each other.'

'Can you not?' asked Roger, genuinely surprised. He shook his head at his friend. 'For a knight, you have some very odd ideas! There is nothing wrong with a bit of innocent bloodsport.'

Geoffrey did not want to argue. He turned his horse around, but his men – faithful Sergeant Helbye and six fellows from his manor of Rwirdin on the Welsh border – were among the gawking spectators, and they blocked his path.

'Come away, Will,' said Geoffrey, addressing Helbye impatiently. 'I do not want to miss a sailing because of a street fight.'

'Attack, boy, attack!' boomed Roger. 'You will not beat him by backing away!'

The older brawler meant business. He feinted to his right and then lunged to his left, so that only the quicker reactions of his opponent prevented him from being skewered. There was a gasp from the crowd as the youngster tottered, then righted himself, holding his injured arm awkwardly.

'Do not retreat!' Roger's voice was loud enough to be heard in France. 'Stand your ground!'

'The staff!' the youngster yelled, when a glance at the crowd told him two knights were among the spectators, and one of them was trying to help him. 'He wants to take the staff!'

'Do not babble!' shouted Roger. 'Concentrate, and do not take your eyes off your opponent.'

'The staff,' pleaded the youngster, gazing at Roger with what seemed to Geoffrey to be desperation. 'Make sure Brother Gamelo does not get the staff!'

'Who is Brother Gamelo?' asked Roger of Geoffrey. 'And what staff does he mean?'

'I have no idea,' said Geoffrey, amused that Roger imagined he would know. 'It is you he is speaking to, not me.'

'Well, I do not know what he is blathering about,' muttered Roger impatiently. He watched the lad parry a blow, and began to bawl instructions again. 'Do not just stand there! Use your dagger!'

'Do not let Gamelo take it!' the young man all but screamed.

He was about to add more, but his opponent dived, a knife flashed briefly and the youngster dropped to his knees clutching his shoulder. There was another gasp from the crowd as he pitched forward and began to roll down the sloping roof. Moments later, there was a soggy crunch as he landed on the street below.

When Geoffrey looked from the crumpled body back to the roof, he saw the older man had taken advantage of the fact that all eyes had been on his stricken opponent, and had escaped. He was nowhere to be seen, and Geoffrey supposed he had slid down the other side of the roof and fled.

The spectators surged forward, wanting to see the corpse of the man who had been knifed before their very eyes, while Geoffrey sighed tiredly and rested his hands on the pommel of his saddle, knowing he would not be going anywhere as long as the mob hemmed him in so tightly. His black and white dog, resenting the uninvited proximity of so many people, growled and nipped unprotected ankles, so Geoffrey soon had a small clearing around him. A few indignant people looked as if they might consider kicking the animal, but a glance at the tall, well-built knight who wore the Crusader's cross on his surcoat and who looked as though he had earned it, made them reconsider.

Roger shook his head in disgust, eyes still fastened on the

spot where the youngster had fallen. 'The boy should not have taken his eyes off his opponent. If he had listened to me, he would still be alive.'

Unimpressed by the whole unedifying spectacle, Geoffrey changed the subject. 'The wind has changed and I doubt any ships will be leaving today. We will have to spend the night here.'

'I know an excellent tavern,' said Roger cheerfully. 'The beds have more fleas than a pack of Holy Land mongrels, but since this is to be our last night in England, we will spend it romping with comely wenches, and will not notice the state of the mattresses anyway.'

'It had better be more pleasant than that place you recommended yesterday,' said Geoffrey, not without rancour. 'I do not want to spend half the night fending off prostitutes, and the other half repelling thieves.'

Roger guffawed. 'You should have done what I did: select one whore and let her fight off the others while you get a decent night's rest.' He leered and gave Geoffrey a dig in the ribs. 'But tonight will be different. Yesterday's offerings *were* paltry and I do not blame you for abstaining. But the lasses in Southampton are famous for their looks and charm.'

Geoffrey had heard this claim before. The big knight was an undiscerning judge of looks and charm, and generally put women into two categories: nuns and ancient dames, who were treated with a rough reverence, and the rest, who were considered fair game for his clumsy advances – whether they were world-weary ladies of the night or other men's wives or daughters. It meant he was not always an ideal travelling companion, and Geoffrey had been forced to use wits, cash, and even his sword to extricate them from a number of delicate situations on their journey towards the coast.

'There he is,' said Roger, when a stretcher bearing the broken body of the young man was carried past. 'He was a fool for fighting on a roof. Still, I suppose we live and learn.'

'He did not,' Geoffrey pointed out. He leaned forward to look more closely. 'That is odd. I saw him stabbed in the shoulder before he fell.'

11

'He was,' agreed Roger. 'And he was skewered because he allowed his attention to stray, instead of watching his opponent as I instructed.'

'In that case, why is there a crossbow bolt sticking out of his back?'

Roger and Geoffrey spent what remained of the short winter afternoon searching for a Normandy-bound ship, while the men trailed behind, bored and tired. Finally, as the daylight faded to shadows of dark grey, and Geoffrey accepted they would have no luck that evening, it began to snow. At first, there were only a few flurries, but then it started in earnest, with falling white disks the size of silver pennies. The first ones melted as soon as they touched the ground, but their successors stuck, and it was not long before the vile black slush of previous snow, churned mud, and sundry other rubbish was hidden beneath a veil of white.

Despite the fact that dusk was approaching fast, Southampton's streets still teemed with people – bands of sailors on their way to drunken belligerence, apprentices wearing the liveries of their employers, and scruffy watchmen hired to prevent breaches of the peace that became too violent or disruptive. But it was not sailors, apprentices, or guards Geoffrey saw when he looked around. It was a brief flash of someone dodging quickly down a lane. Since it was not the first time in the last hour or so he thought he had detected such a movement, he turned his horse and cantered back. However, when he reached the alley, there was nothing to see, and it wound innocently towards the wharfside warehouses. He watched for a while, staring into the shadows, but saw nothing untoward. When he finally left the lane, Roger was waiting for him with a quizzical expression on his face.

Geoffrey explained. 'I keep glimpsing someone who slips out of sight whenever I look around. We are being followed and I do not like it.'

'You worry too much,' declared Roger. 'It is probably just some thief who fancies his chances with our saddlebags when we bed down for the night. Ignore it.'

Geoffrey supposed he was right, although it did not make

him relax his guard. He took some comfort in the fact that the fellow would find dogging their footsteps increasingly difficult with the snow swirling down like a thick mist.

'We will find a ship tomorrow,' said Roger confidently, as though failure was not an option. He blinked water from his eyes. 'I have had enough of this English weather. It will not be like this in Normandy.'

Geoffrey smiled. 'It is likely to be a good deal worse. And unless a favourable wind blows, we will not be leaving here at all.'

'Your men are not happy.' Roger jerked a callused thumb behind him, to where the soldiers and Helbye formed a sullen group, huddled into their cloaks and with their hoods pulled low over their faces. Even the dog seemed resentful. It declined to take its usual place by Geoffrey's horse, and kept company with the men, as though expressing its solidarity with them. The only soldier who did not form part of the morose pack was the idiot, Peterkin; he rode with eyes shining in innocent delight at the flakes that settled on him, his slack mouth hanging open in wonderment.

'You had the pick of the men on your manor,' said Roger, eyeing the soldiers with undisguised disdain. 'Could you not find any who were more promising than this rabble?'

Geoffrey shrugged. 'I could not take men with dependants, no matter how much they wanted to come. These six have no families relying on them to provide their daily bread.'

'That is because two have spent so much time in prison they have not had the chance to woo themselves wives; two like each other more than they do women; and two are stark raving mad. I have never seen such miserable specimens in all my days!'

There was nothing Geoffrey could say, because Roger was right. The Littel brothers were inveterate thieves, and he had pressed them into service because otherwise they were due to hang. They were hard, ruthless men who Geoffrey suspected would desert as soon as they had stolen enough money to make good their escape. Freyn and Tilloy were a good deal more than friends, something Geoffrey considered irrelevant as long as they did not allow their relationship to interfere with their duties. But it was Joab and his brother Peterkin who gave him the most cause for concern. Both had the minds of children, especially Peterkin, and the more Geoffrey came to know them, the more he regretted taking them from their homes.

'That business with the roof-top fight today was odd,' said Roger, when Geoffrey did not reply to his disparaging remarks. 'How did a crossbow bolt find its way into that lad's back when you and I saw him stabbed in the front?'

'We saw him drop to his knees after he was knifed and raise his hand to the injury. Then he pitched forward and tumbled from the roof. However, since he was being attacked from the front, I would have expected him to have fallen *backward*, not forward. I suspect the shoulder wound was a mere scratch, and that the fatal injury was caused by the crossbow bolt in his back.'

'Meaning what, exactly?' asked Roger.

'Meaning someone else came along and shot him in the back, probably a friend of the knifeman.'

'It was a curious thing, that crossbow bolt,' said Roger, after reflecting on the injustice of such cowardly tactics. 'Did you see it?'

'It had been painted red,' said Geoffrey immediately. He had thought it odd that a missile should be so coloured at the time. 'Although I cannot imagine why.'

'I can,' said Roger smugly, pleased to know something his literate, intelligent friend did not. 'It had been dipped in beetroot juice.'

'Why?' asked Geoffrey, not certain whether to believe him. Roger often produced 'facts' that it later transpired had been distilled from something he had not fully understood.

'Because to stain an arrow increases its chances of success,' said Roger. 'A red one ensures you will get a stag or a boar. A white bolt – rubbed with ashes – will let you kill a hare. And one stained blue will bring down a bird from the sky. Everyone knows this where I come from.'

'But the man on the roof was not a stag or a boar. And are you sure you do not know what he meant when he shouted about this staff? He was yelling to you.'

Roger frowned. 'Perhaps he wanted me to throw him one, so he could knock the knife from his opponent's hand.'

Geoffrey did not agree. 'He was telling you to prevent "Brother Gamelo" from taking it, not demanding that you provide him with one.'

'I suppose he could mean Aaron's Rod,' said Roger, after a moment of serious consideration. 'That is the only staff of any importance I can think of.'

'Aaron? You mean Moses' brother in the Bible?' asked Geoffrey, regarding Roger warily and wondering how he had come up with such an odd notion. 'Why would you think he meant that?'

'Because my father always said he would get it for Durham cathedral,' replied Roger casually. 'A big and important place like that needs some good relics. We have plenty of saints, of course, like Cuthbert, Aidan, Oswald, and Balthere, but my father wants something really important.'

'Aaron's Rod?' asked Geoffrey in astonishment. 'But it does not exist.'

'It does,' said Roger. 'Or my father would not have promised it to Durham, would he?'

'That does not necessarily follow,' Geoffrey pointed out. The Bishop of Durham – who was also Roger's father – was as wily and dishonest as his son was guileless, and Geoffrey knew better than to believe anything he said. 'How could Flambard ever hope to authenticate such a find?'

'He will not have to, because people will just *see* its holiness – like they do with St Cuthbert, where the goodness shines from his coffin.'

'Does it indeed?' asked Geoffrey wryly, sure it did not.

'Aaron's Rod is important,' Roger went on. 'God used it to write the Ten Commandments.'

'He did not,' countered Geoffrey immediately. 'He told Moses to wave it about, and it brought some of the plagues that resulted in the Israelites being released from slavery in Egypt.'

'Maybe,' hedged Roger, unwilling to admit he might be wrong. 'But it is a powerful thing nevertheless, and it will soon be in Durham.'

Geoffrey seriously doubted it, but Roger was not an easy man to dissuade once he had made up his mind about something. Moreover, he did not want to spend the rest of the day in a debate neither of them would win. He changed the subject.

'This snow is getting worse. We should find this tavern of yours before everyone else has the same idea and we are obliged to sleep in the stables.'

Roger beamed in the gloom. 'It is called the Saracen's Head – a fine name for a couple of Crusaders like us. My father told me about it, and I always stay there when I sail to Normandy. You will not regret bedding down there, lad! It is not a place you will forget in a hurry.'

Geoffrey suspected that was likely to be true, although he was not entirely convinced that the experience would be a pleasant one.

It did not take a genius to see that Roger's tavern was located in Southampton's seedier quarter – where mercenary soldiers gathered in brawling gangs, where sailors came to spend their pay on the red-wigged whores who touted aggressively for business, and where shady merchants met to exchange goods they had decided were exempt from the King's taxes. The houses were grimy and unkempt, although each had windows that were heavily shuttered against thieves. Here and there, drunks lay in the snow, singing and slopping half-filled wineskins in noisy salutes to passers-by. There were beggars, too, rolled up in their rags against the cold, and calling pitifully for alms.

Shadows flitted back and forth in the darkness, and Geoffrey dropped his hand to the hilt of his sword, ready to draw it should he sense an attack, although he suspected they would be safe enough, even in a rough area like the one Roger was blithely leading them through. Fully armed Norman knights were formidable fighters, and it would take more than the grubby criminals who lurked in the alleys and doorways to best one of them and live to tell the tale. Cut-throats and robbers watched them ride by, then prudently went about their own business.

Geoffrey glanced behind him again, aware that whoever had been following them was still there, betrayed by small, furtive movements that flickered at the corner of his eye. But, he supposed, if the watcher meant them harm, something would have happened by now, and he imagined Roger was right in assuming it was some desperate thief.

As Geoffrey and Roger approached the tavern, their men straggling behind them, a low rumble of voices could be heard from within, broken occasionally by louder calls as the landlord hurried to keep his customers supplied with ale and wine. Roger dismounted, unbuckled his saddlebags, and handed the reins of his destrier to a groom. Leaving the trusty Sergeant Helbye to ensure horses and men were properly settled, he strode towards the door, grinning in anticipation of a meal and hot spiced wine to drive away the chill of a bitter winter evening. Geoffrey followed, his dog slinking at his heels.

The best seats near the fire had already been claimed, and the two knights were escorted to a table at the far end of the tavern. Although not the cosiest spot, it had the advantage of privacy, and was comfortingly distant from the other tables, around which huddled some of the most disreputable-looking characters Geoffrey had ever seen. He could only suppose the sheriff was bribed to stay away, because the fact that crimes were being plotted and reviewed was so obvious that it could not have been more brazen had there been a sign saying 'Felons Welcome' emblazoned over the door.

A harried pot boy slammed down two cups of steaming ale, then left the knights to brush the snow from their clothes. Clumps of soggy ice dropped to the matted rushes on the floor as Roger gave his cloak a vigorous shake.

'Bloody weather!' he muttered, hauling his conical helmet from his head and giving the hair underneath a long, hard rub with his thick fingers. 'I hate the cold.'

'When we are in the Holy Land, you always say you would rather face an English winter than the heat,' said Geoffrey, trying to massage some life into his frozen face. 'And you have told me that snow can isolate Durham for weeks at a time. You should be used to this kind of thing.'

17

Roger grunted noncommittally. He flopped on to a wooden bench, seized his ale and drained it in a single draught. He leaned back against the wall, and wiped his lips on the back of his hand, closing his eyes in satisfaction. 'That is better. There is nothing like a pot of boiling ale to drive the chill from a man's bones.'

Geoffrey sat next to him, enjoying the furnace-like warmth of the room. He snatched up his ale just as Roger was reaching for it, and was allowing its soporific effects to relax him, when he realized his men were still outside.

'Let them be,' said Roger drowsily, grabbing Geoffrey's arm as he stood to leave. 'I expect that idiot Peterkin has lost his saddlebags or some such nonsense. Helbye can sort it out.'

Geoffrey settled back again. 'Poor Helbye. I do not think he would have come with me this time, had he known the kind of rabble I expect him to convert into military men.'

Roger chuckled. 'He is happy enough – more so than had he been forced to watch you ride to the Holy Land while he ended his days hoeing weeds and counting sheep. Helbye is a soldier, and will never be content with farming.' He gave Geoffrey a disparaging glance. 'Unlike you.'

'I am no farmer,' said Geoffrey, startled by the insult. 'I inherited my manor twenty years ago, but have spent less than a week there. I have been a soldier most of my life. You know that.'

Roger looked him up and down critically, his eyes lingering meaningfully on the book that poked from his friend's saddlebags. Roger did not approve of books or the fact that Geoffrey enjoyed reading them, considering such pastimes unknightly.

Geoffrey and Roger had little in common, other than the fact that they were both knights, but they had formed a firm friendship nonetheless. They were physically very different: Roger was huge, red-faced, and cared little for his personal appearance, while Geoffrey was usually neat, if not clean, and had expressive green eyes that showed him to be a man of intelligence with a sense of humour.

Their personalities were even more disparate. Roger loved

nothing more than a good fight, and his other pleasures included making a nuisance of himself in brothels and drinking to a state of rowdy bonhomie with his friends. His view of the world was as uncomplicated as was his personality, and he never suffered from the moral dilemmas that had plagued Geoffrey as the Crusader army butchered, looted, and plundered its way across half the known world. Geoffrey, however, was regarded as something of an oddity among his fellow knights. When city after city fell to the greedy hands of the Crusader army, Geoffrey had declined to steal the gold and precious jewels that most knights considered their right, preferring instead to add to his collection of books and scrolls.

'You might not see your estate for years once we leave,' declared Roger. 'We will be on our way tomorrow and by next week, we will be in Normandy, where we will ride south to Venice to board another ship that will take us to Jaffa. Then it will only be a day's ride to the Holy City itself.'

Geoffrey recalled Jerusalem with pleasure, thinking about the new Crusader church at the Holy Sepulchre with its yellow stones and round-headed arches, and the fabulous Dome of the Rock, resplendent in Turkish mosaics and its great cupola glittering like a glimpse of Heaven itself.

Roger also reviewed Jerusalem's delights and sighed wistfully. 'The brothels are a taste of Paradise, and the wines are like nectar. It is the finest city in the world.'

He gave a sudden bellow to attract the attention of the pot boy, a noise that made Geoffrey jump in alarm and stilled the hum of manly conversation in the tavern as abruptly as if a troupe of nuns had entered. Roger ordered more ale when an alarmed servant came rushing over to see what was the matter, then stretched his legs out in front of him as he rested his back against the wall.

'You usually claim that Durham is the finest city in the world,' Geoffrey observed. 'Have you changed your mind?'

'Hush!' snapped Roger in a voice sufficiently loud to draw startled glances from the unsavoury occupants of the nearby tables. 'It is not wise to mention that place in public these

19

days. It is too closely associated with Bishop Flambard.' He leaned forward conspiratorially, although Geoffrey noticed that the volume of his voice did not diminish. 'He is my father, you know.'

He sat back and folded his arms defiantly, while Geoffrey noted that Roger's incautious declaration had drawn more than one interested appraisal from the other customers. Roger was proud of his father, and never allowed an opportunity to pass without boasting about their alleged consanguinity, despite the fact that Geoffrey knew the details of his ancestry perfectly well.

Flambard had been the previous king's Chief Justiciar, an office that had entailed raising large sums of money for the king to squander. When King William Rufus had been killed in a hunting accident the previous year, Flambard offered to serve the new king, Henry. Henry, however, did not want an unpopular man like Flambard in his court, so the wicked bishop found himself under arrest and incarcerated in the formidable White Tower of London.

Geoffrey suspected Roger was right to conceal his parentage in Southampton, although he thought the big knight would not keep his secret long if he yelled it at the top of his voice in crowded taverns. Whenever Geoffrey considered the relationship between one of the most cunning men in the country and the bluff knight who sat next to him, he could not help but wonder whether Roger's mother had been mistaken. Roger was straightforward and blunt, and political subterfuge was as alien to him as honesty and plain-dealing were to his alleged father.

At that moment, the servant, a skinny youth with a jaw that sagged to reveal yellow teeth, arrived with a tray of food. His apron was dark with spilled grease, tavern dirt, and ale, and Geoffrey was not encouraged to observe him 'cleaning' his hands on it before he unloaded a few sorry-looking lumps of bread and a bowl of onions.

'I want more than that,' said Roger, looking disparagingly at the offerings. 'Bring me some meat, boy. None of your fancy stews, though – I want a real piece of flesh.'

'It is Lent,' said the boy nervously, taking in Roger's size and the array of weapons he carried with him. 'We do not provide meat at this time of year.'

'Rubbish,' declared Roger dismissively. 'I am a Crusader knight – a *Jerosolimitanus* – who fought to free the Holy Land from the infidel, and I expect meat for my pains, Lent or no.'

Intimidated, the lad hurried away. Roger had not needed to tell him he had been on the Crusade; both he and Geoffrey wore white – albeit grimy, especially in Roger's case – surcoats with red Crusader's crosses emblazoned on them. Under these they wore chain mail – knee-length tunics of connected iron rings that were strong and heavy, and allowed the freedom of movement necessary when wielding a heavy broadsword. Their legs were protected by boiled-leather leggings, tucked into boots made from donkey hide. Chain-mail gauntlets and conical metal helmets with Norman nosepieces completed their armour. At their waists were thick belts, to which were attached huge swords, and both had daggers strapped to their legs. Geoffrey's arsenal included a lance, while Roger preferred a mace. It was protection far in excess of what was needed for a port in England, but old habits died hard, and Geoffrey and Roger felt vulnerable without it.

'That told him,' said Roger, satisfied as he watched the pot boy in urgent discussion with the taverner, casting frightened glances to where Roger sat. 'A man needs more than bread and a few onions to stave off the cold of this miserable land.'

The door opened a second time, and a cold draught swept across the room, rustling the rushes on the floor and sending hard pellets of snow swirling towards the hearth. Helbye entered with the recruits at his heels. With an exasperated sigh, Geoffrey saw there were not six men who stood waiting like sheep for Helbye to tell them where to sit, but five, and it was the addle-witted Peterkin who was missing. When Geoffrey pointed out that Peterkin was not there, Helbye's shoulders slumped in weary resignation.

'Damn the boy! He was with us a moment ago. I suppose he is dallying with his nag – you know he prefers to tend her himself rather than leaving her to the grooms. I will go and

21

ferret him out.' He was grey with fatigue, and, not for the first time, Geoffrey wondered at the wisdom of allowing the older man to accompany him to Jerusalem.

'See to the others, Will,' he said, easing him towards a vacant table. 'I will find Peterkin.'

And then I will either kill him myself or abandon him permanently, he thought uncharitably, as he stepped into the swirling snow and headed for the stables. Although the distance between the outbuildings and the tavern was not great, Geoffrey knew Peterkin could lose his way between them.

The night had turned frosty, so the ice-covered ground cracked and shattered like glass as Geoffrey walked. The cosy hum of voices faded quickly as he moved farther from the tavern, the snow serving to smother the familiar sounds of night – the snicker of ponies in their stalls, the yowl of a courting cat, the drunken babble of some sailor who had tumbled into a ditch. As he drew closer to the stables, he saw a flicker of a light under the door, and assumed it belonged to the grooms who would be settling the horses. He supposed Peterkin was with them, ensuring as always that his own evil-tempered mount received better attention than the others.

He pushed open the stable door and strolled inside. Immediately, the stalls were plunged into complete blackness. Horses whinnied and shuffled uneasily. Instinctively, he dropped one hand to the hilt of his sword as he waited for his eyes to grow accustomed to the gloom. To his right, a shadow flitted, and he made his way towards it, moving carefully across the straw-strewn floor. Then there was another movement, as if the person sensed him drawing closer and did not like it. It was cold and late, and Geoffrey did not want to spend the night chasing a half-witted boy who should never have been taken away from his home in the first place. His patience began to wear thin.

'Peterkin!' he snapped. 'Come out at once. You will unsettle the horses with all this prowling around in the dark.'

There was no reply. Geoffrey grew exasperated, torn between leaving the lad to spend the night in the stables, if that was what he wanted, and a nagging concern that he was not fit to be left alone in a place like the Saracen's Head.

'Peterkin!' he shouted. 'Enough of this foolery. Come out!'

But the shadows remained silent, although Geoffrey heard someone breathing unevenly nearby. Irritation with Peterkin began to give way to the feeling that all was not well, and he drew his dagger, wondering whether he was already too late to prevent Peterkin from falling foul of some of the tavern's less respectable clients.

He took a step forward, but then stumbled over something lying in his way. His dagger flew from his hand, and landed in a pile of straw. Cursing under his breath, he crouched down to find it. But it was not cold steel his groping fingers encountered; it was warm flesh that was sticky with what Geoffrey's military experience told him was blood. As he straightened, someone launched himself at him, so violently that both he and his attacker went tumbling to the ground.

Two

It was not easy to best an experienced knight in full battle armour, even when he had dropped his dagger. Geoffrey's attacker, though, was putting up a respectable fight. He feinted this way and that with a long-bladed hunting knife, and used his familiarity with the dark stables to his advantage by ducking in and out of stalls while Geoffrey was forced to grope around blindly.

However, it was not long before Geoffrey was able to grab the man, and then it was only a matter of moments before he had him pinned to the ground. He twisted the man's wrist until he dropped the knife with a cry of pain, then hauled him upright, pulling him to the door so he could see his face in the dim light that filtered through the tavern's windows into the yard.

His assailant was nondescript, with mouse-coloured hair, a sallow complexion, and drab brown eyes. There was nothing unusual or memorable about him, and Geoffrey did not think he had seen him before. He was about to demand an explanation for the attack when he became aware of a still shape lying on the ground nearby. For the first time, Geoffrey was able to see it was Peterkin, and realized it had been his body he had stumbled over when he had first entered the stables. Not releasing his hold on his captive, Geoffrey stared at the boy.

Peterkin's large blue eyes were wide and sightless, and blood gleamed darkly in a puddle beneath him, trailing from the wound inflicted by the crossbow bolt – red in colour – that protruded from his chest. Geoffrey's shock turned to anger when he realized the lad had come to a stupid, meaningless end at the hands of a ruthless robber. He grabbed his captive

24

with both hands, forcing him up against the door so hard that the man's feet barely touched the ground.

'You bastard!' he snarled, further incensed by the blind fear in the man's eyes. 'The lad was a simpleton! He would have given you his purse, had you asked. There was no need to kill him for it!'

The man said nothing, although he gagged and struggled as Geoffrey's hands tightened around his throat. For a few wild moments, Geoffrey considered throttling him there and then, certain the lawless patrons in the Saracen's Head would say nothing if he dispensed instant justice to a thief and left his body in the snow. But killing unarmed men did not come easily, and he decided to let the sheriff deal with the matter. He began to haul the murderer across the yard, intending to hand him over to the town's bailiffs.

He had almost reached the tavern door, when there was a hiss and a thump, and the man jerked convulsively. Geoffrey stared at him in astonishment. A crossbow bolt – red again – protruded from his chest. From the darkness to his left, Geoffrey heard a sharp gasp of horror, which made it obvious that a dreadful mistake had been made and that the quarrel had missed its intended victim.

Geoffrey dropped the dying man and took cover behind a stack of barrels, wondering what connection Peterkin's killers had with the roof-top fighter, and whether whoever had been following them all afternoon – and on reflection Geoffrey realized they had been shadowed only *after* they had witnessed the skirmish – was anything to do with it.

But it was not a good time for analysis. As he peered from behind the barrels, there was a sharp twang, and another quarrel smacked into the ground near his feet. As he ducked back, he saw a figure dart from the stable and race towards the seedy wharves that fringed the river. Geoffrey followed, but his armour was not designed for running and few knights took to their feet for exactly that reason. It was not long before he began to gasp for breath, and his quarry easily outdistanced him. Then an image of the slow-witted Peterkin came into his mind, and he forced himself to run harder, determined that neither of the two murderers should escape justice.

The bowman dodged around the nautical clutter that filled the shore road, a muddy track that ran along the quay and was bordered by a stone sea wall. Ramshackle piers jutted into the river at right angles to the wall, unstable structures of decaying wood that were coated with algae and seaweed. Boats were moored to them, jostling each other as they rose and fell on the swell. These were not the great, proud ships that carried legal cargo, which were anchored in the main harbour, but small, ill-kept vessels that looked as if their owners would carry anything – or anyone – for a high enough price.

The shore road was littered with ropes, broken barrels, the abandoned hulks of boats, and discarded fishing nets, made more treacherous by the film of snow that masked them from sight. Geoffrey tripped and almost fell over a rusting anchor chain, but regained his balance and thundered on. He saw the bowman slow down and zigzag as he reached a chaotic scatter of crates that were awaiting collection. He began to gain on him, and in desperation, the bowman vaulted across the wall, and scampered down one of the battered jetties. Geoffrey was bemused: the pier went nowhere, and once the man had reached the end of it, there would be nowhere left to go – unless he planned on swimming.

The bowman soon realized he was trapped, and glanced behind him in an agony of terror. He reached a watchman's tiny hut, and in the dim light of its lamp, Geoffrey recognized the rodent-like features: it was the older of the two roof-top combatants. Confused, Geoffrey watched him stumble over uneven planks and coiled ropes, wondering why the man should want to kill Peterkin. He broke into a run again, and was almost to the point where he could grab the hem of the killer's flying cloak, when something hit him on the shoulder. It was not a serious blow, and he barely felt its impact through his chain mail, but it was enough to send him staggering towards the water. The timbers were rotten near the edge of the pier, and Geoffrey felt them crumble under his weight. He tried to fling himself sideways before the whole thing gave way, but a shadowy figure emerged

26

from the darkness and gave him a shove. The wood snapped and Geoffrey began to fall.

He hit the river with a tremendous splash. For an instant, he felt nothing, then a searing cold seeped through his clothes and shocked him into immobility. His padded linen surcoat soaked up water like a sponge and his chain mail and sword were heavy anyway. He began to sink like a stone.

Water roared and frothed in Geoffrey's ears, and he could see nothing in the pitch blackness. His instinct was to try to claw his way back to the surface to escape the black seawater that foamed and gurgled all around him, but a distant, rational part of his mind told him it would be futile given how heavy he was in his armour.

Visions of being washed out to sea filled his mind, but then he bumped into something hard. It was one of the wooden piles that had been driven into the river bed to support the pier. He grabbed it in relief, wrapping his arms and legs around its barnacle-encrusted surface, and began to work his way up, climbing it as though it were a rope. It was easier than he imagined, and the vegetation that swept and waved around it helped, because he was able to use it to gain handholds.

Just when he thought his lungs would burst, and he was on the verge of abandoning the sensible approach in favour of a panicky struggle upwards, his head broke the surface. As he took a great gasp of air, a wave slapped into his mouth, making him cough and splutter, retching as the sour, bitter taste of salt stung his throat. Gagging, he heard voices over the soft swish and gurgle of water, and realized his attackers were watching to see if he surfaced. He heard footsteps on the planking as they moved, walking along the pier to ensure he did not emerge farther down.

'Who was he?' one asked the other.

'Who cares?' said another man in the tremulous tenor of old age. 'All I know is that we saw a bullying Norman knight chasing a peasant and we evened the odds in the peasant's favour.'

'I hope he was not a murderer or a traitor,' said the first uneasily, and Geoffrey heard the planking groan above his

27

head. He closed his eyes, feeling as though he were in the depths of some ghastly nightmare. Seldom had he ever felt so helpless, knowing it would take very little for the pair to dislodge his precarious grip on the slippery pillar and send him back to the bottom of the river.

'All Normans are murderers, Ulfrith,' said the old man with grave authority. 'And they are traitors, too – traitors to us Saxons. I was at Hastings thirty-five years ago, battling to keep King Harold on the throne, and I will fight those damned, usurping Normans until the day I die!'

Geoffrey rested his head on the pillar. While he knew many Saxons still resented King William's conquest of England, open hostility towards the invaders was usually confined to sullen glances or occasional hurled clods of mud. Few risked physical encounters, and it was just plain bad luck that he had happened to encounter a couple of patriots while he was in the act of chasing down the man who had murdered Peterkin.

'Actually, what I meant was I hope the man we helped to escape was not a murderer or a traitor,' said Ulfrith. 'This "poor peasant" of yours. I do not want to be accused of abetting a crime.'

The old man spat in disgust. 'The only crime that has been committed here, is that a Norman was chasing a Saxon.'

'How can you be sure he was Saxon, grandfather?' asked Ulfrith doubtfully. 'Or that the knight was Norman? It was impossible to tell in the dark.'

'The knight was screeching obscenities in Norman-French – the Devil's language – while his victim had the thick yellow hair that marked him as one of us.' The old man's voice was firm.

'I did not see yellow hair,' said Ulfrith dubiously.

Nor had Geoffrey. The bowman had worn a hood, but the greasy fringe that poked from beneath it was dark. He had also possessed coarse, rodent-like features that suggested he was probably Norman himself, or perhaps Celtic, but he was definitely not one of the flaxen-haired giants who claimed themselves the rightful inhabitants of England. And Geoffrey had certainly not been 'screeching' Norman-French – there had been no need for shouting, because he had intended to interrogate the man properly when he had caught him, probably in English, which Geoffrey spoke as well as French and several other languages.

'The Norman's victim was a Saxon lord,' elaborated the old man with conviction. 'Perhaps even the Aetheling himself – the true heir to England's throne. And we saved him!'

'No, grandfather,' said Ulfrith firmly, doubtless sensing that someone needed to put a check on the rapidly escalating flights of fancy before they became too grotesque. 'And I wish now we had minded our own business. I did not like the look of your "Saxon" victim, and he did not even have the courtesy to thank us when he made his escape. Now if there are questions asked about that knight's disappearance, it is us who will be blamed, not the real culprit.'

The old man clicked his tongue at his grandson's faint-heartedness. 'There is not a man in the town who will not buy us a drink for ridding our country of a Norman. So, come on, lad. We will celebrate this Saxon victory with a flagon of ale!'

Their voices faded away and Geoffrey sighed in relief, knowing he would be able to climb out of the river without some patriotic veteran laying about him with his walking stick. But leaving the water was not so simple. He was too cold to scale the slippery weed-encrusted pillars any higher, and he could not relinquish his hold to move to a better place because he would sink.

He was considering some desperate options, such as removing his armour and attempting to swim, when he saw rough pegs protruding from the pillar to which he clutched. On closer inspection, he saw they formed a ladder. He grasped the lowest one, hoping it would bear his weight. Hauling himself up was not easy, and he was forced to stop several times and rest. But eventually he reached the top, and rolled on to the snow-dusted planking to lie gasping for breath.

Prompted by a chill wind, he looked around. Nearby was the hut in which, presumably, the patriots had been sitting when they had been roused by his pursuit of the Saxon nobleman. He walked towards it, and pushed open the door. The lamp had been left lit and there was a brazier that had

29

been banked, but that still released a comforting warmth. Gratefully, he stumbled inside, fumbling with the buckles on his surcoat, which felt so heavy he wondered whether it might make him crash through the floor to the river below.

Once he had stoked up the fire and removed his sopping surcoat, he felt better. He jammed the door closed with a stool, and quickly divested himself of his armour and the soaking clothes underneath. While he knew he would not be able to dry them before the Saxons returned from their celebrations, he was able to wring them out, and even felt entitled to steal the rough, but dry, woollen jerkin that hung on the back of the door. On one lopsided shelf was a flask containing a clear liquid, which burned its way down his throat when he swallowed it. He shuddered, supposing it was some powerful local concoction that not only served to intoxicate whoever was rash enough to drink it, but that was also good for lighting fires and clearing blocked drains.

By the time he had re-donned his armour, the act of dressing and a lot of vigorous wringing had restored some warmth to his body, and he began to feel human again. He took another gulp of the potent Saxon wine, flung his surcoat over his shoulder, and began to retrace his footsteps through the snow to the tavern.

The first thing Geoffrey saw when he entered the Saracen's Head was that a number of the tavern's customers had congregated around the hearth. At their centre was a man so old he was bent almost double and a fair-headed giant who was probably his grandson. It did not take a genius to discern that here were Geoffrey's would-be killers, recounting their great victory over the evil Norman empire with a cup of the inn's best ale. Their story, however, was clearly being treated with some scepticism by the audience, some of whom were already drifting away, shaking their heads in amused disbelief.

'But it is true!' cried the old man angrily. 'Every word is God's truth. Is that not right, Ulfrith?'

The younger man nodded, although he did not do so with much conviction. Geoffrey watched from the doorway, tempted to stride over and teach them a lesson for their audacity. It would be an uneven contest, and then it would be Normans who would celebrate a victory over Saxons. But Geoffrey was not the kind of man to pick fights with old men and boys, even ones who had done their best to drown him, and he decided there was greater satisfaction to be had in watching the pair dismissed as flagrant liars by their friends.

'You have been at that bunion lotion again,' scoffed a man with bad skin. 'You are drunk!'

So that was what it was, thought Geoffrey uneasily. Still, it had banished the cold readily enough.

'I have not touched a drop of that since Christmas,' protested the old man indignantly. 'You go and look at the flask in my hut. You will find it full to the brim.'

'Right, I will, then,' said the man, winking at his friends as he left.

Geoffrey grinned and wished he had drunk more.

'I tell you, we drowned a Norman by our jetty,' the old man persisted in a voice that had changed from boastful to wheedling. 'He was chasing a Saxon prince. Tell them, Ulfrith.'

'Yes,' said Ulfrith uncertainly. He blushed to the roots of his yellow hair and refused to look anyone in the eye. Geoffrey could not remember when he had seen a less convincing liar. The lad's fellow drinkers apparently concurred, because more of the audience wandered away.

Some people were not amused, however, and Geoffrey saw Roger listening to the discussion with a troubled expression. Helbye already wore his cloak and helmet, and so did the men, and Geoffrey suspected they were waiting only for Roger to give the word before they went to search for him.

Roger gave a beam of delight when he saw Geoffrey, while Helbye nodded in relief and unfastened the clasp on his cloak. The men also began to relax, while even Geoffrey's dog seemed pleased to see him, something that rarely happened unless there was food involved.

Roger nodded towards the old man and his grandson. 'That pair claim to have drowned a Norman, and Helbye thought

31

their victim might have been you.' He roared with laughter at the improbable notion that a boy and his aged grandfather would be able to best Geoffrey.

Helbye did not join in the hilarity. He had seen the trail of drips from Geoffrey's surcoat and noticed his wet hair. 'What happened?' he asked quietly. 'Where is Peterkin? Those two did not harm him, did they?'

'They would not dare attack any of us,' said the older Littel brother confidently.

'Where is my brother?' asked Joab tremulously. He looked even more peculiar than usual that evening, and his wild eyes bulged with anxiety.

'Someone shot him,' said Geoffrey bluntly. He saw Joab's jaw drop in shock. 'I am sorry. There was nothing anyone could do to save him. He was dead when I arrived.'

Joab shook his head. 'No, he is not dead. You are mistaken. No one would kill Peterkin.'

'He is in the stable,' said Geoffrey. 'Tomorrow, we will . . .'

Before he could finish, Joab had darted from the room. Geoffrey instructed Helbye to follow him, then see that the sheriff was informed of the murder and the body carried to the nearest church. Wary of being out in a dark town with a killer at large, Helbye took the other men with him.

'What is going on?' demanded Roger when they had gone. 'Peterkin is too stupid to die!'

'I was wrong to bring him here,' said Geoffrey bitterly. 'Tomorrow, after he is buried, I am sending Joab home. Perhaps the others should go with him. None will ever make decent soldiers.'

'Never mind that,' said Roger impatiently. 'What happened? *You* did not shoot Peterkin, did you, so his feeble wits will not delay us on our journey?'

Geoffrey was too drained to feel indignation that Roger should consider him the kind of man to murder one of his own soldiers for personal convenience. 'He was shot with a red-stained crossbow bolt, just like the one that killed the youngster on the roof this afternoon.'

Roger gazed at him. 'What are you saying? That the same

32

scoundrel who murdered the boy also murdered Peterkin?' For the first time, he noticed Geoffrey was wet. His astonishment quickly turned to anger, and he whipped his dagger from its sheath, the expression in his eyes murderous. 'I will kill that pair of Saxon villains for this!'

'You will not,' said Geoffrey, pulling him down as he started to stand. 'Their friends will not stand by while you slay them in cold blood, and even you cannot take on a hundred men armed with blades, staves, and God knows what else.'

'I can,' declared Roger in furious determination, starting to stand again. 'You just watch me. And anyway, if I am hard pressed, you will come to my aid, just as you have done in the past.'

'I cannot,' said Geoffrey. 'I am too cold to be of any use to you. And you have eaten all the food, it seems. Did you save me none?'

'We were hungry,' said Roger, reluctantly abandoning the attractive proposition of racing across the tavern and killing the insolent duo who had dared to attack his companion. He reached out and felt Geoffrey's sleeve. 'You will catch your death sitting around in here, lad. You should change. Landlord! Where is our chamber?'

Wearily, Geoffrey followed Roger to where the taverner waited to conduct them to the room they were to sleep in, although Geoffrey hoped Roger did not plan to do so in the company of half a dozen women to celebrate his departure from English soil. He was too tired for high-spirited jinxes that night, and wanted only to lie down and cover himself with as many blankets as he could find.

Two men sat on the stairs, nursing their ale disconsolately. They were the Saxon and his grandson. The old man gazed defiantly at Roger and remained seated, although his grandson quickly jumped to his feet so the knights could pass. Geoffrey gazed at him coldly.

'I hear you murdered a Norman tonight,' he said.

Ulfrith's jaw dropped in astonishment. 'How did you know that?' he whispered, aghast.

'You were bawling it to the whole tavern,' said Geoffrey

dryly, seeing that intelligence was not one of the Saxon's more noteworthy characteristics. 'Why? Was it meant to be a secret?'

'I would kill another, if I could,' said the old man, fixing Geoffrey with a malevolent glower. 'I would run every Norman through with my broadsword – if I could still lift one.'

'Grandfather, please,' said Ulfrith nervously. He smiled uneasily at Geoffrey. 'He means no harm, my lord. He is almost ninety years old.'

'Is being ninety an excuse for rudeness, then?' asked Geoffrey, raising his eyebrows.

The young Saxon nodded earnestly. 'Yes, of course! Do you know any ninety-year-olds who are *not* rude to everyone they meet?'

Geoffrey smiled. His easy nature meant it was difficult for him to remain angry for long, and he was amused by the young man's notion that age justified the old man's ill manners. He was about to reply, when the door burst open and the man with the bad skin entered, waving aloft the flask of bunion medicine in gloating vindication.

'Half empty!' he crowed. 'He *has* been drinking it, and *that* is why he invented his wild story of Saxon princes and murdering Normans!'

The old man's face was a picture of wounded dismay, and he used his grandson's legs to haul himself to his feet before hobbling off to try to snatch the offending phial as his tormentor bandied it about the tavern.

'He promised he would not drink any more of that,' said Ulfrith, troubled. 'It contains all sorts of strong herbs, plus a powerful distillation of wine.'

'It is not poisonous, is it?' asked Geoffrey.

Ulfrith shrugged carelessly, then looked at the surcoat that was draped over Geoffrey's shoulder. 'You have been on Crusade,' he said wistfully, reaching out to finger the damp linen. If his slow mind registered that it was unusually wet, then nothing showed on his face. 'I wanted to fight the infidel, too, when I heard the Pope's call for brave men to travel east.'

34

'Why? Do you like slaughtering unarmed women and children, and stealing their property?'

'I do,' called Roger from the top of the stairs. Geoffrey was not entirely sure he was joking.

'I just want to travel,' said the Saxon. 'But no one will take me.'

'Is there a reason for that?' asked Geoffrey, thinking it might be because the lad had a penchant for murdering Normans – not a characteristic to render him popular on a Crusade, where the main purpose was to kill Saracens, not each other.

'I am overly big to be a sailor,' said Ulfrith ruefully. 'All the sea captains tell me I am too heavy for climbing rigging and furling sails, and the only soldier I know said I would eat too much and be too expensive to keep.'

'Come on, Geoff,' shouted Roger impatiently. 'You will catch a chill in those wet clothes.'

'Wet clothes,' mused Ulfrith. Geoffrey watched in amusement as the connection between a sodden knight and his own escapade on the waterfront gradually formed in the Saxon's mind. 'Oh no!' he breathed, the blood draining from his ruddy features. 'It was you!'

By the following day, the blizzard had abated, and when Geoffrey awoke, a pale sun had already started the messy business of melting its leavings. He leaned out of the window and looked across a town of white roofs and muddy brown paths trampled through carpets of snow. In the distance, he could hear the sounds of the port: yelling voices, barking dogs, whinnying horses, and squawking gulls. Crashes echoed as cargo was loaded, and bells clanged as ships set sail or waited to dock.

The tavern had been lively well into the night, when Geoffrey was sure a good deal of illicit business had been conducted, and its patrons were either at home in bed or collapsed in drunken heaps on the tables downstairs. The noise had not bothered Geoffrey. He had been tired, and had barely stirred even when Roger had slipped into the chamber with a giggling woman in his arms.

'Come on,' he said, slapping the rounded hulk that was Roger, still asleep in the bed.

There was a startled squeak, and two bright blue eyes gazed dazedly at him from a tangle of fair curls. Geoffrey flung the prostitute the dress that had been hurled to the floor in the heat of the moment the night before, and waited for her to leave, while Roger slowly roused himself, scrubbing at his face with thick fingers and groaning as the morning light lanced into his eyes. His bleariness evaporated when he saw the woman.

'Mary, lass,' he said hoarsely, leaning towards her with a lecherous twinkle.

'Maude,' she corrected, a little crossly, fending him off. 'Maude, not Mary.'

'Maude, Mary,' said Roger with a careless shrug. 'What difference does it make?'

'How would you feel if I called you Robert of Bristol?' demanded Maude indignantly, fluffing up her hair in anticipation of an argument.

'Bristol?' bellowed Roger. 'I am not from *that* stinking hell-hole. I am from Durham, lass – a place God Himself would be proud to call home.'

'I would keep that quiet, if I were you,' advised Maude practically. 'The only thing we know about Durham around here is that it is the see of that vile man who claims to be its bishop.'

'What a fine view there is from this window,' said Geoffrey quickly, knowing Roger was unlikely to take such an insult to his father meekly.

'Damn the view!' snarled Roger. 'This whore is maligning the finest man who ever set foot on English soil.'

Maude gazed at him in sheer disbelief, then started to laugh. Geoffrey could understand her amusement, given Bishop Flambard's unhappy reputation.

'Are we talking about the same man?' she asked. 'The toady of King William Rufus, who taxed us to breaking point and who was made Chief Justiciar by dint of his cunning and slippery ways? And I am not a whore, by the way, just a country lass who has lost her way.'

36

'Lost her way to what?' asked Geoffrey. 'The brothel?'

'Bishop Flambard is a great man,' stormed Roger. 'He is an honest, upright soul who has never done a corrupt deed in his life.'

This time Geoffrey joined Maude's laughter. Even Roger, who was a far more loyal son than the devious bishop deserved, could not fail to see that Flambard was about as far from honest and upright as it was possible to be.

Roger glowered and fingered the dagger at his side, so Geoffrey suspected it was only their friendship that prevented the big knight from fighting him. He controlled his amusement and pushed Roger's hand away from the weapon.

'You must be the only person in Christendom who thinks this way,' he said. 'But we should not be discussing Flambard when we have passage on a ship to find. The morning is already half gone.'

'The best thing that happened to England was when King Henry arrested Flambard and threw him in his dungeons,' declared Maude, ignoring Geoffrey's attempt to bring the conversation to an end.

'That is not true!' Roger was outraged. 'He is not in a dungeon. He is being treated with courtesy and kindness, and I will kill anyone who says otherwise!'

He looked dangerous, and Geoffrey hastily stepped between him and Maude. 'You are right,' he said gently. 'The King would not treat a bishop roughly. But the day is passing, and we need to make enquiries at the quay. I want to find a ship while the weather holds.'

'Good luck, then,' said Maude in the tone of voice that suggested the task was hopeless. She nodded at the high, bright white clouds. 'There will be no sailings today; the wind is wrong.'

Geoffrey sat on the edge of the bed and began to tug on his boots. 'Perhaps, but we can still buy passage for when the wind is good.'

'You mean leave this nice warm chamber?' asked Roger, eyeing Maude with lustful hope in his eyes, their disagreement already forgotten – or forgotten sufficiently for him to enjoy a romp.

'You stay here,' said Geoffrey. 'I want to make sure Peterkin is buried first, and that his brother has enough money to return home.'

Roger bounded off the bed. He was fully clothed, and even wore a dagger strapped to his thigh, so Geoffrey could only imagine that Maude had passed a very uncomfortable night.

'I had forgotten about Peterkin,' Roger said, buckling his sword belt and bundling Maude unceremoniously out of the door, slamming it shut behind her. Geoffrey opened it again, and passed the startled prostitute her clothes. She snatched them away and struggled into them before flouncing off down the stairs.

'We must track down Peterkin's killer,' announced Roger, donning his surcoat. 'The one you said looked like a weasel and who also killed that young man on the roof. We cannot have peasants killing our soldiers every time they feel like it.'

Geoffrey smiled. 'And how will we do that? This is a large town, and we have no authority to hunt murderers. All we can do is tell the sheriff, and hope he knows the kind of men who favour red-stained quarrels.'

'Very well,' said Roger reluctantly. 'But it is curious that these coloured bolts keep turning up everywhere. We have now seen three men killed with them. I wonder if they died because of what the roof-top fighter shouted before he was murderously shot in the back.'

'You mean about the staff?' asked Geoffrey. 'I cannot imagine what. You did not even understand what he meant.'

Roger leaned forward to tap his temple. 'You are not using that quick mind you are so proud of.'

'Am I not?' asked Geoffrey, wondering what he could have missed.

Roger looked pleased with himself. 'Just because you know you do not know, does not mean Weasel does not know you do not know. Do you know what I mean?'

'No,' said Geoffrey.

Roger sighed, and began to explain in the patronizing voice he used on some of the dim-witted lads he was occasionally obliged to train as soldiers. '*We* do not know the significance of the young man's words. But Weasel does not know that, does he?'

'You are beginning to think like your father. You see a deviousness and cunning that are not there. We witnessed a brawl, during which two men ganged up on a youngster and killed him – something that probably happens every day in a town like Southampton.'

'What about Peterkin, then?'

'Peterkin was killed by the same two men because he was silly enough to linger in the stables after his friends had left. He was easy prey, and they killed him so they could take his purse.'

'But he had nothing in his purse, except a wooden cross and some glass beads.'

'That is irrelevant. Thieves do not check the contents of purses before deciding whether a robbery is worthwhile. They killed Peterkin first, and *then* discovered he had nothing to offer.'

'But they almost drowned you,' said Roger, refusing to relinquish the notion that there was some despicable plot in motion.

'They did not. That was unrelated meddling by Saxon oafs. But we should look for a ship, or we will still be in this godforsaken place when spring comes.'

Without waiting for a reply, he opened the door and clattered briskly down the stairs. He was not entirely pleased to see Ulfrith sitting in the room below.

The Saxon had taken some pains with his appearance. He wore a relatively clean jerkin that was probably the best he owned, and a pair of thick leather trousers that looked as if they had been taken directly from the legs of a cow. His gold hair had been trimmed into a neat bob, and brushed until it shone. Geoffrey regarded him warily. Ulfrith stepped forward and smiled.

'I am sorry for almost drowning you last night,' he said, not looking sorry at all. 'And I have decided the only way I can make amends for such a misunderstanding is that I offer you my services. You can take me with you to the Holy Land.'

*   *   *

39

'This is hopeless,' muttered Roger disconsolately, as he trailed after Geoffrey that afternoon. 'Every boat here is either already full or sailing somewhere we do not want to go.'

'The bad weather last month means there are more people who want to travel than there are places on ships,' said Geoffrey, looking around to see which vessel they might try next. 'We might have to head farther along the coast, and leave from Pevensey.'

Roger sighed gustily. 'But I want to go to Normandy *today*. I am sick of all this snow and cold. It will be warmer there.' He glanced behind him, to where Ulfrith hovered at a respectful distance. 'Your Saxon is still following us. Why will he not take no for an answer? I am tempted to shove him into the sea right now, just like he did to you last night.'

'I do not think a ducking will put him off. He sees us as a chance to escape a life of drudgery and intends to make the most of it.'

He turned and waited until Ulfrith caught up with them. The Saxon, sensing they had been talking about him and sufficiently naive to be happily optimistic about it, gave a grin as he hurried forward.

'You have changed your mind,' he said in satisfied delight. 'You will take me with you after all.'

'Can you arrange passage to Normandy?' Geoffrey was exasperated with being told there were no berths available and saw he was obliged to resort to other tactics. 'For us, my sergeant, and our four men?'

'Five men,' corrected Ulfrith, not even trying to hide his pleasure. 'Of course I can. I know all the captains here, and they know me.'

'Is that good or bad?' growled Roger uncertainly. He had a point. Not everyone would like Ulfrith's irritating cheerfulness, and a word from him to some of the surly types who slouched near their vessels might do more harm than good.

Ulfrith did not notice Roger was less than optimistic about his chances of success, and made a show of studying the clouds to demonstrate his superior meteorological knowledge.

40

'There will be no sailings today or tomorrow, because the wind is wrong, but I will arrange one for as soon as I can.'

'Remember we want to go to Normandy,' said Geoffrey, thinking that the lad might be so keen to impress that he would buy passage elsewhere if Normandy proved difficult, believing that one foreign place was much like another and they would not notice the difference. 'There is space on ships sailing to the Low Countries and Scotland, but we need to go to Normandy.'

'Aye,' muttered Roger. 'Who in his right mind would want to go to Scotland? It is full of screaming savages intent on stealing English cattle for unnatural purposes.'

'You mean like eating them?' asked Geoffrey, to tease him. Roger's dislike of the Scots was legendary, and he had spent a good deal of time fighting them before he had left for the Crusade.

'You go back to the Saracen's Head and I will sort everything out,' said Ulfrith with a confidence Geoffrey felt was unjustified, given the bald fact that berths on ships bound for Normandy were few and far between. 'Leave everything to me. And I will negotiate a good price too – better than anything you could manage for yourselves.'

He strode away, swaggering with the importance of the task he had been set. Geoffrey turned to Roger and grinned.

'A cup of warm ale, even if we have to drink it in the Saracen's Head, sounds more appealing than spending the day in fruitless discussions with hostile Saxon sea captains.'

Roger followed him back to the inn. The afternoon was turning chilly, with a cold wind slicing in from the north-east. The sky was clearing, too, promising freezing temperatures once darkness fell. Their feet crunched on slushy snow that was turning to ice, and Geoffrey was glad he had decided to walk that day, and that his warhorse was safe inside the tavern's stables. Destriers were expensive animals – it was not any old nag that could carry a fully armoured knight into battle without balking at the noise and the stench of spilled blood – and knights treated them with care and respect. It would be easy for a horse to damage a leg on the frozen, uneven ruts that formed the main road.

'What a dismal place,' said Roger as they walked through streets lined with shabby houses and the smoke from hundreds of cooking fires swirled around them. 'This is nothing like Durham. Durham is magnificent. You would like it, given your obsession with pretty buildings.'

As they moved away from the main harbour, the hectic sounds of trade faded. Geoffrey's dog loped ahead of them, shoving its nose in piles of offal, and wagging its tail in delirious delight. Some of the unwholesome mess through which it rifled was apparently even deemed edible, although Geoffrey tried not to think about what it might be devouring. Suddenly, it abandoned its scavenging and looked back down the road, ears pricked and one foot frozen in mid-step. Geoffrey turned to see what had disturbed it, but the street was empty. He snapped his fingers at it as he passed, to tell it to follow him, but the animal was growling and the hackles at the back of its neck were erect and bristling.

Geoffrey's dog was not known for its courage, and it was as likely to become agitated by a large cat as a hostile intruder. Roger ignored it, and continued to stride towards the tavern, but Geoffrey paused and scanned the silent street. It seemed deserted, but the dog continued to growl. There was a narrow alley a short distance away, and the dog's attention was fixed on it. Geoffrey retraced his steps and peered down it. At the far end was a gate, which swung closed, as though someone had just passed through. He ran towards it, and shoved it open to see where it went.

It opened on to a grassy area, where three cows nuzzled at the crust of snow in an attempt to graze on the sparse vegetation beneath. Coffin-sized bumps and a scattering of rubble suggested that this had once been the site of a church, abandoned when the town had built a new one. Geoffrey walked to the centre of the green and looked in all directions, scanning for signs that someone had fled down one of the many lanes that radiated outwards like spokes on a wheel.

But there was nothing to see. A small group of children kicked an inflated pig bladder around at the far end of the clearing, and two men wearing the glistening aprons of fishmongers talked together halfway down the widest of the streets. Geoffrey considered asking them whether they had seen someone running, but they saw him watching them and gazed back with resentful hostility. Bright straw-coloured hair poked from under the cap of one of them, and Geoffrey decided he did not want more encounters with bitter, dispossessed Saxons who seemed to believe that every Norman was personally responsible for the Conqueror's victory some thirty-five years before.

His dog had followed him, and was happily excavating a mound that Geoffrey was certain was a grave. Ignoring the snarls of outraged protest, Geoffrey grabbed it by the scruff of its neck and dragged it away before it could find itself some bones. The fact that it was no longer growling suggested that whatever had unnerved it had gone. Geoffrey sighed, suspecting he was being oversensitive, and that he should not allow the animal to send him rushing off down seedy alleyways every time it sensed the presence of a cat. The swinging gate had doubtless just caught in the wind, and had misled him into thinking that someone had opened it. He smiled at his own foolishness, and retraced his steps to where Roger waited.

Three

'Dog ran off, did it?' asked Roger as Geoffrey walked towards him after his fruitless foray. 'You should keep the thing on a leash when we are in towns. It is safer – and I do not mean for the dog.'

Roger was leaning against a water pump, oblivious of the fact that his looming presence was causing consternation to two Saxon crones who were hovering with empty buckets. Geoffrey tugged his arm, leaving the women to their well, and continued towards the tavern. He wondered when the hostility between Saxons and the Normans would ease. Usually, it was not a problem: Normans had taken Saxon wives, and their children had united the two peoples. But there were pockets of unrest, particularly among older people, who could still remember a time when it had been Saxon lords who had crippled them with taxes and held them in virtual slavery, rather than Normans.

'I am glad you sent Joab home,' said Roger. 'He was beside himself with grief when we buried his brother this morning. He was unhinged anyway, but today he verged on the lunatic.'

'I would have sent the others, too, but they declined to go. You have filled their greedy heads with too many stories of Holy Land treasure.'

'What did the sheriff say about Peterkin and the man with the weasel-like face? Did you tell him about the red bolts? I meant to go with you to see him, but that whore Mary came back and accused me of not paying her.'

'And did you?' asked Geoffrey. 'It would not be the first time you sent some poor woman away without her earnings. And this one was called Maude, not Mary.'

'How can I be expected to remember such trivial matters as names and whether they were paid?' asked Roger carelessly. 'Anyway, I offered her double if she spent a few more moments in my company, and she left happily enough afterwards – with her silver. But what did the sheriff say?'

'He said he knew of no one who uses scarlet arrows and that he has never heard of the tradition of colouring them in the way you described.'

'Must be something that only happens near Durham, then,' said Roger. 'We do things better up there. It is why we are superior soldiers.'

'Not because you have more practice from skirmishing with the Scots?' asked Geoffrey, smiling. He changed the subject, before Roger could start a tirade against the wicked Gaels and their innocent English victims. 'But the sheriff did not hold much hope for catching Peterkin's murderer. He said there were two other violent deaths last night, and that random killings happen fairly frequently, given the large number of men who gather – sailors, soldiers, traders, and so on.'

'But Peterkin was in your care, Geoff. You must want his death avenged! We shall have to find this Weasel ourselves.'

'How?' asked Geoffrey. 'We do not have time to investigate before we leave, and in any case, we have no idea where to begin. But one of Peterkin's killers paid the price: the sheriff collected the body of Weasel's accomplice this morning. He said he had never seen him before, and that he was not local. He will make enquiries, but I suspect nothing will come of it. The town is too big, there are too many places to hide, too few people willing to talk, and too many men coming and going.'

Roger shot him a puzzled look. 'It is unlike you to stand by while your men are slaughtered. Perhaps *I* should wander the town to see if I can spot Weasel – and then kill him for you.'

'It would be better if you passed him to the sheriff,' said Geoffrey. 'A lot of people will recognize Weasel from that roof-top brawl, and the sheriff noticed the similarity between the scarlet bolts that killed the boy, Peterkin, and Weasel's accomplice.'

'So?' asked Roger. 'What of it?'

Geoffrey sighed. 'He will identify Weasel's body and recall that it was *us* who accused him of killing Peterkin. He will know exactly who murdered the man.'

'But Weasel *did* kill Peterkin,' Roger pointed out. 'He deserves to die.'

'So he might, but it is not for us to take the law into our own hands. The sheriff could hang us for murder, just as he would Weasel.'

'But we would not *be* guilty of murder,' protested Roger. 'Only of dispensing justice.'

'I see,' said Geoffrey, thinking that perhaps Roger and his devious father had something in common after all – an ability to twist the facts to suit their own purposes. 'But I doubt you will find Weasel anyway. He will be lying low, hoping to escape by remaining hidden.'

'So, what did the sheriff make of the roof-top fight, then?' asked Roger, after a while.

'Not much,' said Geoffrey. 'His men questioned dozens of witnesses, but no one has admitted to knowing either combatant. He says the boy and Weasel were probably just passing through Southampton and had a disagreement that turned violent. It happens all the time, apparently. But, if we assume it was Weasel's accomplice who shot the lad – in the back, while Weasel faced him – then we can probably also assume that he killed Peterkin, too. And he is dead – shot by Weasel, who is not as good a marksman, fortunately for me. So, we do not have to worry about *him* evading justice.'

Roger looked around and shuddered. 'I feel as though someone has been watching me all day. I do not like this town. The sooner we leave, the better.'

'Have you *seen* anyone following you?' asked Geoffrey, surprised that a man like Roger should pay heed to such a sensation.

'I thought I saw an odd shadow earlier, but it turned out to be your dog enjoying itself with a chicken.' Roger's eyes lit on a bent figure that limped towards them, and he gripped Geoffrey's arm in mock alarm. 'Here comes

Ulfrith's grandfather! Get behind me, quick, lad! He looks dangerous, and you do not want to be bested by him a second time.'

Geoffrey sighed, seeing Roger was not going to let his embarrassing defeat be forgotten in a hurry. 'I was not *fighting* him,' he pointed out, although he knew it would make no difference to Roger's perception of events. 'He pushed me and I fell.'

'Like a maiden who has been at the ale!' guffawed Roger, loud enough to be heard over half the town. 'She totters all over the place, and will crash to the floor if you tap her with a feather! But the old man is drawing close, Geoff! Will you draw your sword to protect yourself, or would you rather I saved you?'

'Perhaps you should,' said Geoffrey, eyeing the old man warily. 'He has a determined glint in his eye that I do not like at all.'

The old man wheezed his way towards them, gnarled fingers clutching a stick on which he leant heavily. His remaining wisps of white hair were tied behind his head in traditional Saxon fashion, he wore a grimy tunic, and there were leather laces on his home-spun leggings. Geoffrey glanced at Roger, and saw the big knight grinning openly when he saw the exact nature of Geoffrey's victorious assailant in the harsh light of day.

'My grandson wants to go to the Holy Land,' said the old man accusingly, as though it were Geoffrey who had planted the idea in Ulfrith's mind. 'And he says you will not take him.'

'He is right,' said Geoffrey. 'So, you need not worry about losing him.'

He tried to step around the old man, but found his sleeve caught in a claw-like hand. He could have shaken it off, but the old warrior was unsteady on his feet, and Geoffrey did not want to knock him over. He stopped, aware that the bony hand on his arm was as much for support as to prevent the knight from leaving.

'You will not find a stronger lad, nor a finer fish-gutter,' the old man claimed proudly.

'I see,' said Geoffrey, trying gently to pull away. 'But you need not be afraid we will take him.'

'You misunderstand me,' said the old man, securing a firmer grip on Geoffrey's sleeve. 'I *want* you to take him into your service.'

'Useful though a talent for fish-gutting might be in the desert, we must decline,' said Geoffrey, his surprise evaporating when he realized the old man was urging Ulfrith on him so the boy could complete what he had failed to accomplish the previous night. 'I have trained soldiers from my own manor, and do not need more.'

He ignored Roger's snort of laughter at the notion that his men were anything like trained.

'You *do* need more,' insisted the old man. 'I watched you bury a soldier this morning, and I saw another going home. My grandson will take their places.'

'Thank you, no,' said Geoffrey firmly. 'Anyway, I am not in the habit of employing men who have tried to kill me. Or ones who hate Normans.'

'Ulfrith does not hate Normans,' said the old man, a hint of bitterness in his voice. 'I wish he did. I have done my best to make him see that you should not be tolerated in our land, but although he nods as I speak, the fire has never been in him like it was his father. Ulfrith has but one ambition in life, and that is to be part of a crusade.'

'Then he is a few years too late,' said Geoffrey. 'The Crusade is over, and the Holy Land is now under the control of the Christians, God help it.'

'But there are still skirmishes,' said the old man, 'and you still need soldiers to keep the infidel from snatching it back again. Ulfrith is your man.'

'Why are you so keen for him to die so far from home?' asked Geoffrey. 'I thought you were fond of him.'

The old man sighed. 'There is nothing for him here. I was the chief of a village before the Normans came, and I have spent my whole life expecting a wrong to be righted and to be given my lands back. But the Normans' hold on England grows stronger with each passing year, not weaker, and I know my manor is lost for ever. Ulfrith can fritter away his life as a fish-gutter, like his father, or he can make something of himself in the Holy Land. You stole his birthright; at least do not deprive him of this chance to do something noble.'

'*I* will take him,' declared Roger, who, unlike Geoffrey, was moved by this speech. 'I need a squire, and the louts Geoffrey has pressed into service are worse than useless. And I am only half Norman anyway – my mother was Saxon and was a great lady in Dur . . . up north.'

The old man smiled and began to pump Roger's hand, tears glittering in his rheumy eyes. 'Even better! Ulfrith will serve a man with Saxon blood in his veins. I can die with pride!'

'I will train him well,' said Roger confidently. 'You will have good cause to be proud of him once he has learned all *I* have to teach.'

'I hope you know what you are doing,' said Geoffrey to Roger, as they walked away. 'I can tell you from personal experience that Ulfrith has a murderous streak.'

'Aye,' said Roger, pleased. 'And that will make him a better soldier than you, who do not!'

That evening, Geoffrey and Roger sat in the Saracen's Head, discussing whether they should accept the passage Ulfrith had arranged for them on a ship that would not leave for ten days, or whether to ride to Pevensey, to see if they might fare better there.

Roger was for riding to Pevensey, because he did not like periods of enforced inactivity and would rather be doing something else – even something as potentially futile as a multi-day ride to another port where the situation might be no different. Geoffrey thought it was better to wait, maintaining it was foolhardy to squander an assured passage in favour of the vague possibility that they might find a quicker one. The ship Ulfrith had chosen was a sturdy vessel under a competent-looking captain, and the lad had even inveigled them a cabin, an unheard-of luxury as far as Geoffrey was concerned. Usually, when he travelled by ship, he slept on the open deck when the weather was fine or found some miserable corner in the hold when it was rough.

Yet, although the sensible option was to remain where they

were, Geoffrey did not like Southampton, and did not relish the prospect of lodging at the Saracen's Head for the next ten days. He could not shake off the feeling that someone was watching them, and was not easy with the notion that Weasel might be lurking in the shadows. He tried to be rational, knowing that a man with Weasel's inferior fighting skills was hardly a reason to leave the town, but the niggling concern persisted nonetheless.

The inn was hot and stuffy, and smoke from a badly swept chimney swirled around the room and made his eyes smart. He had also drunk too much wine, and wanted to escape the unhealthy atmosphere for a while to clear the fumes from his head. Leaving Roger carousing with the Littel brothers, while Helbye and Ulfrith hovered soberly in the background, he weaved his way across the room and stepped out into the cold night air. His dog followed, and snuffled optimistically at his hand, hopeful for something to eat.

It was a clear night, and he gazed up at the many stars that glittered above, wondering why it was that the more he stared at them, the more there seemed to be. He felt a sudden longing to be done with travelling and fighting, so he could sit in some quiet cloister and read about natural philosophy and astronomy, to understand the mysteries of the sparkling heavens above. But he knew that was never likely to happen. He was too old to become a scholar and the only other option was to forsake his knighthood and take the cowl. He knew he would make a poor monk: he was too independent and did not like people telling him what to do. He also had no intention of keeping vows of chastity, and even the most relaxed of orders would be unlikely to turn a blind eye to flagrant and frequent womanizing.

He snapped his thoughts away from the problems a scholarly life would bring when his dog began to growl deep in its throat, the way it did when it wanted to voice its objection to something, but did not want to make enough noise to draw attention to itself. Geoffrey crouched next to it, peering into the shadows, alert for any movement that might herald the winding of a crossbow. But there was nothing to see, no matter how hard he looked, and eventually the dog's growls ceased and its hackles lay flat again. Geoffrey patted its silky head, while it sat at his feet and gave a bored sigh.

He remained outside a while longer, enjoying the crispness of the winter night, then explored some of the tavern's outbuildings, to assure himself no one was lurking there with red crossbow bolts at the ready. The dog accompanied him happily enough – something it would not have done had it sensed any kind of threat.

After the cool peace of the yard, the tavern seemed noisier and stuffier than ever. It had also become more full since Geoffrey had left, and the area around the hearth was a seething mass of bodies, packed so closely together that it was only just possible for a man to raise a cup to his lips.

The table at which Roger sat was not as busy as the area near the fire, because it was not as warm. When Geoffrey had left, Roger had been engaged in a drinking game with the Littel brothers, but by the time he returned, they had abandoned him, and were dicing with some fishermen in a corner. Their places on the bench opposite Roger had been taken by three Benedictine monks, who sat with drawn cowls that made them look like crows at a funeral. Geoffrey smiled to himself, certain the company of three dour monastics was not the big knight's idea of fun.

'Are you sober now?' Roger asked as Geoffrey sat. 'Did the fresh air dispel that wonderful floating effect that I have been trying to attain all evening?'

'The dog started growling,' said Geoffrey, reaching for the wine jug. 'I thought there might be someone lurking outside.'

'You should have fetched me, in case there was an old man or a Saxon boy intent on besting you in armed combat.' Roger roared with laughter at his own wit.

'I hope to God we can leave this place soon,' said Geoffrey, knowing he would never be able to mention Southampton again without Roger making some reference to his ignoble defeat. 'It is worse than Jerusalem for random violence – at least in the Holy Land the fighting has a purpose of sorts.'

'You do say some peculiar things sometimes,' said Roger,

51

regarding him askance. 'You are a knight. Where would you be without acts of random violence?'

Geoffrey cast him a cool glance. 'Violence is all well and good if it leads to an acceptable end, but not when it causes an innocent like Peterkin to be shot for the price of a jug of ale.'

'I do not know why your overlord, Prince Tancred, tolerates your odd ideas,' said Roger, with genuine disapproval. 'It is not natural for a man to carry on so. It must be all that reading you do.' He folded his arms and pursed his lips in a matronly fashion, every fibre of his being expressing the suspicion and fear that the ignorant reserved for matters they did not understand.

'There are other ways to steal a purse besides killing its owner,' Geoffrey pointed out. 'If Weasel had simply pointed the crossbow at Peterkin and asked for it, the boy would have handed it to him. As I said, I will be glad when we leave this wretched country.'

'That is the land of your birth you are talking about,' said Roger admonishingly. 'It is a fine place, populated by good, honest folk, and every town and village is fit for the saints.'

Geoffrey regarded him suspiciously. 'This afternoon, you claimed you never wanted to set foot on its snow-infested pathways again, and that the sooner you could set sail for sunny Normandy, the happier you would be. What has brought about this sudden transformation?'

Roger shrugged, watching him out of the corner of his eye in a way that made Geoffrey aware that circumstances had somehow altered. 'I thought I might stay a while longer.'

Geoffrey frowned, wondering what had induced Roger to change his mind, when only a short while before he had been all in favour of riding to Pevensey on the remote chance they might find a ship that left England a day earlier than the one in Southampton. Could the prostitute, who had entertained him so royally the previous night, have persuaded him to linger?

Roger gestured to the monastics who sat opposite. 'These men have asked me to do something.'

Geoffrey was immediately wary, unable to imagine anything a monk might say to make Roger want to remain in

England. He regarded the three clerics sceptically, wondering whether he might do better not hearing what persuasive arguments they had used on his friend. He looked from one to the other, noting with detached amusement that the trio provided a perfect example of how men wearing identical clothes could end up looking completely different from each other.

Although all wore the cowled habits that marked them as members of the Benedictine Order, none looked impoverished. The material of their clothes was thick and expensive, and they wore boots of calfskin lined with fur. The monk in the middle seemed to be in charge, although none wore any badge of office. He was a big man, with thick, iron-grey hair and a pair of calculating dark-brown eyes. There were laughter lines around his mouth, suggesting he had found more amusement in his fifty or so years than was likely had he been in a monastery all that time. He also exuded an unmistakable aura of power. Geoffrey had met such men before, and was instantly on his guard, knowing from bitter experience that the less he had to do with them, the better.

The man to the right was tall and sinewy, with short ginger hair. His expression was simultaneously aloof and cunning, accentuated by a thin scar that ran from his lip to his temple. The last one was small and dark. His black eyes were restless, and Geoffrey had the impression that not the slightest detail escaped his attention. He had a narrow face with a sharp, prominent nose, and he held his head at an angle, which lent him the appearance of a curious but malevolent hen. They all looked, Geoffrey decided, like most high-ranking monastics he had encountered – sly, self-interested, and dishonest.

'What do you want?' he demanded of the monk who sat in the middle, not caring that the man's companions clearly thought he should show more respect.

'Nothing overly demanding,' the monk replied. 'But before we discuss it, I should probably introduce myself. I am Roger's father.'

Geoffrey glanced at Roger uncertainly, not sure the man was telling the truth. Roger beamed happily and slipped a conspiratorial arm around Geoffrey's shoulders, drawing him close so he could breathe into his ear in a hot, wine-perfumed whisper.

'He is indeed Ranulf Flambard, the Bishop of Durham. My father.'

Geoffrey looked from the monk to Roger, then back to the monk again. He was spared from making an immediate response by the arrival of a pot boy with some meat Roger had ordered. A sizeable chunk of pork, swimming in a sauce of greasy onions and brown apples, was slapped down, and Roger rubbed his hands in eager anticipation, kinsman forgotten.

'I thought you were in the White Tower of London, My Lord Bishop,' said Geoffrey bluntly. It was not an auspicious start to the conversation, but it voiced the concern uppermost in his mind.

Flambard grimaced. 'So I was until a few days ago. I escaped.'

Geoffrey was startled. 'People do not escape from the White Tower!'

'Ah, but I am not just any old person, am I?' said Flambard with an enigmatic smile. 'I have many friends, a vast fortune, and more intelligence than the whole of King Henry's council put together.'

'Modestly put,' said Geoffrey dryly. 'But you should not underestimate Henry. He is no simpleton. I met him recently, and I can tell you without exaggeration that he is one of the most crafty men I have ever encountered.'

Flambard gave a grin, and Geoffrey saw that the resemblance between him and Roger was unmistakable, particularly in the way the eyes twinkled. Geoffrey glanced around him uneasily, certain it was not wise to be sitting in a tavern with the unpopular bishop at any time, but especially when he had just absconded from one of the King's most powerful fortresses.

'Crafty is a good word for Henry,' said Flambard. 'However, I outwitted him easily over my escape. I befriended the gaolers with my affable charm and ready purse, and ordered a vat of wine, so we could enjoy a night of festivity together.

Concealed in the vat was a rope. Later, while the gaolers snored in drunken slumber, I climbed out of the window, where loyal subjects waited with horses.'

Geoffrey reached across the table, to the startled consternation of Flambard's two companions, and pushed back the sleeve of the bishop's habit. The ginger-haired cleric reached hastily for something in his robe that Geoffrey was certain was unlikely to be of a religious nature.

'It seems your cunning escape might have been more pleasant had your friends also provided you with gloves – or a less abrasive rope,' Geoffrey said, gesturing to the heavily bandaged hands he had exposed. There was a small scraping sound as the ginger-haired man sheathed his dagger. He was right to be cautious, Geoffrey thought: Flambard's ruthless taxes meant that most of the population would dearly love to ram something sharp into the bishop's black heart.

Flambard scowled, looking more like a petulant child than one of the most powerful churchmen in England. 'It is a risk one takes when one is forced to rely on men less able than oneself.' He fixed his companions with a stare that was about as far from episcopal benevolence as it was possible to be. Both looked away, so Geoffrey knew exactly who Flambard held responsible for the oversight. 'But although the skin of my palms remains in King Henry's tender care, the rest of me is about to sail to France, where I shall offer my services to the Duke of Normandy.'

'Geoffrey served the Duke of Normandy,' said Roger through a mouthful of food.

'Really?' asked Flambard, appraising Geoffrey anew. 'Why did you leave him?'

'He sent me to tutor his kinsman, Tancred,' said Geoffrey shortly, not wanting to discuss his military career with a man he instinctively did not trust. He supposed that while Roger had inherited his physique and swarthy complexion from his father, his personality had come from his mother, or Roger and Geoffrey would not have liked each other.

'Tancred,' mused Flambard. 'An ambitious and greedy prince, who went on Crusade for the sole purpose of amassing personal power and fortune. I considered doing the same myself, but things were going rather well at home, and I thought it was rash to risk so much on what might have proved an unprofitable venture.'

Geoffrey turned to Flambard's companions. 'How did you help him escape?' he asked with genuine interest. 'The Tower is supposed to be impregnable – at least, that is what the King tells the citizens of London, who are being taxed to pay for the thing.'

'I put the rope in the wine and arranged for horses to be ready,' the redhead said. 'But the whole thing was Odard's idea.'

Odard demurred. 'Xavier flatters me. I am just a humble monk.'

He looked anything but humble, and Geoffrey imagined him capable of arranging a good deal more than mere prison break-outs.

'Geoffrey wanted to be a scholar,' boomed Roger irrelevantly. 'It was because he ran away to Paris's libraries so often that the Duke of Normandy sent him to tutor Tancred in Italy.'

'What was wrong with a career in healthy slaughter?' asked Flambard, humour glinting again in his eyes. 'Do you prefer books to butchery, Sir Geoffrey?'

'Don't you, My Lord Bishop?' replied Geoffrey evasively.

'I considered a military life when I was younger,' said Flambard, wincing as he used his damaged hands to take a piece of meat from Roger's platter. 'Pork in Lent! Still, it is my favourite meat.'

'It is mine, too,' said Roger fawningly.

'So what prevented *you* from pursuing a career in slaughter?' asked Geoffrey of Flambard.

The bishop chewed thoughtfully. 'It did not take long for me to learn that life as a courtier was far more lucrative. I took holy orders when King William Rufus offered to make me a bishop.'

'I heard the office cost you a thousand pounds,' remarked Geoffrey. It was a fabulous sum of money, beyond the wildest dreams of most folk.

Flambard sighed. 'You are right. I did not relish watching such a large sum disappear, but it will be worth the price eventually. Durham is a great prize. I own huge tracts of land, my own mint, my own court of law, and several castles. It will make me rich.'

'You will miss them, then,' said Geoffrey insolently, 'when you flee to Normandy.' He did not like this gloating, complacent churchman, no matter how much Roger would have him believe that his father was only a miracle or two short of canonization.

'I will not leave them for long,' said Flambard, unmoved by Geoffrey's obvious antipathy. 'Henry is not secure on his throne yet, and may be ousted by a man with a greater claim – like the Duke. Failing that, I am rich enough to win Henry over eventually.'

'You mean you will bribe him to allow you to return?' asked Geoffrey.

Flambard pretended to be shocked. 'Sir Geoffrey! That would be tantamount to the crime of simony, and *I* am a man of God! I was merely proposing that I might offer the King a loan, so he can use the money to protect his kingdom against his enemies.'

'I see,' said Geoffrey, thinking that Flambard was a brave man indeed, if he planned to visit the Duke of Normandy first, to see what might be gained from serving him, and then proposed to return to King Henry if the Duke proved unsuitable. Geoffrey would not have attempted to play such a dangerous game.

'Good meat, this,' said Roger, waving a bone in Geoffrey's direction. 'You should try some. It will fortify you for our journey north, to complete the small task my father asks of us.'

'My journey is east – to Normandy and the Holy Land,' said Geoffrey, as the big knight cracked the bone between his powerful jaws.

Roger shook his head. 'My father wants something first.'

Geoffrey regarded Flambard coolly. 'We are taking a serious risk even to be seen with you. You are an escaped felon, and

King Henry will not look kindly on anyone who helps you. But it would be more dangerous still to run your errands. We will not do it.'

'We will,' said Roger. 'My father needs me.'

Dark-haired Odard gestured around the tavern. 'Where lies the danger? We are three humble monks enjoying a cup of ale in the company of strangers. No one will associate your change of plans – to travel north instead of to the Holy Land – with us. We met purely by chance.'

'No,' said Geoffrey. 'This is no random encounter, but one that has been carefully planned. You knew Roger would be in Southampton looking for a ship to take him to Normandy. You have been following him all day, waiting for an opportunity to speak.'

'What do you mean?' demanded Roger. 'I was just sitting here and he spotted me. I had no idea he would be in this tavern.'

'But he knew *you* would be here,' said Geoffrey. 'It was he who recommended the Saracen's Head as a place to stay, remember? And now I cannot help but wonder whether all those captains were bribed not to sell us passage – to prevent you from leaving before you had been inveigled into doing whatever it is Flambard feels he cannot do himself.'

'How could a mere cleric hold such sway over rough sea captains?' asked Flambard, in a way that suggested rough sea captains posed no problem at all for a 'mere cleric' of his talents and resources.

'We sensed we were being followed,' Geoffrey continued. 'And we were right. The good brothers here were probably doing that – although not very well.'

Xavier was indignant at the criticism, although Odard merely smiled his secret smile. Their reactions told Geoffrey his guess was correct, and his unease intensified. The errand Flambard wanted his son to complete must be important indeed, if he were prepared to go to such lengths to ensure cooperation.

'Father would never do such a low thing,' said Roger defensively, to the startled amusement of Xavier and Odard. Flambard inclined his head graciously, and Geoffrey felt a surge of fury that the man should so casually abuse the blind trust Roger placed in him.

Observing Geoffrey's anger, Flambard fixed him with a cold glower and for the first time, Geoffrey sensed his malevolence, aware he would sacrifice anything and anyone to get what he wanted. He had not risen from obscurity to one of the most powerful positions in England by ability alone, and Geoffrey detected a ruthlessness in him that was chilling.

'Roger is my son,' said Flambard in a soft voice with steel in it. 'When I command him to do something, he obeys.'

'Even when you command him to break the law?' asked Geoffrey, holding Flambard's gaze. His instincts told him to leave immediately, but then what would happen to Roger? The big knight would be putty in Flambard's hands, and who knew what he might agree to do without Geoffrey to advise him? 'Would you have him executed by King Henry because he plots treason on your behalf?'

'Now, just a moment,' objected Roger indignantly. 'He has only asked me to deliver a message. Where lies the treason in that?'

Flambard ignored him and shook his head at Geoffrey. 'You do me an injustice – and Roger, too. Do you put so little faith in his integrity?'

It was not Roger's integrity that Geoffrey was worried about – although integrity was not a word he would have used to describe Roger's straightforward outlook on life – it was his gullibility. Geoffrey knew that Roger genuinely believed Flambard could do no wrong.

'I have intestacy and plenty of it,' declared Roger, earning a bemused look from the others. He beamed at his father. 'You can put your faith in my intestacy all you like.'

Flambard patted his hand and then turned his bright gaze on Geoffrey again. 'I want Roger to deliver a message to my prior at Durham. It contains nothing treasonous or sinister: it is merely a pastoral missive from one cleric to another.'

'Really?' asked Geoffrey sceptically. 'Can I see it?'

'Certainly,' said Flambard, reaching for his scrip.

'He can read,' interposed Roger for Flambard's information. 'He likes to look at books.' He made it sound a pastime akin to sodomy or conjuring up black spirits from Hell.

'What I say to my prior is none of your affair,' said Flambard, dropping his hand away from his scrip as though it had been burned.

Clearly, he had not anticipated that one of the notoriously rough Holy Land knights would be literate, and Geoffrey was more convinced than ever that Flambard's missive was anything but pastoral. He determined that Roger should have nothing to do with it.

'The Prince-Bishop of Durham will not have his private messages perused by nosy knights,' said Odard with courtly disdain. 'I imagine you are not even a knight with property to speak of. You are doubtless an impecunious younger son of a man with too many children.'

It did not take a genius to see that Odard hoped to make Geoffrey feel he was unworthy to read Flambard's episcopal missives, but his guess about Geoffrey's heritage was right to a certain extent: Geoffrey was a fourth son and his tiny manor on the Welsh borders would never make him wealthy. However, he felt himself justified in reading whatever it was Flambard wanted to give to Roger.

'I will not yield to your demand to read my correspondence,' said Flambard haughtily. 'You can go back to Jerusalem, to murder old men and steal from widows too weak to stop you.'

'Very well,' said Geoffrey, standing to leave and thinking that the descriptions of his supposed activities in the Holy Land were more akin to the wrongs Flambard had perpetrated than anything he had ever done.

'Geoff, wait!' cried Roger. 'I cannot do this alone. I need someone to go with me.'

'People journey north every day,' said Geoffrey, hoping Roger would see sense and decline Flambard's mission when he realized he would have to do it alone.

'I need soldiers,' protested Roger, grabbing Geoffrey's arm to prevent him from walking away.

'You have Ulfrith,' said Geoffrey. 'He will protect you.'

Roger's tone became wheedling. 'Please, Geoff! You always said you wanted to see the cathedral in Durham. I will show it to you. And there are other churches, too, not to mention a fine library.'

Geoffrey smiled at Roger's attempts to entice him. 'All the churches and libraries in the world will mean nothing if the King's agents arrest us for carrying secret dispatches from Flambard to his minions. I will have nothing to do with this, and if you have the remotest grain of sense in your thick head, you will not either.'

Flambard stood as Geoffrey picked up his cloak, ignoring Roger's indignant spluttering. 'Very well. I see I will have to take you further into my confidence.'

'No, thank you!' objected Geoffrey hastily, trying to step around him.

A meaty hand grabbed the hem of his surcoat and prevented him from leaving. 'Just listen,' said Roger quietly. 'Listening will harm no one.'

That depended on what you heard, thought Geoffrey. He was certain King Henry would not appreciate the difference between listening to treason and acting on it.

'You consider me a traitor,' said Flambard reproachfully. 'I am not. However, while I was in the service of Rufus, I had occasion to amass a little personal wealth.'

'So I gather,' said Geoffrey dryly. While most taxes Flambard had collected had doubtless found their way to Rufus's coffers, Flambard was far too greedy to have handed them all over, and Geoffrey was not at all surprised to hear he was a rich man.

'I intend to donate most of my gold for the building of my cathedral,' said Flambard. He lowered his voice, so Geoffrey had to strain to hear what he was saying. 'It is not cheap to hire a hundred masons for four decades, yet that is what I must do if my mighty church-fortress is to be completed. We have been working ten years already, and only the chancel is finished. We are just beginning the nave and the transepts. A vast sum will be needed, and *I* have it hidden in a safe place.'

'So, you have set money aside for the cathedral, and you want us to tell the prior of Durham where it is?' asked Geoffrey, not sure he believed it. Coming from a man of Flambard's dubious reputation, it sounded unlikely at best.

Flambard nodded. 'You are a shrewd man, Geoffrey Mappestone. I would feel happier if I knew my son's safety was in your hands.'

'Now, just a moment,' objected Roger, offended. 'I can look after myself. I am no child to be given a nursemaid. I am a *Jerosolimitanus*!'

'I know,' said Flambard soothingly. 'But all men fare better with a friend than alone.'

'That depends on the friend,' said Geoffrey.

Flambard was still gazing at him. 'Your guess about the nature of my message is not quite right. You see, the amount of money we are talking about here is considerable – so considerable I can trust no one person to resist its lure and ensure it goes to the cathedral.'

'You have appointed men you cannot trust to build it?' asked Geoffrey, amused that Flambard was reaping the fruits of his corrupt practices in such a way.

Flambard sighed. 'I would trust them with lesser sums, but this is a fortune beyond the imaginations of most men.'

'Then you should not tell greedy Crusader knights about it,' advised Geoffrey.

Flambard sighed impatiently. 'Listen, and you will understand all. I have drawn three maps on three pieces of parchment. Separately, these maps mean nothing, but together they form a whole and will reveal where my treasure is hidden. I have already sent two parchments by separate messengers – one to the Sheriff of Durham and the other to a goldsmith called Walter Jarveaux. The third, I will send with Roger to Prior Turgot.'

'Who are the other messengers?' asked Geoffrey.

'Men I trust,' said Flambard evasively.

'It would not be these two, would it?' asked Roger, pointing at Xavier and Odard.

Flambard smiled indulgently. 'I have just told you that the

other two messages have already been dispatched. Odard and Xavier would not be sitting here if they had been sent north, would they?'

'I do not understand how this map works,' said Roger, frowning. 'Why are the parchments impossible to inter-pret alone?'

Flambard withdrew something from the scrip at his side, while his two companions regarded it in horror, clearly appalled to see it waved openly in a tavern. Flambard ignored them.

'This is the map for Turgot,' he said, as Geoffrey took it from him 'As you can see, it is blank except for a cross. This cross marks where the treasure is hidden.'

'I see,' said Geoffrey. 'A cross on a blank page is useless, but if it is laid over a map showing rivers, forests, and villages, it will tell you where this fortune is located.'

'Precisely,' said Flambard. 'The second map depicts two streams and a path; the third map indicates the location of a settlement. You might think that whoever has the map with the name of the area has an advantage over the others, but all it will tell him is that the treasure is hidden within a five-mile radius. And even a man desperate with greed cannot dig up huge tracts of countryside on the vague chance that he might discover my hoard.'

'I would,' said Roger. 'I would hire a team of men and promise them a share when it was found.'

'I would explore the area carefully, looking for evidence of disturbed soil,' said Geoffrey. 'If this hoard is as large as you suggest, then burying it would have left a mark on the ground.'

Flambard grinned. 'And that intelligent approach would mean you would be more likely to find it than Roger. But I am not stupid. I employed men skilled in such matters to bury my treasure. It is hidden so well that no one will ever find it without the help of my maps.'

'And what is to stop these "skilled men" from helping themselves?' asked Geoffrey.

'They have been taken care of,' said Odard smoothly.

'You mean you have killed them to ensure their silence?'

asked Geoffrey coldly. 'Is that what will happen to Roger once he has done your bidding?'

'Nothing will happen to him – or you – because you know nothing important,' said Flambard. 'Without the other two, your map is worthless. I know I can trust Roger to do as I ask.'

'You can trust Geoff, too,' said Roger, giving his friend a comradely slap on the back. 'He is less interested in riches than anyone I know. Even if he did come across the treasure, he would probably donate it to the cathedral anyway. He likes a pretty building.'

'Well, that is settled then,' said Flambard, mischief glinting in his dark-brown eyes. 'None of us has anything to worry about. Roger is a good son who will carry out his father's wishes; Geoffrey has no ambition for wealth; and my treasure will be used to praise the glory of God with a great cathedral that will be one of the wonders of the world. What evil is there in that?'

Four

'God's teeth!' breathed Geoffrey in awe, as he and Roger, with their men streaming behind them, crested the rise of a hill and the city of Durham came into view. He reined in his horse to admire the spectacle in front of him. 'That is remarkable!'

The city was several miles away, yet it dominated the landscape. It stood on a rocky peninsula set in a loop of the River Wear. On three sides, it was protected by cliffs and the river; the fourth was defended by the castle, which comprised a double moat, an octagonal keep atop a motte, and a wall. Entry to the peninsula was controlled by sturdy and well-guarded gates.

On the highest point of the peninsula, occupying the best position, was the cathedral. The completed chancel stood like a palace, with layer upon layer of blind arcades and round-headed windows. The foundations were already laid for the nave, which promised to be so large it took Geoffrey's breath away. Once it was finished, Flambard's largess in funding it would be remembered for centuries – and Geoffrey was certain the notion of everlasting fame was not too far from the bishop's mind as he continued what his ecclesiastical predecessors had started.

South of the cathedral was the abbey. Geoffrey saw the community would be a large one, and already boasted a chapter house, a dorter where the monks slept, a frater where they ate, and kitchens. There was also an elegant house with a tiled roof that Geoffrey imagined was where the prior lived. Finally, there was the city itself. The main town clustered around a market square, and its houses were large and well built. Between castle and cathedral were untidy hovels that Roger said would soon be demolished because they posed a fire hazard, while the last part was an ancient community known as the Elvet, located on the opposite side of the river.

'There are bigger and better cathedrals than *that* in the Holy Land,' said Ulfrith disparagingly. 'This is all right, but the Holy Land is . . . well, it is holy.'

Geoffrey wondered how the lad had gained his rosy impressions of Palestine. It was not from any Crusader, who would be more likely to list the Holy Land's less appealing aspects – heat, flies, and inconvenient intestinal diseases. Geoffrey had tried to correct his unrealistic vision, but Ulfrith had declined to believe him. He had also infected the other soldiers with his enthusiasm, and even the unsavoury Littel brothers now talked about Jerusalem in reverently hushed tones. Geoffrey only hoped he would not have a mutiny on his hands when they eventually set eyes on the proverbial land of milk and honey.

'This is the best cathedral on Earth,' declared Roger, peeved. 'When it is finished, it will be a great fortress, with towers for lookouts, arrow slits for archers, and a thick door to keep out the Scots.'

'Will there be room in this church for religion?' asked Geoffrey wryly. 'Or will its function be purely military?'

'Well, there is the Chapel of the Nine Altars, I suppose,' said Roger, after a moment of serious thought. 'The religious stuff can take place there – and there will be a lot of it. The Benedictines have an abbey here and pilgrims will come, of course.'

'Why?' asked Ulfrith. 'They would do better going to the Holy Land.'

'Because we have lots of saints,' said Roger huffily, not pleased to have the importance of his home city questioned by the likes of Ulfrith. 'There is Cuthbert, the greatest of them all, and his friends Aidan and Oswald. And we shall soon have Aaron's Rod.'

He cast Geoffrey a defiant glance. Geoffrey sighed, but declined to become embroiled in another debate about the thing.

66

'Do these saints already belong to Durham?' asked Sergeant Helbye thoughtfully. 'If not, there might be a fight for them, and we could offer our services to the side we think will win.'

'They are all ours,' said Roger loftily. 'Do you not know the story of the cow and the bones?'

'Enlighten us,' said Geoffrey warily, not sure they could believe anything Roger told them about history, coloured as it would be by prejudice and ignorance, but curious nonetheless.

'When Cuthbert died, he was brought to Durham by a cow,' said Roger authoritatively. 'The cow told Cuthbert's friends where to put his body – which was still as fresh as a daisy, even after a thousand years – and instructed them to build a church over it, to keep it nice.'

Geoffrey turned away so Roger would not see him smile. The story of St Cuthbert was one he had read many times. When the monks on the remote island of Lindisfarne were threatened by Viking raids, they removed the body of their founder from its grave to take to a safer place. All were astonished to find the body undecayed after 200 years. It was declared a miracle, and Cuthbert was canonized. The monks spent years wandering with the body, until they followed a girl with a dun cow to a place called Dunholm. The cow stumbled, and the monks interpreted it as a sign that they were to settle. They founded a church and St Cuthbert's relics had rested in it ever since.

'I see,' said Ulfrith, accepting Roger's version of the story without demur. 'And where do Cuthbert's friends St Aidan and St Oswald come into all this?'

'Cuthbert has Oswald's arm in his coffin,' said Roger, unwilling to admit he did not know and fabricating instead. 'They were friends in life and when Oswald died, Cuthbert could not bear to be separated, so usually kept a bit of him somewhere close by, to talk to.'

'Oswald and Cuthbert could not have been friends,' said Geoffrey, reluctant to see the gullible Ulfrith fed such patently false information. 'Oswald died when Cuthbert was a child—'

Roger interrupted with a wave of his hand. 'Details! The point is that my father is going to take the bones of all these saints from that wooden church you can see next to the cathedral, and put them in his glorious new one. And since they are England's best-loved relics, pilgrims will flock to see them. Durham will be rich beyond its wildest dreams.'

'That is why Flambard is willing to pay for the cathedral with his own funds,' Geoffrey explained to Ulfrith. 'He expects returns on his investment.'

'He is a bishop,' said Roger, offended. 'Why should he not build a cathedral? Durham is one of the most powerful sees in the country, and so its bishop should have an impressive church.'

It was not only a cathedral Flambard was raising, Geoffrey noted. In the shadow of the chancel, other structures were springing up, and scaffolding rose around sections of a curtain wall that would eventually surround the whole peninsula. Flambard would be lord of a community comprising castle, abbey, cathedral, and fortified town.

'Right,' Geoffrey said, turning to mount his warhorse. 'I suggest we deliver this map to Prior Turgot and head south. This jaunt has delayed our return to the Holy Land by weeks. It is all right for you, Roger – your overlord is in a Turkish prison – but mine is not, and he expects me back.'

'Then you should not have spent so much time trying to work out which one of your family murdered your father,' said Roger unsympathetically, referring to an incident that had kept Geoffrey in England the previous autumn. 'I would not have taken so long to discover the truth.'

'Would you not,' said Geoffrey, thinking that if someone murdered Flambard, Roger would have, quite literally, thousands of suspects to interrogate. The widespread jubilation that would doubtless accompany news of the unpopular bishop's demise would make the crime – if it could be considered as such – even more difficult to solve.

'We will stay with my sister,' said Roger, when they eventually reached the flat-bottomed ferry that would carry them across the river. 'She will enjoy our company.'

'We will not be here long,' Geoffrey warned. 'Remember what we agreed: as soon as the map is delivered, we leave.'

'I know, I know,' said Roger impatiently. He gestured with a brawny arm at the city, causing the boat to rock precariously, so Geoffrey had to clutch at the ferryman to avoid being tipped into the water. 'But just look at all this, lad. It is God's own land!'

'Perhaps you should stay, if you feel so strongly about it,' said Geoffrey. 'You never did tell me why you joined the Crusade. I had no choice – Tancred wanted to go and I was in his service – but you volunteered.'

Roger sighed. 'Just because I admire a chest of gold does not mean to say that I want to live in one. There is plenty for me in the Holy Land yet. There are cities to be looted, and the infidel still infest some of our most sacred places.'

Once across the river, Geoffrey followed Roger up a steep, rocky path to a formidable stone-built gateway called Owengate. He detected movement through the arrow slits, and knew archers were on duty, ready to fire at anyone who posed a threat. Above them, a covered platform had been constructed to allow defenders to drop missiles on to the heads of anyone attempting to force entry. Geoffrey would not have enjoyed the prospect of storming such a well-defended site.

'I am Sir Roger of Durham,' proclaimed Roger importantly – unable to claim Flambard as a family name because of his illegitimacy – to the guard inside Owengate who demanded to know his business. 'I have returned from fighting God's holy war, and have come to pay my respects to my sister, Eleanor of Durham. Let me in.'

'She is known as Eleanor Stanstede now,' said the guard cockily.

Roger appeared to be startled, although whether by the news that his sister had married in his absence or by the guard's insolence, Geoffrey could not tell. He tensed, ready to grab Roger if he took offence at being so rudely questioned and tried to take the gatehouse single-handed. Geoffrey had not ridden days through snow, rain, and howling winds so Roger could be shot without even being allowed inside.

'How am I supposed to know what my sister has been

doing?' demanded Roger. 'I have just told you I have been fighting – unlike you, who have doubtless been skulking here with your cronies, like the black-hearted coward you are.'

Geoffrey's hand went to the hilt of his sword when the gate was thrown open, and a man strode out. His wariness turned to confusion when the man grinned from ear to ear, and Roger's scowl disappeared like a puff of smoke in the wind.

'Simon, you scoundrel!' Roger bellowed, enveloping the guard in a powerful hug. Simon was not a small person, but even so, Roger's enthusiastic welcome made him wince.

'You villain!' cried Simon in return. 'I never expected to see you again.'

'It will take more than a few Saracens to keep *me* away,' declared Roger pompously.

'Well, I am delighted to see you,' said Simon. 'Although I do not imagine others will feel the same. If you know what is good for you, tread carefully for a while. Some people have long memories.'

'I care nothing for them,' said Roger disdainfully. 'And all that is in the past now, anyway.'

'What do you mean?' asked Geoffrey suspiciously. 'Did you leave Durham under some kind of cloud? Is this man suggesting you might not be welcome here?'

'No!' said Roger indignantly. He remembered his manners. 'This is Sir Geoffrey Mappestone, who comes from near Wales. He is a true friend and a great warrior.' He pulled Simon close to him, adding a whisper Geoffrey would have been deaf not to hear. 'I must warn you that he reads.'

'We let the monks do that around here,' said Simon, eyeing Geoffrey uneasily. 'There are more than enough of them for that sort of thing.'

'My father has expanded Durham's monastery recently,' explained Roger to Geoffrey. 'He wants it to be massive, and rival places like Peterborough, Winchester, and Ely.'

'Then he should watch himself,' said Simon. 'It is unwise to let reading men grow too powerful. Who knows what they might do with their inkwells and their scrolls and their pens?'

He shot Geoffrey a look that was not entirely friendly.

Geoffrey smiled at him, noting the uncanny resemblance between him and Roger. Both had the same deep-set eyes that Geoffrey had noticed in Flambard, and they had broad shoulders and were heavily built. He wondered whether the entire city was populated by the fruits of Flambard's amorous adventures with seamstresses and maidservants.

'Simon Mainard here took his mother's name,' said Roger to Geoffrey. 'He usually tells people he is our father's nephew, although we are actually half-brothers.'

'It does not do for a bishop to have too many offspring,' said Simon with a knowing grin. 'And I am informed that a bishop's "nephews" fare much better than those who confess to being his sons.'

Geoffrey thought it was probably safer for Flambard's offspring to keep their parentage completely to themselves. Admitting kinship with the devious bishop would not make them popular, and might even be dangerous.

'Never mind that,' said Roger, draping a thick arm around his half-brother's shoulders. 'What is this about our Eleanor? She has married, you say?'

'To Haymo Stanstede. Remember him? He is the town's spice merchant. Very wealthy. She did well for herself.'

Roger gazed at him uncertainly. 'Surely you mean *Guy* Stanstede? Haymo is old enough to be Methuselah's grandfather.'

Simon agreed. 'But Guy died of a bloody flux last year, and Haymo found himself without an heir. He put about the news that he was available as a husband, with a view to begetting a son. Eleanor decided to accept the challenge, and they were married last summer, although she expected him to be dead within a few months, thus leaving her his fortune. But Haymo is thriving. In fact, he is more vibrant now than he was as a widower. He must be nearing seventy and married life suits him.'

Roger shuddered. 'Poor lass, having to endure *that* coming at her night after night. But I am here now, and will keep her talking late into the night, long after Haymo Stanstede will need to rest his ancient limbs. He will not seduce my sister while *I* am around.'

'As her spouse, it is his prerogative to seduce her when he likes,' Simon pointed out. 'And you should ask *her* what she wants before you interfere. You know what she can be like.'

'She will welcome rescue,' declared Roger in a voice that indicated the matter was already settled.

'Where do you plan to stay? With me? I can lodge my pig with a neighbour, and the sty is really quite pleasant once it has been mucked out.'

'No,' said Roger rudely. 'I am a *Jerosolimitanus* and I do not sleep in pigsties.' He drew himself up to his full height, although the impression of status and wealth he aimed to project was marred by his filthy clothes and the straw that still clung to his surcoat from their bed in a hayloft the previous night. Simon did not notice, and even seemed awed by Roger's untruthful claims.

'Will you stay with the prior?' he asked doubtfully, apparently selecting the most auspicious lodgings he could think of. 'I do not think he will like that very much.'

'Of course not!' said Roger in disdain. 'We will stay with Eleanor. She always did keep a cosy house, and it will be even better now, if she lives in Stanstede's mansion.'

'He still owns the place just off the market square,' said Simon with a wink. 'But you cannot take this lot with you. Ellie is very particular about who she lets into her private quarters.'

He was looking at Geoffrey's soldiers. Geoffrey understood exactly why he should voice reservations about their imposing themselves on the hospitality of a wealthy lady. They were travel-stained and scruffy, and sported an eccentric array of garments that were a compromise between the armour Geoffrey insisted they wear in case they were attacked, and the additional clothes they had donned to ward off the icy northern winds. They all looked rough and disreputable.

'Can they be lodged in the castle?' he asked. The other option was a tavern, but he did not want the Littel brothers in a place where they could drink themselves into a state of belligerence, then cause trouble in the town. At least the castle would probably impose some sort of curfew on its guests.

Simon nodded. 'Best place for them. And you can leave that here, too, if you like.' He pointed at Geoffrey's dog, which was sniffing the air in eager anticipation of unwary chickens to kill. 'It seems savage, and will not be welcome in a city where livestock roams free.'

'Believe me, Simon, you do not want responsibility for that thing,' said Roger, regarding the dog with dislike. 'Let Geoffrey keep it. He can no better control it than anyone else, but at least he has the funds to compensate people for their losses.' He smiled at Geoffrey. 'But before we make Ellie's day by telling her she has guests, I want you to see something.'

'The prior's house?' suggested Geoffrey hopefully. 'It would be good to deliver that map now.'

'Later,' said Roger.

'Where?' asked Geoffrey reluctantly. He was tired, dirty, and in no mood to traipse around a city on some tour devised by Roger that would probably include seedy taverns and perhaps even a brothel.

Roger looked proud. 'I want you to see our relics – and the shrine my father is building for Aaron's Rod. Then you will believe me when I say it is coming to Durham.'

Roger was not easily dissuaded from a course of action once he had decided upon it, and Geoffrey found he had no choice but to follow him and Simon along a path of yellow mud that led to the cathedral. Once he was close, and could see in detail the elegant windows and the intricate decoration on the façade, his irritation evaporated. He gazed at the mighty edifice for some time, before Roger tugged on his sleeve to lead him inside.

Like many stone churches built by Normans, the interior of Durham cathedral was icy cold. The narrow windows admitted little light, so it was shadowy, too. The walls were vibrant with paintings, some intricate geometrical designs of red and yellow, others depicting fabulous animals from the Bible. Roger hurried Geoffrey through it and out the other side, to where an old wooden church looked decrepit and dirty next to the expanding cathedral. He opened a door that creaked on worn leather hinges and marched down the aisle to the altar, sword clanking against his boots and his footsteps slapping on the flagstones. Geoffrey and Simon followed.

'This will be demolished soon,' Roger announced, his voice loud in the silence. 'The Saxons built it when Cuthbert first came to Durham, and his bones have rested here for ages.'

The altar was made of wood, lovingly carved with scenes from Cuthbert's life by some long-dead craftsman. Behind it were a series of alcoves, each filled with a box, although one was ominously vacant. Roger pointed to it.

'That is where Aaron's Rod will rest – assuming, of course, that it will not go directly to the cathedral. Now, that big coffin you can see in the middle is Cuthbert's. Above him are Ceolwulf, Edbert, and Aidan, while that long casket to the left contains one of Oswald's arms; the other is in with Cuthbert, of course.'

'Of course,' said Geoffrey wryly. 'However, I understood it was Oswald's *head* that was in Cuthbert's coffin, not his arm.'

'You know nothing about this,' said Roger dismissively. 'Oswald's head is . . .' He faltered.

'Yes?' asked Geoffrey.

'Elsewhere,' Roger concluded mysteriously. 'It is not here.'

'I see,' said Geoffrey, assuming that Roger did not know. 'What about Balthere? I thought his relics were in Durham.'

'St Giles' Church,' said Roger. 'He is less famous, but the Saxons are fond of him.'

'They were,' said Simon. 'But he was stolen four years ago and no one has heard of him since.'

'Someone stole Balthere's bones?' asked Roger, horrified. He crossed himself quickly. 'Then someone is bound for the fires and brimstone of Hell and *that* is certain. The saints do not like their mortal remains manhandled.'

'Most people have forgotten about Balthere,' said Simon. 'Especially now we will soon have something to put even Cuthbert in the shade. Everyone will like Aaron's Rod.'

'I am sure they will,' said Geoffrey. 'And I am equally sure they will pay handsomely to pray near it and ask it for boons.'

'Oh, yes,' agreed Roger, rubbing his hands together. 'It will certainly bring in the money.'

'Come on,' said Simon, yanking on Roger's surcoat. 'It is cold in here. I do not want to spend the day gawking at relics – no matter how holy they are. That is for monks and men who can read.'

He gave Geoffrey another unpleasant look, so the knight wondered yet again what it was about literacy that so often provoked hostile reactions from those who did not possess such skills.

He followed the brothers along the footpath that wound back to Owengate. It jigged to the left, and Geoffrey found himself in the marketplace, the heart of the city. The market comprised a rectangle of trampled mud, fringed by the houses of merchants who owned the right to sell their goods there. Some, like the tanner's home, were small and mean, with rotting roofs and walls covered in cheap plaster. Others, like the clothier's establishment, showed signs of recent wealth, and work was in progress to add more storeys and larger rooms. Some even had windows filled with what looked to Geoffrey to be real glass.

To one side of the square was the house of Haymo Stanstede, husband to Roger's sister. Oddly, it appeared as though its occupants were still asleep, even though the sun was already dipping in the west. It was a fine house, with a smart tiled roof. The door was a startling red, while the shutters, closed against the winter chill, were painted in a lively but eccentric pattern of green and yellow. It was not the kind of house Geoffrey usually associated with spice merchants, but supposed the man's trade had allowed him to travel, and his tastes were accordingly exotic.

Simon hammered on the door, which was eventually answered by a woman sleepily rubbing her eyes. She was in her early twenties, and her full figure was only just covered by the tight-fitting lace dress that Geoffrey doubted did much in the way of warding off the cold.

75

Roger treated her to a leering wink. 'Good morning, Agnes. Is my sister in?'

'Roger!' she cried, hurling herself into his arms. 'You are back! The infidel did not kill you!'

'No, lass,' said Roger, treating her to a smacking kiss that made her eyes water. 'But I killed a good number of *them*. Thousands, probably. But do not keep an old warrior out in the wind. Let me in, and tell my sister that me and my friend have come to stay with her.'

Agnes shrieked indignantly as Roger's hand snaked behind her, and then beckoned him inside the house with a coquettish smile.

The house comprised a large chamber on the ground floor with a flight of wooden stairs to one side. The main room was hall-like, with a central hearth and tables and benches set out like those of a tavern. The walls were painted in bright colours, and the rushes on the floor were reasonably clean. Geoffrey was impressed. The house was enormous by any standards, and even his brother's castle in Goodrich did not boast such space.

There were a number of women inside, some wearing little more than their undergarments, although the unannounced presence of two knights did not seem to unsettle them unduly. Geoffrey made an association between their weary insouciance and the bawdy depictions in most of the wall paintings, and realized that while Stanstede might well sell spices, he indulged in an entirely different trade after dark. Geoffrey imagined Roger's sister at the centre of it all, a formidable matron with whiskers on her chin and a ready hand to thump recalcitrant customers into submission should the need arise – a female version of Roger, in fact.

'Eleanor!' exclaimed Roger, stepping forward to greet the woman who walked down the stairs to see who was calling out of hours. 'You look bloody marvellous, lass!'

That was one way of putting it, thought Geoffrey. He found himself gazing at one of the loveliest women he had ever seen. Like Roger, her hair was dark, almost black, although hers hung in a shining sheet down her back, not arranged in dirty short spikes. Her eyes were an arresting dark amber, and were surrounded by long eyelashes that accentuated the alabaster colouring of her skin. She was tall – almost as tall as Geoffrey – but her graceful posture did not make her seem oversized. Geoffrey was very seldom at a loss for words, but he found himself so when he first set eyes on Roger's sister.

That evening, Geoffrey, Roger and Simon sat at a long oak table in the solar, an upper-storey room in Eleanor's sumptuous house, well away from the noisy activities that were taking place in the brothel below. Eleanor waited on her guests, filling a cup here and offering a plate of nuts there, ensuring they were comfortably seated. Ranulf Flambard had evidently ensured his daughter was well trained in courtly manners, because Geoffrey had seldom been so graciously and politely attended. There was a roaring fire in the hearth, and the meal she had provided was delicious.

It was also the first time in years that Geoffrey had dined in formal clothes. Usually, he wore either full battle gear or the light chain-mail tunic and boiled-leather leggings that passed as half-armour. Very occasionally, he dispensed with military regalia and wore the hose and shirt that went underneath, although he only had two sets of each and both were in desperate need of repair and laundering.

Roger insisted that to wear armour would be an insult to his sister's hospitality, and that they should dress in something more appropriate. He donned the shirt of blue silk he usually wore when he visited brothels, a less-than-salubrious garment with a sinister rip surrounding a dark stain on the back that indicated the fate of its first owner. With it he wore red woollen leggings and a handsome jerkin with gold laces on the front – clothes that Eleanor had kept for him while he went on the Crusade.

Geoffrey was pondering which of his shapeless brown hose and stained shirts would be least offensive to female company, when Roger had offered to lend him something. Geoffrey had demurred, not wanting to be clad in clothes looted from someone Roger had killed in battle, or in something so thick with filth that it could stand of its own accord. But he had been astonished to learn that Roger, before he had gone to fight Saracens, had been considered quite a sartorial figure. The day he had left, Eleanor had washed and folded his many fine clothes and packed them in a chest with scented wood balls – and something that smelled a little less pleasant to take care of moths – to await his return.

Nonchalantly, the big knight recommended a few appropriate items for his friend, as a result of which Geoffrey was dressed in dark blue hose that were too big for him, and a shirt of thick linen that was whiter than anything he had owned in his life. He had washed away most of the grime of the journey in a bowl of hot water scattered with rose petals, and had shaved himself with his dagger, making a neater job of it than Roger, whose face was ravaged by crusted blobs of blood and angry red grazes. To complete the effect, Geoffrey's hair was neatly trimmed and brushed, and he had even remembered to scour his fingernails.

'Tell me about your journey from Southampton, Sir Geoffrey,' said Eleanor, wearily breaking into another of Roger's lurid tales of slaughter and looting in the Holy Land.

Roger gazed at her in surprise. 'But nothing happened, except for the odd skirmish with robbers who thought better of it once they encountered real fighting men. All our best stories are from the Crusade.'

Eleanor smiled, revealing small white teeth, and gave her brother an affectionate tap on the cheek. 'But I find it hard to believe that *every* man, woman, and child in Palestine lusts for Christian blood, and that their sole purpose in life is to desecrate Christian shrines.'

'It is true!' protested Roger indignantly. 'Ask Geoffrey.'

Geoffrey did not feel comfortable lying to the lovely Eleanor, but nor did he want to expose his friend as a man who stretched the truth. No matter how much Roger had convinced himself that the butchery and slaughter of the Crusade was just, there had been some appalling acts of inhumanity that still troubled Geoffrey's sleep on occasions. He had barely begun to consider how to extricate himself from his dilemma when Eleanor spoke.

'I imagine these sword-wielding savages you slew by the thousand were like people here would be, if a foreign force invaded their lands,' she said dryly. 'I cannot see the infidel are so different from us.'

Simon gave a snort of derision. 'Do not talk rubbish, Eleanor! The Saxons barely raised a finger when the Normans seized their lands thirty-five years ago.'

'But the Normans did not slaughter as many Saxons as they could find, then set out to ensure the rest led lives of such misery that they would be forced to leave, did they?' said Eleanor sharply. 'The conquest of England and the conquest of the Holy Land are not comparable.'

Roger gave a long-suffering sigh. 'That is because the Saxons are Christians, Ellie. They knew the Normans were coming to make life better for them.'

'So, when the Conqueror seized England, he was doing it out of the goodness of his heart, was he?' asked Geoffrey, amused by the notion.

Simon gave him an unpleasant look. He had taken every opportunity that evening to voice his disapproval of Roger's guest, and Geoffrey was beginning to find his poor manners tiresome. 'The Saxons are an inferior race, and should be grateful we offered them better lives,' he said coldly.

'Simon's mother was a Norman blacksmith's daughter,' said Eleanor to Geoffrey. 'And so he claims pure Norman ancestry. Roger and I, however, had a mother who was Saxon, so, I suppose he is saying he considers himself superior.'

'Our mother was a fine woman,' said Roger, before Simon could reply. 'Our father knows how to select wenches! Every one of them was a beauty.'

Eleanor smiled, and laid an elegant hand on Roger's brawny arm. 'You are trying to prevent us from arguing. You are right. We should not bicker as we celebrate the return of our dearest brother.'

'Exactly,' said Roger, raising a slopping cup in a clumsy salute. 'Drink to my health, Simon! And then I will tell you about the Siege of Antioch.'

'No!' said Eleanor firmly. 'If you keep up these stories, I shall have nightmares all night.'

'Your husband can comfort you, then,' said Roger, disappointed that his colourful tales were to be cut short. 'That is what they are for.'

'Haymo is away. He has gone to New Castle for spices, so I shall be alone tonight.'

'But I cannot stop now,' said Roger, recalling yet another story he wanted to share with his family. 'I still have not told you about when I killed seven Saracens with a single sweep of my sword.'

Eleanor regarded her brother sceptically and then turned to Geoffrey. 'Did he? Then all I can say is that they must have been standing very conveniently close together.'

'Do not ask *him* to verify my bravery that day,' said Roger, flashing Geoffrey a scornful glance. 'He went off to look at books during the height of the slaughter.'

'So he is a coward,' pounced Simon with spiteful satisfaction. 'A man who prefers to read than join his friends in a noble battle against the Devil's spawn.'

'Why did *you* not join the Crusade?' asked Geoffrey, turning on him, and finally tired of his insults.

Roger had been correct in that Geoffrey had declined to take part in the slaughter at Antioch, but most of that had occurred after the battle, in which Geoffrey had acquitted himself as well – and better in many cases – than his fellow knights. He objected to being called a coward, especially by Simon, who had probably never seen a real fight in his life. Automatically, his hand dropped to the hilt of his dagger, only to find that it was not there. It was in another chamber, along with his sword, because Eleanor had taken one look at the arsenal carried by the two knights, even in civilian clothes, and had ordered them away to disarm themselves before sitting at her table.

'I have a bad leg,' replied Simon icily, although Geoffrey had detected no limp. 'I received a near-fatal wound defending Durham from a raid by Scots.'

'That near-fatal wound was a scratch, Simon,' said Eleanor, laughing. 'You men! Why do you always exaggerate? A graze is always a serious injury, and a running nose is a falling sickness. You are worse than children.'

'It was not really a raid, either,' added Roger. 'Two Scottish peasants tried to steal that pig of yours and you fell over attempting to get it back.'

Simon's lips compressed into a hard thin line. 'The thieves outnumbered me and I was injured protecting my property. I—'

Roger guffawed and gave his brother one of his hearty shoulder claps. 'You and that pig! I swear you love the thing more than you would a wife.'

'Why not tell Geoffrey the real reason you did not join Roger on the Crusade?' asked Eleanor. 'It was because you were needed to organize the castle guards. The security of a city like Durham is a considerable responsibility and Sheriff Durnais felt he could trust no one else to do it.'

Simon's glittering gaze was fixed on Geoffrey. 'I am no coward – unlike you.'

'Geoffrey is no coward,' said Roger. 'He fights better than any knight I know, but prefers to kill soldiers, rather than women or unarmed men – for the added challenge, I suppose. At Antioch, there were very few armed soldiers to fight. We crept in at night, you see, when most of them were in bed.'

'That is horrible!' said Eleanor, pulling a face that registered her disgust. She stood abruptly. 'That is enough! You can discuss this tomorrow if you must, but there will be no more tales of killing in my house tonight!'

The rest of the evening passed uncomfortably. Roger had to be interrupted on numerous occasions when he started to relate the kind of tale that was forbidden; Eleanor was angry with him for spoiling a happy occasion; and Simon was sullen because he did not like Geoffrey. His temper expressed itself in a variety of ways, ranging from spilling wine so it dripped in the knight's lap, to making disparaging remarks about his dog.

Reluctantly, Roger described the journey he and his companions had made from Southampton. He was, however, careful to omit the real reason for their visit. Geoffrey had decided that the fewer people who knew about Flambard's maps and the hidden treasure, the safer it would be –

for everyone concerned. Geoffrey had devised a lie that Roger knew he was to tell if anyone asked why he had travelled north.

Roger had done well for himself in the Holy Land, and his saddlebags were full of loot. Geoffrey recommended that he should deposit some of it with the Durham goldsmith, so it would be there for him when he returned home – or would pass to Eleanor if he did not. No one, except the prior, need ever know the true reason for the visit.

'Did you travel through London?' asked Simon in a bored voice, pandering to Eleanor's demand for non-violent conversation. 'It would be the most direct route.'

'We did not,' said Roger sourly. 'We went via Salisbury, because *someone* had an urge to see some standing stones. It added days to our journey.'

'But it was worth it,' said Geoffrey enthusiastically. 'I have read about the ancient stone circle that stands outside the city of Salisbury, although no one knows who put it there—'

'He refused to come with me unless we made the detour,' interrupted Roger. 'He likes looking at that sort of thing.'

'I can well imagine,' muttered Simon disparagingly. 'But why did you want him with you at all? You must know your way from the southern ports to Durham by now.'

'We have enjoyed many adventures together,' said Roger, reaching across the table to take a large piece of meat. His next words were all but indecipherable when he declined to allow speaking to interfere with the more important process of chewing. 'It is good to travel with a man you can trust, and he wanted to see our cathedral anyway.'

'He would,' muttered Simon, eyeing Geoffrey unpleasantly.

'I could tell you about the two horse thieves we met at York,' said Roger, eyeing Eleanor hopefully. 'That is a tale related to our journey from Southampton and not about the Crusade.'

'No, thank you,' said Eleanor. 'Tell me about the city of York instead. Is it true that a great minster is being built, and that the market is the finest in England?'

Roger sighed. 'It is a church, no more. And I did not

notice the market. I am a soldier, not a tradesman. But our journey here was a hard one, and more than once we were in danger—'

'Our journey was uneventful,' interrupted Geoffrey quickly.

'But that one-eyed knight from York—'

'The minster is a fine building,' said Geoffrey. 'It is not as grand as Durham, but it—'

'Since we are talking about York, I *must* tell you about the one-eyed knight,' boomed Roger. Simon leaned forward, interested. 'It is not a tale with *too* much bloodshed.'

Geoffrey resigned himself to the fact that if Roger wanted to tell stories of battles and slaughter, there was very little anyone could do to prevent it – even Eleanor, a forceful lady who knew her own mind. Simon was entranced, though, and it was not long before the comparatively bloodless encounter with the poor one-eyed soldier had become embellished to the point where Geoffrey was not sure whether he and Roger had even shared the same experience.

'Have you lived in Durham all your life?' Geoffrey asked Eleanor politely, feeling obliged to offer an alternative topic of conversation.

She smiled gratefully. 'For most of it. My father sent me to a convent to receive training in some of the courtly arts.'

Her voice was low and far more cultured than Roger's. And, unlike her brother's Norman-French, which was liberally spangled with Saxon words and idioms, hers was perfect.

'And your husband is a spice merchant?' he asked, flailing about for a neutral topic.

She looked at her feet. 'By day Haymo is a merchant, but he has other business ventures that take place at night – ventures of which I do not approve, as it happens.'

And Geoffrey knew exactly what they were. In the hall downstairs, the occasional gust of coarse manly laughter wafted upward, sometimes accompanied by a feminine squeal. While Geoffrey did not object to brothels in principle – on occasions he found them places where an enjoyable evening could be passed in pleasant company – he understood why a woman with pretensions to being a lady would disapprove of one under her own roof.

'Did you not know about his brothel before you married him?' he asked curiously.

She sighed tiredly. 'Of course, but Haymo promised he would give it up for me. However, now he claims that having a wife is more expensive than maintaining a bachelor life, and says he needs the money. But I can assure you, Geoffrey, I would rather be poor than live in a house of ill repute.'

She looked away as a chorus of male voices were raised in the kind of cheer that invariably precedes a woman divesting herself of some of her clothes. Eleanor blushed scarlet.

Geoffrey shrugged. 'It sounds as though there are plenty of customers wanting to avail themselves of what your husband has to offer, so perhaps he will soon earn enough to retire. But brothel keeping is an unusual occupation for a man who is . . .'

'Old?' suggested Eleanor when he hesitated, uncertain how to phrase it. 'Most of the brothel keepers you have met are young, then, are they?'

Geoffrey glanced at her uncertainly, not sure whether she was asking him a question to solicit information, or testing the strength of his moral fibre.

'Simon indicated Haymo is not young,' he said, deftly sidestepping the question.

She sighed again. 'Haymo is almost seventy, but I think he will live another seventy years yet. Not that I want him gone, of course, but I had not expected him to be so . . . agile.'

Geoffrey nodded sympathetically, not sure what to say. He was about to change the subject and ask something about the city, when there was another commotion from downstairs. There was a splintering noise that sounded as if someone had thrown a chair, then jeers and accusing voices suggesting a fight was about to erupt. Geoffrey's dog emitted a low whine and slunk away to a corner with its ears flat against its head. Eleanor pursed her lips and stood up.

'You see why I do not like this business?' she asked Geoffrey. 'Soldiers come from the castle, and sometimes monks escape from the abbey. Warriors and monastics do

84

not like each other, and they fight over the women. And, when Haymo is away, it is me who has to sort it out.'

'I will do it,' said Roger, standing and taking a heavy candle holder from the table. 'I will teach these louts to be unmannerly in my sister's house.'

He was in the process of reaching for the door, when it burst open. He gazed in open-mouthed astonishment as two men rushed in, each armed with a loaded crossbow and with his head swathed in bandages to conceal his face. Eleanor sat as though transfixed, and Geoffrey dived out of his chair and wrestled her to the ground, wincing as a bolt snapped into the table near his head. Simon's reactions were almost as quick, and he hit the floor an instant later. Roger was slower. With sickening clarity, Geoffrey saw one of the invaders raise his crossbow and point it directly at his friend's heart.

Eleanor screamed, startling the man with the crossbow long enough to allow Geoffrey to hurl a wine goblet that hit him squarely on the side of the head. The man reeled, then took aim again with grim purpose. But the danger had penetrated Roger's mind, and he was on the floor, rolling under the table next to Eleanor, and the bowman found his target was no longer there.

Geoffrey bitterly regretted allowing Roger to persuade him out of his chain mail. He did not even have a heavy boot he could tug off and throw. He glanced around quickly, looking for something, anything, he could use as a weapon. There was nothing.

From his position under the table, he saw the feet of one of the men as he walked around it, looking for someone to kill. Geoffrey saw he had two choices: he could lie where he was and wait to be shot like a trapped animal, or he could attack.

Moving so fast the man was taken by surprise, Geoffrey leapt to his feet and dived full-length across the table, knocking the intruder to the floor. His accomplice darted this way and that in panic, trying to find a position where he would have a clean shot. Geoffrey twisted and turned, using the man with whom he struggled as a shield to protect himself.

With one hand, he gripped the crossbow and forced it away, hoping the thing would not discharge during the fracas and kill him anyway. The man fought to point it back at him.

'Shoot! Shoot!' he shrieked to his accomplice.

Geoffrey's dog howled and barked in agitation, while Simon rolled himself into a tight ball and closed his eyes. While the intruders' attentions were on Geoffrey, Roger acted. He surged to his feet like a great bear and hurled himself at the second intruder with all the energy he could muster. Few men were capable of withstanding a frontal attack from Roger, and his opponent crumpled under the impact. His head struck the corner of the table with a soggy crunch, and Roger found himself astride a man who was insensible.

Meanwhile, seeing their ambush had failed and that his accomplice was unconscious, the first man began to panic. Geoffrey saw frightened eyes through the mask, which were vaguely familiar and he had the sense that he had met their owner before. With a strength born of desperation, the man ripped his crossbow away from Geoffrey and aimed it at his chest, so Geoffrey grabbed the cloth that covered the table and hauled with all his might. Pots and cups rained down around them, landing on the floor with tinny crashes. A large pewter jug caught the bowman a nasty crack on the shoulder, and a heavy candlestick struck Geoffrey's head. His senses swam, and he was aware of the intruder pulling away from his weakening grasp and making for the door.

'Do not let him escape!' he gasped, seeing him reach the door.

He tried to climb to his feet, but he was dizzy and only managed a few steps before he stumbled. Roger shoved past him, and Geoffrey heard his thundering feet on the wooden stairs. He was aware that the intruder still had his crossbow, and that Roger was unarmed. Cursing the buzzing blackness that threatened to overwhelm him, he tried to follow, pushing all else from his mind but helping his friend. Eleanor tried to stop him, but her voice was a stream of meaningless sounds. He reached the top of the stairs, clinging to the handrail with one hand when his legs promised to fail, and fending off Eleanor with the other. His vision darkened, and he felt himself lose his balance and start to pitch forward. Thick arms that smelled powerfully of scented wood balls caught him.

'God's blood!' swore Roger, hauling him back into the solar. 'Who in the Devil's domain were they? What did they mean by bursting into the home of a lady with weapons?'

'I think they meant to kill someone,' suggested Simon shakily. He made a valiant attempt to pull himself together and sound as though he was unflustered. 'I take it you did not catch the villain, then? I would have given chase myself, but my bad leg prevented me.'

'Did it really?' said Eleanor coldly. 'Geoffrey knocked himself all but senseless, but that did not prevent *him* from trying to help Roger.'

'Senseless is a good word for him,' Geoffrey heard Simon mutter. If his vision had not still been tipping and swirling, Geoffrey would have taken exception to the comment. Instead, he slumped on a chair and rested his aching head on his arms.

'Well, no one is hurt,' said Roger, unsympathetic to matters like bumps on the head that did not involve plenty of blood. 'Mind you, I thought we were all dead men when they first arrived.'

'We almost were,' said Simon. 'Those were professional killers, hired to kill quickly and cleanly.'

'They made a poor job of it, then,' said Geoffrey, lifting his head cautiously. 'Whoever employed them should ask for his money back.'

'Who would pay men to kill you?' asked Eleanor, appalled. Geoffrey noted she did not include herself in the statement. 'What have you two been up to? You said you only came here to deposit Roger's earnings from the Holy Land.'

'Perhaps they were Saracens,' said Simon, in a hushed, fearful voice. 'Perhaps they followed you to claim vengeance for all that bloodshed you brought about.'

'They were not,' said Geoffrey firmly. 'Their faces were masked, but I saw their hands. They were pale – Saxon or

Norman, not Arab. Anyway, surely you heard them shouting in English?'

Simon glowered. 'If you know so much, then tell us their names.'

Geoffrey ignored him and pointed to the insensible intruder, who still lay on Eleanor's thick rugs. 'He should be able to tell us what we have done to warrant such a welcome.'

Roger knelt and felt the man's neck. 'He will not be telling us anything, unless you can commune with the dead. He must have died when his head hit the table.'

'Damn!' muttered Geoffrey, standing unsteadily and going to remove the bandage that masked the man's face. The features were not familiar. He glanced enquiringly at Roger and Eleanor. 'Have you seen him before? Does he live here?'

Eleanor declined to look, although Simon studied the dead man for a long time. He tested the quality of the man's clothes by rubbing them between two grubby fingers. 'I do not know him, but he is not from around here. This cloth has a southern feel to it. I imagine he followed you from Southampton.'

'Why would he do that?' asked Eleanor, regarding Roger intently, the expression on her face making it clear she had guessed that the real reason for her brother's visit to Durham had nothing to do with depositing his ill-gotten gains with the city's goldsmith.

Roger refused to meet her eyes, and busied himself by picking up plates and cups from the floor. Geoffrey watched, wondering what he could say that would prevent her from interrogating her brother, who would quickly become flustered and reveal all. He suspected she would be safer knowing nothing about Flambard's shady business. If, as seemed probable, the attack had something to do with the map that Roger was to deliver to the prior, then it would be best for all concerned if they were to complete their mission without telling anyone about it, and leave.

'I expect they intended to rob you of your loot,' suggested Simon. 'Your saddlebags were heavy when I lifted them earlier, and I imagine there is a tidy fortune packed inside them.'

'Aye, there is,' said Roger, transparently grateful to be

provided with a plausible excuse for the ambush. 'I expect some footpad saw them on our way north, and decided he would make himself rich. That is what happened.'

'You are lying,' said Eleanor firmly. 'You cannot fool me. I am your sister. Tell me the truth.'

'Well,' began Roger uncertainly, already yielding.

'Roger, no!' exclaimed Geoffrey, appalled that Roger might be about to reveal something that could put Eleanor's life in danger. His thoughts were still fuzzy from the knock on the head, or he would have been able to concoct a story that would satisfy her without putting her at risk. As it was, he found he could not think clearly, and knew he would only arouse her suspicions by telling obvious lies.

'He is right,' acknowledged Roger, reluctantly. 'I cannot tell you.'

'Why?' demanded Eleanor. 'Are you involved in something illegal?'

'No,' said Roger. He caught Geoffrey's eye. 'Well, possibly.'

Almost certainly, thought Geoffrey, if Flambard were involved.

'Is it something to do with our father?' pressed Eleanor. She snapped her fingers in understanding. 'I know ! You went to visit him in prison and he charged you to run some errand for him. Oh, Roger! How could you be so foolish? You know what he is like! He will twist you around his little finger, just like he always does, and his innocent-sounding request will lead you into trouble.'

Geoffrey regarded her with new-found admiration. She was astute and intelligent, and she had read Roger like an open book.

'It will not,' mumbled Roger. 'He only wants me to deliver a message.'

'You stupid oaf!' cried Eleanor in despair. 'Our father has been arrested and imprisoned for treason, which means anyone caught carrying messages from him will also be considered a traitor. Do you want to be executed for crimes against the King?'

'It is not like that,' protested Roger. 'This is innocent!'

Eleanor gave a sharp bark of laughter. 'Nothing associated with Ranulf Flambard is innocent. The man is a cunning, treacherous snake, who is willing to use anyone – even his misguided son – to win him the power and riches he craves.'

'How dare you say such things!' roared Roger, finally angry. Geoffrey closed his eyes, wincing at the noise. 'Our father is a good and saintly man. He is a bishop!'

Geoffrey regarded him doubtfully. Even Eleanor was startled into silence by this assertion.

'What has being a bishop to do with being a good man?' asked Geoffrey eventually.

Roger swung round furiously. 'And you have no right to slander my father's good name, either! He asked me to do something decent and noble, and I intend to discharge my duty with honour.'

Eleanor groaned. 'Why do you always fall for his charms? And now it seems you have dragged Geoffrey into the mire with you.'

'He came willingly,' claimed Roger, although that was not how Geoffrey remembered it.

'He should not have done,' snapped Eleanor, glaring at Geoffrey. 'If he had not agreed to help, you would not be in my solar fighting off attacks from masked intruders.'

'Geoffrey would never desert a friend,' Roger yelled, working himself into a state of righteous indignation.

Eleanor turned away to register her disgust. 'Simon will fetch the sheriff, while you two carry this body downstairs, so it can be removed tomorrow. Meanwhile, I suppose I will scrub the poor man's blood from my table and find him a shroud.'

'Now, just a moment,' began Roger indignantly. 'This "poor man" tried to kill me – and you, too. I have no idea why, but I will not be blamed for it.'

'But you *are* to blame for it,' argued Eleanor. 'You agreed to complete whatever nasty business Flambard charged you with, and you brought death into my house.'

Roger sighed. 'You have not changed, Ellie. You are still a shrew.'

Geoffrey saw tears of hurt glitter in her eyes, before she

stormed from the room. Simon scrambled after her, protesting to her deaf ears that it was not safe to fetch the sheriff while it was dark, and that it would be better if he went in the morning. Regardless of his protestations, Geoffrey heard the door open and then close again as he went to do her bidding. Geoffrey thought it unlikely that the intruder would strike again that night – he would consider himself lucky to be alive – but even so, he understood Simon's reluctance to be out alone so soon after the attack.

Roger grinned at Geoffrey. 'Pay no attention. Tomorrow, she will be sorry she yelled at us.'

'You,' corrected Geoffrey. 'She yelled at *you*. I am the innocent bystander.'

'You are in this every bit as much as I am,' said Roger. 'You wanted to come with me.'

Geoffrey laughed at Roger's ability to remember events in a way that suited him, while Roger eyed him malevolently.

'Help me with this corpse,' he snapped, grabbing the legs and hauling on them unceremoniously. 'Do not stand there cackling like some fiend from Hell, or she really will throw you out of her house. She does not approve of disrespect towards the dead.'

With some difficulty, because Roger was anxious they should not leave a trail of blood and brains on Eleanor's floor, they manhandled the body down the stairs, where they laid it on a bench in the hall. Wordlessly, Eleanor thrust a sheet at Geoffrey and watched him cover the dead man with it, before leaving them alone again.

'She is right you know,' said Geoffrey, as she slammed the door behind her. 'It probably *is* that map Flambard gave you that led to this attack.'

'Rubbish,' said Roger. He began to walk back to the solar, where there was a fire and wine. 'It is Simon who was right, not her. This miserable pair of excuses for robbers was just after my money.'

'I do not think so. And I do not think Peterkin's death in Southampton was a coincidence, either.'

'And why is that?' asked Roger, unconvinced.

91

Geoffrey walked to the table, where the crossbow bolt, fired early in the attack, was still embedded in Eleanor's polished oak. With some difficulty, he removed it, and held it up for Roger to see.

'Peterkin, Weasel's accomplice, and the roof-top brawler were killed by red bolts, remember? Well, here is another, just like them.'

Roger gazed at it. 'But how can that be? That was weeks ago. If tonight's invaders had wanted to kill us for my father's map, then they would have made a play for it long before now.'

'We have not given them the opportunity,' said Geoffrey, sitting at the table and rolling the bolt between his fingers. 'We left early the day after we met Flambard. Most people would have required at least a morning to make the necessary arrangements, but we had no ties or obligations, so were able to head north as soon as it was light enough to see.'

'And that was just as well, given that you wanted to make detours to look at standing stones.'

Geoffrey nodded. 'That may well have saved our lives. Instead of taking the shorter and more direct road north through London, we travelled via Salisbury. It is not a route most people would choose, and these would-be killers were probably horrified when they believed they had already lost us and Flambard's map. They have doubtless been searching ever since.'

'No,' said Roger, shaking his head, although his voice lacked conviction. 'It is all coincidence.'

'In that case, how do you explain these red bolts?' demanded Geoffrey, waving the offending item in front of Roger's nose.

'Lots of people have those. I told you it is common knowledge that scarlet quarrels allow you to kill a stag, a blue one a bird, and so on. It proves nothing.'

'It proves a great deal. The sheriff in Southampton denied knowing about this tradition of staining arrows. That suggests it is a local custom, practised here in Durham.'

'So?'

'It tells us that whoever committed the Southampton murders has some connection with Durham. And since Flambard is Bishop of Durham, it suggests to me that he is at the heart of all this.'

'It might,' said Roger, reluctantly acknowledging that his father might have involved him in something less straight-forward than the delivery of a letter. 'But it might also tell us that Southampton-born Weasel knows good arrows when he sees them and chose to buy from a Durham-trained fletcher.'

'Possible, but unlikely,' said Geoffrey, after giving the matter some thought. 'Fletchers produce arrows they can sell to anyone, not ones with a colour significance that only a few will appreciate. The extra work of staining would be a waste of their time. No, Roger, these bolts, like their owners, came from Durham.'

'Do you think Weasel was the intruder who has just escaped?'

'He is the right height and build, and there was something familiar about the eyes through the mask. I am almost certain it was him.'

'But what is he doing so far from Southampton? I do not understand.'

Geoffrey rubbed his chin. 'Neither of the men who broke in this evening were good archers, or they would have hit at least one of us before things went wrong for them. We know from personal observation that Weasel is not skilled with crossbows, or in hand-to-hand combat, which may be another reason to identify him as the man who escaped tonight.'

'But who is he?' asked Roger. 'Other than a dismal soldier, that is.'

Geoffrey shrugged. 'Some hired man, I suppose. Once we know who employed him, all our other questions will probably be answered. However, Flambard has so many enemies that it will be almost impossible to know which of them is after his treasure.'

'No,' said Roger, after a good deal of soul searching. 'You have this completely wrong. It is nothing to do with my father's maps at all. It is to do with the staff.'

'What staff?' asked Geoffrey, puzzled.

'The staff the roof-top brawler shouted about,' said Roger, pleased with his deduction. 'That is the common thread in all this, and it happened *before* my father chanced to meet me in the Saracen's Head. The map has nothing to do with this.'

'There was nothing chance about that meeting,' said Geoffrey firmly. 'It was carefully planned on Flambard's part. But this staff notion of yours makes no sense. A staff is a long piece of wood, and difficult to conceal in saddlebags. Why would Weasel chase us all the way up the country when it is obvious we do not have it?'

'Aaron's Rod,' said Roger in satisfaction. 'As I have told you before, this is about Aaron's Rod.'

Geoffrey sighed, not wanting to begin that argument again. 'The answer lies in Flambard's map. The common thread in this is Durham – and its bishop.'

Roger said nothing.

'I suspect these two were waiting for us here, anxious we would not come,' said Geoffrey, when no reply was forthcoming. 'When we arrived, they were so relieved, they decided to act immediately, before we disappeared again. There is doubtless a good deal more to this business than providing the prior with information about how to lay his hands on money for the cathedral.'

'Such as what?'

'I cannot begin to imagine. But I have not been happy with this errand from the start. There are too many inconsistencies – such as why Flambard feels the need to share the secret with three people, rather than just telling the prior where to find it.'

'But he explained that: it is because the sight of so much wealth would be too much for one man to bear, but three people would monitor each other and ensure the funds were used properly.'

'But if Flambard does not trust any of these men – prior, goldsmith, and sheriff – why give them the secret at all? Why not keep the treasure hidden until he can dig it up himself?'

Roger was silent again.

'This time,' said Geoffrey, regarding his friend resentfully. 'It is *you* who has dragged *me* into a pit of intrigue and murder.'

Five

The following morning saw a change in the weather. The clear blue skies and pale winter sun were replaced by a cover of solid, dark cloud, which had the dirty brown appearance that preceded snow. It was cold, too, with a searing wind slicing from the north. Geoffrey was glad to abandon his borrowed finery for his own hard-wearing, functional clothes, particularly the padded surcoat. He sat in Eleanor's kitchen, whetting the blade of his dagger, while her servants prepared breakfast.

At first light, just after the abbey bell had finished tolling for prime, there was a sharp rap on the door. Bundling her hair into a cap, Eleanor went to open it. A short, burly man stood there. Geoffrey's dog began to growl, an ominous sound that ended in an outraged yelp as the early-morning visitor aimed a kick at it. Retribution was instant and decisive, however, and Geoffrey saw the animal melt away into the shadows with a look of malicious satisfaction in its glistening eyes, while the visitor swore and rubbed his bitten ankle.

'Cenred,' said Eleanor, shooting Geoffrey a look that suggested that if he did not control the dog, she would – in a way that would be permanent. 'Please, come in.'

'You had better teach that beast some manners,' said Cenred, stepping cautiously over the threshold. 'Or I will have it shot. I will not have wild animals savaging civilians in my city.'

'You are not a civilian,' said Eleanor, leading Cenred to the solar with Geoffrey following. 'You are Durham's under-sheriff, and the man who will step into Sheriff Durnais' shoes later this year. You are a military man of considerable influence in this area.'

Cenred preened himself. He was not an attractive person, and possessed features that were more porcine than human, including an ugly snub nose and small eyes. His clothes were expertly cut, but could not disguise the squat, pugilistic body they adorned.

'Everyone says I am the best man for the position,' he said smugly. 'And they are right.'

Geoffrey leaned against the wall and folded his arms as he watched Eleanor pour her guest a goblet of the warmed ale. In the dim light of early morning, she was even more attractive than she had been by the romantic, golden aura of her beeswax candles the evening before. She wore a dress that accentuated her slim figure and clung to her hips in a way that made it difficult for him to look away. Her dark hair shone, and her complexion was clear and healthy.

'I am here on sorry business,' said Cenred, accepting the ale and taking a noisy gulp. He grimaced when he found it was stronger than he had anticipated. Geoffrey hid a smile, and thought that any under-sheriff worth his salt should have known that ale served in brothels was invariably more potent than that available in normal houses.

'Cenred!' exclaimed Roger, striding into the solar and sitting himself at the table. 'What brings you here at this hour? The lovely ladies downstairs?'

Cenred shot him a nasty look. 'Haunting brothels is not something worthy of a man of my station. It is a pity the same cannot be said for you: it clearly does not promote good health and vigour.'

Geoffrey saw what he meant. There were dark rings under Roger's eyes, and his usually ruddy face was pale, suggesting he had availed himself of the refreshments and feminine hospitality available on the ground floor after his sister had gone to bed. Geoffrey had considered doing the same, given that Eleanor had retired early and he had been unsettled and restless after their encounter with the intruders, but had not thought it would be polite to do so while he was Eleanor's guest. He had assumed Roger would be similarly discreet, although he realized he should have known better.

'You are still alive, then?' Roger continued, addressing

the under-sheriff jocularly. 'I thought someone would have slipped a dagger between your Saxon ribs long before now.'

Cenred gazed at him with dislike. 'You speak as though you have been away for an eternity, but it was only four blissful years. You have not been missed.'

'Cenred will become sheriff soon,' said Eleanor, trying to warn her brother against saying anything to antagonize a man who would hold one of the most powerful positions in the shire.

But Roger was not a man to be impressed by such things. 'Is there no one better for the post?'

'Roger!' snapped Eleanor. She poured her brother a goblet of ale, then slapped a large plate of salted pork in front of him, doubtless hoping food and drink would absorb his attention and shut him up. She offered Geoffrey ale, but he declined: Roger had also reacted with surprise when he tasted the strength of the breakfast brew, and Geoffrey wanted all his wits about him that day.

'So, what brings you here, if not sampling the whores?' Roger asked, draining his cup and slamming the empty vessel on the table with a force that made Eleanor wince.

'I have news for Mistress Stanstede,' said Cenred stiffly.

'You have come about the men who fired crossbows at us,' said Eleanor, rubbing the scratch that Roger had made on her table. 'The body is downstairs and I would be grateful if you would remove it as soon as possible.'

Cenred was puzzled. 'What men?' he asked. 'What body?'

Eleanor made an attempt to hide her impatience. 'The body of the man who died in this very house.' Cenred continued to look blank. 'The men Simon came to see you about last night.'

Cenred's expression did not change. 'Simon did not come to see me last night – about dead men in your parlour or anything else.'

Eleanor released a gusty sigh. 'Damn him! He must have gone straight back to his house to hide!'

'It was dark last night,' Roger pointed out. 'You cannot blame him for being reluctant to be out alone after what happened.'

Geoffrey was amused that the fearless Roger should take

97

the side of his cowardly half-brother. Roger was not a man sympathetic to fear, and always claimed it was an emotion with which he had never been troubled.

'It is very dark *every* night,' retorted Eleanor. 'But I asked him to go to the sheriff and he let me down. He is simply not to be trusted – fey and fickle, like his father.'

'I hope he has not had an accident,' said Geoffrey uneasily. He had not taken to the surly Simon, but that did not mean he wished him harm. Perhaps Simon had tried to do what Eleanor had asked, but had been prevented by Weasel.

'He knows Durham like the back of his hand,' said Roger confidently. 'It would take more than the likes of Weasel to harm him in its streets. He will be safe enough. Eleanor is right – he probably went home, intending to deliver her message in the safety of daylight.'

'It requires more than a good knowledge of a city to evade a crossbow bolt,' Geoffrey pointed out. 'Perhaps we should look for him.'

'Later,' said Roger, eating his pork. 'We have more important business to attend to first.'

He swivelled around in his chair and gave Geoffrey a meaningful wink, to inform him that he intended to visit Prior Turgot and deliver Flambard's map. His gesture was sufficiently obvious that it was observed by Eleanor and Cenred, both of whom looked very interested in what it might mean. Geoffrey cringed, wishing, not for the first time, that Roger would practise a little discretion.

'We need to deposit your Holy Land loot with the goldsmith,' said Geoffrey quickly, trying to conceal his friend's blunder.

'My loot?' asked Roger in alarm. 'With the goldsmith?'

'Yes,' said Geoffrey, although he could see he had only made matters worse. The suspicious expression on Cenred's face made it perfectly clear that he knew Roger had no intention of depositing his gold with any merchant, and that something else was afoot.

Roger's horror gradually gave way to understanding as he grasped what Geoffrey had been attempting to do. 'Yes,' he said, too late and too brightly. 'I need to visit Master Jarveaux, and see what he and I can do for each other.'

Cenred raised his eyebrows. 'Jarveaux is not in a position to do you any favours,' he said.

'Why?' asked Roger curiously. 'What has happened to him?'

'Oysters,' said Cenred enigmatically. 'Unpleasant things, if you ask me, but Jarveaux's mother always kept some for him in her kitchen.'

'I am sure you did not come here to satisfy my brother's unseemly appetite for gossip, Cenred,' said Eleanor, turning her attention to the under-sheriff. 'You said you were here on sorry business. What is wrong, if not the death of a would-be killer in my home?'

Cenred's ugly face became sombre. 'I have some bad news concerning your husband.'

'My husband?' asked Eleanor nervously. 'But he is in New Castle. He left a few days ago on business and is due to come back today or tomorrow.'

'That miserable old lecher,' muttered Roger in disapproval, reaching for the ale Geoffrey had rejected. 'He had no business making advances to my sister. I will teach him a lesson when he shows his wrinkled face here.'

'That will not be necessary,' said Cenred softly. He addressed Eleanor. 'I am afraid your husband and his travelling companions were ambushed on their way from New Castle last night. He is dead.'

Eleanor gazed at the under-sheriff in horror, while Roger's jaw dropped in shock. The colour drained from Eleanor's face, and she became as white as snow. Afraid she might swoon, Geoffrey moved towards her, ready to catch her if she fell. But Roger's sister was made of sterner stuff. She went to the window seat, where she sat with her hands in her lap, waiting for Cenred to elaborate.

'Haymo is dead?' asked Roger, aghast. 'Are you sure it is him?'

Cenred nodded. 'It seems he was one of a party of ten who were travelling south yesterday. There was a problem with a horse, and they left later than they should have done to reach Durham in daylight.'

Roger nodded. 'No sane man travels the New Castle road after dark. There are more outlaws along it than stars in the sky.'

'The survivors say the attack came out of nowhere, just as the light was beginning to fade and they had reached Kymlisworth.'

'That is a hamlet about five miles north of Durham,' said Roger, for Geoffrey's benefit. 'It is a wild place, full of snakes and bogs.'

'Snakes?' asked Geoffrey, startled. 'Not at this time of year.'

'Kymlisworth is near Finchale,' said Roger sombrely. 'And Finchale is famous for its snakes.'

'True,' concurred Cenred. He shuddered. 'Finchale is not a place for God-fearing men. But the attack was not at Finchale, it was at Kymlisworth. Three travellers were killed: Haymo, a Knight Hospitaller and a squire. The others – five women and two grooms from the castle – were unharmed.'

Roger made a disgusted noise. 'But, of course, by the time these people had travelled the last few miles to Durham, the outlaws were long gone?'

Cenred nodded. 'One of my sergeants will go to Kymlisworth this morning, and ask if anyone heard or saw anything, although no peasant with sense would admit to it if he had. Outlaws do not deal kindly with tale-tellers, especially ones in lonely villages who cannot protect themselves.' He regarded Eleanor sympathetically. 'Haymo's body is in the castle chapel.'

'I had better do my wifely duty, then,' said Eleanor, standing slowly. 'I must have his corpse taken to St Giles' Church, and see about arranging his requiem.'

'I will come with you,' said Roger, gruffly kind. 'I will see to everything. You need not worry.'

She gave a weak smile. 'Well, one good thing has come out of this. At least I will not have to endure a brothel in my home. I can be a respectable widow, and put an end to all that debauchery.'

Cenred was horrified. 'Madam, I beg you, do not make

over-hasty decisions while you are stunned by grief. Give the matter some time.'

'I thought you would be pleased,' said Geoffrey, surprised by the under-sheriff's reaction. 'Most towns want to stamp out prostitution, not encourage it.'

Cenred gave him a pained look. 'We have two hundred soldiers at the castle, and a hundred masons and carpenters – not to mention their apprentices – are employed for the cathedral. It does not take a scholar to see that makes for a lot of men. And men need women. Well, most do.' He paused and studied Geoffrey carefully, to assess whether he might be one of the exceptions.

'I like women,' announced Roger enthusiastically.

Cenred continued. 'So, since men will always want women and will go to considerable lengths to lay hands on them, it is better to have brothels we can control. Otherwise, the men run wild among the townswomen and all sorts of trouble follows.'

'That is why Stanstede always employs women from New Castle, rather than Durham,' Roger explained to Geoffrey. 'To ensure he would have no enraged local fathers or brothers hammering at his doors. I expect that was what he was doing yesterday, was it not, Ellie? Collecting whores?'

Eleanor swallowed hard. 'He said he was buying cinnamon, but I knew he was not. I suppose the five women who were travelling with him were his employees?'

Cenred sighed. 'Yes, but since they are here, we may as well see them put to use.' He inclined his head towards the window, where snowflakes were beginning to fall outside. 'This weather means work on the cathedral will stop, and we will have more need of these ladies than ever if we do not want gangs of bored men running riot.'

'So,' said Eleanor weakly. 'I find myself with a brothel to run as well as a husband to bury.'

'I will do it,' offered Roger, rubbing his hands together gleefully. 'I know about whorehouses.'

Eleanor looked doubtful, as well she might. Geoffrey thought she should decline his help, if she had any sense. It would be like placing a fox in charge of a hen coop, and all the wares would be sampled long before the masons or the soldiers had their chance.

'You can think about this later,' he said gently. 'The first thing to do is collect your husband. Roger and I will escort you and arrange a litter.'

'If you go with her, then I can stay here,' said Roger, a predatory gleam in his eye. 'I will make sure things are in order for tonight.'

'Not before you have been to the castle,' said Geoffrey sharply. However Roger might rank his preferences in ways to help his sister, his first duty was to escort her to collect the body of her husband, not leave that task to a comparative stranger. He also had to deliver Flambard's letter.

Eleanor gave Geoffrey a grateful look. 'I am glad you are here – both of you. I might need your services, if the business downstairs becomes as lively as Cenred anticipates.'

Geoffrey, unlike Roger, had no wish to be a brothel warden, but could think of no way to refuse her. He said nothing, but determined to think of an excuse that would allow him to leave in a day or two without seeming rude. Roger was more than capable of maintaining order in a bawdy house, even if he would be disastrous at running one.

'I am sorry to be the bearer of bad news,' said Cenred, setting down his unfinished ale. 'But Durnais is due back soon. I will put the matter in his hands when he returns.'

'Sheriff Durnais has left the city?' asked Roger, astonished. 'But he has never so much as set a foot outside the town gates the whole time I have known him.'

'I know,' said Cenred tiredly. 'And his absence has put something of a burden on me, given that I am obliged to do his work as well as my own. He said he would be gone for seven days, which means he should return today or tomorrow.'

'Where has he gone?' asked Roger. 'New Castle?'

'New Castle is seventeen miles away,' said Cenred heavily. 'Of course he has not travelled such a vast distance on his first excursion in more than twenty years. He has ventured a mere eight miles from his cosy quarters, and has gone to Chester-le-Street.'

'Chester-le-Street?' echoed Roger, even more astonished. He

elaborated for Geoffrey's benefit. 'That is between New Castle and Durham, and has nothing but a church and a few houses.'

'I do not know what tempted him there,' said Cenred, the bitterness in his voice suggesting he was offended that he had not been taken into the sheriff's confidence. 'But what with killers breaking into the homes of merchants, and the murder of travellers on the roads, I wish to God he was here!'

Eleanor, gripping Geoffrey's arm for support, followed the under-sheriff through the muddy streets to the castle chapel. The bitter north wind brought flakes of hard snow to sting uncovered hands and faces, and the stinking muck that carpeted the roads – a putrid combination of sewage, animal dung, and rotting vegetable parings – was already dusted white. Here and there, the gutters that channelled the liquid waste down through the city towards the river were frozen, and the ice caused blockages that spewed evil yellow-brown gouts across the streets. Geoffrey's dog paddled among them in ecstasy.

Roger walked with Cenred, telling him about the ambush in Eleanor's house. Anxious that Roger might inadvertently betray the true purpose of his visit while doing so, Geoffrey listened to the conversation with half an ear, while Eleanor sobbed at his side and regaled him with an improbable list of her late husband's virtues. Sergeant Helbye, puffy-eyed after what had probably been a lively night in the company of other professional soldiers, met them as they walked up the hill. Ulfrith was with him, fresh-faced and bright, suggesting that he, unlike Helbye, had managed an early night.

'I heard what happened,' Helbye muttered, as Eleanor went to walk with Roger. 'Some villains probably saw you go into her house with loaded saddlebags and decided to chance their luck. I always said the north was a dangerous place.'

'The luck of one of them ran out,' replied Geoffrey, deciding not to take issue with him on the subject of dangerous places – their home at Goodrich was hardly a haven of peace and safety, either. He told Helbye what had happened and asked him to take the intruder's body to the castle.

'I will do it,' said Ulfrith eagerly. 'I will sling it over my shoulder and have it there in a trice!'

'I am sure you will,' said Geoffrey, noting the way the Saxon's powerful shoulders already rippled in anticipation of exercise. 'But use a bier instead. It looks more respectful.'

Ulfrith nodded, his fair features grave as he listened to the instructions, then strode away in entirely the wrong direction. Geoffrey sighed.

'Lord save us, Will! Watch him – and keep the horses ready, too. Roger plans to stay, but I want to leave as soon as I can.'

'I thought he was pining for the Holy Land – wine, women and lots of fighting,' said Helbye.

'I do not think those are in short supply here,' said Geoffrey, thinking Roger had made a wise choice to help his sister run her brothel, if wine, women and fighting were his criteria for a happy life.

'I would not stay here,' said Helbye firmly. 'I have been talking to the soldiers at the castle. There is a competition between abbey and bishop to see who can be the least popular.'

'Given that most people believe Flambard is the Devil Incarnate, the abbey must be doing an impressive job, then,' remarked Geoffrey.

'Oh, yes. Especially when you consider St Balthere's bones.' Helbye pursed his lips, and regarded Geoffrey knowingly, although the knight had no idea what he was talking about.

'They were stolen,' he said, recalling Simon talking about the theft of some relics the previous day.

'When Flambard decided to become a bishop – about four years ago – he gave St Balthere's bones to the people of Durham to show them he is a good man. But St Giles' Church had barely finished making a hole in the altar to keep them when they were stolen. The word is that the abbey has them.'

'Why?' asked Geoffrey, puzzled.

'So that all the pilgrims will go there, and the monks will not have to share their revenues with the town. The abbey cannot bear to lose what it considers *its* money.'

'The sooner we leave here the better. If I hear much more about this abbey, I might feel the right course of action is *not* to deliver Flambard's map to the prior, and then where would we be?'

'Embroiled in politics,' replied Helbye disapprovingly. 'Deliver the map, lad, and let us be gone. Do not start considering what is right or wrong, or God knows what might happen.'

It was sound advice. Geoffrey returned his sergeant's salute and rejoined Eleanor and Roger. When they reached Owengate, a guard admitted Cenred and his companions into the castle's bailey. Before Geoffrey could stop him, Roger darted towards an untidy cluster of houses between fort and cathedral, calling over his shoulder that he was going to ask Simon why he had failed to tell Cenred about the attack the previous night. Geoffrey scowled at his friend's retreating back when he saw Eleanor's look of dismay. Cenred shook his head with an expression that suggested he had expected no better from Roger, then led the way to the barbican that protected the castle's main entrance. It lay beyond a series of ditches and banks, and was an impressive stone structure with a wooden archers' gallery running around the top.

Cenred strutted through the gate, giving his soldiers a brief nod as he passed, and entered an area dominated by the wooden keep. It stood atop its motte, and was reached by a flight of makeshift steps. Geoffrey saw that the sentries who patrolled its roof would be able to see for miles across the surrounding countryside. No army of any size would be able to come near without the alarm being raised. And from what Roger claimed, early warning of an attack was something vital in a place where Scots and Saxons alike bided their time to rebel against Normans, and where northern barons were not always loyal to the King.

Cenred strode across the muddy courtyard to the chapel, and opened the clanking door to its dim and silent interior. It was small and intimate, and sturdy columns supported its barrel-vaulted roof. An unusual honey-coloured sandstone had been used for the piers, in which darker yellows swirled around paler ones to create an effect that was almost like marble. At the eastern end was the altar, which comprised a table bearing a single gold cross and two candlesticks. The floor was flagged with grey tiles, and daylight filtered dimly through the small windows to create an intriguing contrast of brightness and shadows. Geoffrey stood still, entranced by its stark simplicity.

Eleanor's attention, however, was on the three shrouded figures by the altar. She stood uncertainly until Cenred gave Geoffrey a poke with his elbow to bring him out of his reverie.

'Do your duty,' he muttered. 'Do not just stand there gaping like a moonstruck calf!'

'I was about to,' whispered Geoffrey testily, reluctantly tearing his attention away from architecture and back to the grim realities of life – or rather of death. 'Which corpse is Stanstede's?'

Cenred shrugged irritably. 'I do not know. You will have to look. He will be the oldest. Proceed.'

Instinct told Geoffrey to ignore such an insolent command, but Eleanor was white-faced, and he did not want to add to her distress by starting an argument with Cenred. He walked to the nearest body, and peeled back the cover that had been placed over its face. And gazed down in shock.

The body was that of Xavier, the monk who had been with Flambard in Southampton.

Geoffrey stared at the still features in confusion. Xavier's flame-coloured hair and scarred face made him quite unmistakable. But he had not been wearing the habit of a Benedictine when he had died; he wore chain mail and a good-quality surcoat that had seen almost as much hard wear as had Geoffrey's. It was marked with a black cross that indicated he was a Knight Hospitaller – an order of soldier-monks founded to protect pilgrims in the Holy Land. The Hospitallers were becoming a powerful force in the east, and their influence was spreading in the western world. Geoffrey regarded Xavier thoughtfully. Why had he worn the habit of a Benedictine in Southampton? And perhaps more importantly, what had he been doing to end up dead in Durham?

'That is not my Haymo,' said Eleanor. 'He was much older than this man.'

Geoffrey realized he had been staring at the body for some moments, and that she was waiting for him to move on to the next one. Cenred, however, was watching Geoffrey.

'Do you know him? You seem startled by what you see.'

Uncomfortably, Geoffrey saw that Cenred was intrigued by his reaction to Xavier's body, and was intelligent enough to sense something amiss. He was relieved Roger was not there to reveal secrets he would rather no one else knew.

'I am not from the north,' he answered vaguely, 'so am unlikely to be acquainted with anyone here.'

'That is not what I asked,' said Cenred, with more astuteness than Geoffrey would have accredited him. 'I asked whether you know him.'

'No,' said Geoffrey shortly. 'I do not.'

It was not a lie: Geoffrey had no idea who 'Brother Xavier' really was. However, he was certain that whatever had transformed Xavier from a Benedictine in a harbour tavern to a dead Knight Hospitaller in Durham was something to do with Flambard and his dubious affairs.

'I see,' said Cenred, equally ambiguously. 'However, even a dim-witted man could not fail to notice that the moment Roger reappears in my city, I find myself with three corpses on my hands.'

'I know my brother has a reputation for brawling,' said Eleanor softly, 'but he cannot be responsible for these deaths. You said the attack took place at dusk, and he was with me at the time.'

Cenred looked as though he would argue, but he nodded to her and turned to Geoffrey. 'Cover him and show Mistress Stanstede her husband, so she can leave this place of death.'

'Do *you* know him?' asked Geoffrey, indicating Xavier. 'Is he a local nobleman?'

Cenred shook his head. 'His name is Xavier de Downey, a knight in the Order of St John Hospitaller, according to a document he was carrying. I have no reason to believe otherwise.'

'Document?' asked Geoffrey, thinking of Flambard's maps.

Cenred made an impatient movement with his hand. 'He had a letter from his Grand Master telling anyone concerned that he was on Hospitaller business. One of the castle clerks read it to me.'

'Was there anything else?' asked Geoffrey.

'Nothing,' said Cenred with a suspicious frown. 'Why?'

Sensing Cenred was not entirely convinced he was innocent of involvement in Xavier's death, Geoffrey knew he should cover the dead knight and leave Durham before he was accused openly. But the questions that tumbled around in his mind were far more alluring, and he found his curiosity begin to get the better of his common sense.

Making up his mind, he hauled the sheet away from Xavier's body and let it drop on the ground, ignoring Eleanor's startled gasp and Cenred's indignant demand to know what he thought he was doing. The first thing that arrested Geoffrey's attention was that Xavier had been shot in the chest. A circle of blood stained the surcoat around a small tear that had been caused by an arrow or a crossbow bolt, although the missile itself had been removed. Idly, Geoffrey wondered if it had been red.

He looked more closely at the wound, and then poked it with his finger. Eleanor gave a horrified cry, and Cenred pushed forward, calling to the soldiers who waited outside. Quickly, Geoffrey stepped away from the body, raising his hands to indicate he had finished.

'Look,' he said to Cenred. 'The surcoat is stained with blood, but when you feel underneath, you can see his chain mail protected him. The tip of the quarrel pierced his skin, but not sufficiently deeply to kill him.'

'What are you saying?' demanded Cenred. 'Of course he died from the arrow wound.'

'He did not. The arrow did not pass through his armour. He died by some other means.'

Cenred stared at Geoffrey with a mixture of unease and distrust. 'And how do you know such things? Are you a surgeon?'

'No, but I have seen many men killed in battle, and I am telling you no arrow killed this man.'

'What does it matter?' asked Eleanor in a small voice. Geoffrey started guiltily. He had forgotten Eleanor in the

108

clamour of questions about Xavier that had been jangling in his mind. 'The poor man is dead anyway. What does it matter whether he was shot by an arrow or killed another way?'

Cenred's pig-like eyes swivelled from Geoffrey to her. 'It matters very much. When Durnais returns, he will claim that a Norman has been slain by Saxon outlaws and revenge killings will follow. I would like to prevent that, if I can.'

'Durnais will not blame Saxons for this,' said Eleanor.

'Oh, but he will,' said Cenred bitterly. 'He has done so before. Durnais is a man who sees everything in terms of Saxon-Norman rivalry. That will not happen when *I* am sheriff.'

He nodded to his soldiers, who began to strip Xavier's body. They did so with such efficiency and deftness that Geoffrey suspected they were no novices at removing clothing from corpses, and that Xavier's was probably not the first to be deprived of its valuables. One of them held up the chain-mail tunic for Cenred to inspect, revealing that two metal rings had been displaced by the arrow, but that the resulting hole was too small to have allowed serious injury. This was borne out by the superficial puncture in Xavier's chest, which had bled a little, but that even the uninitiated could see would not have been fatal.

Cenred looked at Geoffrey coolly. 'So, how *did* he die?'

Now the corpse was naked, Geoffrey was surprised he should need to ask. He pointed to Xavier's neck. 'There are bruises there – as might be made by eight fingers and two thumbs.'

'He was strangled?' asked Cenred incredulously. 'I do not think so! Knights are not the kind of men who allow others to choke the life out of them. You can see for yourself he was armed to the teeth with daggers. If someone had tried to throttle him, he would have run his attacker through.'

Geoffrey was about to say he did not know the answer, when he saw Xavier's helmet. It was well worn, but polished. In it was a dent, and it looked as though someone had struck it, possibly stunning its wearer. He pointed it out to Cenred.

'Perhaps he was knocked from his horse by a stone, then choked while he lay insensible and unable to defend himself.'

Cenred considered for a while, staring down at the corpse and oblivious to Eleanor's mounting distress. 'As under-sheriff, I have seen a few murdered corpses and I am slowly becoming familiar with the clues they offer. I think he was strangled first and shot later. There would have been more blood if he had been alive when he was shot.'

'Why would someone shoot a dead man?' asked Geoffrey, puzzled.

'Who knows? But Saxon outlaws are unlikely to strangle their victims – they would sooner use their bows. Perhaps I can use this fact to subdue rumours of a Saxon atrocity against Normans.'

Geoffrey pulled away the sheet from the next of the bodies. The youthful face that gazed sightlessly at the fine barrel-vaulted ceiling meant nothing to Geoffrey, although his age and clothes suggested he was Xavier's squire. There was no question that he had been killed by an arrow, because the missile had struck him in the face, piercing the skull near the eye. Geoffrey replaced the cover and moved to the last corpse, aware that he had prolonged Eleanor's ordeal long enough, and that he should do his duty and help her take her husband home.

She sighed when she saw the grizzled old face, and leaned down to touch its cheek. Like the squire, Haymo had died from arrow wounds. Tears glistened on her face, and she brushed them away slowly. 'Poor Haymo. He did not deserve this.'

'I am sorry,' said Cenred sincerely. 'I have no words of comfort other than that I will try to find the men responsible for this and bring them to justice.'

Geoffrey declined Cenred's offer of soldiers to carry Stanstede away, and used his own men instead. He watched them fashion a stretcher from twine and two planks of wood, ensured the body was securely fastened to it – seeing it tumble into the mud was something that would do Eleanor no good – and led the grim procession away. Eleanor's face regained some of its colour once she was out of the frigid gloom of the chapel, and she no longer clung quite so hard to Geoffrey's arm.

People watched as they passed, some removing caps and hats as a mark of respect, and Geoffrey heard them muttering, telling those who had not yet heard about the ambush of travellers on the New Castle to Durham road. He heard the words 'Saxon' and 'Norman' whispered frequently, and was astonished that a commonly held assumption was that the Normans had killed one of their own, so Saxons would be blamed. By contrast, a distinguished group of Norman merchants were equally convinced that Stanstede's death was a simple case of Saxon savagery. Geoffrey watched Cenred's porcine features turn grim as he overheard the accusations and counter-accusations. They were just passing through Owengate when they met Roger.

'He has gone,' he announced, aggrieved. 'His house is empty.'

'Who?' asked Geoffrey. His thoughts were still on Eleanor. 'The prior?'

'Simon,' said Roger impatiently. 'His house is deserted and he seems to have left the city. No one has seen him today and I have looked in all the places he usually frequents. He is nowhere to be found. Even his pig is missing.'

'His pig?' asked Cenred, concerned. 'Where is the poor beast?'

'I wish I knew,' said Roger. 'Simon and that pig are inseparable, and if we find the pig, we will find him.'

Geoffrey turned away, so Eleanor would not detect his unease. Perhaps she *had* been wrong to send Simon out to inform the sheriff about the attack, and he was now dead, too. He took a deep breath, smelling the sharp, clean scent of new snow and the sulphurous stench of the open sewers, and wished they had never agreed to help Flambard. He did not like the sensation that events were unfolding all around him, and that he had no control over what would happen next.

It was past noon by the time Haymo's body had been stripped of its blood-stained clothing, washed, shrouded, and carried to the small church of St Giles on the New Castle road. Roger went again to look for Simon, but returned to say that the house was still empty, and that his neighbours had not seen him since the previous evening, when he had told them he was going to dine with Eleanor.

Geoffrey asked Helbye to remain with Eleanor for as long as she wanted to stay with her husband's body in the church and then escort her home. The other men were to guard her house, and to watch for anyone loitering or regarding it with more than a passing interest. The Littel brothers were careless guards, more interested in finding nooks away from the biting wind than in carrying out their duties. By contrast, Ulfrith was overly enthusiastic, unable to recognize the difference between people acting strangely and those who stared at the house because its owner had died violently.

'We should see Turgot,' said Geoffrey to Roger. 'I do not feel safe with that map in your possession. We should rid ourselves of it, then leave while there is still daylight.'

'I cannot abandon Ellie,' said Roger reproachfully, beginning to walk in the direction of the abbey. 'And you will not be going anywhere either. Look at the weather! You will not get far in this.'

Reluctantly, Geoffrey conceded he was probably right. Snow fell thick and fast, settling in a deep blanket across roads, roofs, and fields. If it continued, Geoffrey suspected they might be trapped for days. His dog was already struggling. The snow was deeper than its legs were long, and it panted furiously as it tried to keep up with him. They walked through Owengate and headed towards the monastery. Roger hesitated, then seized Geoffrey's arm to drag him to the huddle of shabby houses that occupied the space between cathedral and castle.

'Before we see the prior, I want another look for Simon,' he said, pulling Geoffrey to a narrow alley with houses built so closely together there was barely room to walk between them. 'Perhaps he found an alehouse and has only just returned.'

'He was very frightened by what happened last night, and may think it better to stay away from Durham until you leave.' And he would have a point, Geoffrey thought. Until the map was out of Roger's hands and in the prior's, he suspected no one would be safe.

Roger shook his head. 'Just because Simon is not a knight, does not mean he is a coward.'

Geoffrey knew perfectly well that not all knights were brave and that not all civilians were fearful, although he strongly suspected that Simon was not the most courageous man in the city, no matter what Roger's loyalty might lead him to claim. Simon had been petrified by the attack – he had rolled into a ball until it was over – and Geoffrey would not have been at all surprised to learn the man had fled. Or was Geoffrey doing him a disservice, and he really had tried to tell Cenred about the ambush, but had met the escaped intruder? Regardless, Geoffrey did not like the fact that he had disappeared.

Roger led the way through narrow lanes, each lined with tiny hovels that emitted the stale, rank odour of poverty, and stopped at a house that was better kept than most of the others. He hammered on the door, so hard that Geoffrey saw flakes of plaster flutter to join the ever-growing blanket of snow on the ground. There was no reply. Roger hauled at one of the window shutters until the hinge buckled, then held it back so they could peer between the thick wooden mullions.

The house was a simple affair, comprising a single chamber and a lean-to cooking area on the ground floor, with a flight of wooden steps leading to a sleeping loft above. Geoffrey saw the lower room had been divided in two. One part contained a table, a stool, and a bench; the other half had been an animal pen, although not so much as a chicken roosted there now. The ashes in the hearth were cold and white, and stray flakes of snow spiralled down from the chimney on to the mat of dirty rushes on the floor. Other than a lump of bread on the table and a pot of cold stew that hung over the dead fire, there was nothing to see. Simon's house was empty.

'Can you squeeze inside and have a look around?' asked Roger, pulling the window shutter open a little further.

Geoffrey stared at the narrow gap between the stone mullions in amusement. 'Not without removing all my clothes and starving for a few weeks. Can you see from here whether the door has been barred from the inside?'

'Why?' asked Roger, letting the shutter close with a snap. 'What has that to do with anything?'

'Because if it has, it means Simon is inside,' explained Geoffrey patiently. 'Perhaps he is asleep upstairs. Is there a back entrance?'

Roger brightened. The notion of finding another way in had not occurred to him, and his previous attempts to enter had involved thumping on the door with sufficient vigour to leave dents in the wood and to yell loudly enough to make the neighbours come to see what was happening.

Geoffrey followed him down a lane so thin he was obliged to walk sideways. It led to a substantial wall built of woven hazel branches and then packed with mud. He supposed Simon kept livestock at the back of his house, and the wall was to prevent them from straying. He said as much to Roger, who gave a bray of laughter.

'Think about where you are, lad: the north of England. And what lies beyond the north of England? Scotland. And what do Scottish heathens crave above all else? English cattle. This wall is not to keep cows in, but to keep Scots out. Anyone in Durham who values his beasts has one of these.'

'I would have thought the castle's defences would suffice to repel the odd rustling party,' said Geoffrey, far from certain the Scots were as good at cattle theft as Roger would have him believe.

'They are devils,' said Roger uncompromisingly. 'But it is not them I am worried about now; it is Simon.' He linked his hands together and crouched down, offering Geoffrey a leg-up.

'You want *me* to go?' asked Geoffrey, startled by the audacity. 'You do it. He is your brother.'

'I am too heavy for you,' said Roger, still holding his hands stirrup-fashion.

'You are not. I can lift you easily.'

Roger gazed at the wall unhappily and scratched his head. 'You first, then, and I will follow.'

'What is the matter?' asked Geoffrey, bemused by Roger's behaviour. Entering other people's property by stealth had never bothered him before, and Geoffrey did not understand why he should object to it now. 'What is there about this particular wall that makes you uncomfortable?'

'Uncomfortable?' demanded Roger, cupping his hands again. 'I am not uncomfortable. Come on, Geoff, lad. It is cold standing here. You go first, and I will be right behind you.'

Geoffrey sighed in exasperation, but placed one foot in Roger's hands. He was propelled upward with unnecessary force, so he almost toppled over the other side. He straddled the wall and reached down to offer Roger his hand. Roger backed away.

'Is the yard empty? Is there any movement in the sheds?'

'Not that I can see,' said Geoffrey, thinking that someone would have to be desperate before they sought any kind of shelter in the rickety sheds in Simon's yard. Even under a blanket of snow, Geoffrey could detect a sulphurous stench that indicated some particularly rank-smelling beast had been lodged there in the recent past.

'Are you sure?' asked Roger doubtfully. 'There is usually a pig.'

'So, you are afraid of a pig, are you?' asked Geoffrey, sensing the real cause of his friend's unease. 'It must be quite an animal if it rattles the formidable Roger of Durham.'

'It *is* quite an animal!' agreed Roger vehemently. 'It is fiercer than any wild boar I have ever encountered, and more treacherous and vengeful than your dog. It will remember me.'

'Will it indeed? And what did you do to it to brand yourself so indelibly on its memory?'

'It was a misunderstanding, and I was only trying to help. But there is no reasoning with a pig. It will see me and bloodlust will blind it to all else.'

'Rather like you in a city of Saracens, then,' remarked Geoffrey. 'Now you understand how *they* feel when they see the likes of you bearing down on them in full battle gear intent on mischief.'

'It is not the same. This is a pig with serious intentions and teeth like scimitars.'

'Then thank you for suggesting I brave the thing alone. But it is cold sitting here. Take my hand and let us get this over with, so we can dump that map on the prior, where it belongs.'

'Someone is coming,' whispered Roger hoarsely, glancing furtively down the alley and ignoring the proffered hand. 'I will keep watch.'

'You do not need to keep watch – we are doing nothing wrong.' But Geoffrey was talking to thin air, and Roger had scuttled to the end of the alley before he could point out that concern for Simon's well-being was no crime and there was no need for stealth and secrecy. Shaking his head in disgust, he dropped into Simon's yard.

It comprised two sheds that had been home to the pig – when it was not occupying half the house, presumably – and an open area that was about the length of ten lances. There was no movement from the lean-tos, and their doors were closed and barred. Roger need not have been afraid that the pig with the personal vendetta would emerge, because it would not have been able to get out.

The snow had changed the yard from what had probably been scrubby grass to a continuous, unbroken blanket of powdery white, and Geoffrey left deep footprints as he walked towards the rear door. He rattled the handle, and found it was locked. However, one of the windows was ajar, so he levered it open and climbed inside.

He found himself in the extension that served as a kitchen. There was nothing in it except a flagged hearth, a stand holding a bucket of frozen water, and a blocked slop drain. It was not the cleanest room Geoffrey had ever seen, and he grimaced at the slippery vegetable parings that squelched under his boots and at the smell of stale grease and burning.

A door led from the cooking area to a passageway, at the end of which was a second door, which led to the main chamber; the stairs to the upper floor were on his right. Geoffrey walked into the main room and inspected the front door, to see whether it had been barred from inside. He saw that it had not, and all that had been keeping Roger out was a pair of substantial locks.

He looked around the room quickly, half expecting Simon to demand why his privacy was being invaded. But the house was empty, and it seemed to Geoffrey that Simon had simply gone out and locked up his belongings, like any man who expected to be absent for a while. He was about to leave when a fragment of yellow-white under the table caught his eye. Curious, he knelt to inspect it.

The table was crudely wrought, more a series of planks nailed together than a real piece of furniture. At one end was a small drawer, where knives and other utensils were stored when not in use, and it was from this drawer that the small corner of parchment poked. Geoffrey crouched down and saw someone had nailed a document to its underside, presumably to conceal it. It was scarcely an original hiding place, and whoever had put it there should have ensured that none of it showed. But, Geoffrey supposed, it was good enough for a will or the property deed of the house – something that needed to be kept safe but that was not necessarily a secret.

It was not his business to pry into the private affairs of Roger's brother, so Geoffrey stood and started to walk towards the yard again, wanting to leave Simon's house and see that Roger delivered the map before anything else could distract them. Then he paused and looked back at the parchment. Something about it was familiar, and he hesitated.

Simon's house suggested he was not a wealthy man, and his antipathy towards Geoffrey from the moment they met seemed to be based on the fact that Geoffrey could read: Simon, like many men, despised literacy and regarded it with a deep suspicion. So, why should he be at pains to hide a document? Furthermore, the parchment that hugged the underside of the table was of good quality – among the best Geoffrey had seen – and not something an illiterate man of modest means would buy.

Puzzled, Geoffrey walked back to the table and squatted next to it, reaching out to touch the document. Tendrils of unease began to uncoil in his stomach when he recalled where he had seen its like before. Roger had a similar piece shoved down the inside of his surcoat: the parchment was, without doubt, exactly the same as that on which Ranulf Flambard had drawn his treasure maps.

117

Six

Geoffrey gazed thoughtfully at the parchment hidden under Simon's table. He had two options: he could leave it where it was, for Simon to reclaim later, or he could inspect it. He was inclined to do what seemed most prudent and leave well alone. But Flambard said there were three recipients for his maps: prior, goldsmith, and sheriff, and since Simon was none of these, he should not have had one. And, if Geoffrey's suspicions were right, and the attack the previous night was connected to the fact that Roger still had Turgot's map, then perhaps it had been Simon who had informed Weasel that Roger intended to spend the night at Eleanor's home.

Geoffrey frowned. Was he doing Simon an injustice by associating him with Weasel's attack? After all, Simon had been as much at risk as Roger and Geoffrey had been. And did Simon even know the incriminating parchment was in his house? Perhaps someone had put it there without his knowledge. Geoffrey rubbed his head, and thought about Xavier, dead in the castle chapel. Was *he* one of the three messengers Flambard had employed? Flambard had denied he would use Xavier and Odard, but the bishop was not a truthful man. He may have lied about his other messengers to protect them, should Roger run into difficulties and be forced to reveal the nature of his mission.

Or had Xavier been in the north on unrelated business? Perhaps *he* had been seduced by the lure of buried treasure, as Flambard feared others would be, and had come to see if he could find it for himself. And what of Odard, the second of Flambard's friends? Was he also dead in mysterious circumstances? And if so, what did that say about Roger's safety?

118

Geoffrey thought about what he knew of Xavier's death. He and his squire had been travelling with eight other people when the party had been attacked. Cenred assumed the ambush had been the work of outlaws who haunted the Durham to New Castle road and that the motive had been theft. But what if he was wrong? What if Xavier had been carrying the map intended for the goldsmith or the sheriff, and the party had been attacked for that reason?

Geoffrey scratched his head. If that was true, then was it possible Simon's map was the one Xavier had carried? Did that mean Simon had killed Xavier? But Cenred said the ambush had occurred at dusk, and Simon had been with Geoffrey then, dining in Eleanor's solar. So, Simon could not have committed the murder or stolen the map himself. Of course, that did not mean to say that he had not known about the attack, or that it had not been carried out under his orders. After all, if Flambard had trusted his son Roger with the secret of the hidden treasure, then why not his son Simon?

Without further ado, Geoffrey reached out, ripped the parchment from its hiding place, and opened it on the grimy table top, smoothing away its creases and wrinkles. It was, without question, one of Flambard's charts. It depicted two wavy lines representing streams, and a darker, bolder one that was a road. He recalled Flambard telling him one of the three documents contained such features.

He could not help but smile at Flambard's cunning. Even with this map and Roger's, they would still not find the treasure without something to tell them where the waterways and paths were located. They could be anywhere, even outside the county, although Geoffrey suspected Flambard would not have buried his hoard too far from the cathedral: the farther it was from Durham, the greater were the chances it would not reach its intended destination. Idly, but without much hope, Geoffrey wondered whether Roger might recognize the courses of the rivers, and thus identify the spot. Then they could dig up the gold, and hand it to Prior Turgot without the need for more subterfuge.

And now what? Geoffrey thought, as he looked down at the

119

parchment. Should he replace it and not become involved in a mystery that had already claimed the lives of several people? Or should he hand the thing to the prior? The notion of the belligerent Simon profiting from the treasure was repellent, so Geoffrey decided to give the matter further thought later, and shoved the parchment inside his surcoat.

He went back through the kitchen, and was about to climb out of the window, when he saw a second set of footsteps lying parallel to the ones he had made while walking across the garden earlier. Someone had followed him.

He froze, listening intently, to see if he could hear anyone else. It was not a large house, and he was astonished he had not heard another person enter. His first thought was that Roger had overcome his squeamish refusal to scale the wall. But Roger would not have slipped in soundlessly, he would have called out. Not only that, but the footprints were about the same size as Geoffrey's, and too small to belong to the big knight.

Moving with stealth, Geoffrey headed back towards the main room, looking for a telltale sign that someone else was inside. It was as silent and still as the grave. Outside, children screamed in delight as they tossed snowballs at each other, and he could hear Roger berating the dog for whining. This told Geoffrey that Roger had seen no one enter the house, or he would not have been bothering with the dog – the whines of which suggested *it* was aware something was amiss, even if Roger was not – but would be coming to his friend's aid.

There was nowhere to hide on the ground floor of the mean little house. Geoffrey checked the alcove next to the hearth, and even peered up the sooty darkness of the chimney, but was not surprised to find them empty. He could only assume that, while he had been examining the map, the person had ascended the wooden steps that led to the sleeping area on the upper floor.

Drawing his dagger, Geoffrey began to climb, surprised that the steps were well constructed and did not creak and groan. It went some way to explaining why someone had been able to sneak up them without Geoffrey hearing. There were two doors on the landing of the upper floor: one led to a room that overlooked the rear garden, and the other to an attic that had a dismal view of the alley at the front. Both were ajar.

Geoffrey opted for the back room first. Standing well back, he pushed open the door until it lay flush with the wall. No one could be behind it, and the room was completely bare except for apples lying in neat rows on strips of linen. Glancing out of the window, Geoffrey saw there were still only two sets of footprints, and that both of them led into the house: since the other person could not have left via the front door without him seeing, he could only assume the person was still inside. And the only place possible was in the chamber overlooking the front.

Alert for an attack, he opened the door, using the point of his sword so he could stand well back and no one could shoot him. But no one fired. No one did anything, because the room was empty, and the window was wide open. With an exclamation of annoyance, Geoffrey dashed across to it and looked out. Just below, someone was scrambling down the wall. Geoffrey leaned down and succeeded in grabbing the merest shred of a hood, but the person jerked away and it snapped out of his fingers. Determined he should not escape, Geoffrey went after him.

The builders of Simon's house had not meant its exterior timbers to support men clambering on them. There was a sharp snap, and the crossbeam to which the intruder clung split. With a shriek, he let go and tumbled in an inelegant flurry of arms and legs to the ground. For a moment, Geoffrey thought the fall had injured him, and that he would be caught, but the soft snow had absorbed the impact and the man was able to struggle to his feet and run away, stumbling and tripping on the ice.

'Roger!' yelled Geoffrey, hoping his friend would catch him.

But Roger did not reply, and Geoffrey saw the man reach the end of the alley. He was going to escape, carrying at least some of the answers to the mystery with him. Geoffrey was about to abandon a cautious descent for a freefall when the matter was decided for him. With a tearing creak, the beam that supported his weight gave way and he, too, fell into the snowdrift under the eaves of the house.

He staggered to his feet, still bent on giving chase, but the man was already out of sight. Geoffrey hobbled the few steps to the end of the lane, but realized it was hopeless when there was nothing to see in either direction. The fellow could have gone anywhere, and Geoffrey did not know the area well enough to know where to start a search. Disgusted, he gave up, and leaned against the wall to recover.

'What are you doing?' demanded Roger, emerging from another alley. He saw the open window and the broken timber on the ground below. 'You could have opened the door from the inside; you did not have to leap from the upstairs window like an acrobat!' His eyes became wary. 'Or did you meet the pig?'

'Did you see him?' asked Geoffrey, not interested in Roger's porcine battles. 'Did you see who climbed over the wall after me?'

'No one did. I was keeping watch.'

'Then you did not do a very good job. Someone followed me inside.'

'But why would anyone do that?' asked Roger, puzzled. 'Surely, if a burglar intended to rob the place, he would have waited until the house was empty.'

'I do not think he was a burglar. I suspect he wanted this.' He handed Roger the map.

'Here, what are you doing with this?' asked Roger in astonishment. He nudged Geoffrey in the ribs. 'My father did not give you one, too, did he? And he did not tell me? Crafty old dog!'

'He did not,' said Geoffrey shortly. 'And I can assure you I would not have taken it, anyway. I found it nailed to your brother's table.'

'Really?' asked Roger, gazing at the map in amazement. 'And how did he come by it?'

'I think Xavier may have been one of Flambard's couriers, and that he died for it. But how this map – possibly Xavier's – came into Simon's hands, I cannot begin to imagine.'

'But my father told us Xavier and Odard were not the other two messengers.'

'Yes, he did,' said Geoffrey flatly.

Roger sighed. 'Was it Odard you saw in Simon's house, then? Or perhaps that Weasel?'

Geoffrey shrugged, frustrated. 'He wore a cloak with a hood, and I did not see his face.'

Roger frowned, and twisted the map this way and that, as though he imagined it might yield its secrets if he studied it long and hard enough. Eventually, he looked up and his face was bleak.

'You think Simon killed Xavier? Is that what you are telling me?'

'I have no idea, but the more I learn about the business the less I like it. I will go with you to the prior, then I am leaving.'

'You cannot,' said Roger grimly. 'I wish you could, because I feel guilty about putting you in danger. But I was talking to one of the castle guards while you were checking the house . . .'

'You said you would keep watch while I was inside,' objected Geoffrey.

'You said there was no need,' countered Roger.

Geoffrey sighed. 'So, this person must have scaled the wall while you were passing the time of the day with the soldier. That is why you did not see him.'

'I only took my eyes off it for a moment,' said Roger, having the grace to appear sheepish. 'And it was your fault anyway.'

'Was it?' asked Geoffrey, startled. 'Why was that?'

'Your dog,' said Roger, shooting the beast an angry glower. The animal, sensing censure, favoured Roger with a malevolent glare of its own. 'The soldier tried to pat the thing and it snapped at him. It damn near took his fingers off. I was obliged to chat with him, so he would not report it to his superiors. Eleanor would not approve of that at all. She does not like lawbreaking, and the keeping of savage dogs in the city is a serious offence.'

'It will not be an issue much longer,' said Geoffrey. 'I

will take him with me when I leave this afternoon. Eleanor's reputation as a law-abiding citizen will remain intact.'

'You will not. That is what I have been trying to tell you. The soldier told me that snow has closed the roads in all directions. The women and the grooms who survived the ambush last night had quite a struggle to get through – they almost abandoned the bodies, because they were beginning to think they would not make it – and everyone who has tried to leave today has been forced to return. Like it or not, we are trapped here.'

The Benedictines were determined to build a substantial abbey to complement the splendid cathedral, and, although thickly falling snow had put an end to outside work, hammers, saws, and mallets rapped out a syncopated tattoo that indicated progress was still being made on the inside. Geoffrey stood for a moment, gazing again at the foundation stones that showed how massive the cathedral would be once it was completed. It spanned the entire width of the peninsula, except for the part occupied by the little church of St Mary le Bow, where the common people would attend weekly services.

The abbey was enclosed on three sides by the wall that ran all around the peninsula, and would be protected on the fourth by the cathedral-fortress when it was finished. Until then, it was separated from the town by a fence that had a gate halfway along it. Roger informed the scruffy lay brother on duty that he had important business with Prior Turgot, and pushed his way inside while the man was still deciding whether or not he should let him in – not that he or the tiny dagger he carried could have excluded the knight anyway.

'That is where Turgot lives,' said Roger, pointing to an attractive building, made from neatly hewn blocks of grey stone that had probably been intended for the cathedral. Its roof was tiled, and it was the only one not laden with snow, suggesting it was probably warm inside. Geoffrey was impressed to note that all the window shutters were open to admit the light, but that real glass kept out the cold. Glass was an expensive commodity, and such luxury indicated that the prior was a man who knew how to look after himself. Roger reached the door, clearly intending to enter regardless of the fact that he had not been invited. A weary-looking monk with ink-stained fingers rushed to intercept him.

'Please,' he gasped, pushing Roger aside and unlatching the door himself. 'I am Algar, the prior's secretary. Before you disturb him, I must see whether he is accepting visitors. He does not like unannounced invasions . . . I mean visits.'

'He will accept *me*,' declared Roger confidently. 'I am Roger of Durham.'

'I know who you are,' said Algar, risking life and limb by inserting himself through the door before him. 'You are the man Bishop Flambard forced to go on Crusade, because the Scottish tribes promised they would never raid Durham's cattle again if you left the country.'

Geoffrey regarded Roger in amusement. Here was a tale he had not heard before.

'The Scots are a lily-livered horde,' announced Roger uncompromisingly. 'I did to them what they did to us, and gave them a taste of their own medicine.'

'Unfortunately, you gave them more than a taste,' said Algar gloomily. 'You gave them an overdose – a fatal one in many cases. The name Roger the Devil is still feared by hapless villagers all along the border, and not all of them are Scots.'

'It is difficult to know where you are sometimes,' grumbled Roger. 'Especially in the dark. But I did not come to talk about my reputation as a fearless warrior. I came to see Turgot on important and private business.'

'Wait here,' said Algar, gesturing to a hallway that contained several chairs and a table bearing a bowl filled with scented leaves. 'I will see whether he is available.'

'If he is in, then he is available,' said Roger firmly. 'I am a *Jerosolimitanus* and an influential man in this region. If I want to see the prior, then the prior I shall see.'

'I will tell him that,' said Algar nervously. 'But wait here first. He gets angry if I grant interviews without his permission, and I intend to be promoted soon. I do not want my chance of advancement ruined because of you.'

'Roger the Devil,' mused Geoffrey, as the ambitious Algar disappeared up the stairs. 'I always wondered why you left Durham when you despise anything not English. Now I know: you were compelled to leave because you harried your neighbours to the point where they agreed to do anything just to be rid of you.'

'Pay Algar no heed,' said Roger contemptuously. 'He refers to things that happened during my youth, and it is not fair to drag them up now.'

'You left four years ago, Roger,' said Geoffrey, smiling. 'You were no youth then.'

'If you say so,' said Roger, his bored tone indicating the conversation was over. He looked around him. 'God's blood! That Turgot knows how to take care of himself. It smells like a whore's den in here with all these scented leaves lying about.'

'The prior will see you,' called Algar uneasily. He indicated the arsenal of weapons Geoffrey and Roger carried. 'I can assure you that you will not need those here.'

'You can never tell,' said Roger, pushing past him to walk up the stairs. 'The prior might want to practise his swordplay with me.' He roared with laughter, and Algar became more nervous than ever.

'Do not worry,' said Geoffrey kindly, wanting to reassure him.

Algar was not convinced. 'That is Roger the Devil. And I have just allowed him to enter Turgot's private apartments fully armed. If anything untoward were to happen, it could ruin my plans to be prior myself one day!'

Prior Turgot sat at a large table that had been placed near the window of his solar, a comfortable room with wool rugs on the floor – so thick that Geoffrey's feet sank as he stepped on them – and rich tapestries on the walls. Soft colours had been chosen, so that pale blues, light greens and primrose yellows gave the room a restful, cosy feel. All the furniture matched, and was the rich red-gold of cherry. A fire crackled merrily in the hearth, while next to the table a brazier filled with glowing coals provided additional heat and ensured the great man would not suffer cold draughts down the back of his neck. Among the parchments that littered the table were dishes of sugared almonds and tiny marchpane cakes, as well as two jugs of wine. It was a chamber that offered all the comforts that might be expected by some cosseted queen, and a far cry from the poverty recommended by St Benedict.

Turgot was not alone. Two other monks were with him, one making copies of confidential letters for the abbey's records, the other muttering in the ear of the first. Geoffrey could hear reverence in his voice when words like 'tithe', 'benefaction', and 'taxes' were uttered.

'Sir Roger,' said the prior, standing to bow as the knights approached. 'To what do we owe this pleasure? You do not usually set foot in places of God when you are in Durham.'

Geoffrey glanced at him sharply, detecting a note of censure. Despite Roger's pride in his home, it seemed he was not overly popular in his father's palatinate. Geoffrey studied the prior carefully. He was small, almost dainty, with soft white hands that fluttered when he spoke. He had a head of bushy white hair, and behind eyebrows that were almost as long as Geoffrey's little finger were a pair of shrewd eyes. Eccentric though he might appear, Turgot was no fool.

'I wish you would visit us more often,' Turgot continued, wincing as Roger grasped one of his delicate hands with a hard, brown paw. 'It would be good for your soul.'

Geoffrey had the distinct impression that he had been about to add it would also allow him to keep an eye on Roger's whereabouts, so trouble could be averted.

'You hold your masses so damnably early in the morning,' said Roger irritably. 'If you had them at noon, you would find the number of people in your congregations would double.'

'I will bear it in mind,' said the prior, his face expressionless. 'So, have you come to ask me to intervene with Bishop Flambard about your banishment?'

'No, I have not,' said Roger shortly. 'And I was not banished. I followed my father's suggestion that I might like to travel.'

'And did you enjoy seeing the world?' asked Turgot,

hopefully. 'If so, then perhaps you should consider journeying a little farther—'

'The Holy Land is a grand place,' agreed Roger, smiling at memories that were more golden than the reality. 'I was on my way back there when I was diverted.'

'Were you?' asked the prior, and there was no mistaking the disappointment in his voice. He forced a smile. 'Then, we will not be honoured with your company for long? You will return to the Holy Land, where there are plenty of heathens for you to kill and enemy villages to plunder and loot?'

'Aye,' said Roger fondly. 'As I said, it is a grand place.'

'I see,' said Turgot. He waited several moments, evidently expecting Roger to state the nature of his business and be on his way. Roger, however, was in no hurry to leave, and began looking meaningfully at the wine in the jugs. Wearily, Turgot nodded to one of his monks, who went to fill cups. Evidently anticipating the visit might be a lengthy one, the prior gestured to his two companions.

'Forgive my manners. Do you recall my fellow brethren? This is Brother Burchard, my bursar.'

Burchard was a large man with a florid, heavy face and a head of coarse black hair that was in need of a trim. His small eyes seemed more petty than intelligent, and he looked to Geoffrey like the kind of man to steal food from the pantries at night and blame it on someone else. Geoffrey imagined that in his youth – the bursar was well into middle age – he would have been an imposing figure. Now he was merely overweight. He nodded a curt greeting to Roger, although Geoffrey noticed it was far from friendly and that he barely bothered to look up from pouring the wine. Something about him reminded Geoffrey of an ape he had once seen in the south of Spain.

'And this is Hemming, my sub-prior,' Turgot continued, pointing to the other monk.

Of the three monastics, Hemming was the most normal in appearance. He was unquestionably Saxon, unlike Turgot and Burchard, who were obviously Norman. He had short, corn-coloured hair that bristled thickly from his tonsure and his eyes were an arresting blue. Geoffrey liked the way humour lurked in them as he watched the bursar fill one goblet significantly fuller than the others and keep it for himself, and thought Hemming would be the most interesting and least priestly of the trio. Hemming half rose from his chair and gave an amiable smile.

'We have never met,' he said in a soft, but pleasant voice. 'But your reputation goes before you.'

Roger regarded him warily, trying to ascertain whether he was being insulted. After a moment, he indicated Geoffrey with a careless jerk of his thumb. 'This here is my friend.'

'Does he have a name?' asked Hemming, his blue eyes gleaming with merriment.

'Sir Geoffrey Mappestone,' said Roger tartly. 'And if you want to know his history as well, he has a manor somewhere near Wales, which is full of sheep, but he is not there often and spends most of his time in the service of Tancred de Hauteville.'

'Are you any relation to Godric Mappestone?' asked Turgot, regarding Geoffrey with interest. 'He was my father's overlord in Normandy and abandoned his French holdings for richer pickings in England after Hastings.'

'My father,' said Geoffrey, wishing that Normandy was not so small and mutual acquaintances not so common. His father was not a man most people had admired, given his propensity for appropriating land that was not his own.

The prior was pleased by the connection. 'How is he? He must be almost seventy by now.'

'Dead,' said Geoffrey shortly, reluctant to tell Turgot what had really happened.

'I am sorry,' said Turgot, and it seemed his sympathy was genuine. All Geoffrey could think was that either the prior had not encountered his father for a very long time, or he was thinking of the wrong person. 'I will say a mass for him tonight.'

'Thank you,' said Geoffrey, not adding that Godric needed all the masses he could get.

'I know the name, too,' said the bursar, and his heavy face creased into a scowl as he struggled to recall where. He snapped his fingers. 'It was a legal dispute – some claim that Godric had unlawfully seized his neighbour's field.'

'Probably,' said Geoffrey. His father regularly treated his neighbours' fields as his own, and it did not surprise him that someone had complained to the courts about it.

'He was found guilty and fined,' the bursar continued. 'I wonder if the scoundrel ever paid.'

'I cannot claim Norman ancestry, and so can embarrass you with no family tales,' said Hemming, grinning at the bursar's appalling lack of tact. 'I am Saxon – a member of the Haliwerfolc.'

'I am one of those, too, on account of my mother,' interjected Roger. He explained to Geoffrey. 'Haliwerfolc are those Durham inhabitants who are Cuthbert's chosen people. We are special.'

'Cuthbert belongs to the abbey now,' said Burchard austerely. 'He is accessible to *all*, not just to Saxon peasants who lay claim to him on the grounds of ignorance.'

The wry humour left Hemming's face, although he responded to Burchard's rudeness only by gazing down at his sandalled feet. Geoffrey looked from him to the bursar, and wondered whether the abbey was the haven of peace and brotherly love it should be.

'Before the abbey was founded, there was a community here called the Church of St Cuthbert,' said Roger to Geoffrey. 'All its priests were married, but they left when Cuthbert was taken from them and given to the Benedictines.'

'Not all,' corrected Hemming softly. 'Some of us remained. My family has a special connection to Cuthbert, because our ancestor was one of the monks who brought him from Lindisfarne. I could no more leave Cuthbert than fly to the moon.'

'We have lots of saints here,' announced Roger boastfully. Seeing him about to list them yet again, Geoffrey tried to interrupt, but Roger was unstoppable. 'Cuthbert is the most famous, but we also have Oswald, Aidan, Eithilwald, Eadfrith, Ceolwulf, Edbert, Billfrith, and the Venerable Bede. And then there was the one who was stolen. What was his name?'

'Balthere,' said Burchard disparagingly. 'He was popular with Saxons, but not with intelligent folk. His bones were in St Giles' Church, but they were stolen. Still, he was only some Saxon hermit.'

Hemming's face was white with anger at the insults to his heritage that dripped relentlessly from Burchard's lips, and Turgot, seeing his bursar had overstepped the mark, intervened hastily.

'It is my hope that Balthere will reappear one day, when he will be displayed with honour and reverence next to Cuthbert.' He sat, and clasped his hands together, steepling his fingers in the way that Geoffrey had noticed religious men often did. 'But you did not come to discuss relics. What can we do for you today?'

Roger treated the prior to a knowing wink. 'What you can do for me is irrelevant. The real question is what can *I* do for *you*.'

'Well?' asked Burchard rudely, when Roger drained the wine from his cup and declined to elaborate. 'We are busy men. Tell us what you want, and let us all be about our business.'

'In good time,' said Roger, fixing the bursar with a cool glare. 'I do not like to be rushed. And I am still thirsty. Give me a drop more wine, and I shall tell you something that will make you very happy.'

'How was the Crusade?' asked Turgot, watching as the bursar resentfully filled Roger's goblet. 'I have heard the slaughter was great and terrible.'

'It was,' agreed Roger appreciatively. 'And I was at the heart of it.'

'That I can believe,' muttered Burchard unpleasantly.

The atmosphere in the prior's solar was uncomfortable. The three monks were growing exasperated with Roger's clumsy game of wait-and-see, but were too shrewd to dismiss him, lest he really did have something that would benefit them. Whatever they might think of the bluff knight, he was a son of the Bishop Flambard, after all.

Geoffrey was loath to intervene, but he was uneasy with the

131

notion of Roger passing the map to the prior in the company of his two companions. Had he been Roger, he would have requested a private audience with Turgot, then if Turgot chose to take the others into his confidence later, that was his choice. There was something about the bursar Geoffrey did not like, while he sensed Hemming was an intelligent man who might well use his Saxon wits against a Norman bishop. Geoffrey fought back the temptation to tell Roger what to do and drank more wine.

'I said a prayer for you last night,' said Turgot conversationally, as Roger drained the cup a second time.

'Good,' said Roger. 'A few of them here and there does no one any harm.'

'We are glad to hear it,' said Hemming, a discreet smile playing around the corners of his mouth again. Geoffrey saw the bursar raise his eyebrows heavenward before slapping the jug back on the table and returning to his seat. Turgot seemed shocked.

'The Holy Land is now in the hands of Christians,' said Roger, as though news of the Crusade's success was something the monks might not have heard. 'We drove the Saracens from our shrines and slaughtered as many of them as we could.'

'I am sure you did,' muttered the bursar. 'Slaughter is about the one thing you do very well.'

'And the looting?' asked Turgot with a smile. 'How was that?'

With a sudden flash of insight, Geoffrey saw exactly where the prior was leading the conversation. He almost laughed aloud. Turgot had surmised – quite wrongly – that the purpose of Roger's visit was to donate some of his plunder to the abbey. Anyone who knew Roger, even slightly, would be aware that he and his booty were not easily parted, and that an abbey would be the last place the knight would consider as a beneficiary.

'There was plenty of looting to be done, I can tell you,' said Roger, pleased to be asked. 'All a knight like me had to do was take it.'

'Really?' asked Burchard, exchanging a keen glance with

his prior. Apparently, he was also wondering whether any of it might be coming their way.

Roger nodded. 'Of course, I had to fight for it. Saracens love their gold, and only yield it to those they consider worthy opponents.'

'Especially the unarmed women and children,' muttered Geoffrey. 'They willingly take on heavily armed soldiers to save their leaking pots and their half-starved livestock.'

'Of course, the infidel learned a thing or two from me,' boasted Roger, ignoring Geoffrey's mumbled comments. 'At the siege of Antioch, I killed seven men with one—'

'You must be tired of hearing about the Crusade,' said Geoffrey, mostly so Roger would hand the map to Turgot, but partly because he saw the prior's beneficent smile begin to look strained. Turgot, like Eleanor, did not want to be regaled with lengthy sagas of bloodshed and mayhem.

'Actually, we have heard very little,' interjected Burchard, ignoring the grateful smile Turgot gave Geoffrey. 'Personally, I find it gratifying to hear how infidel gold passed to Christian hands.'

'You would not think so if you had been there,' said Geoffrey shortly. 'The Crusade did not display our religion in its best light.'

'Are you questioning the sanctity of our holy war?' demanded Burchard. 'It was undertaken at the request of the Pope and had God's blessing. God would not have favoured such an undertaking had it not been morally right.'

'If I thought God approved the murder of unarmed civilians, I would never set foot in a church again,' said Geoffrey coolly. 'But I do not believe He had any say in the matter. I think the Crusader army cut a bloody swath across half the world entirely of its own volition.'

'That is heretical talk!' exclaimed Burchard, coming to his feet with his fists bunched. 'Father Prior! Will you allow this dirty, ill-bred lout to spread lies about God's holy Crusade?'

'Peace, peace!' said Turgot, waving a frail hand that, nevertheless, held enough authority to make his bursar sit again. 'There are many views about the morality of the holy wars, and we should always listen to the opinions of men who have experienced them first-hand.'

'Roger needs to speak to you privately,' said Geoffrey, deciding that if Roger would not take the initiative to end the uncomfortable interview, then he would have to do it himself or risk spending the rest of the day listening to Burchard's ill-informed opinions. 'It is a matter of some urgency.'

'If he wants to confess to misbehaving in his sister's brothel, he can do so to one of the lower monks,' snapped Burchard. 'The prior has neither the time nor the inclination to listen.'

'I have done no such thing!' declared Roger indignantly. 'You have a nasty mind, Burchard!'

Burchard was on his feet again, and the prior intervened hurriedly. 'Perhaps we should accede to Geoffrey's request. I will hear Roger's petition in private, as he asks.'

Burchard made as if to demure, but Hemming took his arm and hustled him outside. Hemming bowed to Geoffrey as he left, and his lack of curiosity suggested to Geoffrey that he was confident he would hear about it later anyway.

'Now,' said the prior, smiling warily at Roger once they were alone. 'What do you want?'

'My father charged me to bring you this,' said Roger importantly, reaching inside his surcoat and rummaging around.

'Flambard?' asked Turgot, watching Roger search his person. 'But he is in prison.'

'He has escaped,' said Roger with a satisfied grin. 'He will be in Normandy by now.'

'Escaped?' echoed Turgot in astonishment. 'But how? The White Tower of London is one of the most secure prisons in the country. No one escapes from there.'

'Well, he did,' said Roger, still hunting for the map. 'But that is irrelevant. What is important is that he sent something . . . God's blood! I cannot find the damned thing!'

The cursing, groping, and patting went on for some time before Geoffrey realized he would have to help. Turgot sighed in exasperation, and glanced meaningfully at the hour candle. However, once Geoffrey had unbuckled Roger's surcoat, the

134

parchment fluttered to the floor and Roger snatched it up with relief.

'Thank God for that!' he exclaimed. 'I thought I had lost it. And then what would have happened to my father's cathedral?'

'What is it?' asked the prior, examining the thin parchment in puzzlement.

'It is a map,' said Roger gleefully. 'And the "X" marks the spot where treasure is buried.'

'That is all very well,' said the prior. 'But a cross is no good on its own.'

Roger explained Flambard's plan, adding irrelevant asides and unnecessary details that only served to confuse the prior, so it was some time before he understood what Flambard intended.

'It is the kind of plot he would devise,' Turgot said eventually. 'I wondered whether he might do anything useful with the fortune he amassed during his years at court.'

'You know about the treasure?' asked Roger.

Turgot shrugged. 'I know he is a rich man, and that he managed to retain a good portion of his wealth when King Henry seized the rest. But I do not know where it is.'

'It is around here somewhere,' said Roger. 'It must be. It would not have been safe to cart great chests of gold around the country.'

'True,' said Turgot. 'But Flambard is a remarkable man. It would not surprise me to learn he had done it.' He gave a wry smile. 'I travelled to London with Hemming not long ago, to visit him in prison, and persuade him to help us with the cathedral. Perhaps that was what gave him the idea.'

But Flambard had not trusted Turgot, then, thought Geoffrey. Flambard trusted no one – not even the loyal Roger – with the location of his hoard.

'Where are the other maps?' asked Turgot. 'As you have explained, one is worthless alone.'

'One is to be delivered to Walter Jarveaux, and the second to Sheriff Durnais,' said Geoffrey, thinking about the map hidden in his own surcoat and wondering whether to pass it to Turgot immediately, or whether he should send it anonymously, so no one would ask how he came by it.

Turgot pursed his lips and regarded Geoffrey sombrely. 'Then Flambard's clever plan is already in trouble. Yesterday, I received news that Durnais, who has gone to Chester-le-Street, never arrived, and no one knows where he is.'

'Did he receive his map before he left?' asked Geoffrey.

'Not that he told me.'

'So, does that mean it arrived *after* he left for Chester-le-Street?' asked Geoffrey. 'Or that it has not arrived at all?'

'I will ask,' said Turgot. 'Although I suspect the latter. Cenred would have told me had a message arrived concerning the cathedral. But Durnais is not the only thing wrong with Flambard's plan.'

'Well?' asked Geoffrey, aware of a sinking feeling in the pit of his stomach.

'You said the third missive was to be passed to the goldsmith,' said Turgot. He sighed and rubbed the bridge of his nose, as if his head ached. 'Jarveaux died two days ago – he choked on an oyster.'

Geoffrey and Roger sat in silence as they thought about the prior's revelations. Turgot steepled and unsteepled his fingers as he considered the problem, splendid eyebrows waving to express their owner's anxiety. Roger scowled at the map – crumpled and dirty from resting so long in the unsavoury depths of his surcoat – as if it were personally responsible for the misfortunes that had befallen the men who were to realize his father's plan. Still, Geoffrey thought, at least he now knew the reason for Cenred's odd comment in Eleanor's house when Roger had announced his intention to deliver his gold to Jarveaux: Cenred, like every other Durham inhabitant, knew Jarveaux was dead.

The news of the goldsmith's death and the sheriff's disappearance gave recent events a yet more sinister turn, and added credence to Geoffrey's notion that there was more to Flambard's plan than he claimed. There had already been seven deaths Geoffrey thought were connected to the treasure: the young roof-top brawler, the accomplice of Weasel who had invaded Eleanor's parlour; Peterkin and the man who had probably murdered him, Xavier and his squire, and now the goldsmith.

Was Jarveaux's death a coincidence? Accidents happened, and Geoffrey knew it was dangerous to look for patterns in events that were random. But, it seemed that Flambard's venture had been doomed from the start. Even before Roger had accepted Flambard's commission, Peterkin had been killed. Someone had known or suspected Roger would be entrusted with one of the maps, and had been determined to take it from him, even then. Poor Peterkin had probably been questioned by Weasel, and had been killed when he had been unable to answer.

And what did the missing Simon have to do with the mystery? How had one of Flambard's maps ended up pinned under his table? Had Simon put it there himself? Or had it been hidden without his knowledge, and he was dead in some ditch with a red quarrel embedded in his cowardly heart?

All the evidence suggested that someone did not want Turgot, Jarveaux and Durnais to receive their maps – or rather, that the treasure should not be used to build the cathedral. Geoffrey stood, and went to stare out of the window, looking to where the chancel rose out of the snow.

On the nearby table were some drawings, anchored at the corners by an assortment of goblets, lead seals, and inkwells. They were the plans for the completed building. Geoffrey knew he should not linger in Turgot's house, and that he should make it clear that he and Roger had discharged their obligation to Flambard, but architecture fascinated him, especially when conducted on as grand a scale as at Durham. He studied the plans, tracing lines on the parchment with his finger.

'How curious!' he said, Flambard's maps forgotten as he became absorbed. 'The Lady chapel will be at the west end, rather than the east.'

'It will be known as the Galilee Chapel,' said Turgot, coming to stand next to him. 'We wanted it at the east end, but every time we try to build there, the foundations crack.

The Chapel of the Nine Altars, which is next to where we wanted the Lady chapel, is also unstable.'

'Just before I left four years ago, a good part of the Chapel of the Nine Altars fell down,' said Roger, going to refill his cup again.

'All that has been rebuilt,' said Turgot. 'Even the floor has been repaved.'

'My father says Cuthbert will be moved into the cathedral soon,' said Roger. 'And, of course, if the Lady chapel were to be built next to the Chapel of the Nine Altars – where Cuthbert will be – it means there will be women.' He looked at Geoffrey as though that explained everything.

Geoffrey, however, did not understand the point he was making. 'What have women to do with it?'

'Is it not obvious?' demanded Roger impatiently. 'Lady chapels are frequented by women. And if the Lady chapel is built at the east end of the church, then women will walk very close to where Cuthbert will lie.'

'So?' asked Geoffrey warily, sensing he was to be regaled with yet another of Roger's contorted theories. 'I do not see the connection.'

Roger sighed gustily. 'Use your imagination, man! How do you think Cuthbert will feel if there are women in the next room, all chattering and flaunting their wares.'

'Even a saintly man like Cuthbert cannot be afraid he will succumb to temptation after being dead for four hundred years,' said Geoffrey, amused at the image Roger had created. 'And women will not go to the Lady chapel to "flaunt their wares", as you put it, but to pray.'

'Cuthbert's body was uncorrupted,' persisted Roger. 'It came out of its grave as fresh and whole as the day it went in. Of course he will still be tempted by the charms of a good woman.'

'But the good women are unlikely to feel the same way,' argued Geoffrey. 'You will find most of them prefer their lovers alive.'

'Well, it is Cuthbert who is making the foundations crumble,' said Roger firmly. 'And it is because he does not want women near his shrine.'

Geoffrey started to laugh at the ludicrous nature of Roger's claim, but Turgot nodded agreement. 'The stonemasons also believe this, but we will not be alive to see what will happen – that part of the cathedral will not be built for decades yet.'

'Aaron's Rod will be in the Chapel of Nine Altars as well,' added Roger, not willing to let an opportunity pass without mentioning the relic he was sure was coming Durham's way.

Geoffrey was surprised to see Turgot nod agreement to that, too. 'Flambard has promised to secure it for us. It and Cuthbert will attract many pilgrims our way.'

'How can he provide you with Aaron's Rod?' asked Geoffrey, astonished that an educated man like Turgot should believe such nonsense. 'No one can know what happened to it.'

'Well someone did,' said Turgot. 'It is an instrument of great power, and it is impossible to imagine it was just lost or forgotten. Flambard says a Crusader brought it from the Holy Land, and one day it will be here.'

Geoffrey was not usually sceptical of relics, but the whole idea that the Rod should reappear after thousands of years, only to fall into the hands of Flambard, was just too much. He was sure Turgot and Roger were mistaken, but did not want to argue, so turned his attention back to the builders' plans.

'The cathedral's enormous height will mean it will be visible for miles around,' he said, awed, tapping the parchment with his finger. 'Its towers will make it taller and larger than the castle. This is not a place of worship; it is a statement of Norman authority in the north!'

Turgot smiled from under his coxcomb eyebrows. 'Most men see only a big church when they study these drawings, but you have the vision to look further. When it is finished, it will be the most glorious building in Christendom, and people will view it with wonder for thousands of years. Mortals will come and go, but it will remain.'

Geoffrey continued to assess the plans, increasingly impressed by the sheer scale of the building that Flambard intended to raise. Until then, finishing it had been a distant objective, and even his vivid imagination had not allowed him to appreciate

139

its full scale. Now he did understand, he felt its completion should transcend the sordid plotting of men like Flambard. He studied the prior for a moment, assessing the shrewd eyes under the white caterpillars that crawled across his forehead, and came to a decision. He withdrew the parchment he had discovered in Simon's house.

'We found the second of Flambard's maps by chance this morning,' he said, handing it to the prior. 'It was in Simon's house.'

'But you said the three recipients were me, the sheriff, and the goldsmith,' said Turgot, staring at it in confusion. 'Simon is none of these.'

'Perhaps he is one of the three couriers,' said Geoffrey, knowing he was not. 'But that is irrelevant. What is important is that you now have two parts of the puzzle, and that brings Flambard's treasure a little closer to the cathedral's coffers.'

Turgot took the parchment, and placed it on top of the one Roger had given him. All three men studied it intently. The cross on Roger's map was clearly visible through the thin material, but it still did not tell them where the treasure might be hidden.

'It is hopeless,' said Turgot, looking up eventually. 'We have streams and a road, but unless we have some landmark – a village, church, or some distinctive feature – these are meaningless. Flambard is clever: his parchments are indeed useless unless all three are viewed together.'

'You can understand why,' said Geoffrey. 'If two maps were sufficient to locate the hoard, then there would be nothing to prevent one of the three recipients from persuading another to share information and divide the spoils in half.'

'But his cunning has been wasted,' said Turgot heavily. 'I have my map, but Jarveaux is dead and Durnais is missing.'

'True,' agreed Roger. 'Nor do we know whether that dead Hospitaller – Xavier – was to deliver his message to the sheriff or the goldsmith.'

'We do not know he was to deliver one at all,' Geoffrey pointed out. 'We can only surmise that he was one of the couriers: we cannot prove it. He might have come to ensure

140

you did not try to persuade the prior to go digging for personal gain in the middle of one night, Roger.'

'I would never do that,' declared Roger hotly.

'But does Flambard know that? He trusts no one, not even his prior.'

'A Hospitaller is dead?' asked Turgot, looking from one to the other uneasily. 'Would it be one of the trio who often accompany Flambard around the country?'

'Trio?' asked Geoffrey thoughtfully. 'There are three of them?'

Turgot nodded. 'Xavier, Odard, and Gilbert Courcy. Their Grand Master sent them to Flambard four years ago, to act as his personal bodyguards.'

'I know a child called Gilbert Courcy,' mused Roger irrelevantly.

'You know them?' asked Geoffrey, ignoring Roger. A child could have no bearing on this affair. 'Was Xavier red-haired with a scar?'

Turgot nodded, 'And Odard is small and dark, but his fighting skills are reputed to be prodigious. Gilbert is younger, and is being trained by the others.'

Was Gilbert the 'squire' who had died with Xavier? Geoffrey wondered. Or was he elsewhere, perhaps in league with Weasel? And did that mean Flambard had lied, and Xavier and Odard were indeed the other two couriers? Geoffrey rubbed the bridge of his nose and marvelled at the webs of lies and deceit Flambard had woven. No one could trust anyone else, and no one was what he seemed.

'Xavier was killed with Haymo Stanstede last night,' said Roger.

'I heard about the ambush,' said Turgot. 'But I did not know one of the victims was Xavier. These Hospitallers usually melt into the background when Flambard is at Durham, so I doubt whether he will be known to anyone outside the abbey. They always go hooded and cowled, sometimes wearing Benedictine habits. They are mysterious men.'

Cenred had not known Xavier, Geoffrey thought. 'Why did Flambard choose Hospitallers to serve him? Why not Benedictines?'

141

Turgot shook his head. 'Who knows? Hospitallers are renowned for their blind loyalty, so perhaps that appeals to Flambard. But let us assume that you are right and that Xavier was one of Flambard's couriers. You, Sir Roger, are the second. That means that the third is probably in the city wondering how to fulfil his mission – Jarveaux is dead and the sheriff is missing.'

Roger scratched his head despondently. 'Then our journey has been a waste of time. The third messenger cannot deliver his map, and without it the treasure may just as well be on the moon.'

'Our only hope is that Durnais returns, and that *his* courier is not the man dead in the castle chapel,' said Turgot, although he did not look optimistic. 'It is a pity. King Henry will not readily forgive Flambard for all the evil things he has done, and he will not be allowed to return to England very soon – if ever. Our funds are low, and unless we raise more money soon, building will have to stop.'

'Tax the people,' said Roger with a shrug. 'That is the usual solution to problems like this. Although they complain bitterly, they always come up with the goods.'

'We could,' said Turgot. 'But the people have been too heavily taxed already. No, if Flambard's treasure cannot be found, there will be nothing we can do but to stop building.'

'That is life, I suppose,' said Roger stoically. 'But I had better get back to my sister. She needs a hand with the brothel.'

The prior winced. 'I am sure she does, and I am also sure you are the man to help.'

Roger took that as a compliment. He gave Turgot a conspiratorial grin, and was halfway to the door when he stopped. A thought had occurred to him.

'Geoff is good at solving mysteries,' he said, ignoring the agonized glance Geoffrey directed at him. 'He sorted out an unholy muddle involving a plot to kill the Advocate of Jerusalem last year, and then he uncovered a diabolical scheme involving the death of his father. He is good at sniffing out trouble and making all end well.'

142

'Is he now?' asked Turgot thoughtfully. 'I thought there was more to him than the average knight. Most of *them* are not interested in architecture. And most would have kept my map *and* the one from Simon's home, and set about hunting down the third – and the cathedral would have been doomed.'

'Oh, yes,' said Roger proudly. 'Geoffrey Mappestone is the man you need to help you with your problem. *He* will be able to find out what happened to this missing map.'

Seven

There were times when Geoffrey did not like Roger very much, and when he found the big knight's lack of tact a sore trial. One of those times was now, with Roger boasting to Turgot how his friend would be able to solve the mystery concerning Flambard's treasure. Geoffrey did not want to become any more entangled in Flambard's plans than he was already. Men had died, and Geoffrey had no desire to become the next victim of a convoluted plot hatched by the devious bishop.

'This could be the answer to my prayers,' said Turgot. 'I confess I was beginning to doubt whether Flambard's hoard would ever find its way to its rightful place.'

'Geoffrey will see justice done,' said Roger, slapping his friend on the back with such vigour it hurt.

'Good,' said Turgot. 'Will he start immediately, or would he like another cup of wine first?'

'No,' said Geoffrey firmly, not liking the way they talked about him as though he was not there. 'I do not want wine and I do not want to meddle in Flambard's affairs. It is too dangerous.'

'I thought you had been on the Crusade,' Turgot pointed out. 'Surely our little city cannot compare to marauding Saracens and mighty battles on the walls of the Holy City?'

'I assure you it can,' said Geoffrey. 'Especially if Flambard is involved. But I agreed to accompany Roger until he delivered his message and that was all. As soon as the weather eases, I am leaving.'

'But do you not realize what this treasure will mean for the cathedral?' cried the prior, grabbing Geoffrey's arm as he started towards the door. 'Without it, all building will stop within weeks. Then who knows what might happen? It may never be completed!'

'I am sorry,' said Geoffrey, disengaging his arm. 'But I am in Tancred's service, and I do not think he will approve of me acting for other men.'

'Tancred risked his life to take God's holy kingdom from the infidel,' argued the prior, determined to use every tactic he could think of to make Geoffrey change his mind. 'He will not object to you acting on behalf of a cathedral raised to God's glory – especially since you are trapped here anyway.'

'Aye,' added Roger. 'Look at the weather. In Durham, when the snow falls this heavily, the roads are closed for days – sometimes weeks. You might as well make yourself useful.'

'But I do not want to,' objected Geoffrey. 'If I have as much time to fill as you seem to think, then I will spend it in the library, reading.'

'There will not *be* a library unless the third map is discovered,' said Turgot slyly. 'My monks will be sent to other foundations and Durham's books will be left to rot.'

'Rubbish,' said Geoffrey, knowing that a wealthy order like the Benedictines would never allow such an asset to slip through its fingers so carelessly. 'The library will be moved to another location. It happens all the time.'

'Then you are welcome to use it all you like – after you have discovered the third map.'

'No,' said Geoffrey, exasperated. 'Use one of your monks.'

'My bursar has a tenacious and greedy mind, so I will set him to look for it. But you are a knight, and able to go to places where a monk cannot. We stand a better chance of locating the treasure if two of you search.' Geoffrey shook his head and grabbed the handle of the door, but Turgot stopped him. 'If you will not willingly agree to help, then I shall use less pleasant means of persuasion.'

Geoffrey gazed at him in astonishment. Turgot's voice had hardened, and the eyes had lost their benign quality. The Benedictine Order was powerful, and Geoffrey saw he was naive to imagine that a man could claw his way into such a position of influence by being gentle and kindly. There was an iron core in Turgot that was as strong and unbendable as that in any ambitious nobleman or courtier.

'How?' Geoffrey asked. 'I have committed no crime, so you cannot threaten me with arrest.'

'Not you,' said Turgot, turning to fix Roger with eyes that were as cold as ice. 'Your friend.'

'Just agree to help him, Geoff,' said Roger, suddenly furtive. 'It will not be too taxing, and I will be with you to make sure nothing dreadful happens.'

'What have you done that leaves you open to blackmail?' demanded Geoffrey, wondering why Roger had brought him to Durham when he seemed to have so many secrets to hide. Geoffrey was not entirely sure he wanted to know, given that Turgot seemed to consider it sufficient cause for having his own way, and Roger was uncertain and embarrassed.

'Roger committed a dreadful sin,' said Turgot harshly. 'Why do you think he went on Crusade?'

'You went to atone for a sin?' asked Geoffrey, regarding Roger uneasily. 'You said you joined because you were interested in the looting. And the prior's secretary believed you went because you made a nuisance of yourself with the Scots.'

'That is what most people think,' said Turgot, a hint of spite in his voice. 'An envoy from the Scots *did* offer a truce – they would leave us alone provided we sent Roger away – and Flambard *did* agree to it. But there was another reason, too, wasn't there, Roger?'

'I suppose there was,' mumbled Roger.

'Why did you not tell me before?' asked Geoffrey, not liking the fact that Roger's lack of openness was about to impact on his own life. 'I thought we were friends.'

'We are friends,' said Roger with a sigh. 'I did not tell you, because I did not want you to think badly of me. But the truth is that my father told me to go on Crusade to salve a guilty conscience.'

'That does not sound like you. You committed murder, pillage and God knows what other crimes on the way to the Holy City, and none of those seemed to have preyed on your mind.'

'This was different,' muttered Roger sheepishly, prodding at a rug with a scuffed boot.

'It was indeed,' agreed Turgot nastily. 'You see, Roger is a desecrator of holy relics!'

Later that day, Geoffrey and Roger sat in Eleanor's solar, while outside the snow continued to fall. In some places the drifts had reached the sills of the lower-floor windows. Wind rattled the shutters, hurling pellets of ice against them, and howling down the chimney to make the fire gutter and roar.

The streets were deserted. Shops were closed, no work was possible in the fields, livestock had been herded into the safety of byres and stables, and even beggars had been driven to take shelter wherever they could find it. A dog barked somewhere, and the abbey bells still chimed when it was time for the monks to attend their offices, but as dusk approached, the city grew ever more silent, as though the snow was suffocating it.

Geoffrey edged closer to the fire, trying to warm his hands by cupping them around his half-empty goblet of mulled ale. For all his protestations that he wanted to be out of the city, he was glad he was not on the road in the foul weather that raged outside. Riding would be impossible, not to mention unpleasant, and he would have to walk and lead his horse in case it stumbled and injured itself.

He looked at Roger. The big knight had acquiesced to Eleanor's insistence that no armour was to be worn in her house, and was dressed in thick red leggings and a crisp white shirt with scarlet laces down the front. Over it he wore a curious fur garment he said he had acquired during one of his Scottish raids. It looked like a wolf pelt to Geoffrey, and smelled like one, too. Why Eleanor objected to armour, but allowed the odorous jerkin into her presence mystified Geoffrey.

Bearing in mind the attack of the night before, Geoffrey had declined to abandon all his armour, even to please Eleanor, and wore thick leather leggings and a light chain-mail tunic. He had left his sword in the room on the upper floor where the men of the household slept, but he still

147

carried a large dagger in his belt and a smaller one in his boot.

Eleanor knelt between them, stirring a pot of pork and bean soup that simmered over the hearth. She had pestered Roger relentlessly about his business in Durham, asking him questions and changing the subject, and then asking questions again. It was not long before she had confused the big knight into telling her all about Flambard's maps, despite Geoffrey's attempts to stop him. Her reaction was predictable: she was disgusted that Roger should have been so easily persuaded to help Flambard, and claimed that no good would come of it.

He studied her as she knelt to tend the soup. Her dark hair shone in the firelight, and the flames painted her eyes deep gold. He admired her clean, fresh complexion and the way her dress fitted her slender figure, and thought it a pity she should be in mourning. He thought it an even greater pity she had married old Haymo Stanstede in the first place, because a young and attractive woman deserved better than the wizened specimen he had seen in the castle chapel. He hoped the wealth she would inherit would give her the freedom to make a better choice when the obligatory period of mourning was over. Had he not been obliged to return to Tancred, and had she not laid out her husband's corpse only a few hours before, Geoffrey would have considered paying court to her himself. It would be a lucky man indeed who captured the heart of Eleanor.

'He did not do it with malicious intent,' she said defiantly. 'He made an honest mistake.'

'I am sorry?' asked Geoffrey, startled from his reverie. 'Surely you do not mean Flambard?'

She sighed. 'Who have I been talking about this last hour? Have you not been listening?'

Geoffrey had not, and had been concentrating on the way her clothes clung to her body when she leaned over to stir the broth. He knew she had been talking, but Roger had been answering, and he had supposed a contribution from him was not required.

'It was unfair to force Roger go on the Crusade for what he did,' said Eleanor, stirring the beans vigorously, as though she wished the spoon were a weapon. 'He should not have been punished.'

'It *was* an honest mistake,' agreed Roger, gazing down into his goblet with sorrowful eyes. 'And I am sorry for it, believe me.'

Geoffrey did believe him. He knew Roger well enough to know he would not willingly have desecrated one of the most sacred relics in the country – not because he was respectful of the Church and its authority, but because he was a superstitious man who believed strongly in a divine power that would strike down anyone who treated holy relics with irreverence. Geoffrey also knew Roger was not a clever liar, and that if he claimed the affair was a misunderstanding, then it was likely to be true. He was too straightforward, and too easily caught out in untruths.

Yet he had lied about his reason for going on the Crusade. Geoffrey could only assume that once Roger had started to tell people that his motive was to accumulate wealth, he had eventually come to believe it himself. It would not be the first time he had remembered events in a way to suit his own requirements, although Geoffrey would not have called it lying exactly. Geoffrey supposed that by the time they had met, Roger had already forgotten the real reason for being on the Crusade, but nevertheless he wished Roger had confided in him, and was angry that his friend's actions had forced him to become the prior's agent.

'The way Turgot treated Roger was grossly unfair,' Eleanor went on furiously. 'He should have known he would never do such a thing deliberately.'

'True,' agreed Roger morosely.

'And then he threatened to tell everyone about it,' said Eleanor, sitting back on her heels to look at Geoffrey. Drips from the spoon splattered on to her dress, but the perceived injustice of Roger's treatment was so great that she was unaware of them.

'Would that have been so bad?' asked Geoffrey, deciding he had better enter the conversation before her tight dress distracted him again. 'If everyone already knew, then Turgot would not be able to blackmail Roger now.'

Eleanor made a disgusted sound at the back of her throat and waved the spoon at him. 'That is a stupid thing to say. You have only to look at the Crusade to see the ends to which men will go in order to protect the things they consider holy.'

Geoffrey did not think religious fervour was what motivated most Crusaders. A few were holy men, who genuinely believed Jerusalem should be in Christian hands, but they were in a minority.

'If people had known what Roger had done, he would have been held responsible for every mishap that befell the city,' Eleanor went on. 'People always want someone to blame when things go wrong.'

'Securing a scapegoat is a way folk deal with situations beyond their control,' agreed Geoffrey, carefully neutral.

'Quite,' said Eleanor. 'Roger would have been held responsible for *everything* unpleasant – the harvest failing last year, the tithe barn catching fire. He could never have lived here in peace again.'

Geoffrey suspected that was true. Many people were superstitious and simple-minded. Roger *would* have been blamed for all manner of misfortunes, and while it probably would not have been possible for a mob to lynch him, life would not have been easy for him or for his family, including Flambard. No wonder the bishop had been so keen to send his son to the Holy Land.

'It was an honest mistake,' said Roger, yet again. 'I needed a candle holder.'

Geoffrey tried not to smile. 'And the item you chose just happened to be St Oswald's skull – one of the most revered and holy relics in the north of England.'

'I did not know the shiny silver box in my father's chamber was a reliquary,' objected Roger, as if he imagined it had been placed there for the sole purpose of confusing him.

Roger had taken Geoffrey to see Durham's relics again after their interview with the prior. The reliquary containing Oswald's head, however, was conspicuous by its absence – something Geoffrey had asked Roger about when they had first visited the shrine. Sheepishly, Roger informed him that it had been put inside the high altar, so it could recover from the indignities it had suffered at his hands. Geoffrey knew that many saints were manhandled in their often-turbulent post-mortem travels, and thought there was no need for the abbey to be so protective.

'You have not heard my side of the story,' said Roger unhappily.

'I have – several times,' said Geoffrey.

Roger cleared his throat, and began to tell his tale yet again, as though Geoffrey had not spoken. 'I had just finished an evening in a tavern and decided to visit my father. He was busy, so I waited in his office. The careless servant did not provide me with a light, and I was damned if I was going to sit in the dark, so, I lit a candle, but it kept falling over.'

'He needed a candle holder, you see,' elaborated Eleanor. 'He did not intend to commit an act of sacrilege. It was all perfectly innocent.'

'I looked for ages,' continued Roger. 'Then I saw this silver box on the table. I decided to see whether there might be a dish inside – and there was. I found a wooden one.'

'St Oswald's skullcap,' said Geoffrey.

'But it did not look like a head,' objected Roger. 'It looked like a bowl. And how was I to know St Oswald would be on my father's table?'

'When Flambard arrived and saw what Roger had done, he was aghast,' said Eleanor, shaking her head anew at the unfairness of it all. 'He would not even listen to Roger.'

'He was unreasonable,' agreed Roger. 'I offered to put Oswald back the way I found him, but he said I would be struck down if I touched it a second time. He and Turgot both said the only way I could make amends for such an act of desecration was to join the Crusade.'

Geoffrey rubbed his chin. Although he could hardly admit it, he saw the humour in Roger blundering around drunkenly in the dark and not stopping to consider the fact that a candle holder was unlikely to be stored in a silver casket. But using saints' bones as dishes was not something encouraged by the Church, and Geoffrey understood why bishop and prior had thought a pilgrimage necessary to absolve Roger. And Geoffrey was certain that sending Roger on a long and dangerous journey that would take him away from the Scots had also been taken into consideration. Flambard had killed three birds with one stone: he had made sure Roger did not mention his desecration and bring retribution down on his family; he had ensured Roger was absolved; and he had taken advantage of Roger's absence to agree to the Scots' truce.

'Our father did not give Turgot the exact details,' said Eleanor. 'But he mentioned a desecration. Turgot promised to keep the secret and to my knowledge, he has – until now, that is. It was unfair of him to tell you.'

'It was,' agreed Geoffrey wholeheartedly. 'I wish he had kept it to himself.'

'A story was put about that the Scots wanted Roger to leave,' said Eleanor. 'We have not had a raid since Roger left, so perhaps they really did make some arrangement.'

'So, you cannot be angry with me,' said Roger. 'I have atoned for my sin. If St Oswald is no longer cross with me, you have no right to be.'

'I am not angry with you about that,' said Geoffrey. 'I am angry because you volunteered my services to Turgot. You told him I would find the third map *before* he resorted to blackmail.'

'I was trying to help,' protested Roger. 'I thought you liked the cathedral and might want to play a part in its completion.'

'Not like this, and I have a bad feeling there is more to Flambard's plan than finding his treasure.'

'What do you mean?' asked Eleanor. 'What else could there be?'

'I do not know,' said Geoffrey. 'But I wish we did not have to find out.'

'You are looking too deeply into what is a simple affair, Geoffrey,' said Eleanor, as she ladled the soup into pewter dishes and placed horn spoons on the table. It was now pitch dark outside, and the wind had picked up even more, whistling down the chimney and making the rugs twitch and shudder as though they were alive.

'It all seems so elaborate,' said Geoffrey, picking up a

152

spoon. 'Turgot seems an honest enough man. Why not just *tell* him where the treasure is buried? Why all the secrecy and subterfuge?'

'If there is enough gold to buy a hundred masons and carpenters and their supplies for the next four decades, then we are talking about a lot of money,' Eleanor pointed out. 'And if folk know Flambard owns such a vast hoard, it is not surprising there are greedy men who want it.'

'*I* would not want it,' said Geoffrey vehemently. 'King Henry would hear about any fabulous increases in wealth, and his commissioners would be on the recipients like hounds after a fox. The King is not a man to let anything stand between him and money, and a thief would not enjoy his new-found wealth for long.'

'You are different from other men,' said Eleanor. 'You are better.' She blushed when Geoffrey looked at her, startled by the unexpected compliment, and studied the spoon in her hand.

'It is decent of you to stand by me, Geoff,' said Roger. 'I would not like that relic business to be made public – I would never be able to show my face here again.'

'That was not the only reason I agreed to comply with Turgot's demands,' said Geoffrey. 'It was for Eleanor, too. She had nothing to do with your careless choice of candle holders, but that will not prevent her from becoming the victim of vengeful townsfolk.'

Eleanor smiled, a rosy flush still dappling her cheeks, while Roger looked from one to the other sharply. 'My sister is a widow of less than a day, Geoff. I do not want her reputation besmirched by hopeful suitors.'

'I can take care of my own reputation, thank you,' said Eleanor stiffly. 'I am not some silly girl who needs the likes of *you* to tell me how to behave. I am a grown woman who knows her own mind.'

Geoffrey, looking at the determined glint in her eyes and the defiant jut of her chin, was sure she did. The more he saw of Roger's sister, the more he admired her. He wished he might come to know her better, and thought it a pity he would not have the opportunity.

'So,' she said, standing to fill the bowl Roger had already drained. 'What shall we do to find Turgot's treasure? Shall we see if we can find Sheriff Durnais, or shall we question Jarveaux's family, to see if he received one of these maps?'

'*We* will do neither,' said Roger firmly. 'Geoff and I will handle this. You can stay here and do what widows are supposed to do.'

'Can I now?' asked Eleanor archly. 'And what is that, pray?'

'You can sit in your solar and cry. That should keep you busy.'

'It will not! Do you think me some mindless simpleton, who has nothing better to do than to sit at home and pretend to be something I am not?'

'Are you not distressed by the violent death of your husband? You were married to him, woman!'

'Of course I am shocked. And I will grieve for him. But he was murdered in the ambush that also killed the knight – Xavier – who you think may have carried one of these maps. If I want to avenge Haymo, then the best way I can do that is by helping you.'

'But it would not be seemly for you to be out and about with us when we make our enquiries.'

'I was not thinking of accompanying you "out and about",' said Eleanor haughtily. 'But I can go to places you cannot – I can listen to women's gossip at the well, and, as a recent widow, I can talk to Alice Jarveaux on the grounds that we have both recently lost husbands.'

'But you are in mourning,' objected Roger, returning to what he considered his central argument. 'You cannot gossip at wells while your husband's corpse is still warm. Have you no respect?'

'I have every respect for Haymo,' snapped Eleanor angrily. 'Although even you must see that being married to a man three times my age was not easy.'

'You chose him,' countered Roger. 'You need not have done. I always said *I* would look after you.'

Eleanor gave him a sad, tender smile, and reached out to touch his bristly chin. 'You did. And I am sure you would have done all you could. But you were on the Crusade, and rumours came back to us about diseases and battles and starvation and God only knows what else. I did not know whether you would return.'

'I might not have done, given the number of battles I was in,' said Roger carelessly. 'But if I had died, I would have asked Geoffrey to make sure that you got all my loot.'

'And how would you have done that, if you were dead?' asked Eleanor archly. 'But we are wasting time. We need to decide how to recover the third map, and I shall help whether you like it or not. We are both responsible for Geoffrey being dragged into this – you because of your act of sacrilege, and me because he acted in my interests when he agreed to the prior's demands – so we must both assist him in any way we can.'

'Roger is right to keep you out of this,' said Geoffrey gently, hoping his quiet reason might succeed where Roger's bluster had failed. 'We agreed to help Turgot because we wanted to protect you, not so you can become more deeply involved.'

'Well, that is too bad,' said Eleanor haughtily. 'I *will* help, and that is the end of the matter. People will be kind to me because I grieve for my husband, and will tell me things they would not tell you. You *need* me.'

'We will manage,' insisted Roger. 'But Turgot said he was going to set the bursar to discover the third map, too, because he is tenacious. What does "tenacious" mean exactly? Is it something to do with singing in tune?'

'Burchard?' asked Eleanor. 'You do not want *him* helping you. He is hated by the townsfolk, and if *he* has been told to find the third map, you may as well abandon all hope of ever seeing it again. People would rather see it destroyed than have it in his hands.'

It was difficult to know where to begin in their quest for the missing parchment the following day. The roads were well and truly closed, so Geoffrey and Roger could not travel to Chester-le-Street in search of Sheriff Durnais, which would have been the obvious place to start. The next option was to visit the home of Walter Jarveaux, to try to ascertain whether he had received a message from Flambard before he had died. It was eventually agreed that Eleanor, with Geoffrey in attendance, would visit his wife.

Meanwhile, Roger was charged to frequent the city's taverns in search of his half-brother. He was delighted with the assignment, although Geoffrey had grave misgivings, afraid he might damage their chances of learning something useful with his overenthusiasm. His worries intensified when Roger said he would take Ulfrith with him. Ulfrith was no more subtle than Roger, and Geoffrey winced when he imagined the pair of them reeling from tavern to tavern in an indiscreet bid for information.

When Eleanor went with Geoffrey to visit Mistress Jarveaux, he found himself staring at her again. Her cloak was a simple affair of blue, but even that cumbersome garment served only to enhance the slenderness of her figure and accentuate her height. She took his arm as they walked along the snowy streets, clutching it hard when her shoes skidded on the slick surface. It had been a long time since he had escorted a woman somewhere – unsatisfactory evenings with females whose names he could not remember did not count – and he found he was enjoying the experience, despite the bitter wind and the threat of more snow.

His dog slunk along behind them, panting with the effort of moving through the drifts. It growled when it reached the first corner, and Geoffrey saw Tilloy and Freyn huddled in an alleyway, still guarding Eleanor's house against possible attackers. He cautioned them to be especially watchful when the house was empty, and continued the walk from the market square to Owengate, where they would cross the river to reach the pleasant cluster of houses known as the Elvet.

The guards at Owengate had heard about the murder of Stanstede, and were solicitous as Eleanor stepped into the ferry. One offered her a dirty cushion to sit on.

'We are sorry, Mistress,' said the other, who had removed his hat as a mark of respect and was bareheaded in the bitter wind. 'That New Castle road is dangerous, but every-one knows Master Stanstede provided a valuable service and those outlaws should have known better than to attack him.'

'Thank you, Ned,' said Eleanor, a little stiffly.

'That is true,' agreed the first guard, stepping back quickly from where he had been fussing with his cushion. The dog had decided to sit on it, and its savage demeanour did not make him willing to argue. 'I am surprised the outlaws did not see his cart was full of women and leave it be.'

'Perhaps they fired first and realized their mistake later,' said Eleanor.

Geoffrey shoved the dog off the cushion so Eleanor could sit and then knelt next to her, watching the oarsman ease his little craft into the strong, fast-flowing current. The guards' words were revealing. They indicated Stanstede had been a popular and well-known figure locally. So, either the men who had ambushed him were not locals, or they did not care whether he provided a service or not. Geoffrey strongly suspected the real target had been Xavier, and that Stanstede's death was incidental. But that conclusion did not answer the real question: who had perpetrated the ambush? It could not have been Weasel, because he had been attacking Eleanor's solar at the time.

It was not long before the ferryman had transported them across the river, and Geoffrey helped Eleanor on to the opposite bank. She took his arm again, and they walked into the Elvet.

The goldsmith had been a wealthy man. His home was built of stone, and all the windows had glass, although these were shuttered against the foul weather, giving the house an oddly abandoned look. Geoffrey's rap was answered by an ancient, sparse-haired woman who was almost bent double with age. White gums showed that she had long been without teeth. Her eyes were filmed with blue, so Geoffrey wondered if she was sightless, as well as toothless. She stood on the doorstep squinting and peering, her jaws working rhythmically on nothing.

'It is Eleanor Stanstede, Mother Petra,' said Eleanor politely. 'I have come to share my grief, as a widow, with Alice.'

'Grief?' queried Mother Petra. 'I thought you would be

157

dancing on the table to be rid of Haymo! Why you married that old lecher is beyond me.'

'He was a good man,' said Eleanor, quietly dignified, 'and it is not nice to speak badly of him now he is not here to defend himself.'

'Aye,' said Mother Petra, standing aside to let her enter. 'I will be joining him in Purgatory soon enough, and I can tell him what I think then. It is a terrible thing for a woman to have a son like him. Had I thought he would grow up to become a brothel keeper, I would have drowned him at birth.'

'You are Haymo's mother?' asked Geoffrey, a little confused. If Stanstede was seventy years old, as everyone said, then the old crone who stood in front of him must be verging on ninety – a great age indeed when most people considered themselves lucky to reach fifty.

'Who are you?' demanded Mother Petra. 'You speak English like a Norman – carefully and with a hint of native French. You are no Saxon.'

'His name is Geoffrey Mappestone,' said Eleanor patiently. 'He is Roger's friend, and offered to escort me here to make sure I did not fall in the snow. May we see Alice?'

'If you are coming in, then hurry up,' snapped Mother Petra, when Geoffrey was slow in following Eleanor over the threshold. 'You are letting the heat escape, and I do not want to spend the rest of the day in a cold house.'

Jarveaux's home was even more luxurious inside than out. The walls were decorated with murals, mainly geometric designs, while the floors were covered in thick carpets that made even the prior's comfortable domain seem inferior. The old woman led them along a passage, and up some stairs to a cosy chamber on the upper floor.

'Wait here while I fetch her,' she instructed. 'She is sculpting marchpanes. It seems that the deaths of my two sons have not made a great impact on their wives – you are out visiting, while she laughs and jokes in the kitchens.'

'*Two* sons?' asked Geoffrey, bewildered. 'You are the mother of Stanstede *and* Jarveaux?'

Mother Petra cackled, revealing her toothless gums. 'I had seven sons from five husbands. I was a beauty once, and men courted me from far and wide. But I have lived to see them all in their graves, husbands and sons. The last was Haymo. I always said I would outlive them, and I was right.'

'I am sorry,' said Geoffrey, thinking grief must have turned her mind.

'Why?' asked the old woman. 'The only good one among my whole litter was Thurstin. Now there was a man after my own heart!'

'Thurstin was Flambard's father,' explained Eleanor in a low voice. 'And my grandfather.'

Geoffrey's mind reeled. 'She is related to Flambard as well? God's teeth, Eleanor! She seems to have produced half of Durham!'

'She is Flambard's grandmother,' said Eleanor in a whisper. 'At least, that is what she says. Thurstin was a priest, and not supposed to have children. But Flambard has always been solicitous of her, and it is possible they are related. He bought her this house when he became bishop here.'

'He did,' confirmed Mother Petra proudly. 'And ask yourself: why would a great man like a bishop bother with the likes of me unless she were his grandmother.'

'She is cantankerous,' muttered Eleanor. 'No one would agree to have *her* nearby unless there was some family obligation.'

'Eh?' croaked the old lady. 'Speak up. I cannot hear when you mumble.'

'I was just telling Geoffrey how fond Flambard is of you,' said Eleanor in a loud voice.

'He is my grandson,' said Mother Petra. 'The best of all my grandchildren. But I will fetch Alice for you, and you can sit together and count your blessings that you are now both widows.'

She hobbled away, although Geoffrey suspected that she was a good deal more sprightly than she would have them believe. The fact that she had answered the knock to the front door before the servants suggested she was alert and curious, and that she was sufficiently agile to reach it before a second knock had been required. If she were responsible for the cunning vested in Flambard, then Geoffrey suspected she was a formidable figure, despite her great age.

'So, you are Jarveaux's sister-in-law,' he said to Eleanor when she had gone. 'If Jarveaux and Stanstede are her sons, then you and Alice are sisters by marriage.'

Eleanor shrugged. 'Durham is a small city – most people are related in some way or another.'

Geoffrey had wondered why Jarveaux had been chosen as a recipient for one of the maps, and now it transpired he was Flambard's uncle. And Flambard's other uncle – Stanstede – was Flambard's daughter's husband. Geoffrey scratched his head, and questioned whether such a liaison was legal or proper. He also wondered how many more of Durham's population had some family tie to the unchaste bishop.

'Eleanor!' came a low voice from the door. 'I heard what happened. I am so sorry.'

Geoffrey saw a woman in the doorway, offering Eleanor outstretched hands that were covered in flour to the elbows. Heedless of the white smears they left on her cloak, Eleanor slipped willingly into the woman's embrace. Because he had the impression the goldsmith was as old as Stanstede, Geoffrey had anticipated a middle-aged woman, who would bear her grief stoically. Alice Jarveaux, however, was not middle-aged. She was in her twenties, and exquisite in the way only Saxon women could be: small and delicate, with silvery gold hair arranged in two neat plaits rolled in circles above her ears. Her eyes were a deep sapphire-blue, and her complexion as perfect as a Christmas rose.

'I have had a terrible day,' she announced. 'Walter ordered horses for today, and the groom made me pay for them, even though Walter is dead and will not be going anywhere.'

'He hired them from the castle?' asked Eleanor sympathetically. 'Those men drive a hard bargain.'

'The groom said it was not his fault Walter died, and that he should not have to suffer financially because of it,' said Alice. 'Insensitive brute!'

'This is Alice Jarveaux,' said Eleanor, pulling out of the embrace and turning to Geoffrey.

'Haymo and Walter seem to have done well in acquiring

themselves young wives,' said Geoffrey, thinking he should consider moving to Durham when he became too old and infirm to fulfil his duties as a soldier.

Eleanor smiled. 'As I said, this is a small city, and the choice of husbands is not great. It is better to have one who is old, than none at all. Is that not so, Alice?'

'Only if he is rich, too,' said Alice. She looked Geoffrey up and down with the eye of a professional. 'So you can rid yourself of any designs on me. You are comely and of an age where you are young enough to be active but old enough to be interesting, but you clearly have no money.'

'I have a manor,' said Geoffrey, resenting the implication he was a fortune-seeker. 'And I have no intention of taking a wife, anyway – young or otherwise.'

'Do you prefer men, then?' asked Alice bluntly. She looked him up and down again. 'You do not look the type, but appearances can be deceptive.'

'I prefer their company to that of prattling women,' retorted Geoffrey, feeling a discussion of his sexual preferences was not an appropriate topic in the home of a recent widow. No wonder Roger had been happy for him to accompany Eleanor to visit Alice: Roger had known the woman was a shrew.

'Do you,' said Alice acidly. 'We women are often accused of mindless chatter, but you need only to venture into a stable to know that is not true. Men blather far more than women, and on the most tedious of topics – shoeing horses, how sharp a hoe needs to be, how leather-soled shoes slip on cobbles, or the optimum size of cartwheels. But women discuss matters of interest and importance.'

'Like what is the best flour for marchpanes and how difficult it is to see to sew by candlelight?' asked Geoffrey coolly.

Alice studied him, hands on hips. 'It will not be long before we fall out. Who are you, anyway?'

'He is a friend of Roger's,' said Eleanor. 'But do not argue with him, Alice. He saved my life – some louts broke into my house and shot at us with crossbows.'

Alice nodded. 'I heard about that, too. It was all over the city, like the news about Haymo's death.'

'I will miss Haymo,' said Eleanor sadly. 'I know I complained about him, and several times I wondered whether I was wise to marry such an old man, but he was always kind and gave me everything I asked for.'

'Well, now you will not have to ask him for anything,' said Alice practically. 'If you want something, you can have it, because his fortune is at your fingertips. But do not delve into it for a few days yet. Wait a week or two, for the sake of appearances, then start to enjoy yourself. We will show this city how to live, you and I!'

Eleanor gave a wan smile. 'Alice has always known she would outlive Walter,' she explained to Geoffrey. 'She has been looking forward to the day when she is free of him.'

'When I was fourteen, my father presented me with a number of potential husbands,' said Alice. 'I chose Walter because he was the oldest and wealthiest. For a dozen years of discomfort, I knew I would secure myself a life of contentment and freedom.'

'I see,' said Geoffrey, trying not to show surprise that a child could be so calculating. 'But will your family not make you marry again?'

'They will not!' said Alice fiercely. 'I can manage my own affairs, and need no family to meddle. It has all worked out rather well. It was me who recommended that Eleanor take Haymo. Like Walter, he was old and rich, but unfortunately he was rather more vigorous than his half-brother, and led her something of a merry dance until his sad demise.'

'Cenred wants me to continue running the brothel,' said Eleanor tearfully. 'But I do not think I can. You know I do not approve of that side of his business.'

'I will help,' offered Alice generously. 'Cenred is right: we do not want bands of lust-crazed men marauding the city. It is better that a proper service is provided to eliminate that sort of thing.'

'You should not offer your expertise for a day or two,' advised Geoffrey. 'It will be considered unseemly for a woman whose husband's body is still warm to take up employment in a brothel.'

Alice shot him an unpleasant look. 'I offered to help with

162

the administration, not as one of the whores. But I have neither time nor inclination to waste my day with the likes of you.' She turned to Eleanor. 'I am sorry you are sad, but remember that Haymo had a good life, and was happy with you. It is a pity he died with an arrow in his chest, but better that than choking his last while enjoying his conjugal rights on top of you.'

It was not a pleasant image. Eleanor swallowed hard and Geoffrey winced. Alice was a woman who did not mince her words, so Geoffrey decided not to mince his. The whole point of the visit was to solicit information that might help them locate the third map, and that was what Geoffrey was going to do, no matter how much his questions might offend or annoy the abrasive Alice.

'How did your husband die?' he asked. 'And when?'

'What business is that of yours?' asked Alice in amazement. 'You have no right to enter my home and ask me that kind of thing!'

'I heard he choked on an oyster,' said Eleanor quickly, seeing it would not be long before Geoffrey and Alice insulted each other to the point where further conversation was futile. 'Is it true?'

'*He* is probably one of King Henry's commissioners,' said Alice, regarding Geoffrey with dislike. 'He heard I have a fortune from my husband, and has been sent to see whether I killed him. He plans to claim Walter's estate for the Crown and have me wrongfully convicted of murder. I know how the King's "justice" works for us Saxons.'

'Geoffrey is Roger's friend,' said Eleanor gently. 'He has never even set eyes on King Henry.'

Geoffrey had actually met King Henry on a number of occasions, but he said nothing.

'Well, Norman?' demanded Alice when Geoffrey remained silent. 'Do you think I deliberately choked Walter to get his gold? Is that why you came here?'

'It is possible,' he replied coolly. 'Although I think it more likely that you drove him to suicide with your nasty opinions and comments.'

'Please,' said Eleanor, coming between them as Alice's

pretty face became dark with anger. 'Do not argue. Answer his questions, Alice.'

'Why? And why does he want to know, anyway?'

'It is not for him, it is for me,' said Eleanor. 'Haymo was murdered. I want to set my mind at ease that his death and Walter's, so close together, are just coincidence. That is all.'

'Very well,' said Alice, after a few moments of studying Eleanor's face as though she might read the truth there. Geoffrey was glad it was not he subjected to such close scrutiny, because he was not certain he would have passed the test. 'Walter choked on an oyster four days ago. You know how fond he was of oysters. It was an accident, nothing more.'

'How did he choke?' asked Eleanor. 'What was he doing at the time?'

'One moment he was charming us all with an account of how horse dung is better for a garden than cow manure, and the next he was on his feet clutching his throat,' said Alice. 'I had warned him before about talking and eating at the same time, but, like all men, he thought he knew better. Anyway, that was the end of him. We tried to help, but he still died.'

'How did you help?' asked Geoffrey.

'We banged his back and tried to make him drink wine to wash the thing away, but it was no use. He started to flail around in his panic.' She pointed to one of the windows that overlooked the street. 'He smashed that with his fist, as though there was not enough air in the room for him to breathe.'

Geoffrey saw one of the panes had indeed been broken, and the jagged hole had been stuffed with rags so the heat would not escape. 'Did he receive any letters before he died, perhaps delivered by a knight – or at least by a messenger you had not seen before?'

'He had letters every day. He was a goldsmith and in great demand. In fact, he had so much correspondence that he hired a clerk to see to it all.'

'Can we speak to him?'

'Why?' asked Alice. 'Do you intend to steal Walter's list

164

of customers and sell them inferior work when they believe they are purchasing high quality pieces from Walter and his apprentices?'

'If I did, I would not ask you to provide me with the means to do it,' said Geoffrey tartly. 'I want to know because your husband may have received something that belongs to the prior.'

'The prior?' asked Alice, narrowing her eyes. 'You said you wanted to set Eleanor's mind at rest about Haymo. Now you claim you are acting on Turgot's behalf.'

'Turgot is also concerned by two deaths within such a short space of time,' said Eleanor calmly.

'Turgot is a greedy, grasping hypocrite!' declared Alice. 'I will say nothing to help him!'

'He is the head of a monastery,' said Geoffrey. 'It is his job to be a greedy, grasping hypocrite.'

Alice glared at him for a moment, then laughed uncertainly. 'You are right, but I will not help Turgot to grab any more of the city for his abbey. Now, Eleanor, you may stay and talk if you like, but I shall waste no more time with your impecunious knight. I have marchpanes to finish.'

'Then I bid you good day, madam,' said Geoffrey with a bow. 'And I hope your marchpanes provide you with all the entertainment you could hope for.'

Eight

Eleanor wanted to stay with Alice, and engage in the kind of deeply meaningful talk of which men were apparently incapable, so Geoffrey left the Jarveaux household alone. He was reluctant to abandon Eleanor, but was informed bluntly that she had lived most of her life in Durham, and had no need of a knightly protector in a city where most inhabitants either knew her or were kin. Given Flambard's procreational abilities, not to mention the peculiar relationships that originated with Mother Petra, Geoffrey imagined she might be related to more people than she knew.

He recrossed the river and began striding along a path he thought led back to the marketplace. It was snowing again, and the flakes were so large it was difficult to see where he was going. His dog panted as its legs sunk into drifts that reached its belly, and shot him a resentful glance. He was aware of the hazy shapes of houses on either side as he went, but none looked familiar. He supposed he should stop at one, and ask whether he was on the right path before he became lost, but he wanted to be alone for a while, to think about what he had learned and how his investigation might proceed, and did not wish some kindly soul to offer to accompany him.

Treading in snow that was knee deep in places, he considered the aggressive Alice and her dead husband. Was it chance that sent the half-brothers to their graves within a few days of each other? And what about Mother Petra? She did not harbour deep maternal sentiments for her offspring, with the possible exception of Flambard's father, and Geoffrey thought she was certainly crafty and cunning enough to indulge herself in murder. But her age meant she was also frail – not so much as she would have people believe, but she would not be able to shoot men on the New Castle road.

So engrossed was he in his thoughts that he had ploughed some distance before he realized he had left the city and was on a footpath that went east. Instead of houses lining the street, there were fields, each carefully dug, so the frost would break up the larger clods and ease the work to be done in spring.

He was about to retrace his footsteps, when he saw a dark mass looming ahead. It was a church with a tower and an overgrown churchyard liberally smattered with people-sized mounds. Geoffrey picked his way across them, intending to shelter from the blizzard for a while and sit alone with his thoughts. He pushed open a wooden door that clanked, and entered. The dog ignored his command to wait outside, and was past him in an instant, disappearing into the shadows to sniff and explore.

Geoffrey closed the door and peered around him. It was dark. The windows were little more than narrow slits in the wall, and the shutters on every one had been closed to keep out the snow. An attempt had been made to provide some light, and cheap tallow candles had been placed in holders along the walls, which flickered and jumped in the draughts that whistled under the door, and through the holes in the roof. It was a simple building: there was a nave with a high altar and a Lady chapel from which came a low murmur of prayers.

He reached the Lady chapel and stepped inside. It was more brightly lit than the nave, because two coffins rested there on trestles, each with a thick beeswax candle at either end. They by far exceeded the quality of the spluttering tallow candles that lit the rest of the building, and shed a warm golden glow. Each coffin comprised an oblong wooden box draped with a cloth; the lids leaned side by side against a wall, waiting to be nailed down when the time came for burial.

It did not take a genius to discern that here were the bodies of Jarveaux and Stanstede, waiting for the weather to improve so they could be interred in the graveyard. Geoffrey recalled that Stanstede had been taken to St Giles' Church, and Helbye, who had been directed to stay with Eleanor while her husband was laid out, had complained that it was a dismal and cold building.

There was a faint odour that was far from pleasant, although the dog's tail wagged as it sniffed at the air. Jarveaux had been dead for four days, and the scent of the candles, the chill of the church, and the bowls of dried flowers on the altar could not quite mask the fact that it was time he was buried. However, Geoffrey suspected this would be difficult as long as the snow continued to fall, and no one would want a corpse put in a hole that was shallow and attracted wild animals.

Kneeling between the coffins was a priest, and it was his prayers that whispered around the church. His Latin was good, although his threadbare habit and the fact that Geoffrey could see white feet through the upturned soles of his boots suggested that an education had not brought him much in the way of material wealth. He glanced around as Geoffrey entered, and his words faltered. Not wanting to disturb him, Geoffrey backed away, and went to inspect the rest of the building.

There was little more to see. The high altar was a table with a wooden cross on top. A square niche was cut into it, and a wreath of holly leaves rested inside. Geoffrey went to sit at the base of a pillar in the nave, careful not to let his sword clank and make a noise that would bother the priest. The hiss and mutter of Latin in the otherwise silent church made Geoffrey feel as though he was truly in a House of the Dead. While he listened with half an ear, he tried to decide what he should do next.

By craning his neck, he could see the corpses from where he sat. He knew that a lot could be learned from the dead, and here were the bodies of two men whose deaths he suspected were related to Flambard, no matter what Alice claimed about oysters. He decided that it would do no harm to inspect them, to see what secrets they might yield. But he could hardly do so while the priest knelt with them, so he settled himself down to wait; he sensed it would not be long, given how the man was shivering. The dog lay beside him, resting its head on its paws. Its ears flicked back and forth as the wind rattled the shutters and doors, and Geoffrey relaxed, knowing it would growl should anyone else enter.

No more than an hour had passed before the priest, shuddering almost uncontrollably from the cold, nodded to Geoffrey on his way out. The knight unlatched one of the window shutters and watched him disappear into a small house nearby. Almost immediately, smoke started to drift from the chimney, indicating that the priest had added a damp log to his fire. Geoffrey suspected he would not return before he had made himself something warm to drink, and perhaps not even at all that day.

Alone at last, he walked towards the coffins and raised one of the sheets. Stanstede gazed at him with wide eyes, as though he had imagined Death was not something that would happen to him. Geoffrey knew the body had been prepared by Eleanor, so did not expect to discover anything too unusual. It had been dressed in a cream-coloured shift that reached its ankles, and its hands clutched a wooden cross. Eleanor had been lovingly thorough: she had shaved his face, washed him with scented oil, and even trimmed his beard. Geoffrey had the feeling Stanstede looked a good deal better in death than he had done in life.

Surreptitiously, and conscious he would have a lot of explaining to do if he was caught, Geoffrey eased the shroud away from Stanstede's neck, wanting to know whether he, like Xavier, had been strangled. Then he pulled the shroud up as far as it would go, and even turned the body in its coffin so he could inspect its back. The only mark on Stanstede was the hole in his chest where the arrow had been. Geoffrey had seen enough wounds to know that this one would have been almost instantly fatal, and would probably have pierced the heart.

He put the body back as he had found it and turned his attention to the next one. Unlike Stanstede, whose face was pallid, Jarveaux's was dark purple. The half-closed eyes had an opaque quality about them, like a dead fish, and the skin was mottled. Geoffrey had never seen the body of a man who had choked on his dinner, so was not in a position to say whether the ugly, dark features were what would be

169

expected from such a cause of death. He took out his dagger and prised open the goldsmith's mouth, deciding the only way to know for certain if Alice's claim was true would be if he were able to retrieve the offending oyster. He was just moving into a position where the light was better when the dog stiffened, its eyes fixed on the darkness of the nave.

Geoffrey abandoned his examination, watching as the hackles arose on the back of the dog's neck. He could hear and see nothing, but something had disturbed the animal. Still holding his dagger, he walked briskly down the nave, peering into the shadows at either side to see whether anyone was hiding. But St Giles' was a small church, and it would have been difficult for a person to conceal himself in it. As far as Geoffrey could tell, he was alone.

The dog, however, continued to growl, and Geoffrey saw its attention was fixed on one of the windows. He ran towards it and ripped it open, ready to use his dagger if anyone was there. But the graveyard was deserted, and Geoffrey could see nothing moving. He closed the shutter and conducted another search of the church, deciding the dog must have heard something from outside – a cat or perhaps the wind.

When he returned to the bodies, the dog lay with its head on its paws looking bored, and whatever had made it uneasy had evidently gone. Geoffrey took a deep breath to steady himself, and went back to Jarveaux. Fighting down his distaste, he held open the dead man's mouth and pushed his fingers into it, trying to reach the back of the throat. He found nothing, except that the throat was swollen. Whether this happened in cases of choking, or was even something that happened naturally after death, Geoffrey did not know. Growing exasperated, he took one of the candles and held it close to Jarveaux's face, to see whether he could see the oyster.

He almost dropped the candle when its flickering light revealed the inside of Jarveaux's mouth. It was a mass of tiny, reddened blisters. Geoffrey stared at them, wondering whether the goldsmith had been one of those men who had violent reactions to certain kinds of foods, and that shellfish was something he should not have eaten. But Alice said he

170

had liked oysters and ate them often. If he regularly indulged himself, then he should not have had an aversion to them, and they should not have poisoned him.

Puzzled, Geoffrey looked at the dead man's hands. There were blisters on his fingers, too, and three fingernails were broken. He turned his attention to the neck, and saw it was streaked with scratches, where the dying man had clawed at his throat.

Geoffrey replaced the candle and rearranged the shroud so no one would know what he had been doing. His thoughts whirled with questions and suppositions, and he wished more than ever that he had not travelled north in the first place. He found a pile of snow next to an especially loose shutter, and rubbed his hands in it, trying to remove the stench of the dead man's mouth. Then he went back to the base of the pillar, sat, and drew his cloak around him, although he knew the chill that seeped through him had nothing to do with the temperature in the church.

He was no physician, but he had seen enough dead men to tell one cause of death from another, and this one was obvious. Jarveaux had not choked on any oyster while lecturing to his household on the joys of manure. He had been poisoned.

Once daylight began to fade, night set in quickly, bringing an earlier than usual end to the winter day. The heavy, grey-brown clouds and the swirling snow made it almost impossible to see, and Geoffrey realized it would be a while before he was able to leave the church and return to Eleanor's warm and welcoming solar. He glanced up at the sky, hoping the flakes that fell so thickly, swept horizontal by a furious wind, would soon stop, and that he would be able to leave.

He went back to the pillar and sat in the gathering darkness, watching the way the tallow candles shed their flickering light in feeble pools of gold. Despite the cold, he began to feel drowsy, and was on the verge of sleep when a noise roused him. The dog was growling again, and Geoffrey had drawn his dagger before he was even aware of what he had done. He stood and waited in the shadows.

171

But the pattering footsteps that slapped briskly down the nave belonged to the priest, who had come to secure the church for the night. He was startled by the presence of a knight in his domain, and stumbled in his haste to run away. Geoffrey caught his arm and prevented him from falling.

'Leave me alone!' squeaked the priest, struggling to free himself. 'I have nothing to give you! This is a poor church – you can see that. Even our relic has gone.'

Geoffrey studied him. He was a thin man with a spotty, oily complexion and a pallid face, both of which indicated a poor diet. His clothes also attested to the fact that he had little money: not only were his boots so holed that Geoffrey wondered whether he might be better off barefoot, but the cloak he wore over his threadbare habit was patched and frayed. Geoffrey saw he was exactly what he appeared – an impoverished priest eking a meagre living by burying the dead, and marrying and baptising his parishioners. Geoffrey imagined that the funerals of Stanstede and Jarveaux, both wealthy men whose widows might be generous with funds for masses for their souls, would provide an unlooked-for but welcome boon that winter.

'I mean you no harm,' said Geoffrey gently, releasing his arm and sheathing his dagger. 'I am here to pay my respects to Master Stanstede. I am staying in the house of his widow.'

'Oh, it is you,' said the priest, relieved as he recognized Geoffrey in the candlelight. 'You are Sir Roger's friend. I saw you praying here earlier. I am Brother Eilaf.'

'What did you mean when you said that even your relic had gone?' asked Geoffrey curiously.

'Brother Wulfkill died trying to protect it. At least, we think that was what happened. His arrow-pierced body was found the same morning the relic went missing.'

'I heard something about a stolen relic,' said Geoffrey, struggling to make sense of the priest's rambling dialogue. He nodded at the niche in the altar. 'Is that where it rested?'

Eilaf nodded. 'Bishop Flambard gave us St Balthere's bones four years ago, so we Saxons could have our own saint when the abbey took the others. Balthere was a hermit, and miracles often occurred around his shrine. He may not be Cuthbert, but we loved him.'

'My sergeant said the abbey had something to do with the theft.'

'Prior Turgot denies it, but my parishioners believe the abbey is behind the loss, because of the foundations.'

'I beg your pardon?' asked Geoffrey, bewildered. 'What foundations?'

'The foundations in the Chapel of the Nine Altars cracked a few nights before Balthere was stolen,' explained Eilaf. 'Us Saxons believe God was expressing His displeasure at the way His saint was about to be treated. And it is not as if the cathedral needs another saint – it has Cuthbert, Oswald, Bede, and Aidan to name but a few, and Bishop Flambard has also promised it Aaron's Rod.'

'Oh,' said Geoffrey flatly. 'That.'

Eilaf studied him in the gloom. 'I see you are sceptical about its existence. So am I, but you will not be popular if you say so here. But I am gabbling. You startled me when you emerged from the shadows. I immediately assumed that you were some lout employed by *him*.'

'By whom?' asked Geoffrey, confused again by the priest's chaotic conversation.

'Burchard. He was here yesterday and today, poking around the deceased like a carrion crow.'

'The abbey bursar?' asked Geoffrey, wondering what Eilaf was talking about now. 'Why would he poke around Stanstede's corpse?'

'It is not Stanstede he is interested in,' said Eilaf. 'It is the other one – Jarveaux.'

'Why?' asked Geoffrey, although he knew exactly what Burchard had been doing, given that he had just done the same thing himself.

'He is convinced that Jarveaux had an important document that has gone missing. He made me strip the corpse to see if it was there.'

'And did he find it?' asked Geoffrey.

'Of course not. Alice paid me to prepare her husband's

body, and if I had found anything, it would have been passed to her, along with his other effects.'

'*You* prepared Jarveaux?' asked Geoffrey, straining to see the priest's face in the dim light. Was Eilaf an honest man? Had he given everything he had found to the widow?

'Eleanor insisted on tending Stanstede herself, but Alice declined to see to Jarveaux. I suspect they did not have a close relationship, but I was grateful for the money she paid, and dealing with the dead holds no terrors for me, as it does for some people.'

'Not Burchard, apparently,' said Geoffrey.

'I wish there *had* been something to find,' Eilaf went on. 'Because then Alice might have paid me more when I returned it to her. It will be a long, lean winter without Jarveaux to pay me.'

'What do you mean?' asked Geoffrey, wondering whether hunger was responsible for Eilaf's randomly meandering discourse.

'Alice will not hire me to write for her, like her husband did. She will sell his business to one of the other goldsmiths, and settle back to enjoy her wealth.'

'You were Jarveaux's scribe?' asked Geoffrey, thinking that here was the man who might know whether the goldsmith had received a missive from Flambard.

Eilaf nodded miserably. 'I was. The money I had from him was important, too. He was good to me – he always came to me for his scribing, even though most people use the ones at the abbey and parish priests are ignored.'

'Why did he employ you? Kindness?'

Eilaf gave a bitter laugh. 'No! It was because he did not want the abbey familiar with his business. He knew I needed his money, which forced me to be a discreet servant.'

'Jarveaux did not approve of the abbey?'

'Who does? They are a greedy, scheming rabble, interested only in power and wealth. The rich merchants in the city hire their own scribes – as Jarveaux employed me – but the poorer ones are forced to use the abbey's.'

'Why?'

'They have learned they lose customers if they do not.'

'Why would the abbey want its scribes used for town business when they should be illustrating manuscripts and suchlike?'

'For two reasons. First, it brings additional revenue and the bursar loves money. And second, it allows him to know what is happening among the city's tradesmen.'

Geoffrey's mind raced. Was there any significance in the fact that Flambard had chosen a merchant who did not trust the abbey to receive one of his maps? And was there any significance in the fact that he had chosen the prior to receive one of the others? Perhaps that was how Flambard intended to keep them in check – by choosing men who treated each other with healthy scepticism.

'Perhaps Eleanor will be able to find you something to do,' suggested Geoffrey. 'She might need a clerk now she is responsible for her husband's business.'

Eilaf gave a sharp bark of laughter. 'I am sure she will, and she can scarcely take that custom to the monks! But what would my bishop say, if he knew I was making my living by acting as clerk to a brothel?'

'Very little, I imagine. Flambard is not a man overly endowed with inconvenient moral standards.'

'That is true,' admitted Eilaf ruefully. 'Then the only thing standing between me and starvation is my conscience. Do not let yours bother you, or you will find it leads to all manner of dilemmas.'

'I am a knight,' said Geoffrey wryly. 'Consciences seldom bother us.'

Eilaf chuckled softly. 'Then be careful: too much thinking in Durham can be dangerous, too.'

'In what way?'

There was a sudden hiss of wind that rattled all the window shutters, blew open the door, and had the dog galloping down the nave barking furiously. Geoffrey drew his dagger and ran to the door, rushing into the darkness of the churchyard and looking around to see whether their discussion had been overheard. He could see no one. Snow still swirled, although it was easing, and some discarded rags fluttered in an eddy

175

between the churchyard wall and the gate, but they were all that moved.

He was about to assume the sudden noise was nothing more sinister than a strong gust of wind, when he saw fresh footprints leading across the churchyard to one of the windows and back again. He knew the prints had not been made by him, and the set that went towards the church were less clear than the ones that led away, suggesting that whoever had made them had remained near the window for some time. When Geoffrey looked more closely, he saw they were at the window the dog had growled at earlier. Someone had indeed been watching Geoffrey while he inspected the bodies. It was possible that someone had even followed him to St Giles' – and had listened to his conversation with Eilaf.

A quick circuit around the outside of the church told Geoffrey that the only footprints other than the eavesdropper's were the priest's: whoever had been spying on him had gone. For the time being, he and Eilaf were alone. He left the dog outside, knowing it would bark if anyone else tried to approach, then returned to the priest, intending to learn more about the abbey. He was irritated to hear that it dabbled in a heavy-handed manner in the city's affairs, and that Roger had not mentioned it.

But Eilaf had had enough of Geoffrey and his questions, and was busy extinguishing the candles so he could lock up the church and go home. A change had come over him since he realized someone had heard what he had said. He was nervous, and his hands shook when he blew out the flames.

'You were telling me about the abbey,' said Geoffrey, following him as he walked to the high altar. 'Why do you recommend I leave the city?'

'I can say nothing more,' said Eilaf fearfully, all but shoving Geoffrey out of the way in his haste to finish his duties and leave.

'You clearly know a good deal about the city and its relations with the abbey. Why will you not tell me about them?'

'It is not my place to gossip. It is too dangerous.'

'Dangerous?' queried Geoffrey. 'Is the situation so dire that even talking is considered risky? That is an unhealthy state of affairs. Perhaps I can help.'

'No,' said Eilaf brusquely. 'You will make things worse if you meddle, so leave me alone before anyone else hears us. I do not want to wake up to find my house burning, or that someone has let the sheep at my winter cabbages.'

'Someone would do that, just for speaking to me?' Geoffrey was astonished. He knew the abbey was powerful, but other foundations held a similar sway over their neighbouring towns, yet people there were not afraid of reprisals because they said what they thought.

Eilaf did not reply, and pushed him out of the way to ensure a window was secure.

'If you are right, the damage is already done,' Geoffrey went on practically. 'Someone heard us talking, so you have nothing to lose. Perhaps something can be done to break the abbey's power.'

Eilaf sneered. 'Who will do that? You, who will soon return to the Holy Land, and forget about us? Sheriff Durnais, a man so deep in Turgot's purse he is almost a monk himself?'

'Durnais favours the abbey?' If that were true, then Geoffrey's notion that Flambard had sent his missives to three men who would monitor each other was wrong: if the prior ruled the sheriff, then Durnais would not be keeping anyone in check. He would allow Turgot to do whatever he liked.

Eilaf walked down the nave, pinching the candles between a moistened thumb and forefinger to extinguish the flames. Geoffrey caught his arm and stopped him.

'I promise I will arrange employment so you will not starve. But I need you to tell me about the abbey. Is the bursar at the heart of the problem?'

Eilaf tried to struggle out of Geoffrey's grip, but he was too weak. After a few moments, he gave up and stared miserably at his boots. 'Burchard offers protection to the city's merchants: they pay him and he ensures nothing nasty happens to them or their businesses.'

'Extortion?' asked Geoffrey, startled. 'Does Turgot know?'

Eilaf took a deep breath. 'I hope not, because he does not seem to be a bad man. I have often wondered whether to tell him, but as soon as I set foot in his house, my courage fails, and I tell myself he would have to be a fool not to be aware of Burchard's methods, so complaining to him would be useless – even dangerous.'

Was Turgot aware of Burchard's activities? wondered Geoffrey. He did not know the prior well enough to hazard a guess. Turgot was desperate to see the cathedral – and the abbey – completed, and was fully prepared to use blackmail to ensure Geoffrey's cooperation. He was a churchman, which should ensure some standard of ethics, but so was Flambard and that did not stop *him* from indulging in immoral activities. Geoffrey did not know what to think about Turgot.

'Have your parishioners complained to you about all this?'

'Of course. They asked whether they should unite and refuse to pay, but I knew the abbey would respond by declining to buy their goods, and would pressure others to do likewise. The rebelling merchants would soon find themselves destitute.'

'Has Burchard actually acted, or does he just threaten?'

'He acted. Those who were particularly outspoken against him had accidents – a house collapsed on one and another cut his foot on a carelessly placed spade. Nothing was ever said, but . . .'

'Was Jarveaux similarly threatened, because he used you rather than the abbey scribes?' asked Geoffrey, wondering whether the bursar's talents ran to armed raids on the New Castle road.

Eilaf shrugged. 'Not that he told me.'

'You were his clerk. Do you know if he received any unusual letters or messages recently?' Geoffrey wanted to know whether he had seen the map. With luck, it would have arrived, and Eilaf would know where Jarveaux had put it. Then, all Geoffrey would have to do was take it – by force if necessary – and hand it to Turgot. Then he would be free to leave the city and its nasty secrets, taking Roger with him.

'Perhaps,' said Eilaf, taking the last of the candles and

using it to light his way down the aisle. 'He had an odd missive two days before his death. Normally, he showed me everything – because he would not know what they contained unless I read them to him – but he did not show me this, which I found strange.'

'I see.' Geoffrey experienced a surge of hope. If the message contained a picture or symbols, like the other two maps, then there would be no need for Jarveaux to ask a scribe to explain it to him.

Eilaf stopped suddenly, and gazed at Geoffrey with frightened eyes. 'He *did* choke, did he not? I mean, that missive – whatever it was – did not lead him to an unnatural death?'

'Choking is hardly natural,' said Geoffrey evasively, not wanting to unnerve the man by telling him Jarveaux had been poisoned. 'Was this letter delivered by a knight?'

'Oh, yes,' said Eilaf. 'He had a mop of reddish hair and a scar on his face.'

Xavier! thought Geoffrey, pleased. So, Xavier *had* been one of Flambard's agents, and he *had* completed his mission before he was strangled on the New Castle road. But why had he died? What was the point of killing the man *after* the message was delivered? Xavier's role in the affair would have been over once the map was with Jarveaux. Or would it? Geoffrey realized there was a serious flaw in his logic.

Xavier had been with Flambard in Southampton, and had helped him to escape and flee the country. He was a trusted friend, and Geoffrey thought Flambard would be unlikely to use him as a mere courier. So, had Xavier delivered the map or had he visited Jarveaux for some other reason – perhaps to ensure he followed Flambard's instructions? Geoffrey rubbed his head, and realized there were more questions to answer before he could draw any firm conclusions.

Eilaf glanced around him nervously. 'I will tell you one more thing: be wary of Burchard. I see him creeping about the city at night, when my parishioners summon me for last rites.'

'Alone, or are other monks with him?'

'Both. Maybe he is out with the abbey's blessing, but

maybe not. But if you really want to find out, you can hide by the abbey's back door, and when he slips out, you can follow him.'

'You know a lot about Burchard's nocturnal habits,' observed Geoffrey, wondering whether Eilaf was the innocent he seemed.

'I am not brave, and when I go out at night, I hide if other people come towards me. The bursar does not, so I often see him. I know it is him, because he has a distinctive gait. He lumbers, like an ape.'

'Thank you for your help,' said Geoffrey. He handed the man a silver coin. 'I will mention you to Eleanor. Perhaps there are parts of the spice business she might need help with, and you can leave the brothel administration to the likes of the bursar.'

Eilaf grinned, then rummaged in the scrip that hung at his side. 'I will not be needing this, and Alice has not asked for it. Keep it, and see what you can discover in your quest against the abbey.'

He handed Geoffrey a key, then waded through the snow to the meagre comfort of his home. Tiredly, Geoffrey lifted his dog over his shoulder and began the difficult trek to Eleanor's house, wondering whether he would have the nerve to use the key to break into Alice's house and rifle through her husband's personal belongings in search of Flambard's third map.

'Where have you been?' demanded Roger angrily, as Geoffrey was shown into Eleanor's solar by one of her servants. 'We have been worried!'

Geoffrey felt they had good cause. The blizzard that had started when he had left Alice's home had intensified by the time Eilaf had made him leave the church, and it had been hard work walking back to Eleanor's house carrying the dog. He was cold, wet, and exhausted.

'I came home hours ago,' added Eleanor accusingly. 'We were afraid something dreadful had happened to you.'

'We have more dead men than we can count, and Durnais and Simon are missing,' Roger went on. 'We are supposed to be working together, not wandering off alone and alarming the others.'

'This is not a safe city,' said Eleanor before Geoffrey could reply, so he began to feel that the opportunity to tell either of them where he had been would never come. 'You should have taken some of your men with you if you wanted to go for a walk.'

'Earlier today, you told me it was safe,' said Geoffrey quickly, seeing Roger open his mouth to continue their duet of recriminations. 'I did not want you to come home alone from Alice's house, but you told me you would be fine.'

'Durham is safe for women,' said Eleanor impatiently. 'It is not for men.'

'Why not?'

'Because of the monastery,' said Eleanor tersely. 'Men who speak out against it have accidents.'

'But I have not spoken out against it,' Geoffrey pointed out. 'On the contrary, I have been ordered to work for it. I cannot be at risk from that quarter.'

'If you think it is that simple, then you are a fool,' said Eleanor sharply. 'You are making the assumption that everyone at the abbey wants the same things as the prior. I am sure they do not: there are factions and parties inside it that want only what suits them.'

'That is true,' said Roger grimly. 'Monks like that bursar strut about the city as if they own it, and make threats to force the townsfolk to do as they ask – especially where money is concerned. Did I tell you that, Geoff?'

'Not really,' said Geoffrey shortly. 'But I wish you had, because then I would never have agreed to come with you in the first place.'

'Just as well I forgot, then,' said Roger practically.

'The abbey's treatment of the town is no secret,' said Eleanor. 'Merchants are cajoled into selling goods at ridiculously low prices to the abbey. Those who decline find that hitherto reliable customers have been "persuaded" to take their business elsewhere. Burchard offers "protection" too, even though the abbey is what most folk fear the most.'

'Never mind that,' said Roger. 'What have you been doing

all day, Geoff? Ulfrith and I had a good time in the taverns, but we learned nothing of interest. No one has any idea where Simon might be.'

'I learned nothing from Alice, either,' said Eleanor. 'She mellowed after you left, but she either does not know or is not telling whether Jarveaux had his map. I hope your day was more successful.'

'I have been in St Giles' Church,' said Geoffrey, reluctant to discuss with Eleanor what he had discovered about Jarveaux. She and Alice were friends as well as sisters-in-law, and he did not want to put her in a position where she might experience divided loyalties.

'You can tell the truth,' said Eleanor, reading his thoughts with an acuteness he found disconcerting. 'All I want is for this map to be found so Roger will be safe. I will not tell Alice anything to risk that.'

'Aye, you should not,' said Roger vehemently. 'She has always had too much to say for herself.'

'Unlike you, I suppose,' retorted Eleanor. 'You have been talking all afternoon.'

'About what?' asked Geoffrey.

'Who killed who during the Crusade, mostly,' said Eleanor, shooting her brother a glance that suggested she did not consider it nice.

'You disapprove of the Crusade?' said Geoffrey.

'I did not want Roger to go, because I knew what it would make him. He left a gentle, peace-loving man, and he has returned a hardened killer.'

Geoffrey regarded Roger doubtfully. The two knights had met near the beginning of the venture, before the slaughter and bloodshed that was to follow, and Geoffrey recalled Roger had been overly ready for a fight even then. On no account would *he* have described Roger as gentle or peace-loving. Not wanting to argue, he changed the subject.

'What do you know about the priest of St Giles'? Is he honest?'

'The poor love him because he charges less for his services than the monks,' said Roger. 'He was Jarveaux's scribe, although he will lose that income now. Why do you ask?'

Eleanor smiled in understanding. 'Because Geoffrey has been questioning Eilaf about Jarveaux and whether he received his map, and wants to know whether the priest's testimony is trustworthy. Well, you can believe Eilaf. What did he say?'

Geoffrey relented, and decided to tell her what he had learned after all. He sensed he could trust her to act in the best interests of the brother she so obviously adored. 'That Jarveaux received a message before he died, which may well have been our map. He did not show it to Eilaf, which suggests it was pictorial and therefore did not need to be read.'

'Like the two we have already seen,' said Roger.

'He also told me it was delivered by a knight whose description matches Xavier.'

Roger sighed. 'Good! Now we can tell Turgot that Jarveaux had the map before he died and *he* can get it from Alice. And that will be an end to the matter.'

'I wish it were that simple,' said Geoffrey. 'But the reality is we do not know for certain whether Jarveaux received the map, or even whether that was why Xavier visited him. We can only surmise. And there is another thing. Jarveaux did not die by choking on his oysters: he was poisoned.'

Eleanor and Roger gaped in disbelief. Then they exchanged a glance that suggested they thought he might have broken his snowy journey with a sojourn in one of the town's taverns.

'It is true,' objected Geoffrey, irritated by their response. 'When Alice said her husband broke the window in an attempt to get air, it was the poison that was choking him and making him flail around, not an oyster in his windpipe.'

'Poisoned by whom?' asked Roger, his voice loaded with scepticism.

'I do not know. I am not even sure why, although it probably has something to do with this damned business of Flambard's.'

'No,' said Eleanor firmly. 'Alice would never tolerate her husband poisoned at her own table.'

The obvious response to that objection was that Alice had poisoned him herself. It would not be the first time an elderly man had been dispatched by a young wife, or vice versa, and

Jarveaux's death might be no more than a badly timed murder on Alice's part.

Eleanor sat next to him. 'I do not feel comfortable with any of this. I would order you away from the city tonight, but Cenred told me that all roads are totally blocked by snow. If this bad weather continues, you will be here for weeks!'

'I would not leave you alone, Ellie,' declared Roger chivalrously. 'And when I leave for the Holy Land, you will come with me.'

Geoffrey regarded him dubiously. 'A fortress filled with Crusaders is no place for a lady.'

'We will find lodgings in the city,' said Roger. 'She will keep house while I go looting. You can sit at home and earn the odd penny by scribing.'

Geoffrey laughed, amused by the image Roger had concocted, and his own feeble role in it. But for all that, it was more appealing than helping the prior locate Flambard's treasure.

'It all sounds very comfortable,' said Eleanor with rank disinterest. 'But I do not want to live in a place where I will be obliged to thrive on the proceeds of slaughter. And anyway, none of us will be going anywhere unless we reason some sense into the muddle of facts you have accumulated. We should spend a few minutes going over what we have learned.'

Roger groaned. 'Must we? My head aches.'

'It always does when there is thinking to be done,' said Eleanor unsympathetically. 'Go and fetch some of that cold pork from the kitchen, then, while Geoffrey and I sort this out.'

'Right,' said Geoffrey, watching Roger heap portions of meat on three trenchers, then pour generous goblets of wine to wash it down. 'This business started with Flambard. He charged three messengers to take three maps to three different people. Of these, we can only prove one reached its intended recipient: the prior had his from Roger.'

'Aye,' agreed Roger, downing the contents of one cup and refilling it before passing the others to Geoffrey and Eleanor.

'My father should have given all three to me and not bothered with the others. By now the treasure would have been safe.'

'It is safe now,' Eleanor pointed out, 'because no one knows where it is. Continue, Geoffrey.'

'To return to Southampton, I believe Peterkin was killed because it was assumed *he* was one of Flambard's messengers, saddling up to ride north immediately. I imagine Weasel and his friend were searching his body for the map when I disturbed them.'

'You gave chase, but Weasel shot his accomplice by mistake and escaped,' continued Roger, adding more wine to Geoffrey's already brimming cup so he could feel justified in replenishing his own. 'Then there was that roof-top fighter, also killed with a red bolt. Do you remember him shouting about a staff?'

'What did he mean?' asked Eleanor. 'What kind of staff? A bishop's crook?'

'He died before he could explain,' said Geoffrey, before Roger could hold forth about Aaron's Rod. 'So we do not know. We do not even know whether his death is related to the others, only that he was killed by a missile similar to that used on Peterkin and by Weasel when he invaded your solar.'

'Then there *is* a connection,' said Eleanor. 'Those stained quarrels are expensive and not often used these days. They hark back to pagan times, when a witch put a spell on arrows to allow an archer to kill the prey he wanted. It is a Durham tradition; I have never heard of it elsewhere.'

'Are they sufficiently unusual that the fletcher might know who bought them?' asked Geoffrey.

Eleanor shook her head. 'They are not made by specific fletchers. They are plain quarrels that someone has paid a witch to chant incantations over. We would be better off trying to find the witch.'

'Good idea,' said Roger. 'There are not many witches these days who still know the arrow spell.'

'That sounds an appealing way to spend a morning,' said Geoffrey unenthusiastically.

'It might help us to learn who Weasel is,' said Eleanor.

She picked up a knife and began to saw more chunks from the cold pork Roger had brought from the kitchen. With it was fresh bread and a sauce made from pickled apples. 'You and I will do that tomorrow, Geoffrey.'

'I will stay here and organize the ladies downstairs,' said Roger nobly. 'It is the workmen's pay day tomorrow, and therefore the busiest day of the week for brothels.'

'Damn your father,' mumbled Geoffrey, sipping from the overfull cup and slopping wine on his shirt. 'It is all his fault we are in this mess. If there were any justice, he would still be in prison.'

'Wait a moment,' began Roger offended. 'My father is a good man—'

'Flambard is my father, too,' interrupted Eleanor, 'but I see him for what he is: a selfish opportunist, who does not care who he destroys or exploits as he claws his way to greater power.' She saw Roger about to argue and raised her hand to stop him, continuing with her analysis of what had happened. 'After Peterkin's death, you two travelled to Durham by an unusual route because Geoffrey wanted to see Salisbury, and you left early, so Weasel and his cronies missed you. They were obliged to wait until you arrived at Durham before ambushing you. Was he watching the gates, to see when you arrived and where you went?'

'Possibly,' said Geoffrey, not wanting to say he believed Simon was responsible for that.

'Meanwhile, Xavier had already visited Jarveaux and possibly left him a map,' continued Eleanor. 'Jarveaux was poisoned at his dinner table, and Xavier was strangled as he travelled from New Castle.' She swallowed and shot Geoffrey a fearful glance. 'You do not think Haymo was involved, do you? It *was* him, Xavier, and the squire who were killed, while the women and the grooms were unharmed.'

Geoffrey shook his head with a conviction he did not feel. Haymo was Jarveaux's half-brother and Flambard's uncle, and so might well have been given a role to play in the devious bishop's plot. But there was no need to voice his concerns to Eleanor before he had proof. It would only serve to distress her. He found he was becoming ever more fond of her, and was sorry he was not in a position to do anything about it. Because he was a knight, bound in service to Tancred, he could not settle down with a woman, whether he wanted to or not. He was destined to take his women where and when they arose, but never for long. It was a lonely prospect, and for the first time it occurred to him that it was a bleak one.

'There is no reason to believe Haymo had anything to do with it,' he said, pushing the thought from his mind. 'Perhaps the ambushers mistook him for Xavier in the dark.'

But there was a flaw in his reasoning: Eilaf said Jarveaux had been visited by Xavier two days before Jarveaux had died. Therefore, by the time Xavier was killed, the map had been with Jarveaux for at least four days, and Geoffrey was sure he would have heard had Jarveaux's house been raided during that time. Was this evidence that Xavier had *not* delivered a map to Jarveaux and that it had still been in his possession when he was strangled? As far as Geoffrey knew, it had not been found on his body, so did that mean whoever murdered him had it?

'What about the women and grooms Haymo travelled with?' he asked. 'We should question them about what happened.'

'I will do the ladies,' said Roger, with a predatory gleam in his eye. 'You see the grooms.'

'Tomorrow,' said Geoffrey. 'They may be able to tell us why Xavier was strangled, but Stanstede and the squire were shot.'

'It is simple to sneak up behind a man and choke him,' said Eleanor. 'They probably throttled him to save arrows.'

'You would not be able to choke us,' said Roger. 'First, we would hear you coming and be ready for you; and second we know how to fight, so you would be unable to retain your grip.'

'Right,' said Eleanor, sensing a challenge. 'I will prove it to you – not now, when you are expecting it, but at some point when you are thinking about something else.'

'Please do not,' said Geoffrey firmly. 'You might be hurt before we realize it is you.'

'But it will prove my point,' insisted Eleanor.

'Then we believe you,' lied Geoffrey. 'But we should be thinking about these mysteries, not discussing how easy it is to strangle people. There are still a lot of unanswered questions: how did the second map come to be in Simon's house? Was it the one intended for the sheriff or Jarveaux? How can we prove Xavier gave his to Jarveaux?'

'And what about Durnais?' said Eleanor. 'He is friends with Turgot. Is that relevant?'

Geoffrey shrugged. 'We do not know whether his unusual and prolonged absence is because he has had an accident or whether he, too, has fallen foul of people who want his map. We also do not know whether he received it: his might be the one nailed to Simon's table.'

'I think Durnais *is* involved in this,' mused Eleanor thoughtfully. 'He never leaves the city, and I think it significant that he should choose to do so now, while there is treasure to be found. Perhaps he received his map first, and immediately went to see whether he could find the hoard.'

'Yes!' exclaimed Roger, reaching across the table for more pork. 'That is exactly where he is! I bet if we asked people who saw him leave they would say he took a spade with him.'

'I doubt it,' said Geoffrey. 'To hold the post of sheriff for so many years must mean he has a modicum of common sense. If he did take a spade, then it would not have been cocked over his shoulder like a peasant setting out for a day in the fields. But Eleanor may have a point about the connection between his absence and the treasure.'

'Of course she does,' said Roger uncertainly, looking bewildered. 'But explain anyway.'

'We have two of the three maps. One contains a cross, while the other shows two rivers and a road. The third will record some geographical feature – the name of a village or a distinctive hill – that will identify the general area in which the treasure is hidden.'

'Yes,' said Eleanor thoughtfully. 'The sheriff might have the map with *that* on it, and he has gone to the area to see whether he can find evidence of something recently buried.'

'But he would never find it,' said Roger. 'My father said you need all three maps to ensure success.'

'He is probably right,' said Geoffrey. 'In fact, knowing Flambard, he is certainly right. But if you were given a map with the name of a village written on it, and you knew that a treasure trove large enough to allow the building of one of the most magnificent buildings in Christendom was nearby, what would you do?'

'I would set out for that village and look for it,' said Roger without hesitation.

'Quite,' said Geoffrey.

'The word is that Durnais has gone to Chester-le-Street,' mused Eleanor. 'That is doubtless a ploy to confuse people, and his real destination is a secret. I always knew there was more to that crafty old man than meets the eye.'

'Perhaps it was Durnais who ambushed Xavier and his party,' suggested Geoffrey. 'It makes sense. He probably wanted to see whether Xavier had another map.'

'But Xavier had already delivered it to Jarveaux,' said Eleanor. She smiled, pleased with their deductions. 'I was confused by all this at first, but now it is much clearer.'

'Good,' said Geoffrey, who felt there were still more questions than answers.

'But there is still Simon to consider,' said Roger. 'I cannot imagine why he would have one of these maps in his house. I will be happier when I know he is safe.'

So would Geoffrey, so he could be sure Simon was not one of the men trying to kill him. He looked out of the window and hoped with all his heart that the snow would stop falling, so they could complete their investigations and leave the city while they were still able.

Late that night, when the city was dark and silent, Geoffrey slipped out of Eleanor's house and plodded his way through the snow to Owengate. Apparently, the guards considered the bad weather protection enough, because they were nowhere to be seen, and Geoffrey was able to unbar the wicket door and slip through it to the river. Awkwardly, for it had been many years since he had rowed a boat, he sculled across the Wear to the Elvet houses on the other side.

When he reached Jarveaux's home, he stood for a long time in the shadows, thinking and watching. When he was certain the household slept, he crept to the door and inserted the key that Eilaf had given him. It did not fit. Puzzled, he peered at it in the darkness. It felt rough and was rusty with age, whereas the lock had the cool, silken feel of new metal. He rubbed his chin thoughtfully. Someone, it seemed, had very recently changed the locks.

Nine

Geoffrey's hopes for a break in the weather were dashed when more snow fell that night, so by the morning the city was almost unrecognizable. Thick drifts transformed the seedy hovels near the cathedral into great waves of white, some so deep that nothing could be seen of the houses at all. Geoffrey heard heartbroken sobs, and looked out of the window to see the corpse of one man being dug from a drift by a woman; he had frozen to death where he had fallen the night before. More people were shovelling around a cottage, where a whole family was feared dead because the weight of the snow on the roof had caused it to collapse.

All work was at a standstill on the cathedral. It was too cold even for the carving that usually proceeded whatever the weather, although one or two men had taken blocks of stone to the tents in the bailey that provided their lodgings, and rhythmic tapping could be heard from within.

The cold weather brought another danger, too. To combat the cold, fires were built that were too large for the hearths. At least one house had erupted in flames during the night, creating a blaze so fierce it had devoured the snow-covered building in moments, long before the alarm could be raised. It was not frozen corpses that were brought from those smoking ruins.

People formed lines to scrape snow from the roads so some trading could continue, but it was not long before fresh falls covered them again, and the work was for nothing. Few stalls opened on the marketplace, and those that did were staffed by miserable apprentices, who stood blowing furiously on cold hands and stamping their feet.

Geoffrey wanted to ride to Chester-le-Street, where the

sheriff was supposed to be. He was keen to know whether the man really did have legitimate business there, or whether Durnais was happily digging up half the countryside in search of Flambard's treasure. But with drifts on the main roads reputed to reach a horse's withers, Geoffrey knew that any attempt to locate Durnais would be a waste of time. His consolation was that digging for treasure would also be made more difficult by the falling snow, and the sheriff would have serious problems without the benefit of the other two maps anyway.

Since riding was out of the question, Geoffrey concentrated on what he could do inside the city. Early that morning, he wandered around the market square, making desultory conversation with those few traders who gathered there. But he learned nothing new about the possible whereabouts of Simon, and the only information he gained about Durnais was that the sheriff did tend to do what the prior wanted, and that it was unusual for him to leave the city.

It was much easier to draw the townsfolk out on the subject of the bursar. Indeed, it was difficult to make them stop once they had started. Poor frightened Eilaf might have been reluctant to tell tales about the abbey's least popular monk, but others were more than happy to vent their spleen to a willing listener. Burchard was not the only villain in a Benedictine habit, it seemed. Sub-Prior Hemming hired cheap labour to tend the abbey's fields, so local men found themselves without the means to support their families; and Prior Turgot had an unpopular habit of evicting tenants who were more than three months behind with their rent, when most landlords tended to allow a longer period of grace.

By the time he had heard enough, Geoffrey had a large group around him, everyone with his own story about how the abbey had done him harm. Some complaints were genuine, but others merely wanted to blame bad luck on the Benedictines, and Geoffrey decided that while the abbey was probably an intolerant and harsh overlord, Durham's citizens were an outspoken and resentful brood. It was also apparent that Burchard usually carried out many of the abbey's less popular duties, and had become an obvious focus for hatred.

Eleanor had gone with Roger to St Giles', and Geoffrey had agreed to accompany her later to meet some witches and ask them about red-stained arrows. It was not a quest he regarded with much enthusiasm, because he was afraid one might take a dislike to him and put a curse his way, but he was eagerly anticipating the prospect of spending time alone with Roger's lovely sister.

He was making his way across the market to return to her house, when he spotted a familiar figure emerging from one of the shops. From the sign outside, Geoffrey saw it belonged to the apothecary.

'Good morning, Mistress Jarveaux,' he said politely. 'The paths are slippery today, so may I escort you?'

'No,' she replied shortly, tucking a parcel under her arm. 'Go away.'

He fell into step beside her, aware that her courtly but impractical shoes were making hard work of walking. This worked to his advantage, because she was unable to move quickly enough to shake him off. Alice was not someone whose company he would willingly have sought, but the fact that she had visited an apothecary's shop – and everyone knew that powerful substances could be purchased from them – combined with the fact that her husband had been poisoned, made Geoffrey want to question her about his death.

'I did not know it was possible to buy oysters at this time of year,' he said, having no idea whether that was true or not, but unable to think of another way to broach the subject. 'I would like some for Eleanor. Can you recommend a good fishmonger?'

'Any will do. They are all controlled by the abbey, so none is any better or worse than the next.'

'Do you like them? Oysters, I mean? I find them slimy and tasteless.'

'Why buy them for Eleanor, then?' she shot back. 'Or do you always express gratitude for hospitality by giving something you consider "slimy and tasteless"?'

'Not everyone would agree with me,' he replied, unruffled. 'Some people consider them a delicacy – your husband, for example.'

'He was a glutton for them,' she said distastefully. 'And look what happened to him. If anyone ever has cause to doubt whether greed is a sin, they should look at Walter.'

'What did you say happened? How exactly did he die?'

She glanced at him sharply and he caught her arm when she skidded and almost fell. 'You have a nasty sense of curiosity. Surely, even a knight must see that discussing a man's death with his widow is unkind. It is painful for me, and I will not chatter about it to satisfy your ghoulish nosiness.'

'You did not seem distressed by it yesterday. I had the impression his death was a relief.'

She stopped dead in her tracks and glared at him. 'And what is that supposed to mean? Are you accusing me of something untoward? If you are, you can come with me to the under-sheriff and lay your accusations before him. Everyone knows Walter died by choking, and Cenred is likely to throw you in prison for levelling such a gross charge.'

Geoffrey suspected that even Durham had not yet reached the point where people were arrested for observing that a young widow shamelessly rejoiced in the death of an aged husband. 'Did anyone examine your husband's body, to ensure it really was the oyster that choked him?'

'I have no idea,' said Alice coldly. 'I did not ask Cenred what he did with Walter once he left my home. I paid a priest to lay him out, and will bury him when the weather breaks.'

'Eilaf asked me to give you this,' said Geoffrey, taking the key the priest had given him from inside his surcoat. 'He said you would not be needing his skills now Walter is dead.'

'He need not have bothered.' She made no move to take it. 'I had a new lock fitted yesterday.'

'Were you afraid someone might break in?' asked Geoffrey. He wondered whether she knew Jarveaux had been given a treasure map, and that the real reason for the change of locks was to prevent anyone from using stray keys to enter her home and get it.

She gave a gusty sigh. 'The old one stuck, and Walter was too mean to buy another. Life is too short to waste on temperamental locks. And it is also too short to waste on talking to you.'

'What do you have in that parcel?' asked Geoffrey as she started to walk away. He nodded to the bundle she held under her arm. 'Shall I carry it for you?'

She stamped her foot in a display of temper and almost took a tumble. 'You are outrageous! What business is it of yours what I buy or when I change my locks?'

'Supposing it was not the oyster that killed Walter,' he said, watching her carefully. 'Supposing it was something else. Surely, you would want to know?'

'What are you talking about? Walter died scoffing his dinner.'

'Who else, other than you and him, were eating these oysters?'

'No one!' she said, exasperated. 'We always dined alone, but there were servants present, all of whom rushed to help when Walter choked. And I do not like oysters – Walter ate them all himself.'

So that explained one thing, Geoffrey thought: all the oysters could have been poisoned, but if Walter was the only one who had eaten them, then he would have been the only one to die. He gazed down at Alice's fair face, trying to gauge whether her temper was a defence against questions she knew might lead to a charge of murder, or whether her indignation was innocent. He realized he had spent too much time with liars and cheats, because he felt he could no longer tell the difference between honesty and untruths.

'I know what you are thinking!' she spat. 'You suspect I killed Walter so I could enjoy his money.'

'You do not seem overly saddened by his death.'

She was very angry now. Her feet skidded as she tried to move away, and Geoffrey saved her a second time from falling. Her face flushed, and her eyes sparkled with tears of outrage that threatened to spill. Geoffrey saw that some of the apprentices, who shivered at their masters' stalls, were watching the exchange with mounting interest, and wondered whether he had pressed her too far. While he was not especially concerned at the prospect of being mobbed by youths, he did not want to demean himself by brawling in public.

'I grieve for Walter in my own way!' she yelled, pushing him away from her, then flapping her arms furiously in an attempt to regain her balance. 'And how I do it is none of your affair.'

'Is he bothering you, Mistress?' asked one of the apprentices, regarding Geoffrey nervously. 'If so, I will ask him to leave.' The lad did not speak with much conviction, as if he knew there was not much he could say to make Geoffrey do anything unless Geoffrey was willing.

'Yes, he is,' shouted Alice. 'Make him go away.'

'Er,' began the apprentice uncertainly, addressing Geoffrey. 'Perhaps, sir, you might . . .'

'I will go when I know what is in that parcel,' said Geoffrey, wondering whether her refusal to tell him was an indication that it contained something sinister, or whether she was merely angered by his impertinent questions.

'What have the parcels of a Saxon lady to do with you, Norman?' asked another apprentice in a valiant attempt at bluster. There was a murmur of approval and encouragement from his friends, and he looked pleased, proud to be the defender of one of the city's wealthiest widows. In a crude attempt at chivalry, he grabbed Alice's arm and caused her to stagger. The parcel fell to the ground, where it burst open to release a billow of grey-white powder. There was a label on it, giving the name of its contents and brief instructions for its use.

'Root of green hellebore,' read Geoffrey aloud, bending to inspect it. 'To be mixed with food and left as bait for the killing of rats.'

Even Geoffrey, who knew little about plants and their toxic effects, could see the apothecary had provided Alice with enough hellebore to dispatch an entire plague of rodents. So could the apprentices, and there was a communal exclamation of shock. Feeling he had won his point and that the woman who gaped in dismay at the spilled powder was not the innocent they imagined, Geoffrey was about to ask why she needed poison now her husband was dead, when she started to swoon. The apprentice made a half-hearted lunge for her, but missed. She swayed for a moment, evidently to give him a second chance, but seeing he was either too slow-witted or bewildered to act, she sank gracefully and carefully into a neat heap in the snow.

The apprentices stared at the still figure in confusion, and seeing Alice could expect no help from that quarter and she was likely to freeze to death before they realized they should assist her, Geoffrey scooped her into his arms and looked for somewhere he might take her to 'recover'. He was unable to hide a malicious smile when he saw one of the people who had emerged from the warmth of their houses to see what was happening was none other than the apothecary.

Geoffrey strode over to him and asked whether he might take Alice into his shop until she felt well enough to go home. He was not at all surprised to see an irritable frown cross her pretty features, or to see her fists clench in annoyance. He carried her across the threshold and deposited her in a chair near the fire, while the apothecary looked for a clean cup to fill with wine. Several of the apprentices followed, and stood in an uncertain semicircle, reluctant to miss any excitement. Alice remained where Geoffrey had put her, eyes closed and head drooping, although a muscle twitching in her cheek revealed that she was not as insensible as she would have people believe.

'Mistress Jarveaux dropped her hellebore,' said Geoffrey. 'She will probably need more.'

'I will prepare some, then,' said the apothecary generously. 'She has had terrible problems with rats recently. She ordered fifty units last week, and is still having difficulties. It must be the cold weather. Rats are not usually so resistant to my green hellebore.'

'Not all rats are, I am sure,' said Geoffrey dryly. 'Especially the very large ones.'

As if on cue, Alice stirred, raising one hand to her head and opening tear-filled eyes. 'Where am I?'

'Poor lady,' said the apothecary, kneeling next to her and offering the wine. 'You are quite safe here. Stay as long as you want, then a couple of my lads will escort you home.'

'What happened?' she said in a low voice. 'I do not remember anything.'

'Really?' asked Geoffrey, amused by the performance. He turned to the apothecary. 'What are the symptoms of poisoning from green hellebore?'

'In rats, the symptoms—'

'In people,' interrupted Geoffrey. 'What would happen if a person took it?'

'But a person would not take it,' said the apothecary. 'It is poisonous!'

'What if he ate it without knowing?' pressed Geoffrey. 'What if it were in his food?'

'I am going to faint again,' whispered Alice, leaning back in the chair. 'I feel very dizzy.'

'I am sure you do,' muttered Geoffrey.

'Perhaps she inhaled poison when the packet broke,' suggested an apprentice. 'It went everywhere.'

'Aye,' muttered another, his voice barely audible as he regarded Geoffrey with dislike. 'It would not have happened if that Norman had not upset her.'

'Dizziness is not a symptom of poisoning from green hellebore,' said the apothecary, making Alice sip his wine. 'It blisters the mouth and eventually makes the heart stop.'

'I see,' said Geoffrey, watching Alice. 'Blisters in the mouth. I have seen a dead man with blisters in his mouth recently.'

'Have you?' asked the apothecary, startled. 'Not in Durham, I hope. Of course, there are many other substances that might damage the tongue and gums. The bites of snakes, for example, and some metals, like lead or quicksilver.'

'I *do* have a problem with rats,' said Alice weakly, appealing to the apothecary with big blue eyes. 'This knight suspects I had other uses for the hellebore. But I have rats. Ask my servants.'

'There is no need for that,' said the apothecary. 'We have known each other for a long time, and if you say there are rats in your granaries, then I have no reason to disbelieve you.'

198

'Thank you,' said Alice, gaining confidence from the apothecary's support and beginning to abandon her helpless lady role. 'Everyone in Durham knows I have an infestation of rodents, and some people have seen them for themselves – great brown things, the size of cats.'

'I have,' offered an apprentice with short, greasy hair. 'My dog is a good ratter, but even he will not take on one of the monsters in the Jarveaux barn.'

Alice gave Geoffrey a mocking smile. 'My rats are legendary. It is only natural for me to take steps to eradicate them. That is why I need hellebore.'

Her expression was confidently smug, especially when the apprentices began a lively discussion with the apothecary regarding how they might help Alice dispatch her giant pests. The time she had gained from her fainting act had allowed her to think, as well as to gather the sympathy of onlookers. Geoffrey knew he would not be able to bully her into confessing to murder now – not only did she have no reason to do so, but he doubted very much whether the townsfolk would allow it. Most of the apprentices had the fair complexion of Saxons, and would resent her being harried by a Norman.

Geoffrey left her to the tender mercies of her admirers, and walked to the end of the market square, where the ground dropped away sharply towards the river. He stood for a while, looking at the water and thinking. It was far too convenient that Jarveaux had died with a blistered mouth a few days after his wife had purchased a poison known to cause such damage to the tongue and gums. That, coupled with the fact that Alice was pleased by her husband's death, was too much of a coincidence. Geoffrey knew Jarveaux had been murdered, and he had ample evidence to suggest that his wife was the culprit. But why? Was it exactly how it appeared – that she wanted rid of an old spouse so she could enjoy herself? Or did she have other reasons, such as obtaining a treasure map?

A few moments later Alice emerged. She had successfully evaded any offers of an escort and was alone. She walked carefully, not wanting to slip on the ice that coated the path, but she did not look like a woman who had recently fainted. Her gait was confident, her head was held high, and there was arrogance in her step. She was, Geoffrey thought, exactly like a woman who thought she had just got away with murder.

When Geoffrey returned to the Stanstede house, Eleanor was in the kitchen, already wearing a thick cloak and sensible boots in anticipation of a morning visiting witches. The Littel brothers had just finished a spell of guard duty, and were talking to her as she gave them their breakfast.

'Are you sure?' she was asking. 'You could not have been mistaken?'

The older brother shrugged and shovelled a spoonful of oatmeal into his mouth, so his answer was all but indecipherable. 'No mistake. The pig is nowhere to be found.'

'Pig?' asked Geoffrey, wondering what they had been talking about together.

Eleanor nodded. 'Simon's pig. He is very fond of it. Most people would have sent the vicious beast to the butcher to deal with, but Simon will not hear of it.'

'Is this the pig Roger is so wary of?' asked Geoffrey.

'The pig and Roger do not see eye to eye,' said Eleanor with a smile. 'Thinking he would save Simon some trouble, Roger tried to take it to the slaughterhouse. But the pig must have caught the scent of blood, and there was a fierce battle of wills in the market, with Roger trying to pull the pig forward and the pig trying to go home.'

'I see,' said Geoffrey, trying to imagine Roger thwarted by a pig. 'I assume the pig won?'

'It was never a real contest,' said Eleanor. 'That horrible beast will outlive us all – at least, it will live as long as Simon is here to protect it from the cooking pot. Cenred is another who has fallen for its piggy charms. Both love it dearly.'

'When Simon is away, the pig usually lodges at the castle,' said the younger Littel, reaching across the table to take some bread. 'As Mistress Stanstede says, Cenred adores that pig.'

'That is because he looks like one,' said his brother, and they filled the room with raucous laughter.

200

'What makes you two experts on Cenred's penchant for Simon's livestock?' asked Geoffrey.

'The soldiers at the castle have been telling us about it,' said the older Littel. 'Cenred is a bit odd about pigs, apparently, and his love of them is often a topic of conversation at meal times. When he heard Simon had gone, he went to get the pig, so he could look after it until he comes back again.'

'But the pig is missing, too,' finished his brother. 'Cenred is far more concerned about the missing pig than he is about the missing Simon. He is angry, too, because he offered to buy the animal, and Simon has always refused to sell. Now he fears for its safety.'

'I see,' said Geoffrey. 'So, when Simon ran away, because he did not want to become embroiled in Flambard's plans, he took his beloved pig with him. It means he knew he might be gone for a while and did not want to be deprived of its company.'

'Or it might mean harm has befallen Simon *and* the pig,' said Eleanor, frowning anxiously. 'I do not think he ran away because he did not want to help Flambard. I think he was already involved, because you found the map in his home. Why would he hide that, then flee?'

Geoffrey rubbed his chin and looked at the Littel brothers. 'Later, when you have rested, you can visit the butchers and ask whether a large pig has been slaughtered recently. I imagine that once we know the whereabouts of the animal, we will have a better idea about what has happened to Simon.'

'That will be a waste of time, 'said Eleanor. 'I would have heard if it had been killed. It is famous in Durham, and if some harm has come to it, everyone would know.'

'Well, ask anyway,' Geoffrey instructed his men. 'It will do no harm to be sure.'

The brothers nodded. Personally, Geoffrey thought Simon and the pig were happily ensconced in some tavern somewhere, waiting for a time when it would be safe to return to Durham. He turned his attention from matters porcine as Eleanor prepared to leave the warm kitchen.

'I can only think of three witches,' she said as they walked towards Owengate, although he was more aware of her hand on his arm than of anything she said. 'But they will probably know others, so we can ask them for names. What shall we tell them?'

'The truth,' said Geoffrey. 'I suspect it is always wise to be honest with witches. We will say that several people have been shot with red-stained arrows, and we want to know whether they have been asked to put spells on weapons recently. You seemed to think it was a practice more popular in the past than in the present, so hopefully there will not be too many suspects.'

'First we will visit Moon Mary, who lives near the river,' said Eleanor. She gave Geoffrey a warning glance. 'She is a little odd.'

Moon Mary was more than a little odd in Geoffrey's opinion: she was stark raving mad. Her round hut stood near the leper hospital, and the door comprised a knee-high hole that obliged visitors to enter on hands and knees. There was no chimney, and smoke from the hearth swirled thickly inside. The atmosphere was so dense that Geoffrey's eyes smarted and he could barely breathe. Moon Mary was naked with the exception of a piece of string knotted around her waist, and she was busily chewing on leaves that Geoffrey thought were at least partly responsible for her peculiar behaviour.

Eleanor tried hard to encourage Moon Mary to speak to them, including an offer of coins and bread, and the right to catch toads from the pond at the bottom of the Stanstede garden. Moon Mary regarded her with a dull, glazed expression, moving only to insert leaves into her mouth at regular intervals. Eventually, becoming dizzy from a lack of clean air and reluctant to waste more time on a one-sided conversation, Geoffrey indicated they should leave.

'I see the serpent near you,' Moon Mary hissed as Geoffrey was all but out of the door. Eleanor was already outside, taking deep breaths and shaking her cloak to try to remove some of the stench of burning wood from it.

'I am sorry?' asked Geoffrey, startled.

Moon Mary nodded. 'Forget your red-stained arrows. They are powerless against the serpent.'

'Right,' said Geoffrey, easing himself all the way out. 'Thank you for your time.'

'Beware the serpent,' Moon Mary howled from inside. 'I sense him near.'

'She has been chewing leaves for so long her brains are scrambled,' said Geoffrey in disgust, brushing dirt and dried grass from his clothes. 'I am not sure we will learn anything from these witches of yours, Eleanor. Moon Mary would not remember whether anyone had asked her for red-stained arrows or an incantation to summon the Devil. She is too addled.'

'Perhaps she was not a good idea,' admitted Eleanor. 'But she is a famous seer in these parts, and I thought we should at least try to see whether she had anything to say. She foresaw the death of King William Rufus three months before it happened.'

'So did a lot of people,' said Geoffrey. 'He was so unpopular that it did not take a genius to see it was only a matter of time before he had an "accident".'

'You are a bad-tempered old sceptic, Geoffrey,' said Eleanor, smiling as she took his arm to walk along the path that led past St Giles' Church and back to the city. 'But next we will visit Ida the Witch, who lives near the abbey. She is more rational.'

'Ida the Witch?' asked Geoffrey doubtfully. 'That is her name?'

'Oh, yes,' said Eleanor. 'She has always been a witch, and there is no point learning a profession if you do not tell people what it is, is there? You have Jarveaux the goldsmith and Sheriff Durnais. Why not Ida the Witch?'

'Because witchcraft is not tolerated by the Church, and if she advertises her profession so brazenly, she might find herself burned in the market square.'

'Not in Durham,' said Eleanor loftily. 'We are not so narrow-minded.'

'Then what about the abbey? You said the monks meddle in all aspects of town life. What is to stop them from persecuting a self-confessed witch?'

'They would not dare,' said Eleanor, although she sounded

203

less certain. 'Although, perhaps we should suggest she calls herself Ida the Healer instead.'

She led the way through Owengate, where more soldiers offered gruff sympathy for her recent loss. They saw nothing odd in the fact that Eleanor told them she was going to visit Ida the Witch, and one even suggested a lane she should avoid on the way because of the danger of falling icicles. They were just approaching the jumble of houses between cathedral and castle, when they were hailed by Cenred. He puffed across the ice to meet them, eyes narrowed against the glare of sun on snow and his cold-reddened, squat nose making him seem even more pig-like than usual.

'I have had no luck hunting your husband's killer,' he said without preamble. 'No one knows any outlaws who would attack a party of ten that included a knight and a squire. I am beginning to think they were travellers themselves, and that they have already moved on.'

'What about the sheriff?' asked Geoffrey. 'Is he back yet?'

Cenred shook his head. 'I cannot imagine why he never arrived at Chester-le-Street. Perhaps, after fifteen years, he grew restless with his duties and decided to take a break.'

'Without telling you? Is he the kind of man to abandon his responsibilities because he is restless?'

'No,' admitted Cenred. 'But the shire is large, so perhaps he has decided to inspect some of the more far-flung regions. Usually, I do that, but maybe he wanted to see them for himself.'

'Again, without telling you what he planned?' asked Geoffrey. 'Surely he would have sent a messenger telling you what he intended?'

Cenred gave a hearty sigh at the interrogation. 'I am sure he has his reasons. But whatever they are, you can be assured they are none of your affair.'

That, thought Geoffrey, depended on whether Durnais was busily digging up the cathedral's treasure. The more he considered the situation, the more likely it seemed that the sheriff's unusual absence was indeed connected to Flambard's hoard. He studied Cenred thoughtfully. Did the under-sheriff know more than he was admitting about Durnais' absence? Were they working together to discover the whereabouts of the treasure? Geoffrey did not think so. He imagined if that were the case, then Cenred would have gone out with his map and spade, while Durnais stayed at home.

'You are acting as Prior Turgot's agent,' said Cenred, fixing Geoffrey with a cool stare. 'You think that grants you the right to interrogate anyone you please about missing maps, but it does not. I do not care about this fabled treasure, and I know enough about Flambard to doubt whether it even exists. It is probably some vile Norman plot against the Saxons.'

'How?' asked Geoffrey, wondering what bigotry he was about to hear next.

Cenred pursed his lips. 'It is obvious. There is no treasure, but the Normans – prior, bursar, and sheriff – will claim us Saxons stole it. It will provide them with an excuse to tax the Haliwerfolc to pay for this damned cathedral.'

Was that it? thought Geoffrey. Could it be that simple? It made sense, and Flambard was certainly the kind of man to devise such a scheme.

'Turgot said you might know whether Durnais ever received one of Flambard's maps,' he said, deciding to assume for the moment that Cenred was wrong and that the treasure did exist. 'Did he?'

'I do not know,' said Cenred stiffly. 'Durnais did not tell me.'

'Did he receive *any* messages before he left?' pressed Geoffrey. 'Was one brought by a knight, or perhaps by a monk in Flambard's service?'

'All the abbey monks are in Flambard's service,' said Cenred heavily. 'And the Norman sheriff likes to maintain good relations with the Norman abbey, so there are always monks at the castle.'

'Jarveaux was murdered, you know,' said Geoffrey, wanting to say something that would make Cenred realize that regardless of whether Flambard's treasure was real, people connected with it were dying. 'If you look inside his mouth you will see it was no shellfish that killed him.'

Cenred stared at him. 'You have a nasty way of passing

your time. First you study corpses in the castle chapel, and now you confess to meddling with the ones in St Giles' Church.'

'I hope you did not meddle with my husband,' warned Eleanor sternly. 'It took me a long time to lay him out nicely, and I do not want my hard work destroyed by you.'

'I did not destroy your work,' said Geoffrey evasively. 'But you should inspect Jarveaux, Master Cenred. You will see I am right.'

'Of course you are right,' snapped Cenred irritably. 'I know he was poisoned by green hellebore, and that he did not choke on his dinner. I am the under-sheriff and responsible for keeping law and order. Do you think I am unaware of who has been murdered and who died naturally in my city?'

Geoffrey regarded him uncertainly. 'You know about Jarveaux?'

'I have just said so. And I have my own ideas about who killed him and why.'

'Who? Since Jarveaux was one of the intended recipients for Flambard's maps, his murder might be relevant to—'

'I will tell you when I have enough evidence,' said Cenred stiffly. 'I will not risk warning the murderer by gossiping before my investigation is completed. You will have to wait and see.'

Ida did not look like a witch to Geoffrey. She was a comfortable woman in her middle years, who wore a spotless white wimple and had a kind, motherly face. She was gentle with Eleanor, and gave her a pomander of herbs she said would bring about restful sleep if placed under the pillow, and offered practical advice about the early stages of widowhood.

'We came to ask whether you have sold any red-stained arrows recently,' said Eleanor, settling by the blazing fire in Ida's clean and cosy home.

'Red-stained arrows?' echoed Ida. 'My dear child! No one has asked for those in many a year. They never did what was claimed; only the foolish bought them and only the unscrupulous sold them.'

'No one has asked you for any recently, then?' asked Eleanor, disappointed.

'Of course not,' said Ida. 'And if he did, I would tell him to dispense with such foolery and practise in the butts. The only way to be a good hunter is to learn to shoot. Charms do no good at all.'

'I thought witches were supposed to dispense charms,' said Geoffrey, thinking that Durham had a very peculiar selection of witches: Moon Mary was too addled, while Ida was too sensible.

'That is what people think,' corrected Ida. 'And some dishonest folk no doubt dabble in that sort of thing. But all I do is help heal the sick and give sound and practical advice when it is needed.'

Eleanor stood to leave. She hesitated, then told Ida all about the missing maps and Flambard's treasure, and how she thought Sheriff Durnais' disappearance might be connected to them. She finished by asking the witch if she could suggest where to look next.

Ida shook her head. 'I cannot see into the future; you must visit Moon Mary for that. However, I am often summoned to the castle for my healing skills, and I think I saw something you may find useful. It was about ten days ago now – just before Durnais left for Chester-le-Street. I was tending a man with falling sickness, who was in a chamber near the sheriff's office. I stayed with him all night, and in the small hours, I heard a stir. I was curious, so I went to see what was going on when honest folk were sleeping.'

'And?' asked Eleanor.

'A visitor had arrived, and the guards were trying to persuade him to wait until dawn to see Durnais. The visitor, however, was determined to see him immediately, claiming he had come a long way.'

'Go on,' said Geoffrey, when Ida paused. 'This could be important.'

Ida shrugged. 'The visitor was insistent, so the guards agreed to wake the sheriff. I saw the visitor enter Durnais' bedchamber and he did not emerge until noon the next day.

207

I had the impression he had discharged his mission and that he spent the rest of the night asleep.'

'With the sheriff?' asked Geoffrey cautiously.

'The sheriff left that room shortly after the visitor went in, and worked all night in his office before riding away at dawn. That is partly why I remember the incident – Durnais *never* leaves the city.'

'This is odd,' mused Eleanor. 'Most messengers would not be permitted to sleep in the sheriff's bedchamber. They would be sent to rest with the soldiers in the hall, or perhaps in the kitchens.'

'Not if that messenger was carrying information Durnais did not want him to share with anyone else,' said Geoffrey. 'Then it makes perfect sense. What happened to this visitor?'

'As soon as he woke he mounted his horse and rode away. I have not seen him since.'

'What did he look like?'

'He wore a Benedictine habit, but given the apparent urgency – secrecy – of his mission, it was probably a disguise. He rode like a man born in the saddle, which made me think he was no priest. He was small, like a bird, with black eyes and a habit of tilting his head to one side. He had an air about him that suggested he was used to being obeyed.'

'Brother Odard,' said Geoffrey immediately. Ida was more observant than Geoffrey had been in Southampton: she had seen through the disguise, and Odard was a man 'born in the saddle' and used to obedience. Odard, like Xavier, was a Knight Hospitaller.

And something else struck Geoffrey. Flambard had needed three couriers for his maps, and Prior Turgot had told Geoffrey that Flambard had had three Hospitallers – Xavier, Odard, and Gilbert Courcy. He surmised that the young man shot on the roof in Southampton may have been Gilbert. Roger said he had once known a child called Gilbert Courcy, but Roger had been away for four years, and boys grew into young men. Roger had known the child, but did not recognize the youth, although the youth had recognized Roger, and had shrieked his last desperate message to the son of the man he served. And once Gilbert was dead, Flambard had been short of a messenger. Geoffrey had assumed Flambard had deliberately orchestrated the meeting in the tavern, but it had been a stroke of good luck for the bishop when he had spotted Roger. He had set the two surviving Hospitallers to follow him until a meeting could be arranged. Poor Roger really had been in the wrong place at the wrong time.

Next, Geoffrey considered the sheriff. Durnais was due to relinquish his office to Cenred. That Durnais lived in the castle and not the city suggested he had no family or fine house. Had one of Flambard's maps – and it had to be the one with the name of a village or a geographical feature on it – offered him an opportunity to take something for himself before he resigned? It seemed to Geoffrey that Cenred was panting hard at Durnais' heels, and the talk of who would be the next sheriff was all around the town. But even the map with the village marked was unlikely to allow him to locate the gold, if the other two were anything to go by.

Or had Odard played a more active role in delivering his map than Xavier or Roger? Had he decided he did not know whether Durnais could be trusted, and so had devised a test? Had he given Durnais a false map, with more information on it than the real one, to see whether the man would do his duty by Flambard and meet with prior and goldsmith or whether he would rush off in a frenzy of greed to find the treasure himself?

The more he thought about it, the more Geoffrey realized that this was indeed what Odard had done. The prior had two of Flambard's maps in his possession, but *he* was not in a position to begin digging. Flambard had been very insistent that it would take all three documents before the location of the treasure could be identified, so Odard might well have given the sheriff a different map, one that would make him believe he had a chance of finding the treasure.

So, if Odard had not given Durnais the real map, did that mean he had passed the original to the prior? In which case, was Turgot already in possession of all three? But then why had Turgot charged Geoffrey and the bursar to search for it? Or was Odard's map the one Geoffrey had found under Simon's table?

'So, Odard was the third messenger after all,' he said aloud.

'You know him?' asked Eleanor. 'Was he delivering the map to Durnais, do you think?'

'I imagine so. Flambard said Xavier and Odard were not his couriers; he lied.'

'That man cannot speak without uttering a falsehood,' said Ida in some disgust. 'You should not have agreed to do his dirty work – for dirty work it will be if he is involved.'

'We know Roger gave his map to the prior and Xavier visited Jarveaux,' summarized Geoffrey. 'And now we know Odard delivered something to the sheriff – who left Durham the following dawn. Odard did not stay long: as soon as he had rested he rode away before anything dire could befall him.'

'Why would he think it might?' asked Eleanor, puzzled.

'Probably because he knows there are people who do not want Flambard's treasure to reach the cathedral, and who will stop at nothing to get the maps for themselves. And he is right: Jarveaux and Xavier are dead, and Roger was attacked – twice if you count the incident in the stables in Southampton where Peterkin was killed.'

'I am no soothsayer, as I told you,' said Ida softly. 'But I still sense that danger surrounds you both. Be wary and be watchful.'

It was sound advice, and Geoffrey fully intended to follow it.

With Eleanor walking beside him, talking about Ida's miraculous cures for warts, Geoffrey thought about Odard, trying to recall details about him from their brief meeting in Southampton all those weeks before. But he could remember nothing of use. He was still engrossed when they took the ferry across the river to the Elvet, and made their way along the slippery footpath to the houses that lay to the east. He barely heard what Eleanor was saying, and when she stopped outside the home of the third witch, he gazed at her in astonishment.

'But this is Alice's house,' he said.

'I know,' said Eleanor tiredly. 'Have you listened to nothing I have been saying? I told you that the third of Durham's witches is Mother Petra – my great-grandmother. I do not know if she is a real witch, or if people assume she is one because of her age. But it is her we have come to see.'

'Perhaps I should wait outside,' said Geoffrey, backing away. 'I have already had an encounter with your friend Alice this morning, and neither of us wants another.'

'I will protect you from her,' said Eleanor, pulling him towards the door. 'And anyway, her bark is worse than her bite. She will not harm you.'

'I am not *afraid* of her,' said Geoffrey tartly. 'I just think it would be better if we avoided each other. Besides, Mother Petra is more likely to talk to you alone than if I am with you.'

'Rubbish,' said Eleanor, rapping sharply on the door. 'She has an eye for handsome men. She is far more likely to talk to you.'

Mother Petra answered the door almost immediately, suggesting she had probably been watching their approach from a window.

'Alice is out,' she said. 'She went to buy rat poison from the apothecary, then she was going to pray by Walter's corpse in St Giles' Church. It is a waste of time, if you ask me.'

'Do you mean praying in general or for Walter's soul in particular?' asked Geoffrey.

Mother Petra gave an inappropriate cackle. 'Both, I imagine. Well, will you come in, or would you rather keep an old woman freezing on her doorstep?'

'Has anyone bought any red-stained arrows from you recently?' asked Eleanor, as they followed her into a large room where a fire blazed in the hearth and a massive pot of mulled wine bubbled and steamed over it. Mother Petra ladled herself a cup, but did not offer any to her guests. Geoffrey decided that age definitely had its advantages – there was Ulfrith's grandfather, the old Norman-hater who had escaped retribution for pushing Geoffrey in the river because he was almost ninety, and now there was Mother Petra, guzzling her hot wine and not bothering to share.

'Why do you want to know?' asked Mother Petra, blowing on the wine so hard that some of it sprayed out of the cup and across the rugs.

'Because it may help me learn who killed my husband,' said Eleanor.

'I do not know his name,' said Mother Petra. 'But I can tell you he was small, with pointed features, dark greasy hair, and nasty yellow teeth that pointed backwards.'

'Weasel!' exclaimed Geoffrey. 'I *knew* it was him who tried to kill us in your solar.'

'You do weasels an injustice. "Rat" would be a better name. I do not like rats.'

'I understand you have an infestation of them,' said Geoffrey. 'Alice is buying enough green hellebore to kill half the rats in England.'

'Ours are particularly hardy,' said Mother Petra. 'I asked her to buy the hellebore, although I am beginning to think we shall need something stronger.'

Was that true? Geoffrey wondered. Had Mother Petra told Alice to purchase the poison? And had Alice then realized that what killed household pests would also dispatch unwanted husbands?

'What do you know about Weasel?' asked Eleanor. 'Do you know where he lives?'

'The abbey,' said Mother Petra. 'He is a monk.'

'What?' exclaimed Geoffrey. 'Are you sure?'

Mother Petra eyed him shrewdly. 'He is not one of those dolts who process around pretending to be godly, but one who comes and goes as he pleases at all times of the day and night. An abbey spy.'

'Weasel is the prior's man?' asked Geoffrey, startled. 'But how can that be true? We first met him in Southampton, and that is a long way from here.'

But, he recalled, Simon had examined the cloth on Weasel's dead colleague and claimed it had a 'southern feel' to it. What did that prove? Geoffrey knew the answer to that was nothing: Simon could have been bluffing, pretending superior knowledge of matters he did not understand. Or Weasel's accomplice could have purchased a new tunic while on his travels, to spend the money he had been paid to commit murder and mayhem. Or had Simon deliberately tried to mislead Geoffrey by suggesting the would-be killers were not local?

'Men travel great distances when it is worth their while,' said Mother Petra, as if reading his thoughts. 'You only need look at the Crusade to see that is true.'

Geoffrey rubbed the bridge of his nose, trying to piece the facts together. Weasel worked for the abbey, and had been in Southampton when Flambard had given the maps to his messengers. Did that mean someone at the abbey – perhaps Turgot – had known that Flambard was making moves to have a treasure hoard excavated? Was that possible, given that everyone thought Flambard was incarcerated in the White Tower at the time? The news of his escape was not general knowledge at that point.

So who had paid Weasel to kill Roger? Was it Turgot, who might well employ subversive means to maintain his position of authority? Was it Burchard, who had a reputation for hiring henchmen to do un-monk-like things? Was it Hemming, who resented the superiority of his Norman colleagues? Or was Weasel acting on his own initiative because he wanted the treasure for himself?

'You will see your rat-faced friend if you visit the abbey,' claimed Mother Petra, breaking into his thoughts. 'He disappeared in January and February – shortly after he asked me to put the magic potion on his arrows – but he is back now.'

And Geoffrey knew exactly where he had been: in Southampton, firing his charmed arrows at Gilbert Courcy, Peterkin, and Geoffrey himself.

'Do many people want their arrows painted?' he asked, wanting to be certain there was not another rodent-featured man who liked spells on his ammunition.

'Not now,' said Mother Petra sadly. 'Back in the old days, no self-respecting hunter would leave his home without his arrows properly blessed. But in these modern times, people have forgotten the powers of the old gods. It is only the wise, like me, who remember.'

'And rat-faced clerics who should know better,' muttered Geoffrey.

'He was desperate. He is an abysmal archer and needs all the help he can get. I charged him a penny an arrow and he went away happy enough.'

'And he wanted them for hunting deer?' asked Geoffrey. 'Red is for a stag, is it not?'

'A stag or an enemy,' corrected Mother Petra. 'We used them at the Battle of Hastings, to shoot the Saxons. If more of us had used them, the battle would have been over much sooner.'

'You were at Hastings?' asked Geoffrey in astonishment.

She nodded. 'I went with my son Thurstin. It was a glorious day. I shot seven Saxons myself.'

'Lord!' muttered Geoffrey.

'I was surprised your Weasel even knew about arrow painting, but he claimed he read about it in the library, so, I suppose that vile place is good for something. But it is a great injustice that my granaries are overrun with rats, while the abbey is free of them.'

'Speaking of poisoned rats, do you know how your son died?' asked Eleanor, somewhat tactlessly. 'Were you there the day he choked at the table?'

'Not me,' said Mother Petra. 'I do not like oysters, and I did not like the company of my whining son at dinner. I learned what had happened later. Why? Do you suspect Alice of killing him with green hellebore?'

Geoffrey was not sure how to answer such a blunt question. 'We do not know how he died,' he said, which was at least partially true. They still did not know for certain who gave him the poison, although Alice was top of the list as far as Geoffrey was concerned.

'Well, he managed almost sixty years without choking himself, so I do not see why he should have started now,' said Mother Petra. 'Perhaps he was poisoned. Perhaps he poisoned himself.'

'Why would he do that?' asked Geoffrey uncertainly.

'Perhaps he thought it would be a better fate than being the recipient of one of Flambard's maps,' said Mother Petra, wickedly casual.

'You know about those?' asked Geoffrey, startled.

'Ranulf Flambard is my grandson,' said Mother Petra, gratified by his surprise. 'He always confides in me.'

Then he should be more careful in future, thought Geoffrey, if the old crone was going to talk openly about his secrets to people she barely knew.

'Why would Flambard's maps make Jarveaux want to kill himself?' he asked.

'I would not want one in *my* possession,' said Mother Petra wisely. 'There are too many greedy and ruthless men around.'

Geoffrey was sure she was right.

Ten

That evening, when he was sure they would be awake, Geoffrey went with Roger to talk to the women who had been with Stanstede and Xavier when they had been ambushed. Stanstede's brothel was very different from the luxurious debauchery Geoffrey had enjoyed in the Holy Land. There, small private chambers were available for hire, should a man decide to pay for the company of a woman. Stanstede offered no such comforts, and men apparently took turns to use two dirty mattresses in an adjoining room, or, if they preferred, slipped into the garden, where there was a wall. Geoffrey supposed that a lack of facilities would make for a more rapid turnover, which might reduce conflict should demand exceed supply, but he found the whole set-up sordid. Had he felt the need for the services of a woman, he decided that Stanstede's establishment would be the very last resort.

The women lounged around in attitudes of boredom. Some picked lethargically at bowls of nuts that had been placed on the tables, while others were evidently already well on their way to insensibility with Eleanor's powerful ale. All were – or had been – pretty, and were healthy and well fed. Roger said they were well paid, and that much of their money was sent to families in desperate need. Yet there seemed something distasteful about the whole business, although Geoffrey would have been hard pushed to identify exactly what. Perhaps it was the fact that they seemed to have lost hope, and that they knew life as a whore lasted only as long as they had their health and some of their looks.

'It is too early for us to start,' complained one woman as Geoffrey and Roger entered. She was a blowsy redhead with stained teeth. 'We do not work before dark.'

'An hour or so with me would not be work, Cath,' quipped Roger, who had spent some time preparing himself for the interview and wore his best brothel shirt. 'It would be fun.'

Cath looked him up and down disinterestedly, and evidently did not concur. He sat on a bench and consoled himself by inching one meaty hand closer and closer to the thigh of a woman who wore so few clothes Geoffrey was certain she must be frozen. She watched Roger's clumsy attempts at subtle seduction with weary detachment.

'Tell us what happened the night Haymo died,' said Geoffrey, thinking they had better learn what they could before Roger became unmanageable. 'Then we will leave you alone.'

'What, *again*?' asked Cath with a sigh. 'We have gone over this a hundred times with the under-sheriff, not to mention our customers. *Everyone* wants to hear the story. We know life here is dull, especially in winter, and folk need something to liven up their lives, but we are tired of telling this tale.'

'I will reward you handsomely for it,' said Roger, leering at the half-naked woman. The expression on his face suggested he would not be paying in cash, but had something else in mind. Not surprisingly, no one showed much interest in his generous offer.

'You are not very good whores,' he cried in dismay, when the woman tired of his clumsy advances and went to sit elsewhere. 'You are supposed to make me feel as if I am the only man in the world.'

'Unfortunately,' said Cath in her world-weary way, 'you are not. There are thousands of you, all pawing and drooling, and you are all exactly alike.'

'You cannot say that kind of thing to our customers,' said Roger, appalled. 'Ellie and I will be out of business in a week.'

'We do not say it to the customers,' said Cath. 'When night comes, you will find us properly bawdy and jolly. But we are off duty now, and do not want men fawning over us in our spare time.'

A murmur of agreement accompanied her words. 'And you are not a customer until we see the colour of your money,' added a woman with hair that had a curious green sheen. 'You still owe me from last night. Just because you are Eleanor Stanstede's brother does not mean you get us for free.'

'I am more than that,' said Roger indignantly. 'I am her business associate.'

A groan went around the room. 'You mean we will have to put up with you indefinitely?' asked Cath, not at all pleased by the prospect.

'Hopefully, we will not be here long,' said Geoffrey, wanting to hear the story and leave. He had not yet sunk so low that he needed to force his company on women whether they liked it or not. 'Tell us about the night of the murder.'

'I do not want to,' said Cath petulantly. 'We did not see the attackers, because they kept themselves hidden, and we know nothing we have not already told Cenred, so do not think you will find Master Stanstede's killer where he has not.'

'We would not presume,' said Geoffrey. 'We want to hear the story for ourselves, because Mistress Stanstede would like to know more about what happened to her husband.'

Cath relented at the mention of Eleanor. 'There is not much to tell. There were five of us, plus Master Stanstede, in a cart. A knight, his squire and two castle grooms were on horses behind us.'

'Did you know these men?' asked Geoffrey. 'Had you seen them before?'

'We knew the grooms. They are regulars here, although they are as dense as pea soup. They had been visiting their sister in New Castle. We did not know the knight or his squire, though.'

'What did they look like?'

'The knight had a scar on his face that made him look sinister, and he had red hair like me. His squire was young and comely.'

Definitely Xavier, thought Geoffrey, who had wanted to be sure. 'And then what happened?'

'We were riding along quite happily together. Us women were singing, and the grooms and the squire were joining in the chorus. The knight did not, but he seemed to be enjoying it anyway.'

'How far into the journey were you when you were attacked?' asked Geoffrey.

'We were at Kymlisworth, which is about five miles north of Durham. Near Finchale.'

'Finchale?' asked Geoffrey.

'I told you about Finchale,' said Roger with one of his significant looks. 'It is the place with dangerous snakes and deep bogs. Nasty area. No one goes there if he can avoid it.'

'Kymlisworth has about thirty villagers,' added Cath. 'But none of them were among our attackers.'

'How do you know?' asked Geoffrey. 'You said you did not see any of them.'

'Because Frances has family there, and she would know if any had turned robber,' said Cath. Green-hair nodded affirmation.

'When exactly did all this happen?'

Cath gazed at Geoffrey. 'What odd questions you ask! Everyone else wants to know how much blood there was, and how deep the arrow went into Master Stanstede. But it was almost dusk. We had left late because of a problem with a horse. Normally, Master Stanstede would never travel after dark, but the knight and his squire joined us in Chester-le-Street and he thought we would be safe.'

'Chester-le-Street?' asked Geoffrey. 'Not New Castle?'

'We stopped to water the horses at Chester-le-Street, and the knight and his squire asked to go with us,' said Frances. 'Everyone knows outlaws are unlikely to attack a party of ten, and that it is safer to travel in big groups. The arrangement suited us all.'

Was it significant that Xavier had joined Stanstede's group at the place Durnais had claimed to be visiting? Did it mean Xavier had killed the sheriff for trying to find Flambard's treasure, then coolly joined the prostitutes to ride to Durham? Or was it the other way around, and Durnais was responsible for the attack on Xavier? Or was Geoffrey reading too much into the train of events, and the role of Chester-le-Street was irrelevant?

'Master Stanstede had decided to stay overnight in Chester-le-Street when he saw how late it was,' said Frances. 'Then the knight asked to come with us, and he saw he could save the cost of beds. He believed outlaws would not dare attack if a knight was with us.'

'But he was wrong,' said Cath bitterly. 'Very wrong.'

'What happened when you were attacked?' asked Geoffrey. 'Was the knight targeted first?'

'No,' said Cath. 'We were riding along, singing, when there was a hiss and poor Master Stanstede pitched forward. When we pulled him up, there was an arrow in his chest and he was dead.'

She paused, and Geoffrey saw the glitter of tears. For all her insouciance, she had been distressed by what had happened, and grieved for the man who had hired her. She gazed down at her beringed hands, unable to speak. Frances took up the tale.

'There is not much more to tell. The knight and his man went into the undergrowth with their swords drawn, looking for the outlaws. They told us to wait.'

'Then what?' asked Geoffrey.

Frances shook her head. 'And then nothing.'

'Did you hear anything?'

'Not a thing. Not a leaf stirring or a twig snapping.'

'It was the snow,' explained Cath. 'It muffled sounds, and made everything silent.'

Frances spoke again. 'After a while, when the knight did not come back, we told the grooms to look for him. They found him and his man a stone's throw from our cart.'

'Do you know how they died?' asked Geoffrey. 'How were the bodies when they were found?'

'Hang on,' snapped Cath impatiently. 'We cannot answer if you do not give us time to speak. We do not know exactly what happened to them, because we were not there when they died. But both were dead from arrow wounds. The grooms found them lying in the snow.'

'Did you go to see the bodies yourselves, or did the grooms just bring them back to the cart?'

'Of course we went to see them,' said Cath, giving him the kind of look that suggested she thought he was simple. 'You do not think those stupid oafs would know what to do in such a situation, do you? It was *us*, not them, who carried the bodies back to the cart – *and* we had to tell the boys to stay with us, not run away like frightened chickens.'

'So much for men,' muttered the half-naked woman from across the room. 'They were all but useless, and it was down to the women, as usual, to sort things out.'

'What did you see when you found the bodies?' asked Geoffrey. 'Precisely?'

Cath sighed. 'They were lying side-by-side, and both had arrows sticking out of them.'

'Did you notice whether one had been strangled?'

'No,' said Cath, eyeing him warily. 'It was dark, and we had just been ambushed. We put the bodies in the cart and headed home as fast as we could. We did not look at the corpses very hard.'

'And then?'

'After a long, hard journey through the blizzard, we went straight to the castle. We told Cenred what had happened, and, although he sent men out immediately to investigate, our attackers had long since disappeared.'

'And so much snow had fallen that the soldiers could not find tracks to follow,' added Frances.

'You saw nothing more?'

'No!' said Frances, exasperated. 'We did not *hear* anything after the first hiss of an arrow. And we *saw* no one – we were expecting outlaws to come and make claims on our virtue, but they never came.'

She sounded disappointed. So was Geoffrey. Their story told him little, other than that Xavier had joined them in Chester-le-Street and not New Castle and Stanstede had been killed first, perhaps to lure Xavier away from the others. He thanked the women and left, although Roger decided to linger a while, much to their displeasure. Geoffrey returned to the solar and sat by the fire, thinking about what he had learned. The more he tried to reason some pattern into it, the more the details became a blur in his mind.

He was about to give up and retire to bed, when he heard the faintest of sounds behind him. He was instantly on his feet with his dagger in his hand, ready to defend himself. Eleanor stood there with a piece of rope in her hands. He replaced his blade in its sheath with an angry sigh.

'I asked you not to try that. Had you succeeded in putting that rope around my neck, I would have stabbed first and identified you second. You should not attempt such foolery just to prove a point.'

Eleanor's face was slightly pale. 'I am sorry. But Roger can be so arrogant sometimes. I just wanted to show him he is fallible.'

'Then why pick on me?'

'Because you are smaller, and I thought I could manage you better. I should have tried my luck on Roger after all – he is bigger, but he is also slower.'

'I would not risk it if I were you,' said Geoffrey tartly. 'It would break his heart if he were to harm you – and harm you he would if you tried that trick on him.'

She smiled at him, her eyes dark and alluring in the candlelight. 'I am sorry. Sleep well, Geoffrey.'

The following day saw no improvement in the weather, and Geoffrey began to despair of ever leaving Durham. He decided to go to the abbey, to speak to the bursar, and see what *his* investigations had told him. As far as Geoffrey was concerned, they were on the same side, and he saw no point in replicating what the bursar had already done, especially since he was loath to spend long and fruitless hours tramping around in the snow.

'We will search the abbey for Weasel when we see Burchard,' declared Roger as they ploughed through the drifts together. 'We will have this man with a noose around his neck today, monk or no. That will teach him to attack *me*!'

'No,' said Geoffrey. 'We cannot burst into the abbey and demand he is handed over. We only have Mother Petra's word he is the man we want, anyway. And she is old.'

'So? She is wiser than anyone else around here. She is also my great-grandmother.'

'Yes, I suppose she is,' said Geoffrey, thinking it astonishing that the simple and straightforward Roger should lay claim to such devious progenitors. 'But leave Weasel for now. We know where he can be found, should we decide to question him later. First, though, I want to know what Burchard has discovered.'

'Damned monks! Why do they always make things so complicated and sinister? It is because of all that writing, you know. I have always said no good would come of it.'

'You sound like Simon. He also distrusts men who read.'

'Quite rightly,' said Roger firmly. 'If we were meant to make scratches and spots on bits of parchment, we would be born with inkwells attached to our hands. I know you like to dabble in those black arts from time to time, but it is different for monks – they spend all day doing it, and it turns their minds to the ways of the Devil.'

'Does it now?' said Geoffrey mildly, his mind on other matters as Roger ranted.

'Just look at the evil those maps have wrought. Men have died because of them – Peterkin, the roof-top brawler, Xavier and his squire, Jarveaux, Stanstede, and Weasel's two friends.'

'That is not the fault of the maps – it is the fault of the man who made them and the people who want to steal his gold.'

'I have been thinking,' said Roger, declining to continue a discussion that maligned his beloved father. 'The prior said one of my father's three Hospitallers was called Gilbert Courcy. I remember a lad of that name – a freckled-faced brat with big teeth.'

'He grew up. I think he was the young man fighting on the roof-top in Southampton.'

Roger stared at him in surprise. 'How did you guess that when I have only just reasoned it out for myself? He was my father's ward, and must have joined the Hospitallers as a novice. He would have been the right age for the fellow on the roof. I did not recognize him at the time, but there was something about him that was familiar: he had the same mop of brown hair.'

'He recognized you, though.'

'I know, and he was trying to tell me something. He wanted me to ensure that Aaron's Rod did not fall into the wrong hands – "Brother Gamelo's", if I recall correctly.'

'Not this again,' said Geoffrey tiredly. 'Flambard cannot give Aaron's Rod to the cathedral because there is no evidence it existed after Aaron died.'

'I suppose you *read* that, did you?' asked Roger scathingly. 'Well, your books misled you, and I know I am right. Gilbert Courcy was telling me to save Aaron's Rod from evil-doers.'

At the abbey, they asked whether the bursar was available, and were shown to the prior's house, where Burchard was ensconced with his superior. Once again, the two knights waited in the hallway, while Algar, the ambitious secretary, went to see whether Burchard might grace them with his presence. Burchard, however, was in no hurry to see them, and Geoffrey was on the verge of leaving before he finally came downstairs.

Burchard was not pleased that Geoffrey and Roger had disturbed him, so to appease him Geoffrey told him most of what he had learned. He omitted his suspicions about Simon, did not mention Alice was his prime suspect for the murder of Jarveaux, or tell him that Mother Petra said Weasel was a monk. Burchard listened carefully, but was not helpful in return. He declined to share anything he had discovered, then began to question the veracity of Geoffrey's conclusions.

'Who said Jarveaux was poisoned?' he snapped. 'Where is your evidence?'

'The blistering on his tongue and hands,' said Geoffrey patiently. 'Go and see for yourself if you do not believe me. There must be men in the abbey who can deduce such things from corpses.'

'Are you accusing us of harbouring poisoners?' demanded Burchard.

Geoffrey sighed. 'You know I am not. I am trying to help.'

'I do not need your help,' said Burchard, putting his sweaty face close to Geoffrey's in a way that was intended to be menacing, but that merely succeeded in annoying him.

'And I do not need yours,' he said calmly. 'But the prior charged us with a task, and I imagine it will be easier for both of us if we cooperate.'

224

'Cooperation is not in the best interests of the abbey. I would rather you ceased your meddling and left everything to me.'

'There is nothing I would like more,' said Geoffrey. 'However, that is for your prior to decide.'

'Do not take that attitude with me. I am no snivelling apprentice you can frighten with your vile Holy Land ways, like those lads in the market square.'

Geoffrey was nonplussed by the accusation. As far as he knew, he had intimidated no one – unfortunately, not even the untruthful Alice. 'I am not trying to frighten anyone,' he said. 'I only—'

'I do not want you here,' grated Burchard. 'You poke about corpses that have been prepared for burial, you frequent brothels and the houses of loose women—'

'Here,' began Roger, offended. 'I hope you are not talking about my Ellie . . .'

'So do I,' said Geoffrey, genuine menace in his words. He was not prepared to stand by and allow Burchard to insult Eleanor. Seeing he had overstepped the mark, the monk hurriedly pressed on with his litany of grievances.

'You make women faint in the marketplace, and you spread scurrilous lies about the abbey. You are a bad influence here, and I wish you would leave, never to return.'

'We have spread no rumours about the abbey,' said Geoffrey.

'You have been gossiping with the priest of St Giles'. And do not deny it: you were overheard.'

So, Geoffrey thought, someone *had* heard his conversation with Eilaf – and watched him examine the bodies of Jarveaux and Stanstede – and the footsteps in the snow *had* been those of an eavesdropper in the pay of Burchard. Was it Weasel, whom Geoffrey knew liked to sneak around in the dark, or another spy? Or was it even Burchard himself?

'Overheard by whom?' he asked coolly. 'Was it you creeping around like a thief, listening to other people's private discussions?'

Burchard bristled. 'I do not perform such lowly tasks myself. I hire others for that.'

On reflection, Geoffrey was not surprised. The bursar was too clumsy for such activities. He would have made heavy work of running away through the snow, and Geoffrey would have seen him.

'Eilaf will pay for his indiscretion,' Burchard went on nastily. 'No one will use *him* as scribe again, and his parishioners will come to *me* for burials and weddings. That will teach him to tell lies.'

'You are a petty, spiteful man,' said Geoffrey in disgust. 'The priest is not the only one who told me how you intimidate merchants into giving you money, and how you punish those who speak against you by destroying their businesses.'

'I do no such thing,' shouted Burchard, incensed.

'But you have just described how you plan to deal with Eilaf, because he had the courage to voice what everyone else thinks anyway. No further proof is needed of the way you conduct yourself.'

Burchard glowered. 'And *you* pose a threat to the security of my abbey. I do not want you investigating the maps, so leave them alone. I will tell the prior of your decision.'

'Very well,' said Geoffrey, raising his voice to the point where he knew it would be heard in the solar above. 'Inform Turgot that Roger and I are no longer acting for him – on your instructions.'

His tactic worked, because there was a thump of hurried footsteps and the sound of a door opening. Turgot stood at the top of the stairs with Hemming behind him.

'Wait,' he called. 'What is going on? What do you mean you are no longer helping me?'

Geoffrey turned to face him. 'I did not want to investigate this ungodly business, and I only agreed because of Roger. Your bursar believes he can solve the mystery without my help, and I am more than happy for him to do so. Good morning, Father Prior.'

'Stop!' commanded Turgot in such a voice of authority that Geoffrey turned in surprise.

'I was only—' Burchard started.

'I know what you were doing,' said Turgot coldly. 'You were countermanding my orders.'

'No,' objected Burchard. 'I was trying—'

'Geoffrey and Roger *will* continue to look into this matter,' said Turgot icily. 'And so will you. You said you knew the whereabouts of the lost map last night. Why is it not in my possession now?'

'You have found it?' asked Geoffrey.

'I did not say I knew *precisely*,' hedged the bursar, red-faced with shame at having been caught out in a truthless brag. 'I said I was *close* to finding it.'

'Close is not good enough,' said Turgot, his blue eyes bright and hard under his monstrous eyebrows. 'I want that map and I want it soon.'

'That should not pose too much of a problem,' said Geoffrey. 'Roger and I know where it is.'

Roger, Burchard and Hemming gaped at Geoffrey in astonishment, while Turgot's eyes held a gleam of avarice.

'Steady on, lad,' whispered Roger hoarsely. 'We do not want my father's treasure falling into just anyone's hands. I would sooner slit my own throat than tell the likes of *Burchard* what we have discovered. Whatever that is,' he added uncertainly, making it clear his own deductions had not been successful in that quarter.

'I am not just anyone,' snapped Turgot. 'I am the man who will realize your father's plans and see his cathedral is completed. Where is the map?'

Geoffrey leaned against the wall and folded his arms. 'Of the three maps, the only one in the hands of its intended recipient is the one Roger gave you. The second – found in Simon's house – I believe is the one that *should* have been delivered by Odard to Durnais.'

'How do you know that?' demanded the bursar, a disbelieving sneer on his face. 'Durnais has been missing for days. He is probably dead in a ditch somewhere, given how many people connected with this treasure seem to meet with unpleasant ends.'

That was very possible, Geoffrey thought. But it was equally possible the sheriff was happily wielding a spade in some godforsaken spot or other, hoping to find gold.

'Let him speak,' said Turgot, silencing Burchard with a wave of his hand.

Geoffrey continued. 'Odard was seen visiting Durnais in the middle of the night ten days ago. Durnais left Durham the following dawn, although everyone tells me he never usually strays outside the city. I conclude that something very important seduced him out of his stronghold: Flambard's hoard. However, I also think Odard did not give him the real map, and he is looking in the wrong place.'

'How have you reached that conclusion?' asked Hemming, bemused.

'One map alone will not reveal where the treasure is hidden – Turgot has two, and he still does not know where it is. Thus, Durnais would not have gone racing off to look for the treasure with only one of the things. *Ergo*, I think he was fed false information by Odard, perhaps to ascertain whether he would be tempted into trying to cheat Flambard.'

'And he has failed the test,' mused Hemming. 'Flambard wanted prior, goldsmith, and sheriff to search for the treasure together, and Durnais has shown himself disloyal and greedy.'

'The map you found in Simon's house was the one he was *supposed* to have had?' asked Turgot.

Geoffrey nodded. 'Although I do not know how it came to be there. Simon is Flambard's son, so perhaps Odard trusts him.'

'Where is he, then?' asked Hemming. 'Simon, I mean. He is said to be missing.'

'Fled, I suspect, taking his pig with him,' said Geoffrey. 'He is fond of the animal, and if anything bad had happened to him, it would still be in its sty. I suspect the disappearance of the pig at the same time as the disappearance of Simon is more than coincidence.'

'This is all rubbish!' declared Burchard. 'You can conclude nothing on the basis of a missing pig. The beast was not popular, and someone has probably killed it. It's absence tells us nothing about Simon.'

'I cannot believe we are discussing a pig while my cathedral stands on the brink of disaster,' said Turgot, closing his eyes in exasperation.

'But the pig is irrelevant,' said Burchard insistently. 'Its whereabouts have nothing to do with Simon, because Simon was seen in the city *last night*. You think he is missing, but he is not.'

'You saw him?' asked Roger eagerly. 'Was he well?'

'He was seen,' replied Burchard enigmatically. He treated Roger to an unpleasant look. 'All your trawling around insalubrious taverns with your stupid Saxon servant did you no good at all. You went to the wrong places and asked your questions of the wrong people.'

'Then obviously Roger is not as well acquainted with insalubrious taverns as you are,' said Geoffrey provocatively.

Turgot silenced Burchard's outraged spluttering with a raised hand. 'So, Geoffrey, I possess the maps intended for me and for Durnais. Where is the one intended for the goldsmith?'

'The priest of St Giles', who is an honest man, saw Xavier visit Jarveaux, which suggests that the third map probably did reach its intended destination.'

'You have not answered my question,' said the prior with an impatient sigh. 'I asked where the map is *now*.'

'Eilaf helped me to determine that,' said Geoffrey, fixing Burchard with a cool stare.

'He is a good man, and will find his reward in Heaven,' said Hemming with a smile.

'I would just as soon he had his reward here, on Earth,' said Geoffrey, knowing he was in a position to demand favours and fulfil his promise to the impoverished priest. 'He should be found regular work as a scribe, and someone should ensure he has enough to eat.'

'I will do it,' said Hemming quietly. 'I shall see he does not starve.'

'But the man is a gossip,' objected Burchard. 'Rewarding him for treacherous talk will encourage disobedience and revolt among the townspeople. It will not do!'

'Sometimes it is wiser to listen to the voices of discontent than try to silence them,' said Hemming. 'Perhaps I should look into the cause of Eilaf's unhappiness – with your blessing, Father Prior?'

'No, do not do that,' said the bursar quickly. Hemming smiled an unreadable smile.

'Why not?' asked Turgot. 'If I do not know what makes people angry, how can I redress the problem?'

Geoffrey watched the exchange carefully. Did Turgot's willingness for Hemming to investigate Burchard's nasty activities mean he did not know how his bursar boosted the abbey's finances? Eilaf wanted to believe Turgot was innocent, and Geoffrey had been sceptical, thinking that even a man tucked inside a monastery could not fail to be aware of what was happening in his city. But perhaps Geoffrey had been wrong.

'It will be a waste of his time,' blustered Burchard, guilt making him more belligerent than ever. 'We have better things to do than listen to the ramblings of poverty-stricken priests.'

'I will decide that for myself,' said Turgot. He regarded his bursar thoughtfully. 'I hope I will not hear tales of oppression. That would not do at all. I want people to love the abbey, not fear it.'

'I will start immediately,' said Hemming. His smile was serene, and it was clear he was looking forward to doing something that would show Burchard in a poor light, and in so doing probably increase his own standing in abbey and town.

Turgot addressed Geoffrey, and his voice was hard and angry. 'The whereabouts of the map, if you please.'

'It was handed to Jarveaux by Xavier about a week ago, probably a day or so after Odard delivered his to the sheriff.'

'These Hospitallers did not travel together, then?' asked Hemming.

Geoffrey shook his head. 'That would have been too dangerous. If they had been attacked, the thieves would have been in possession of two of the three maps. They travelled separately.'

'If Xavier delivered this map a week ago, why was he killed two days later?' demanded Burchard.

Geoffrey wished he knew, because he did not want to admit to Burchard that there were aspects of the affair he still did not understand. 'Xavier joined Stanstede's travelling party at Chester-le-Street. I think he probably travelled there looking for the sheriff.'

'But Durnais did not go to Chester-le-Street,' said Hemming. 'The villagers say he never arrived.'

'Xavier probably did not know that.'

'The answer to all this is obvious,' said Burchard smugly. 'Xavier went to Chester-le-Street to kill Durnais, who had gone there to dig for our treasure.'

'But it was Xavier who died,' Roger pointed out.

'True,' said Burchard. 'But perhaps he killed Durnais first.'

'These questions are impossible to answer as long as we are trapped in Durham by the snow,' said Geoffrey. 'But regardless, Xavier was killed *en route* to Durham. Maybe his murderer thought he still had the map. Eilaf said Xavier delivered Jarveaux's message discreetly, so it is possible the killer did not know he no longer had it.'

'Then he was killed for nothing?' asked Hemming in a soft voice. He crossed himself and muttered a brief prayer. 'How sad, and how pointless.'

'So, Jarveaux *did* have his map, but then he died, too,' said Geoffrey. 'Murdered by hellebore.'

'Really?' asked Hemming, fascinated. 'By whom? And why?'

'We are not interested in the sordid details of Jarveaux's death,' snapped Turgot, on the verge of losing his temper completely. 'We only want to know one thing: where is the map?'

'Still in Jarveaux's house, of course,' said Geoffrey.

Once the prior had the information he wanted, Geoffrey and Roger were unceremoniously dismissed, and the harried secretary showed them out.

'Why did you tell them where it was?' asked Roger accusingly, as they left the abbey and cut through the cathedral. 'I do not understand you at all.'

'Because now we are free of Turgot and his nasty quest. He cannot blackmail you any more.'

'But now Burchard will find the map, and he will take the credit for *our* hard work.'

'Burchard is welcome to undertake the dangerous task of burgling Alice. I do not relish the prospect of ransacking her house while she is in it – and I like even less the notion of doing it while she is out and her coming back and catching us.'

'But we have a key,' said Roger. 'Eilaf gave you one, remember?'

'She changed the lock. Had the key fitted, the map would have been with Turgot by now.'

'Assuming *she* has not done something with it,' muttered Roger. 'I do not like her.'

'It is certainly possible she knows about the map and has hidden it somewhere else.'

'I do not trust that Burchard, either,' persisted Roger, aggrieved. 'He is stupid.' Coming from Roger, this was damning indeed. 'He is so dense that I do not think he will find the map, even if it is staring him in the face.'

'I think he is very good at discovering things. He will find it.'

'But he might keep it for himself,' objected Roger. 'Then, if Turgot does not get his map because Burchard has stolen it, he will tell everyone that I misused Oswald's skull and the cathedral will never be finished.'

Geoffrey smiled at him. 'We will let Burchard hunt for the map in Alice's house, then all we have to do is take it from him while he is walking back to the abbey.'

Gradually, a grin of pure delight spread over Roger's face as he began to appreciate the subtle simplicity of Geoffrey's plan. 'We let Burchard take the risks, then step in and steal the glory? I like that, Geoff. I like it very much!'

As they walked through the cathedral, the sounds of hammering and sawing echoed from the eastern end, where the Chapel of the Nine Altars was located. Intrigued, Geoffrey went to see what was happening, waylaying a carpenter, who stood with folded arms watching his apprentices rig scaffolding around the nine round-headed alcoves.

'We cannot work outside because of the snow,' the craftsman explained. 'But we can work here, on the shrines for the saints.'

'And Aaron's Rod,' said Roger.

'That too. We will have it in the middle, in a long box carved from the finest oak and studded with precious stones. Cuthbert will lie next to it.'

'And when will it grace Durham with its presence?' asked Geoffrey, thinking that the carpenter's handsome reliquary was going to be empty for a long time.

'Perhaps it is here already.' He gave the two knights a knowing look. 'Bishop Flambard said it was, when he gave me his plans for the shrines.'

'Where is it, then?' asked Geoffrey, unconvinced.

'He said it was in a safe place. As soon as the shrines are ready and all the saints are here, Aaron's Rod will join them.'

'And when will that be?' asked Geoffrey.

'Soon,' replied the carpenter vaguely. 'Poor Bishop Flambard is clapped in irons, and it would not do to celebrate its arrival when he is not free to join us.'

'But he *is* free,' said Roger. 'He escaped. I have seen him myself.'

The carpenter's face split into a delighted grin. 'Really? That is good news! I knew God would not let wicked King Henry prevail against My Lord the Bishop for long.'

'You admire Flambard?' asked Geoffrey, certain the man must be out of his wits.

'He is a saint. He pays us well, you see.'

'And that makes him a saint?'

'Yes,' replied the carpenter firmly. 'He said he will give Turgot enough money for us to work for the next forty years. I told him to be careful, though. I do not know if Turgot can be trusted – he might use the funds for his abbey, instead.'

Had the carpenter's distrust encouraged Flambard to devise his elaborate plan? Geoffrey wondered. Flambard had few admirers, and so perhaps he had taken to heart the warning of one of them about Turgot's honesty. He stared at the scaffolding that slowly rose around the chapel, and for the first time began to consider seriously the possibility that Flambard really did have Aaron's Rod to put in it. The Christian world contained many relics, some unquestionably false, but others genuine. Why should one not be one of the most powerful symbols of the Old Testament? But how could such a thing be owned by Flambard? Geoffrey rubbed his chin thoughtfully.

That night, Roger and Geoffrey crouched behind a low wall. A short distance away was the abbey's back gate, guarded by a lay brother who could be heard pacing and jumping up and down in an attempt to ward off the chill. Meanwhile, Geoffrey could not recall when he had last been so cold. Despite wearing his warmest clothes, the winter night seeped into his bones and he, unlike the lay brother, could not exercise to start his blood moving again. If he did, he would be seen, and the bursar would abandon his plan to burgle Alice's house.

Somewhere in the town, a bell chimed and the night watch changed. There was some jocularity as the incoming guards told the others they were in for a frigid time, and the outgoing ones claimed they had filled themselves with their colleagues' ale, so would not feel the cold. The sound of nailed boots crunching in snow eventually faded away and all was silent again. A cat yowled, suddenly and sharply, making Geoffrey jump, and a rat strutted boldly across the path that led to the hovels that lay between castle and cathedral. Time passed slowly.

Just when Geoffrey was about to suggest Burchard must have been put off by the freezing weather and that they should come back the following night, the gate opened and a burly figure slipped out. It was Burchard, and he was accompanied by Hemming. Geoffrey smiled, suspecting Hemming did not trust Burchard to find the map alone – or trust him to hand it to the prior if he was successful. Or perhaps it was Turgot who was distrustful, and had sent Hemming to keep an eye on his bursar.

Geoffrey and Roger followed the two monks along the

little-used path that ran around the rear of the abbey, between river and curtain wall, and that avoided Owengate. They fell into a familiar pattern where Geoffrey led and Roger checked they were not followed. Geoffrey's part was absurdly easy – there were tracks in the snow, and anyone but a blind man could have followed them. Geoffrey recalled with a smile how Eilaf had described the bursar's gait – that he lumbered like an ape. Burchard did indeed lumber.

The monks were brazenly confident, and walked side by side without even bothering with the occasional glance behind to ensure they were alone. Evidently, they were not anticipating problems. Geoffrey was also in danger of becoming overconfident, and had to force himself to be patient with their stately progress.

Then a sudden movement caught his attention, and he slipped quickly out of sight. Three men eased themselves from the shadows of the castle wall, and proceeded to make their way stealthily after the monks. Geoffrey gestured to Roger, to indicate that there might be trouble ahead, then concentrated on keeping both the monks and their pursuers in view without being spotted himself.

It was easier than it should have been, considering the stakes were so high. Burchard was in a bad temper, and whispered angrily to Hemming. His voice carried in the silence of the night, and Geoffrey could hear fragments of the monologue. Burchard had apparently been slighted by the prior at dinner. It had something to do with who had been offered wine first, and Burchard was incensed. His furious diatribe stopped when he reached the river, but began again as soon as he had rowed across it.

Once Burchard and Hemming had secured the boat on the opposite bank and walked towards the Elvet, the three men climbed into a second boat and paddled after them. Geoffrey's eyes narrowed as he studied their shapes in the darkness. He was almost certain one was Weasel, and wondered whether he was in Turgot's employ, paid to watch Burchard and Hemming. Or was he Hemming's man, and was ready to help him against Burchard? Or was he hired by Burchard, lest Hemming proved difficult? Or did he belong to some other faction in the abbey, which Geoffrey had not yet encountered?

'Now what?' whispered Roger, looking at the black waters of the river. 'Do we swim? Durham only has two ferries, and they are now both on the other bank.'

'There must be fishing boats we can use.'

'But that would be stealing,' said Roger, horrified.

'We only want to borrow it. And anyway, you are an accomplished thief – all your loot was originally the property of someone else.'

'God wanted me to have that,' said Roger loftily. 'That is why he placed it in the hands of the infidel in the first place. But I do not steal in my own city!'

'I see,' said Geoffrey. 'Well, God probably wants you to cross the river and take the map from Burchard before Weasel does, too. So where are the other boats? Hurry, or we will be too late.'

Roger led them upstream, to where several coracles were hauled up on the muddy shore. They were small, circular craft comprising skins stretched over a wooden frame and sealed with pitch. They stank of fish, and were steered by means of a single paddle. Roger pushed one into the water, and surprised Geoffrey by showing he knew how to manage it. Geoffrey had expected to be swept a long way downstream, and was pleasantly pleased that Roger was able to land them in the shadows of some trees a short distance from where the others had disembarked.

Alice's house was in darkness. Geoffrey saw Burchard and Hemming observe it for a few moments, then Hemming knelt on the ground while the bursar climbed on to his back. Hemming's gasps of pain and complaints about Burchard's weight were probably audible at the abbey. Geoffrey laughed softly to himself as he watched, amused also by the looks of startled disbelief that were exchanged by Weasel and his cronies, as if they could not believe the monks' incompetence.

Roger gestured he would move to the other end of the street, so they would be able to prevent anyone – monks or their pursuers – from escaping should the need arise, while Geoffrey pressed himself deeper into the shadows of someone's doorway.

Slowly and inelegantly, Burchard eased himself up the side of Alice's house, aiming for a window on the upper floor. At first, Geoffrey did not understand why he should choose to break in upstairs, when the ground floor would have been easier. Then he recalled that Alice's solar had a broken pane – the one Jarveaux had smashed in his death throes. The bursar was aiming for that, doubtless hoping to slip his hand through, unlatch it, and squeeze inside.

Eventually, after a lot of heavy breathing, swearing, and clanking of latches, Burchard managed to open the window. Geoffrey, Roger, Hemming, and Weasel's little band all smiled at the sight of two fat legs waving helplessly in the air when he became stuck. In the end, Hemming was obliged to climb the wall, too, and push hard at the large rump until it disappeared inside the house. Why the more agile Hemming had not gone in the first place was a mystery to Geoffrey, and he could only suppose that Burchard did not trust the sub-prior to find what they were looking for. Or perhaps Hemming suspected that Burchard would be an inadequate partner and did not want to be the one caught inside when the occupants realized a burglary was in progress.

Once Burchard was in the house, silence reigned again. Somewhere in the city, a dog barked, and Geoffrey wondered if it was his, resentful at having been left behind. He shivered as he waited, wishing Burchard would hurry up, so he and Roger could relieve him of the map, take Weasel and his companions into custody, and leave the whole business in the hands of prior and under-sheriff.

After what seemed like an age, and when Geoffrey was beginning to wonder whether Burchard had decided to wait until dawn so he could see what he was doing, the monk appeared, clutching something that he waved triumphantly to Hemming. Hemming gestured impatiently for him to climb down, and Burchard began the laborious process of prising his bulk back through the window.

Suddenly, things happened. Geoffrey heard the unmistakable sound of a crossbow being wound, and saw Weasel aim his weapon at Burchard. Not wanting to be accused of the murder Weasel was about to commit – he was afraid Turgot would claim that only Geoffrey and Roger had known Burchard planned to visit Alice's house – Geoffrey abandoned his hiding place and raced towards the spy, bowling into him so hard he knocked him from his feet. The snow was slippery, and Geoffrey immediately lost his footing, too.

Then Roger appeared from the far end of the street, and wrestled Hemming to the ground for some unaccountable reason. Weasel's companions quickly recovered from their surprise, and one of them drew a knife and struck at Geoffrey, who was still trying to scramble to his feet on a patch of ice. Geoffrey jerked backward, feeling the tip of the weapon catch on the sleeve of his chain mail, and stumbled again. Weasel was scrabbling for the crossbow he had dropped, while one of his friends stabbed wildly with a short sword. The whole tableau was conducted in complete silence, as though it was in everyone's interest to keep the skirmish a secret.

Fists flew and daggers flashed. Parrying blows from two sides, Geoffrey managed to climb to his feet. He saw Roger wrestling with Burchard, while Hemming floundered in a snowdrift, where he had been pushed. But it was a mistake to look elsewhere: one of Weasel's men took advantage of Geoffrey's lack of concentration and darted forward with his sword. Twisting to avoid the hacking blade, Geoffrey slipped again and fell heavily against a wooden shed. It was rotten and unstable, and he heard a rushing sound before something landed on him with all the force of a mass of dropping stones. For a moment, he thought the whole structure had collapsed, but then his mouth, eyes, and nose were full of snow, and he realized that the force of his stumble had dislodged the thatch of snow from the roof.

He began to struggle, Weasel and his men forgotten as he tried to claw his way out of the frozen, solid mass so he could breathe again. It was pitch-black, and he was confused about which way was up. And he was cold. He struggled more fiercely when his lungs began to burn from lack of air. And then everything went black.

Eleven

Daylight slowly invaded Geoffrey's consciousness. He opened his eyes, then closed them quickly when the brightness made his head ache. He rubbed them, opened them cautiously, and sat up. He found he ached all over, and tried to remember what had happened to him. He was in Eleanor's house, and opposite was Roger, sprawled in a chair and snoring with his mouth agape.

He remembered following Burchard and Hemming to Alice's house, and the curious, silent fight between three parties who wanted to keep their presence at the scene from curious eyes. And then there had been the snow. Geoffrey shuddered at the memory of the intensely cold, airless blackness. Unsteadily, and feeling as though he had been trampled by a herd of cows, he walked across the room to Roger and shook him awake. The big knight yawned.

'Are you all right, lad?' he asked, relief showing in his face when he saw Geoffrey on his feet. 'I thought you were done for when you disappeared under that snow.'

'So did I,' said Geoffrey ruefully. 'What happened?'

Roger shook his head. 'I am damned if I know. One minute the bursar was cramming himself through the window with the map, and the rest of us were watching. Then Hemming drew a dagger and moved towards Burchard as though he meant business . . .'

Geoffrey gazed at him. 'Hemming was going to attack Burchard? Why would he do that?'

Roger shook his head. 'Beats me. I thought they were on the same side.'

Geoffrey rubbed his chin. 'But they are not. We have been told there are competing factions within the abbey, and that was patently obvious yesterday – Hemming offered to investigate Eilaf's complaints and expose Burchard as an extortionist.'

'But that assumes Turgot does not already know,' said Roger astutely. 'He is not stupid: I am sure he has guessed exactly how Burchard raises money.'

'You are probably right. Turgot's own authority doubtless lies in the fact that as long as he keeps his minions at each others' throats, none will accrue sufficient power to challenge him. What a vile state of affairs, Roger. I wish we had never come to this godforsaken place.'

'That is my home you are talking about,' said Roger huffily. 'But I told you from the start that the abbey harbours evil men – men who can read – and you would not believe me. Now who is right?'

'It is more complex than that,' said Geoffrey tiredly. 'But tell me what happened after you saw Hemming about to stab the bursar.'

'I considered doing nothing – it would be easier to take the map from Hemming than Burchard, and I do not like Burchard anyway. But I am a knight, and it goes against the grain to hang back in the shadows and watch a monk murdered. So, I knocked Hemming from his feet. Unfortunately, I hit him harder than I intended, and the breath was knocked out of him. He gagged and retched, and did not enter the affray again.'

'Hemming was not the only one with designs on Burchard's life,' said Geoffrey. 'I leapt at Weasel because *he* was about to shoot the man.'

'That does not surprise me,' said Roger sagely. 'Burchard is a nasty piece of work. Hemming and Weasel would have done the world a favour by getting rid of him.'

'But we thwarted them and Burchard lives to see another day. At least, I assume he did?'

'After I shoved Hemming over, Burchard himself appeared, not knowing I had saved his miserable life, and started fighting *me*.'

'What were Weasel and his men doing while all this was going on?'

'Playing around with you. I saw one with a sword and another with a dagger, but we know they are poor soldiers, and I was not seriously worried about leaving you to contend with them. I was wrong.'

'I was holding my own,' said Geoffrey, offended.

'You were not. When I next looked to see how you fared, you had allowed them to bury you. Really, man! How could you let pathetic specimens like that overpower you? First there were the Saxons in Southampton, and now this. The sooner we get you back to the Holy Land the better – you are losing your skills here.'

'The snow dropped from the roof,' said Geoffrey stiffly. 'It would have buried me no matter how good a fighter I am.'

'So you say,' said Roger disparagingly. 'I would not have let myself get into such a situation.'

Geoffrey shook his head. 'Arguing is getting us nowhere. What happened next? I do not remember anything except that I thought I was going to suffocate.'

'That worried me, too,' said Roger. 'So, I decided saving you was more important than engaging in push-and-shove with Burchard. I threw one good punch that bowled him head-over-heels, and came to your rescue. When they saw me coming, Weasel and his louse-ridden companions melted away like shadows in the night.'

'Did you not give chase, to find out where they went? It would be helpful to know if Weasel really is from the abbey, or whether he is someone else's hireling – Odard's, perhaps, or even the sheriff's.'

'Turgot's, more likely,' said Roger practically. 'Weasel *expected* Burchard and Hemming to go burgling last night. How could he know unless the prior had told him? Having Burchard shot while committing a crime would be a good way for Turgot to rid himself of the man.'

'Possibly,' conceded Geoffrey reluctantly. 'Although Turgot is clever, and I am sure he could devise a less embarrassing way of ousting Burchard than having him killed burgling someone's house. There is something about your explanation that does not feel right.'

'Feel right?' echoed Roger in disbelief. 'You are a knight,

man, not some youthful damsel. You cannot dismiss my reasoning because it does not "feel right". It fits the facts.'

Geoffrey did not feel up to an argument. 'So what happened after Weasel left?'

'I brought you here to thaw you out. I have no idea what happened to the monks.'

Geoffrey sighed. 'Damn! We do not even know whether they are alive or not?'

'I did not hit them that hard!'

'But Weasel may have done – and then taken the map.'

'I did not care what happened to the monks,' declared Roger stiffly. 'I was afraid you would die if I did not bring you home. This damned business is not more important than the life of a friend, and I would rather be revealed as the greatest desecrator of relics in the land than leave you to freeze while I chased after the likes of Burchard.'

'Thank you, Roger,' said Geoffrey politely. 'But I was only stunned, not on the verge of death. Did anything else happen?'

'I had the Devil's own job of sneaking you in here without Eleanor seeing. She would not approve of us attacking monks, and I thought we should keep the whole business from her.'

'So monks and Weasel escape, and we are none the wiser about anything. Although we saw Burchard waving something in the air as he climbed out of the window, we do not *know* it was the map. It might have been anything.'

'I have the answer to that,' said Roger carelessly, as though it was of such little importance it had not been worth mentioning sooner.

Geoffrey stared at him. 'How?'

Roger gave him a knowing wink and rummaged inside his surcoat. The first thing to emerge was a chicken bone, apparently secreted there for future enjoyment – or perhaps to feed to Geoffrey's dog to see if he could bring about its demise. But the next item out was a stained and crumpled piece of parchment, which he held aloft triumphantly.

'What is that?' asked Geoffrey stupidly. He rubbed his head, wondering if the avalanche had knocked some of the wits out of it, because he knew exactly what Roger was brandishing.

'It is the third treasure map,' said Roger proudly, placing it on the window sill and attempting to smooth it out with his thick, rough fingers.

'The last time I saw it – or what I assume was it – it was in the grubby hands of our friend the bursar. What is it doing here?'

'He dropped it,' said Roger casually. 'When I knocked Hemming off his feet, Burchard jumped in fright and it fluttered to the ground. I grabbed it before it got buried.'

'Did anyone see you?' asked Geoffrey, certain that if they had, it would only be a matter of time before the killers homed in on Roger to get the thing back.

'No,' said Roger smugly. 'Weasel and his friends were concentrating on you. Hemming was in the snow with his eyes closed, and Burchard was gaping at him, like the stupid ox he is.'

'Gaping at Hemming? Why was he not looking for the map he had just dropped?'

'I do not know,' said Roger crossly. 'I suppose he thought Hemming was dead and he was about to be next. Anyway, moments later, he was groping around in the snow, hoping to find it again. No one knows I have it except you.'

'Good,' said Geoffrey with feeling. 'Let us keep it that way. Do not even tell Eleanor. We do not want people breaking into her house while we are out and demanding it from her.'

'No, we do not,' agreed Roger wholeheartedly. 'I will order Helbye and Ulfrith to stay with her today. And by tonight, the danger will be over anyway.'

Geoffrey regarded him uneasily. 'Will it? Why?'

'I have a plan,' announced Roger, pleased with himself. 'I will need a little help from you, but I know exactly what we should do next and how we can bring an end to all this treachery.'

'Oh, Lord!' breathed Geoffrey nervously.

While Roger went to the pantry to scavenge bread and ale for an early breakfast, Geoffrey gazed out of the window and tried to assemble his thoughts. Who had sent Weasel after Burchard and Hemming? Was it one of the high-ranking monks or someone outside the abbey? And now that Roger had the map, did that mean they could anticipate attempts on their lives until the treasure was recovered and secured in the cathedral's coffers? And more immediately pressing, what was the plan Roger was so determined to carry out? Geoffrey hoped it would not prove too impractical.

'Here we are,' said Roger, pushing open the door with one foot as he balanced an impressive haul of food in his hands. 'This should stave off the hunger for a while.'

'I should say,' said Geoffrey, alarmed. 'Eleanor will be furious when she sees what you have taken. There is enough here to feed a garrison.'

'Nonsense,' said Roger, taking a loaf and ripping it in half. 'Your dog will help us out if I have overestimated what we need. That beast will eat anything.'

To prove it, the dog made a sudden leap and Geoffrey saw a slab of ham dragged under the bed.

'Oh, no,' muttered Roger, heading after it. 'Ellie smokes wonderful ham and that was for me.'

There was a brief tug-of-war, after which the dog emerged with the larger piece, and Roger retreated to the window seat nursing a bleeding thumb.

'What is this plan of yours?' asked Geoffrey, taking some cheese. 'We cannot keep this map, Roger. It is too dangerous. We must hand it to the prior today – preferably with some witnesses, so everyone will know we do not have it.'

'My plan is better than that,' said Roger, rubbing the ham on his hose to rid it of dog saliva, then taking a bite. Reluctantly, he offered some to Geoffrey, who declined. 'Never mind passing the map to the prior. That will not make us safe. I intend to give the prior the treasure itself.'

'How?' asked Geoffrey warily. '*He* has the other two maps, remember?'

'But I have this one,' said Roger, reaching for the third parchment with greasy fingers. 'And he does not. And no one can do a thing without it.'

Geoffrey took it from him. It was a simple affair, made

from the same high-quality parchment he had observed in the first two. It was mostly blank, but in the middle was a word, a drawing of an oddly shaped tree, and what he thought was supposed to be a snake.

'It says Finchale,' said Roger, watching him. He pointed to the writing on the map. 'Finchale.'

Geoffrey stared at his illiterate friend. 'How do you know that?'

'The prior can read, but Jarveaux could not and neither can Durnais. My father would not send them maps they could not understand, would he?'

'He might. It is not impossible to ask a clerk, you know.'

'But that would mean taking someone else into your confidence,' said Roger. 'And my father would not want that. So, he gave his clues in pictures, too, as well as words.'

'A tree and a snake? How does that help?'

'I keep telling you about Finchale, and you keep forgetting what I say,' said Roger irritably.

'Snakes,' said Geoffrey in understanding. 'Snakes and bogs.'

'Exactly. Finchale is famous for snakes. It is also famous for an oak tree that wood sprites inhabit. It was struck by lightning and split in half, just like the drawing here. The sheriff and Jarveaux would know the tree and its story.'

'That is clever,' said Geoffrey, impressed. 'And, as we surmised, no one with this map alone would be able to locate the treasure, unless he was prepared to dig up huge tracts of countryside. Finchale is not a village; it is an area.'

'Right. Now, here comes the part where you help. How well do you remember the other maps we had? For example, if I gave you a blank piece of parchment, could you could plot the cross on it?'

Geoffrey nodded. 'It was folded absolutely geometrically – in half, in half again, then in half a third time. The cross lay on one of the creases. But why do you ask? Even with that and the name of the area, it will be difficult to pinpoint exactly where the treasure lies.'

'You underestimate a little local knowledge, lad,' said Roger smugly. 'I had a good look at the map you found in Simon's house and committed it to memory – using the creases, like you did with the cross. There were two streams and a path. I spent a long time trying to think of a place where two streams ran parallel and a path cut across them. Then I saw *this* map, which says they are at Finchale.'

'You know this area well, then?' asked Geoffrey. 'Snakes and all?'

Roger nodded. 'I fished there when I was a boy – my father told me fishing was a waste of time.' He chuckled. 'If only he knew! But, you see, I know exactly which two streams and which path the second map depicted. I can scratch them on this map, just like you can do with the cross.'

Geoffrey smiled and shook his head. 'Flambard is not so clever after all. You outguessed him.'

Roger looked pleased. 'It takes more than a bishop to outwit me! But his choice of hiding places was more cunning than you think. Finchale is not somewhere most people want to visit.'

'Why?' asked Geoffrey as Roger pursed his lips, a difficult feat with a mouth full of meat.

'Snakes,' mumbled Roger. 'You can see that from this map. There is a picture of one.'

'Not in the winter, surely,' said Geoffrey sceptically.

'This is a special kind of snake, so large and strong that it can live wherever it likes, no matter what the weather,' said Roger grimly. 'There were all sorts of stories about Finchale's serpents when I was a lad. They are as thick as your thigh and can swallow a sheep.'

'But you still went fishing there as a child.' Geoffrey was unconvinced. 'Did you ever see any?'

'Well, no,' admitted Roger reluctantly. 'But my mother did not like me going much. It is a desolate place, full of reeds and ghosts. But the fishing is good – probably because the snakes like to keep a decent stock of fish to eat.'

Geoffrey glanced out of the window. 'It has stopped snowing. We can go today.'

The dog was just snuffling up the last of the crumbs on the floor when they heard angry hammering on the front door.

'It is early for visitors,' said Roger, startled. 'Only just past dawn.'

'Perhaps it is a customer for the brothel. You had better deal with him before he wakes Eleanor.'

Roger went to the window and flung open the shutter so that he could lean out. 'Lord help us!' he breathed. 'It is Alice Jarveaux – and she does not look happy!'

The insistent knocking was soon replaced by raised voices – women's voices. Eleanor had answered the door and Alice had burst in, to stand in the hall and give vent to her rage. Eleanor's softer tones could be heard when she paused for breath, but Alice was doing most of the talking.

'Wash your face,' Roger advised Geoffrey. 'It is filthy, and if *they* see it, they will know we were up to something last night.'

'So what? We did nothing wrong.'

'Listen,' said Roger, cocking his head on one side. 'Alice is here because she says someone broke into her house last night. She must have heard something.'

'She would have been deaf not to,' said Geoffrey, laughing. 'The bursar made enough noise to wake people in New Castle, let alone inside her house! I am surprised no one came to challenge him there and then, especially Mother Petra, who seems watchful and astute.'

'We do not want Alice to think *we* were involved.'

'Well, we *were* involved. You have her property in your hand even as we speak.'

'We did not steal it, though,' objected Roger, dropping the parchment quickly, as if not touching it might make a difference. 'That was Burchard.'

'We told him where to look.'

'What does she want it for anyway?' asked Roger, peeved. 'It was not intended for her.'

'Perhaps she, like everyone else in this city, wants the treasure. She may even have killed her husband for it.'

'But why suspect *us*? No one saw us, and the fight was over within moments.'

'We had better be very careful when we speak to her. Do not tell her *anything* – not about the maps, the prior, and especially not the fact that we know where the treasure is

247

hidden. Is that clear, Roger? This is important.'

'Stop blathering and wash your face. You look like a man who has been up to no good. Hurry, or they will catch us!'

'We are *Jerosolimitani*,' said Geoffrey indignantly. 'We have faced Saracens and fought the bloodiest battles the world has ever known. I am not afraid of your sister and I will wash when it suits me.'

'Roger!' came Eleanor's voice, quiet with the intensity of her anger. 'Come here at once!'

'Where is the water?' asked Geoffrey.

His reflection in the bowl that stood on the window sill told Geoffrey his face was indeed covered with dirty marks from the snow that had fallen on him, and his hair had dried in unruly spikes. He washed away the muck as best he could, and tipped the incriminatingly filthy water out of the window. He ran his fingers through his hair in a futile attempt to render it more tidy, then followed Roger into the solar.

Eleanor and Alice were in it, sitting stiffly in two chairs next to a fire that had only just been lit. The flames popped and hissed feebly over the wet logs, and the room was almost as icy as the frigid atmosphere the two women had created. Alice glowered at the knights as they entered.

'Is this what you learned from the infidel?' she demanded. She stood, and Geoffrey saw her face was white with fury. 'Did they teach you how to break into the houses of poor widows and steal?'

'How dare you accuse my brother of such a vile crime!' shouted Eleanor. 'He does not steal.'

'It is true – we have stolen nothing,' said Geoffrey to Alice quietly. 'And we did not break into your house, I can assure you.'

'Well, someone did!' snapped Alice. 'The frame on my solar window was buckled, suggesting that whoever prised himself through it was a large man – like you two, in fact.'

'There are plenty of big men in the city,' said Eleanor coldly. 'Half the monks at the abbey are fat, given what they eat. Being heavy is no grounds on which to accuse my brother of being a criminal.'

'Perhaps it was not your brother,' said Alice, her eyes

flashing dangerously. 'He does not have the wits anyway. It was probably his friend.'

'Geoff did not break in,' said Roger loudly, determined that Geoffrey should not be blamed. 'We were only watching—'

He faltered and Geoffrey shot him a withering look, wishing the big knight would keep quiet if he could not manage a sentence without admitting they had been at the scene of the crime.

'Watching what?' demanded Alice. 'What were you going to say? Where were you last night?'

'Out,' said Roger, saying it in such a way that even the least curious of people would have wondered where. Alice pounced.

'You were burgling the homes of innocent citizens. You should be ashamed of yourselves!'

'We did not burgle your house,' said Geoffrey with quiet reason. 'Really, we did not.'

'Someone climbed up to my solar window and managed to unlatch it through the broken glass,' said Alice, her temper only just under control. 'He ransacked my property and left the same way, although he made so much noise that he woke Mother Petra. She saw him lose his footing and fall. So, you see, there is a witness to your crime.'

'What makes you think it was us?' asked Geoffrey. 'There are many people who would benefit from robbing the house of a wealthy widow. I mean no offence, but you have nothing I want.'

'No, I do not!' yelled Alice furiously. 'Because *you* have already taken it. You have left me with nothing!'

'What did Mother Petra see, exactly?' asked Roger nervously. 'Faces?'

'She saw a large man prising himself through the window, and she saw shadows scrambling about in the snow below it. I am not stupid, Roger. Your friend has been pestering me ever since he arrived. He made me faint in the marketplace with the vileness of his accusations, and he has been asking horrible questions about me in the city.'

Her voice had risen to the point where she was almost screaming. It was a shrill sound, harsh and grating. Geoffrey supposed he was still fragile from his brush with death the night before, because he found his head was beginning to ache from the noise. He raised his hand to rub it.

'There!' shrieked Alice triumphantly, striding across the room and pushing back his hair. 'That is what happened when he fell from the window after committing his crime! He is bruised!'

'Am I?' asked Geoffrey, surprised. He rubbed his forehead, but could feel no tenderness. Then he looked at his fingers and saw they were black. He had managed a less than adequate job of washing and had missed a patch. He flailed around for an excuse as to why he should have soot on his face.

'Oh, Geoffrey!' cried Eleanor, her face dissolving to a heart-wrenching hurt. 'I believed you when you said you had nothing to do with this. You lied to me!'

'No!' said Geoffrey, dismayed to think she should doubt his word. 'We did not burgle Alice's house last night, and that is the truth.'

'Will you swear you had nothing to do with it?' pressed Eleanor, her face pale. 'Will you take a sacred oath that you have not stooped so low as to attack the home of a vulnerable widow?'

'She is not vulnerable,' said Roger, casting Alice a wary glance. 'And why are you taking her side against us, Ellie? You know what we are up against here.'

'What does he mean?' demanded Alice immediately.

'Nothing that warrants him behaving like a common criminal,' said Eleanor. She stood facing Geoffrey, hands on hips. 'Roger has always been easily led, so *you* must have persuaded him to indulge in thievery. You are a wicked man, who has led my sweet brother into evil ways!'

If it had not been Eleanor making the accusation, Geoffrey might have found the situation amusing. It was grossly unfair that he should be blamed, especially given that it was invariably him who urged moderation on Roger, not the other way around. Geoffrey was not the one whose saddlebags were full of other people's property.

'It is not funny!' Eleanor snapped, scowling at Roger when he showed less self-control and started to grin. 'You think you

250

are on some boyish adventure – like the Crusade – and you do not care who you hurt while you have your fun.'

'I told you it was them,' said Alice spitefully.

Eleanor went to Alice and took her hands. 'I was wrong, and for that I apologize from the bottom of my heart. I will never believe a word these two tell me again.' She turned on Geoffrey and Roger, her eyes as hard as steel. 'I want you to give it back right now.'

'Give what back?' asked Geoffrey, determined that if they were to part with the map, he would force Alice to admit that she knew exactly what it was, and so prove to Eleanor that her role in the affair was far from innocent.

'You know,' replied Alice coldly. 'If you do not give it to me, I shall tell the under-sheriff what you have done, and he will arrest you for larceny.'

'Tell us what you want, and we will see whether we have it,' said Roger, thus intimating that they had in fact burgled her house – a slip that was not lost on Alice, who turned to Eleanor in fury.

'You see? It is obvious they are guilty, yet they still try to deceive us. If they do not return it by the time I reach the door, I will go to Cenred, and then they will not think this is such a lark.'

She began to storm out of the solar, although Geoffrey thought she did not walk as quickly as she might have done had she seriously been considering a visit to the castle. Eleanor turned to Roger and took his big red hands in her slender white ones.

'Give Alice her things, Roger,' she pleaded. 'I do not want this to bring my home into ill repute.'

'But you run a brothel,' Geoffrey pointed out before he could stop himself. He closed his eyes, horrified. He was not usually given to making offensive remarks to women he wanted to impress.

'Ignore him, Roger,' said Eleanor, giving Geoffrey a look of disgust. Yet again, he realized that Eleanor was becoming a lot more dear to him than was wise, although the events of the morning were hardly serving to make the feeling mutual.

'Yes, ignore him, Roger,' said Alice, still inching towards

251

the door. 'You are no evil, grasping Norman, but an honourable man with Saxon blood. If Eleanor had any sense, she
would eject Geoffrey from her home and let him stay with
those vile louts at the castle, if they will sink so low as to
admit him into their fold.'

'I might,' said Eleanor. She cast Geoffrey another glance
full of hostility and then turned her attention to Roger. 'Give
Alice back her jewellery.'

'Her what?' asked Roger, bemused. 'What jewellery?'

Alice abandoned her ultimatum. 'Do not play the innocent
with me. You know what was stolen.'

'But I do not,' said Roger, and his bewilderment was
sufficiently genuine that Geoffrey saw Eleanor having second
thoughts.

Alice, however, was unconvinced. 'Then I shall list the
missing items for your benefit. I want my rings, including the
one I wore on my wedding day; I want the silver necklaces
that belonged to my mother; and I want the ruby pendant my
husband gave me last year. You can keep the silver bangle. If
you are so desperate for money, I will not deny you that.'

'Jewellery was stolen?' asked Roger, astonished. 'But why
would he steal jewellery?'

Geoffrey's mind was working more quickly than Roger's.
Was that why Burchard had been so long inside Alice's
house? Because he was not only looking for the map, but
taking advantage of an opportunity to swell the abbey's
coffers with a little unexpected plunder? Or was he planning
to keep it for himself? It explained why he was slow
to look for the map after he had dropped it – he was
probably checking first that he had not lost any of Alice's
baubles.

'Please, Roger,' said Alice, standing next to the big knight
and trying a different approach. Her blue eyes softened,
and her face took on an angelic quality that Geoffrey saw
through, but that had Roger scratching his head and shuffling
in agitation. 'These things are not worth much, but they are
all I have to remember my mother and my husband. I do not
want to lose them.'

Geoffrey did not think her memories of Walter Jarveaux

were especially fond, but it was a clever tactic to use on the soft-hearted Roger.

'But we do not have them,' said Roger, dismayed. 'Really, we do not. Burchard must have them.'

'Burchard?' asked Alice, startled.

'I think you had better tell us the truth,' said Eleanor, leading her brother to sit next to her by the fire. 'No, do not look at Geoffrey to tell you what to do. Speak for yourself.'

Roger opened his mouth to confess all, despite Geoffrey's instructions that he was to say nothing. Geoffrey knew he had to prevent him from revealing to Alice that they planned a foray to Finchale that day, but did not know how. Desperately, he floundered around for a solution. The mild headache that had started with Alice's screeching became worse from the tension, and he raised his hand to rub it.

'Lord! My head hurts,' he muttered.

And then a solution came to him. Alice, Eleanor, and Roger glanced up just in time to see him collapse on to the floor.

'Geoffrey, speak to me!' cried Roger, distraught and tugging at his friend's surcoat to try to shake him awake. 'What is wrong with him, Ellie? I do not understand what is wrong!'

'Calm down,' said Eleanor sharply. 'Panicking will do no good, so pull yourself together. Alice can stay with him while you fetch the physician; I will bring water to bathe his head.'

'He is dying!' whispered Roger in a choked voice. 'That snow killed him.'

'Nonsense!' said Alice brusquely. 'He will be perfectly all right in a few moments. Summon the physician, if you want to help him.'

'No!' yelled Roger, clutching Geoffrey protectively. '*You* fetch the physician.'

'Very well,' said Alice reluctantly. 'But we should loosen his clothes first. Let me do it. I know how these things are done.'

'You can search him for your jewellery later,' said Eleanor in a cold voice, as Alice's expert hands began to feel around the inside of Geoffrey's surcoat. 'He is hardly in a position to abscond with it now, and it is not honourable to take advantage of him when he is insensible.'

Alice sighed. 'He is a common thief. As far as I am concerned, he no longer merits the kind of treatment we would afford honest men.'

'He is not a thief,' shouted Roger, tugging at the buckles on Geoffrey's surcoat. 'See? There is no jewellery. If you knew him at all, you would know he is not interested in riches anyway. If you had claimed a book had gone missing, then I might have my suspicions, but he has never been fond of gold or precious stones.'

'All right,' said Alice frostily, apparently satisfied that her jewels were not on Geoffrey's person. 'I will go for the physician, but I am coming back. Just because he does not have my belongings with him does not mean that he has not stolen them. He has hidden them somewhere.'

She stood and Eleanor followed her out. Their voices faded away as they clattered down the stairs, so Geoffrey opened his eyes and sat up.

'That was close,' he said. 'You were about to tell them everything we know, and I specifically told you to keep quiet.'

Roger gaped at him. 'I thought you were a dead man!'

'So I might have been had you told Alice we have the third map and can pinpoint where the treasure is hidden,' said Geoffrey, climbing to his feet and going to look out of the window to make sure she had left. 'What were you thinking of? Have you no sense at all?'

'You are alive!' cried Roger. 'I thought the time you spent in the snow must have done something dreadful, then Alice saw that bruise . . .'

'That was dirt. And it would take more than a few moments in the snow to do me serious damage. But you were about to do something that might have proved dangerous for Eleanor, and I could think of no other way to stop you.'

'Let me get this straight,' said Roger slowly. 'All that fainting was just to create a diversion, so I would not tell Alice about the treasure?'

Geoffrey grinned. 'It worked rather well, did it not? It was Alice herself who gave me the idea. She swooned in the marketplace when the situation became uncomfortable, thus extricating herself from an awkward position *and* buying time to think of answers to my questions.'

'Her swooning was an act, too?' asked Roger wearily. 'It was the talk of the city yesterday, and everyone assumed she had fainted from grief.'

Geoffrey gave a wry smile. 'Hardly! But I have seen a number of women swoon when it suits them, and I have always wanted to try it myself. I will have to remember it for future use.'

Roger put his head in his hands. 'Then please tell me in advance next time, lad. I thought you were done for. Remember Richard de Blunville, who received a head wound during the fall of Antioch? We all thought he would recover when he regained his senses the following day, but he dropped down dead within a few hours.'

'I remember,' said Geoffrey soberly. He had liked Richard de Blunville. 'I am sorry if I alarmed you, but something had to be done. We do not know Alice's involvement – perhaps she is innocent, but the odds are against it.'

'I am sick of this gold!' declared Roger, suddenly vehement. 'You were right about it from the start: it is evil, and evil people want it. I am inclined to grab our horses and ride away from here right now. I am tired of all these deceptions and accusations. Even you are doing it – pretending to be ill so that things happen the way you want them to.'

They sat in silence for a while, each wrapped in his own thoughts.

'Do you believe her?' asked Geoffrey eventually. 'Do you think someone stole jewellery from her house last night? Or do you think what she really missed was the map?'

'Lord knows!' sighed Roger. 'What a mess! The bursar might be a crafty, lying fellow, but he is still a monk, and monks do not usually steal.'

'I think the salient word there is "usually". I would not put a little opportunistic fortune-raising past that man.'

'Nor would I, I suppose,' said Roger wearily. 'After all,

the man does read, so who knows to what depths the Devil might lead him to stoop?'

'The question is: what do we do now? You told Alice it was Burchard who broke into her house, and she is the kind of woman to storm up to him, accuse him of theft, and demand her treasure back. Burchard will deny everything, and we both know Alice will not go meekly back to her house and accept her loss.'

'Aye,' agreed Roger. 'It does not matter whether she wants this jewellery or the map; she will not rest in peace until she has it.'

'I cannot decide whether she is party to Flambard's plan or not,' said Geoffrey. He rubbed his head. 'She was Jarveaux's wife, and he may well have confided in her.'

'Here comes Ellie,' said Roger, as footsteps sounded on the stairs. 'Lie down and try to look poorly, or she will suspect she has been hoodwinked – and then you will be a dead man for certain.'

Geoffrey was startled to hear from the physician that he had narrowly evaded death, and that he should avoid eating meat for a month so excessive blood should not build up, cause a superfluity of choler, and bring about a relapse. Eleanor fussed about him, bringing cushions and goblets of watered wine, so he wondered whether she repented her accusations, and did perhaps harbour a small liking for him. Nevertheless, it was not pleasant to be the centre of such attention by means of a deception, and he began to feel uncomfortably guilty.

Alice did not care whether he lived or died. She stood in the doorway with her hands on her hips, and demanded to search his belongings. Eventually, Eleanor eased her out of the house, although she was reluctant to go, then sat grim-faced while she listened to Roger's account of the previous night's escapade. Whether she genuinely believed his many protestations that they knew nothing about any jewellery, Geoffrey could not tell, although neither knight had the courage to admit that Geoffrey had pretended to faint to prevent Roger from speaking earlier.

'Right,' he said, when Eleanor finally left him to rest,

ostensibly watched over by Roger. 'We should go to Finchale while the weather holds. The more I think about it, the more I like your notion of presenting Turgot with the treasure and not merely the map.'

'I know *I* would rather have a chest of gold than a bit of parchment,' said Roger with conviction.

'I am sure you would. But, as more of this plot unfolds, I find myself questioning the prior's role in it. Perhaps he is what he seems – an ambitious and competent man building what will be a powerful Benedictine foundation – but perhaps he is not. So, let's go.' Geoffrey buckled his surcoat. 'The day is wearing on.'

'It is too late,' said Roger, glancing out of the window. 'We do not want to be at Finchale when night falls. We wasted too much time with that physician.'

'And whose fault was that?' demanded Geoffrey archly. 'But I am not staying here all day: there is too much to do and too many questions remain unanswered. And, more importantly, we cannot be certain no one saw you collect Burchard's map from the snow.'

'I do not think anyone saw me,' said Roger, although he sounded less certain than he had done.

'What about Mother Petra?' asked Geoffrey. 'Supposing she did?'

Roger sighed. 'I did not look at the house. I only watched to see what the monks and Weasel were doing.'

'I want to know who Weasel is working for,' determined Geoffrey. 'And why Flambard gave his maps to Turgot, Durnais, and Jarveaux, of all people. None of them strike me as honest, especially Durnais, who is probably digging up half of the county, even as we speak.'

'But we know why he chose three men. It was so they would be forced to collaborate to get the treasure, and therefore not be able to steal it for themselves.'

'I can understand one being Turgot – he is overseeing the work on the cathedral, and will probably see that most of the hoard goes towards its construction – but why the other two? Why the goldsmith and the sheriff?'

'Because they represent civil authority and merchants?'

suggested Roger with a shrug. 'Those are the most powerful agencies in the land – Church, State, and Commerce.'

'All very neat, but why bother with State and Commerce at all? Why not use three monks?'

'Perhaps there were not three he could trust.'

'It is a large abbey, with perhaps a hundred monastics and as many laymen. It is a poor state of affairs if there are not three among them who can be trusted to see their cathedral built.'

'You know what monks are like,' said Roger. 'Would you trust them with your Holy Land loot? Or in your case, your Holy Land books?'

Geoffrey considered. He would certainly not trust Burchard, and from what he had seen the previous night, he could not trust Hemming, either. But Eilaf seemed an honest man – certainly honest enough to pass a piece of parchment to a prior without demanding something for himself. He rubbed his head, more convinced than ever that there was something oddly sinister about Flambard's plan.

'I would like to know how the second map came to be under your brother's table, and I would like to know *exactly* where Durnais is.'

'If you are right, and Odard gave him a false map to test his honesty, he could be anywhere.'

'Except Chester-le-Street,' said Geoffrey. 'We know he is not there. When the weather clears, we can search for him in some of the more remote and inaccessible areas. Odard will not have sent him to a village or a town, where other folk would learn what he was doing and start their own treasure hunts.'

'Here,' said Roger, as a thought occurred to him. 'Three men were supposed to get these maps, right? Of these, Jarveaux is dead and Durnais is missing. Ergo, the prior must have killed them, because he is the only one left.'

He looked pleased with himself, and Geoffrey did not have the heart to tell him that he had already considered that possibility and discounted it.

'I do not think Turgot would have poisoned Jarveaux without first learning where the last map was.'

'Perhaps Durnais fed him toxic oysters, then,' said Roger. 'We have assumed he is digging up the county with a false map, but he might be hiding somewhere, biding his time.'

'He may be biding his time,' agreed Geoffrey. 'But I do not see why he should feel the need to go into hiding to do it. But we need to do something, not stay cooped up here while time passes by.'

'You should have thought of that before pulling your swooning-maiden trick,' said Roger unsympathetically. 'Anyway, as I said, if we go to Finchale, we need an earlier start than this.'

'We will set off at first light tomorrow, then,' determined Geoffrey, reaching for his sword. 'But meanwhile, I am going to the abbey. Keep Eleanor talking while I slip out. Tell her I am asleep and should not be disturbed.'

'But you cannot,' objected Roger. 'The physician said—'

'The physician is a charlatan,' said Geoffrey. 'There is nothing wrong with me. And, unless we want to be attacked again, we need answers as soon as possible – before we go to this snake and ghost-infested bog of yours.'

'But you will need me with you if you are going into that den of thieves and killers that calls itself an abbey.'

'No,' said Geoffrey, knowing the last thing he needed was Roger's blustering honesty when he went to see the prior and his monks. 'Stay here and make sure nothing happens to Eleanor.'

Twelve

All was quiet when Geoffrey walked through the city to the abbey, but then he realized it was Sunday, and what little trading had survived the snows was forbidden. The window shutters on the houses he passed were tightly closed, and he imagined families inside huddled around their hearths, perhaps telling stories to while away the day, or playing games of chance. He reached the abbey and was escorted to the prior's house. This time, there was no long wait, and he was conducted to Turgot's solar almost immediately. Burchard and Hemming were already there.

'Well, now,' said Turgot, raising his impressive eyebrows. 'It seems there was something of a misunderstanding last night.'

'You could say that,' said Geoffrey, looking closely at Hemming and Burchard to gauge their reactions to his presence. Both were uncharacteristically blank-faced, and Geoffrey found he was uncertain about how the interview should proceed. He decided an offensive stance was better than a defensive one, and that prevarication and denials would be a waste of time – for the monks as well as him. 'We followed your bursar and sub-prior when they left the abbey last night, because we wanted to ensure their safety. What happened?'

Hemming gaped at him. 'You tell us! We had the map when Roger suddenly attacked. It was lost during the ensuing skirmish.'

'We did not attack,' said Geoffrey, ignoring the fact that Roger *had* launched an assault on Hemming. 'Three men followed you, armed with swords, crossbows and daggers. It was them who fought you – and fought me, too.'

260

'I do not believe you!' said Burchard with a half-laugh of incredulity. '*I* saw no one but Roger. He hurtled out of the darkness and all but knocked Hemming senseless. Then he went for me.'

'I also saw no one except Roger,' concurred Hemming. 'He was like a mad dog. No wonder the Scots wanted him gone from Durham and he was known as Roger the Devil.'

'He was trying to protect you from men with loaded crossbows,' said Geoffrey, watching the three monks to see whether one might betray himself with a flicker of unease that Weasel had been seen. Predictably, there was nothing, although all appeared surprised by the assertion.

'The only man with weapons last night was Roger,' said Burchard firmly. 'And now we have lost the map. I dropped it when Roger came at me like a fiend from Hell, and even though I searched for it most of the night, it is nowhere to be found.'

'I do not suppose you picked it up, did you?' asked Hemming, giving Geoffrey a searching look.

'No,' said Geoffrey. He favoured Hemming with a searching look of his own. 'But Roger saw you with a knife, going towards Burchard in a way that suggested your intentions were not friendly.'

'He saw no such thing,' said Hemming impatiently, while Burchard regarded his colleague warily. 'He saw me move towards Burchard with a dagger certainly. But Roger could not possibly know what my intentions were.'

'Well, what were they?'

'Burchard's sleeve had caught on the broken glass in the window. If he had tried to free it by brute force – which I sensed he was likely to do – the glass would have broken and smashed on the ground. You will appreciate I did not want that to happen: it would have woken the occupants of the house and alerted them to our presence.'

'My sleeve did catch,' admitted Burchard, showing Geoffrey a rip in his greasy habit, 'when I was trying to squeeze through the window.'

'I was planning to toss the knife to him so he could cut

himself free,' said Hemming. 'It seems Roger jumped to entirely the wrong conclusion.'

Geoffrey regarded him uncertainly, not sure what to believe.

'Why did you have to meddle?' demanded Burchard, turning on him. 'Everything was going well until you arrived. You should have left us alone.'

'Now what are we going to do?' sighed Turgot, pacing in agitation. 'We had the map in our hands and we lost it!' He regarded Burchard in disgust. 'How could you drop something so important?'

'I did not do it deliberately,' protested Burchard. 'And I spent most of the night trying to find it.'

'So did I,' said Hemming bitterly.

'Was the map all you lost, Burchard?' asked Geoffrey. 'Or did you manage to keep the rest of your haul from Alice Jarveaux's solar?'

'What do you mean?' blustered Burchard, while prior and sub-prior regarded him warily.

'Alice paid us a visit this morning, and she accused Roger and me of stealing jewellery last night.'

'I hope you are not accusing *me*,' snapped Burchard, his small eyes flicking nervously from his prior to Geoffrey. 'I have no need for jewellery.'

'That is true,' said Turgot, evidently deciding he had better defend his abbey by supporting his bursar. 'Monks do not steal trinkets.'

'Quite,' said Burchard, gaining confidence. '*You* must have taken the rings and necklaces.'

'How do you know it was rings and necklaces that were missing?' pounced Geoffrey. 'I did not tell you what Alice said was gone, but yet you know anyway. Why is that?'

The bursar stuttered and swore, but was unable to refute the accusations. Eventually, his unconvincing protestations of innocence petered out and an accusing silence reigned.

'I saw Roger digging in the snow like a dog after a buried bone,' said Hemming after a while of allowing the bursar to squirm. 'I surmised you were under it. I wanted to help, but Roger was making such a racket that Burchard was afraid we would be seen, and it would have been difficult to explain what we were doing there at that hour of the night. We were obliged to hide, but I was sufficiently concerned that I planned to visit you today, to make sure you were unharmed.'

'You were?' asked Geoffrey, thinking that such an encounter would have been awkward with Eleanor still angry about the missing jewellery.

'I sensed someone behind us when we left the abbey,' Hemming continued. 'I assumed it was you, and decided you did not mean us harm, or you would not have told us where the map was in the first place. But now you say there were others following us? I confess I do not know whether to believe you. Roger went for *us*, not them, and I certainly saw no one else.'

'Nor did I,' said Burchard, grateful not to be the centre of accusing attention. 'As soon as Roger had ferried you across the river, Hemming and I returned to Jarveaux's house to look for the map. We saw no one but you all night.'

'Perhaps the map was stolen by these archers,' suggested Turgot. 'It is the only logical conclusion.'

'But they do not exist,' declared Burchard. 'He is making them up.'

'They exist,' said Geoffrey. 'In fact, they may be in the abbey even as we speak. One has been dogging our footsteps ever since Flambard first inveigled Roger into acting as his courier. I do not know his name, but he looks like a rat: small, dark-haired, with pinched features and backward-pointing teeth.'

'That sounds like Brother Gamelo,' said Hemming, startled.

Gamelo, thought Geoffrey. Where had he heard that name before? Then it came to him: the roof-top fighter – Gilbert Courcy – in Southampton had mentioned a Gamelo. He had pleaded, almost desperately, for Roger to make sure Brother Gamelo did not take the staff.

'Gamelo was a mercenary before he took the cowl,' said Turgot thoughtfully. 'It is possible he heard about the cathedral's treasure and decided to look into it himself.

He has never been obedient, and I have serious reservations about the sincerity of his commitment to our order.'

'He is one of Burchard's rent collectors,' said Hemming, shooting the bursar an unpleasant glance. 'Thus he has permission to be away for long periods of time with no questions asked. The abbey owns property all over the county, you see.'

Burchard's eyes narrowed in anger. 'Do not hold me responsible for what Gamelo may have done. He carries out my orders, and that is all I know about him.'

'Well, *I* would have nothing to do with such a man,' declared Hemming fastidiously.

'Can I speak to him?' asked Geoffrey.

'You can try,' said Turgot. 'But he will not answer you.'

'And why is that?' asked Geoffrey, wondering whether the man had been threatened into silence by one of the three who stood in front of him.

'Because he is dead,' said the prior.

Gamelo was indeed Weasel. Geoffrey would have recognized the mean, narrow features anywhere, even though the body in the chapter house was dressed in a Benedictine habit and not the greasy jerkin Weasel usually wore. So, Mother Petra had been right: she said the man who had brought her the arrows to be stained had been a monk.

Geoffrey stared at the waxen features, wishing the man could give him the answers he needed. Had he been in the pay of the abbey? And if so, was his master Burchard, who regularly hired louts to frighten people into doing what he wanted? Or Turgot, who was determined to have the gold at all costs? Or Hemming, who was engaged in a power struggle with the bursar? Or was it coincidence that he was a monk? Was he acting for the sheriff, or even Jarveaux? And if it was Jarveaux, had Alice continued to use his services after her husband's death?

The news of Gamelo's death had seemed as much a surprise to Hemming and Burchard as it was to Geoffrey. Both monks had immediately begun a barrage of questions that the prior had stemmed by raising an authoritative hand. Wordlessly, he had headed for the chapter house, leaving the others to follow. After exchanging a mystified glance, Hemming and Burchard had hurried to catch up, while Geoffrey brought up the rear. Hemming muttered a brief prayer when he saw the still, cold features, although Turgot and Burchard did not seem to consider such niceties necessary. The sub-prior's own face was white, and Geoffrey wondered whether he might swoon. Concerned, he took the man's elbow.

'Forgive me,' Hemming whispered, so the others would not hear. 'Sudden death always affects me like this. I have a crushing sense of how fragile life is, and how easily it can be snuffed out. Do you ever have that sensation?'

'Thankfully not,' replied Geoffrey. 'It would not be a useful emotion for a knight, given the number of violent deaths we encounter.'

'Of course,' said Hemming, smiling ruefully at himself for asking such a question. 'I chose a monastic career to avoid such sights, but even monks confront death on occasion, although bloody ones are rare – mercifully.'

'What are you two muttering about?' demanded Burchard.

'We were wondering how Gamelo died,' said Geoffrey.

The prior snapped his fingers, and his secretary approached. 'Algar here discovered the corpse and has been investigating the matter for me. Well? What have you learned?'

Algar swallowed hard. 'I hope this will not affect my chances of promotion to—'

'If you have discovered why Gamelo died, then I will reward you accordingly,' said the prior ambiguously. Geoffrey would not have trusted such a vague promise for an instant.

Algar opened Gamelo's mouth. Inside was a mass of small blisters, and Hemming turned away with an exclamation of horror. The bursar and the prior were less expressive, and gazed down at the corpse with detached interest.

'The abbey physician thinks the poison he swallowed was green hellebore,' explained Algar. 'It blisters the mouth, and he says it is the right time of year to harvest the stuff.'

'Suicide?' asked Geoffrey. 'Or did someone give it to him?'

Algar licked dry lips. 'It seems someone gave it to him.'

265

'How do you know that?' asked Turgot, surprised.

'Because his was not the only death this morning,' said Algar. 'Just moments ago, two lay brothers were discovered dead from the same cause.'

Hemming gazed at him. '*Three* men were poisoned? Are they the trio Geoffrey says followed us last night, do you think? It seems likely, if one was Gamelo, as he maintains.'

'Did *you* give them poison?' asked Burchard of Geoffrey. 'You may have been the last person to see them alive, since you admit to fighting with them. Cenred will be very interested in this.'

'Oh, yes,' said Geoffrey facetiously. 'In the middle of a fight, I asked them to lay down their weapons and take poison instead. They willingly complied, of course, and I always carry a cup of hellebore with me for just such occasions.'

'Death is nothing to mock,' said Turgot sharply. He addressed Algar. 'Where were the other bodies found?'

'Gamelo was near the ferry. I found him when I went to buy fresh fish for your breakfast. The others were in the woods nearby. I think all three must have drunk the poison at the same time, which explains why they died so close to each other.'

'A secular person committed this crime,' announced Burchard. 'It could not have been a monk, or they would have perished in the abbey grounds.'

'Not necessarily,' said Geoffrey. 'I imagine your brethren are a little more circumspect than that. However, it is obvious they were killed by someone they knew, or they would not have accepted whatever was given to eat or drink.'

'Arrange for masses to be said,' Turgot ordered Algar. 'And continue to ask questions of anyone who might know what happened. I want to know what happened here, Algar.'

'But no one knows,' squeaked Algar, loath to undertake an impossible task. 'And I do not—'

But Turgot was already walking away. The more compassionate Hemming took pity on the man, and made suggestions as to how he might solve the crime, while Geoffrey

266

left the chapter house and its odour of death to wait outside. Burchard stood behind him, so close that Geoffrey felt uncomfortable.

'These murders were committed by someone in the city,' he hissed menacingly. 'You will not blame the abbey, or I shall make you sorry.'

'Do not threaten me,' said Geoffrey, turning to meet his eyes. 'I am not one of Durham's merchants, too afraid to stand up to you.'

'I am not threatening you,' said Burchard slyly. 'But I hear you harbour a liking for Stanstede's widow. Do not forget she will remain here long after you leave for the Holy Land to resume your life of bloody slaughter. I am sure you would not like to think of her at risk after you have gone.'

'You bastard!' exclaimed Geoffrey, appalled that he should hear such words from a man who wore the garb of a monk. 'You would not dare!'

'Would I not?' asked Burchard softly. 'Eleanor is a brothel keeper. Such women have no place in our city. The abbey could drive her out, if it felt so inclined. Who would speak up for her?'

'Cenred, for a start,' said Geoffrey immediately. 'He knows the usefulness of a brothel in a place filled with soldiers, carpenters and masons. He sees it as a way of keeping the peace.'

'But unless Turgot finds his map, there will be no cathedral for these men to build and guard,' said Burchard. 'But that is irrelevant, because we *will* have our treasure. And you will do nothing more to interfere. Remember Mistress Stanstede the next time you meddle.'

'You disgust me,' said Geoffrey, turning away. 'You, a man of God, would threaten an innocent woman just to protect your abbey?'

'I would threaten St Cuthbert himself to protect my abbey,' said Burchard softly.

There was nothing more to be learned from the monks, so Geoffrey left the monastery. The deaths of Gamelo and the two lay brothers had unsettled him, and he was not inclined to return to Eleanor's house and spend the rest of the day pretending to be ill. He avoided the market and began to walk along the path that led out of the city past St Giles'. The snow made walking awkward and unpleasant, so he abandoned the exercise and settled for a spell of solitary contemplation in the church instead.

As usual, it was gloomy, and most of its window shutters remained closed against the elements. The ones in the Lady chapel were open, partly to light the chancel, but mainly because the two bodies that lay there had now been dead a week, and, although the cold weather helped, it could not totally dispel the miasma of death that permeated the building.

Geoffrey avoided the chapel and sat in the nave, looking at the high altar with its niche for St Balthere's stolen bones. He recalled what Eilaf had told him about them: that Flambard had presented the bones of a Saxon hermit to the church, so the abbey would not claim all the revenues from pilgrims who flocked to pay their respects.

It was not unknown for relics to be stolen, especially by monastic institutions that wanted to increase their own importance, or by people who made their livings peddling such items. Flambard himself had probably employed such a person to get him Balthere in the first place, and would doubtless do the same to acquire the mythical Aaron's Rod. But it was unusual for stolen relics to disappear so completely: they invariably turned up somewhere else, where the new owners denied shady dealings and announced the saint had arrived by miraculous means – something difficult to disprove in a country where people believed in divine interventions.

'It is a sad sight, is it not?' came a soft voice behind him. It was Eilaf, who had dispensed with his useless boots and was barefoot. His feet were red and swollen from the cold, and his face was more pinched and hungry-looking than ever. 'That niche should hold Balthere, not a wreath of holly.'

Geoffrey nodded. 'Did anyone ever investigate the theft?'

The priest shook his head. 'None of my parishioners are brave enough to confront men like Burchard and demand them back. He has always claimed the abbey is innocent, and since poor Balthere has not been seen since, perhaps he is telling the truth. There would be no point in stealing them if the abbey did not put them on display, would there?'

'Flambard must have been annoyed. Presumably, he paid for them himself?'

'He did, yes. And he was furious when he heard what had happened, although he promised to get them back for us as soon as they made a reappearance. Unfortunately, they never have.'

'For the sake of good relations, why does the abbey not lend you a bone? It owns plenty. What about St Oswald's head? Since it is not with the other relics, that would not be missed, surely?'

'Oswald is far too prestigious to be loaned to the likes of us. And anyway, his skull is safely tucked inside St Cuthbert's coffin, where it belongs.'

'Roger told me it has its own reliquary, inside the high altar,' said Geoffrey.

Eilaf shook his head, smiling. 'Roger has always confused his saints. Do not listen to him. But why have you come here? Did you want to see me?'

'I have been to the abbey and felt the need for some peace.'

'Then I will leave you. I am busy anyway: Jarveaux is to be buried today. The grave is not as deep as I would like, because the ground is frozen. A few extra pennies will probably see it soften miraculously, but Alice will not hear of it.'

'That I can believe.'

'She claims she has already paid for a hole, and objects to being asked for more. But it will have to do. Walter has been dead for a week and is beginning to be a problem.'

'I noticed,' said Geoffrey.

'Eleanor wants her husband buried decently, though. She has been hoping for a break in the weather, but I do not think her prayers will be answered. I will wait two more days, but no longer. My parishioners object to too many stinking rich corpses lying in their church.'

'They have a point.'

Eilaf sighed. 'I must nail Jarveaux inside his box. His

mourners will not appreciate being asked to wait while I finish, and Alice might order me to bury it open unless I hurry. She has already told me to make the service as short as possible.'

'Then I will leave,' said Geoffrey, thinking he did not want to be caught hale and hearty when Alice came to bury her husband in his shallow grave.

As he closed the door behind him, he saw a solemn procession coming towards the church. In the lead was Alice, clad in a new cloak lined with soft, white fur and a pair of boots made of calf skin. Apparently no expense had been spared for her funeral attire, in stark contrast to her niggardliness over her husband's grave.

Not wanting a confrontation, Geoffrey stepped behind a buttress to wait for the procession to pass. Alice picked her way delicately through the snow and opened the porch door, glancing up at the sky as she did so in a way that suggested she had better things to do than listen to Eilaf's mass. Mother Petra followed, bundled into a cloak that dragged along the ground behind her. She gave a sudden grin and nodded a greeting to Geoffrey's buttress. For a moment, he was disconcerted, wondering whether her status as a witch really did give her supernatural powers, but then he noticed the footprints he had left in the snow – large ones made by a man wearing heavy armour.

Other people followed them inside. There were three restless apprentices, eager to be back in their warm workshop to while away their day in idle chatter by the fire. Cenred was accompanied by a woman who looked even more like a pig than he did, while the apothecary's billowing cloak wafted the scent of his herbs and potions around him as he walked. Bringing up the rear was Hemming, representing the abbey, and the only one of the mourners whose entire demeanour did not suggest he was keen to be elsewhere.

Geoffrey waited until the door closed before moving on. From inside the church, he heard Eilaf hammering nails, a mournful sound that echoed across the snowy graveyard like thunderclaps. In one corner, a pile of earth represented the shallow trough that was to be Jarveaux's final resting place.

Geoffrey walked away quickly, leaving the dead goldsmith to his mean grave, his hasty requiem, and his smattering of reluctant mourners.

Roger spirited Geoffrey upstairs via a back door just as Eleanor was rushing through the front one to make an appearance – albeit a late one – at Jarveaux's funeral. Geoffrey told him what he had learned at the abbey, and they spent the afternoon asking questions neither could answer and planning their foray to Finchale the next day, agreeing to travel on foot rather than attempt to ride. Then Roger claimed he was hungry. He had just returned from the kitchen with a substantial hunk of pork when there was a commotion in the street outside. They pushed open the window shutters, and leaned out to see what was happening. A procession made its way towards the castle, while people thronged, voices raised. Roger and Geoffrey were about to join them when Eleanor entered the room.

'You should not be up,' she said admonishingly to Geoffrey, removing her cloak and stamping snow from her boots. 'Lie down at once.'

'What is going on?' he asked. 'Why have all those people gathered?'

'A group of merchants have managed to make their way from Chester-le-Street by using the path that runs along the river instead of the road,' she replied. 'The river path is longer, but the merchants thought it might be easier to travel.'

'Is that it?' asked Roger scathingly. 'A band of traders have braved the snow and arrived in Durham? How did I ever manage to leave this place of high excitement?'

'They had travelled a little more than half way, when they found Sheriff Durnais,' said Eleanor stiffly, not liking the implication that her city was dull. 'That procession you saw is his body being taken to the castle.'

'How did he die?' asked Geoffrey, feeling as though events were suddenly beginning to whirl out of control. Gamelo and his companions had been murdered, and now Durnais had reappeared.

'Drowned,' said Eleanor. 'I suppose the poor man must have lost his way to Chester-le-Street in the snow and stumbled into the river by mistake.'

'You cannot lose your way on the river path!' said Roger in disbelief. 'You just follow the water. Even a Saracen could do it, and they are not noted for their intelligence.'

'I meant he must have lost his footing,' said Eleanor. 'If the path was slippery, he may have fallen and hit his head, and then drowned when he was unable to climb out of the water.'

'Was he alone?' asked Geoffrey. 'I thought a sheriff would have had an escort.'

'He took only a manservant apparently, but the man probably went the same way as his master, and his body was swept away by the river and washed out to sea.'

'So that explains why he never arrived in Chester-le-Street,' said Roger. 'He was dead.'

But when had he died? Geoffrey wondered. Had it been while on his way to dig for Flambard's treasure, or on his way home? And if the latter, had he found the hoard or not? And there was another problem: Durnais had left a week before Geoffrey and Roger had arrived in Durham, when the weather had been cold but not snowy. There had been no reason to take the river route to Chester-le-Street. He said as much.

'Perhaps he felt the need for an adventure,' suggested Roger. 'It must be tedious doing all that administration. Perhaps he wanted to stretch his legs and see something of the countryside.'

'In the middle of winter?' asked Geoffrey. 'With only a manservant and the King's highways riddled with out-laws who would dearly love to attack a sheriff? And any-way, that does not ring true with what I have been told about Durnais. People say it was unusual for him to leave the city.'

Roger slapped his forehead as an idea occurred to him, and gave them a grin. 'I know exactly what he was doing on the river path.'

'Do you think you might share this information?' asked

Eleanor, when Roger was so pleased with himself that he merely smiled and made no further attempt to explain.

'It all boils down to local knowledge,' said Roger proudly. 'You see, *I* know what lies part-way between Chester-le-Street and Durham on the river path!'

So did Eleanor, but the knowledge did not seem to enlighten her in the same way as it did Roger.

'What are you talking about?' she demanded. 'There is nothing there but woods and bog. There is no reason Durnais should want to go there.'

'And these woods and bog go by the name of Finchale,' said Roger, casting a meaningful glance at Geoffrey. 'And we all know what is at Finchale.'

'So,' mused Geoffrey thoughtfully. 'Durnais *did* receive a map and decide to look for the treasure before anyone else. But this means that we were wrong about Odard: we thought he had given Durnais a false map, to lead him astray, but if Durnais was at Finchale, then Odard must have provided him with the real one after all.'

'Durnais would have to be insane if he thought he could locate the treasure just by knowing it was at Finchale,' said Roger doubtfully. 'It is a big place and he might spend weeks digging and still not find it.'

'People are blind to logic when they are bedazzled by the promise of gold,' said Eleanor. 'You and I know that going to Finchale and digging randomly is futile, but a greedy man might not be so rational. It is like the games of chance I see played in the brothel.'

'In what respect?' asked Roger, puzzled.

'The men who play know they will lose eventually – they always do. Yet they sit there night after night hoping for the win that will answer all their prayers. It is the same with treasure. The possibility, even a distant one, of owning fabulous wealth causes men to lose their reason, and makes them do irrational things – like trying to excavate all of Finchale.'

'Flambard would agree,' said Geoffrey. 'That is why he declined to confide in one person.'

'He was right,' said Eleanor grimly. 'The sheriff could *not* be trusted. Meanwhile, Jarveaux also received his map, but made no attempt to contact the others. I am sure he was waiting for them to tell him what *they* knew, then intended to deny receiving his own.'

'And then he could have gone to Finchale to recover the hoard at his own convenience,' said Geoffrey, nodding. 'And even Turgot's motives are a little suspect. I do not think he will steal the treasure for his personal use—'

'Why not?' interrupted Eleanor. 'You have only to look at his lovely house to see that not all abbey funds have been used for the community. How much of Flambard's wealth would be used for the cathedral, and how much for the abbey – or even himself – if the prior has sole control over it?'

That was true, Geoffrey thought. He regarded Eleanor and Roger sombrely, saddened that in all of Durham, Flambard did not know three men sufficiently honest to give the hidden treasure to the cathedral. He was only a little heartened by the knowledge that this was more a reflection on Flambard's choice of acquaintances, than on the city itself.

Eleanor fussed over Geoffrey like a mother hen for the rest of the day, so he deeply regretted his choice of ruses to prevent Roger from revealing all to Alice. Eleanor took her ministrations far enough to try to feed him fish soup that evening, a culinary delight that held some sinister connotations for him, since someone had once tried to kill him with some. He declined to drink it, she insisted, and eventually he capitulated simply so she would leave him alone. The insipid broth made him genuinely sick, and he was more than happy to retire to bed early, reduced to chewing the herbs in the washing water to try to rid his mouth of the rank flavour.

Since Geoffrey was Eleanor's prisoner, Roger went to the castle chapel to view Durnais' body. There was little the big knight could do to ascertain the cause of death without raising suspicion, but the monk who had been hired to lay him out declared that half the River Wear was in the man's lungs, and there was a lot of water on the stone floor underneath the body.

The monk also said it was impossible to tell when the

274

sheriff had died. He had last been seen eleven or twelve days before, but the monk claimed the appearance of the body indicated he had not been dead the whole time. Misconstruing Roger's interest for a shared fascination with the dead, the monk proceeded to regale him with an account of how cold weather tended to preserve corpses, something Roger felt he did not need to know, especially in such enthusiastic detail.

He went to the soggy pile of belongings. There, among river-soiled hose, shirt and cloak, was a piece of parchment. Pursing his lips in disapproval that he should have to do what Geoffrey normally did, Roger picked it up and unfolded it. His face broke into a grin. It was another map, although different from those he had seen already. This one depicted Finchale, but also included one or two landmarks and a cross. Geoffrey had been right: Odard had provided Durnais with a false chart. He replaced it carefully and went to stand over the body, wanting to know what else might be learned.

He watched the corpse stripped and washed, but could see nothing to indicate that the sheriff had fallen foul of a killer. There was a scratch on his hand, washed clean of blood by the river, but swollen and reddened nevertheless. It was the only mark on an otherwise unblemished body. Eventually, having earned himself a reputation as an insatiable ghoul by others who came to pay their respects, he went home.

The following day, Geoffrey was awake long before dawn, and donned leather leggings and a light mail tunic. He had considered wearing full armour, but he did not want to fall into the river and drown like the sheriff. He also knew it was a several-mile walk along the river bank to Finchale, most of which was likely to be slow going, and he did not want their progress to be unnecessarily impeded by heavy garments. He prodded Roger awake, waited for him to dress, and then followed him down the stairs to the door.

The dog worried around his legs in anticipation of exercise, but Geoffrey did not think it would be able to wade through the snow, so shut it in the kitchen, hoping Eleanor would feed it later. Loud cracking sounds emerged before he had even closed the door, and he opened it again quickly to see the animal with a substantial ham bone between its front paws. Geoffrey gazed at it in horror.

'You will be in trouble,' said Roger with a chuckle. 'Eleanor was going to send that to Alice, on account of her burying her husband yesterday.'

Geoffrey seized the dog by the scruff of its neck, and took it across the yard to one of the outhouses, where he hoped it would be able to do no harm until he returned. The first was a pantry, in which more hams and meat joints were stored. The dog slathered in delirious delight. Geoffrey deftly swapped the gnawed ham for a new one, locked the dog in another shed, and left the pristine meat in the kitchen, in the hope that Eleanor would not notice the difference. Perhaps she would think one of Alice's gargantuan rats had savaged the other when she eventually found it. Roger and Geoffrey gathered weapons, spades and cloaks, and were gone before Eleanor woke and tried to stop them.

There was a moon, which gleamed silver over the white countryside. Branches and twigs sagged under the weight of snow, and every leaf seemed to have its own precipitous avalanche waiting to drop. The land was totally silent, the thick blanket serving to still all life, so it was like walking through a vast tomb. Their footsteps were the only sounds, crunching through the rime that had formed over the snowy surface when temperatures had plummeted the previous night.

They did not speak until they were well clear of the city. The path kept closely to the edge of the river, which was wide, deep, and fringed with ice where the slower-moving parts had frozen. In one place, it had set solid from one side to the other, although Geoffrey would not have tried walking across it. In other parts, it had been frozen for days, because there were scratches on its marbled surface where children had skimmed across it on skates made from bones.

Once past the last houses that huddled on the city's outskirts, walking became more difficult. The merchants had forged a way, but the ground had refrozen since, and the holes their feet had made formed treacherous potholes. The two knights pressed on, skidding and stumbling. Roger fell once, twisting his ankle, so Geoffrey thought they might have to forgo their expedition until the snow had melted. But Roger insisted on continuing, and gradually they made headway. Geoffrey's legs burned and ached, and he did not like to imagine how they might feel on the way home. The landscape around them began to brighten, and the sun rose, shedding a pink sheen over the white world around them. Geoffrey stopped to admire it, until prodded on by an impatient Roger.

'I expect this treasure will comprise mainly jewellery,' Roger mused. He was interested in loot and its component parts. 'There will be crowns and bracelets, all studded with rubies and emeralds.'

'I imagine it will be coins,' said Geoffrey practically. 'Flambard implied it was skimmed from his cash-raising ventures for the King, and not many folk pay their taxes with bracelets and the like.'

'How will we carry it back to Durham?' asked Roger, worried. A predatory gleam came into his eyes, and he lowered his voice conspiratorially. 'We may have time to take a small commission. We have been to considerable trouble over these maps, and I would like to be paid for my pains. We will fill our pouches and the abbey can have what is left.'

'We will do no such thing,' said Geoffrey, horrified. 'Your father will have counted every penny and will know if you pilfer from him. And anyway, it is for the cathedral, and even you would not steal from God. Would you?' he added as an uncertain afterthought.

Roger considered. 'Perhaps not this time,' he said eventually. 'Although each circumstance needs to be considered on its own merit – as you yourself have told me on a number of occasions.'

'Not where this kind of thing is concerned,' said Geoffrey firmly, who thought stealing from Flambard was likely to be a lot more dangerous than stealing from God. He stopped abruptly and held up his hand to warn Roger to be silent.

Both listened intently. A duck flapped across the water, sending silver droplets scattering as it went. Then all was silent again. Relieved, they resumed walking, alert for any sign that they were being followed or that someone was waiting for them ahead.

The journey was long and laborious, but uneventful. Once or twice, Geoffrey thought he heard sounds, but each time there was a bird in the undergrowth or a plop from the river as a fish surfaced. It would be a foolish or desperate man to be out anyway, thought Geoffrey. The weather was bitingly cold, and even struggling through uneven, frozen snow did not warm him properly.

Eventually, they reached a bend in the river, and Roger stopped. The previous night, he had drawn the two streams and the path on the map they had seized from Burchard, and Geoffrey had marked the cross on it. He tugged it from his surcoat, squinting at it from a variety of different angles to prove he knew what he was doing, then gestured to the opposite bank.

'Finchale,' he announced. 'Over there.'

Geoffrey regarded the fast-flowing water uncertainly. 'I sincerely hope there is a ford.'

'This *is* the ford,' said Roger. He gave his friend a conspiratorial wink. 'Do not worry about getting wet, lad. You will be warm enough once we start to dig up the treasure. Digging is hard work.'

Geoffrey crouched down and pointed to where the snow had been churned up and the weeds at the water's edge were trampled and torn. 'I wonder if this was where those merchants found the sheriff.'

Roger nodded. 'I think so, judging from what I was told when I inspected his body yesterday. He must have fallen in as he was about to cross. Should we see if we can find the servant who was supposed to be with him?'

Not averse to delaying the unpleasant prospect of wading through the icy water, Geoffrey and Roger separated to poke about in the undergrowth with their swords. Geoffrey did not seriously expect to find anything: if Durnais had fallen into the river and drowned, then his servant would have gone for help, not remained nearby. Therefore, when he heard Roger's yell, he was taken by surprise.

'Here he is,' said Roger, prodding at a half-buried body

in a drift. 'His elbow was showing, and when I shovelled the snow away, there he was. Poor devil.'

'How did he die?' asked Geoffrey. 'He did not drown – he is too far from the river.'

'Aye, but this is Durnais' man right enough. Jacob the Pike. I have known him since he was a lad. It is a pity. His mother is a widow and he was her only son.'

Geoffrey scraped away more snow, revealing a young man wearing a bright yellow jerkin.

'There is not a mark on him,' said Roger, watching Geoffrey conduct a quick examination. 'No sign he was shot, no wound to the head. Perhaps he died of the cold.'

'Or perhaps he was poisoned,' said Geoffrey quietly, pointing out a small wound on one of Pike's hands. It was blackened and swollen, and streaks ran from it up his arm.

'Poisoned?' asked Roger. 'How could he be poisoned all the way out here?'

'Snakes?' suggested Geoffrey, not knowing what to think. 'You said Finchale's serpents are different from the ones in the rest of the country.'

Roger jumped on to a fallen tree trunk and looked warily at the ground. 'Be on the lookout, Geoff. We do not want the same thing to happen to us.'

Geoffrey continued to stare at the body, not understanding at all what had happened. 'This is very odd. We have the sheriff and his man dead on a deserted path: Durnais drowns but his servant is poisoned. Meanwhile, we have Xavier and his man killed on another deserted road: Xavier is strangled but his squire is shot. Why did they all die so differently?'

'You ask too many questions,' said Roger, after a few moments of pondering failed to provide the answer. 'What does any of this matter?'

Geoffrey rubbed the bridge of his nose. 'I do not know. It just seems as though it is significant.'

'I have just remembered something.' Roger continued to look at the ground, as if anticipating some monstrous serpent would come slithering along it towards him. 'When I saw Durnais yesterday, I noticed a swollen cut on his hand, too.

I did not consider it important at the time, but now I see that it is.'

'So, both men show signs of poisoning,' said Geoffrey thoughtfully. 'Perhaps Durnais staggered into the river and drowned before the poison got him.'

'These snakes are dangerous beasts,' said Roger, raising his sword in a way that suggested he intended to chop one in half, should it be rash enough to make an appearance.

'I hope you are right,' said Geoffrey uneasily. 'Because if Durnais and Pike were not killed by snakes, then it means a person poisoned them. And, because they died here, it means their killer knows roughly where Flambard's treasure is hidden. He might be watching us now.'

'So, you have finally worked it out,' came a gloating voice from the trees. 'Congratulations!'

The bursar's voice brought Geoffrey to his feet with his sword at the ready, and he and Roger stood back to back, trying to ascertain where the voice had come from. The undergrowth around them was still and silent.

'Burchard?' called Roger. 'Come out where we can see you!'

'No, thank you,' replied Burchard with a startled laugh. 'You would cleave my head from my shoulders and claim those snakes you have been talking about did it.'

'With their swords, I suppose?' asked Geoffrey, wondering how many archers the monk had hidden in the undergrowth with weapons trained on him and Roger. 'We will not harm you. All we want to do is find this treasure and take it to Turgot.'

'As much as it galls me to say so, I believe you,' called Burchard. 'I heard you discussing it on the way here. I confess I am surprised: I assumed you agreed to help Flambard solely so you could steal it for yourselves.'

So, someone *had* been following them, thought Geoffrey, angry with himself for not being more vigilant. The times he had heard noises must have been Burchard, blundering along the river path in his ape-like manner.

'It is you who wants to steal,' said Roger, peering into the bushes in an attempt to spot the man. 'You want the treasure for yourself.'

'I want it for my abbey,' said Burchard. 'As I told Geoffrey yesterday, I will do anything for it.'

'Even threaten women,' said Geoffrey in disgust.

'What women?' demanded Roger. 'It had better not be Ellie, or I *will* remove your head from your shoulders and tell everyone a snake did it.'

'I am prepared to reach an agreement on that,' came Burchard's disembodied voice. 'A truce. We find the treasure together and *I* will present it to the abbey. And Eleanor will enjoy my protection for as long as she chooses to remain in Durham.'

'And if we decline?' asked Geoffrey.

Burchard gave a short, nasty laugh. 'Life can be unpleasant for women who run brothels. They are often driven out of their homes and their goods confiscated.'

Geoffrey put his hand on Roger's shoulder, to prevent him from storming the trees with a whirling sword. He did not care who presented Turgot with the treasure, just as long as it reached its intended destination. If Burchard agreed to leave Eleanor alone, then Geoffrey thought the bargain was good enough.

'We agree to your terms,' he called. 'But if I hear that you have reneged, I will return to Durham – no matter where I am – and I will kill you. Is that understood?'

Burchard cleared his throat nervously, realizing Geoffrey meant what he said. 'Perfectly.'

'Then come out where we can see you,' said Geoffrey, still holding his sword at the ready.

'With pleasure,' said Burchard, stepping away from the bushes and raising his hands to show he carried no weapon. 'Do I have your assurance you will not slay a lone, unarmed man of God?'

'As long as we have your assurance that you *are* unarmed and alone,' said Geoffrey in return, still watching the trees for signs that Burchard had posted archers there.

The monk allowed Roger to search him. 'I am unaccompanied. Check if you want.'

While Geoffrey remained with the bursar, Roger crashed about in the undergrowth, slashing wildly at the vegetation with his sword. Eventually, he returned to say that Burchard was telling the truth.

'I knew where the treasure was buried long before you fathomed it out,' Burchard crowed, eyeing Geoffrey challengingly. 'I am surprised you are not still in Durham, scratching your stupid head.'

'How did you work it out?' asked Geoffrey, refusing to be provoked. 'And when?'

'After we visited Jarveaux's house. Did I mention that the silly man hid his map under a floorboard? That is the first place a thief would look.'

'And you would know,' said Geoffrey, thinking about Alice's jewellery.

The bursar gave him a look of dislike. 'Baubles are better used for an abbey than adorning vain widows. And anyway, Alice can afford to lose them. She is a wealthy woman.'

Geoffrey saw that particular topic was not going to get them far, so changed the subject. 'But you lost the map. How did you manage to guess the location of the treasure without it?'

Burchard looked so smugly superior that Geoffrey felt like thumping him. 'I lost *one* of them. Jarveaux had made a copy. I put that inside my habit, and I held the other in my hand for Hemming to see. He told me I was not to leave until I had found it, you see, because he did not want to come back again the following night. Unlike me, there are limits to what he will do for the abbey treasure, and a second night raiding the Jarveaux home was well past them.'

'The *abbey's* treasure?' asked Geoffrey wryly. 'Not the cathedral's?'

'It all goes to glorify God,' said Burchard quickly, realizing he had misspoken.

'Not in the same way,' said Geoffrey. 'Abbeys and bishops vie with each other for power. Flambard would never donate gold to build an abbey that will then become strong enough to defy him. He will want all his money to go to the cathedral – his ecclesiastical seat of power.'

282

'What he wants is irrelevant,' growled Burchard nastily. 'In case you had not noticed, he is not here.'

'I do not understand you,' said Geoffrey, shaking his head. 'You say you want the treasure for the abbey, so why did you conceal the second map from Turgot yesterday?'

'Turgot is an ambitious man. I do not want *him* taking the credit for my hard work by digging up the gold himself.'

'Whereas, if *you* take *him* the treasure, everyone will know you found it,' said Geoffrey. 'You will be a hero.'

'Quite. And it will allow me to do an inventory first – to see exactly what there is. I will not have some of it going to fund secret meetings – to which I am not invited – between Turgot and other powerful men.'

'Most noble of you,' said Geoffrey. He thought about what Burchard was saying. At first, he had been suspicious of the bursar's motives, but the more he heard him speak, the more he was certain the man was telling the truth. Burchard was someone who believed any means justified an end. He was happy to lie and steal, as long as he believed that it would ultimately benefit his abbey.

'You are alone and unarmed,' said Roger. 'How do you know we will not kill you?'

'Because I told Hemming exactly where I was going, along with the fact that you might join me at some point. If I die or disappear, he will know where to start asking questions.'

'How did you know we would come here at all?'

'Jarveaux's map was definitely not in the snow by his house, so there was only one other thing that could have happened after I had dropped it: Roger had grabbed it. I knew you would come here.'

'But you said you did not credit us with the intelligence to work out where the treasure is buried.'

'Yes and no,' hedged Burchard, reluctant to acknowledge their success. 'But, we are all here now, and since we want the gold safe inside the abbey before it gets dark, we should make a start on the digging. I do not want to spend the night here.' He shuddered and glanced uneasily around him. 'Not at Finchale.'

* * *

Roger led the way across the ford. The water was so icy that it made Geoffrey's head ache, and by the time he had splashed through the shallows to the opposite bank, he could barely feel his legs. Shivering and stamping his feet in a futile attempt to warm himself, he followed Roger up the bank and surveyed the wilderness in front of them.

Roger was right when he had deemed Finchale a desolate place. It was a long way from any settlement, and exuded the aura that it had been the kingdom of stunted trees, marshy ponds and thick tangled undergrowth since time began. Except for the occasional flap of agitated wings as a duck or a moorhen took flight, and the occasional call of birds, Finchale was a silent place. Geoffrey saw exactly why it had given rise to tales of serpents and snakes. It had an air of desolation, as though it was somewhere people were not supposed to be.

'Right,' said Burchard, rubbing chilled hands together before rummaging in his scrip and producing a scrap of parchment. 'We should begin. I made copies of the first two maps last night, then added the information from Jarveaux's.'

'Why the delay?' asked Geoffrey. 'Why did you not duplicate them sooner?'

Burchard sighed. 'Is that all you are going to do? Ask questions? I had to wait for the prior to leave his office, if you must know, so I could do it without being seen. And then there was that business of Gamelo to sort out.'

'Did you find his killer?'

Burchard shook his head. 'But no one at the abbey can be responsible. We have no green hellebore at the moment, because our physician does not approve of using herbs of Saturn during February.'

'The apothecary keeps some,' said Geoffrey.

The bursar nodded. 'But he sold it all to Alice Jarveaux.'

'And what do you deduce from that?' asked Geoffrey. 'That *she* enticed Gamelo and his friends to take poison in the woods near the river that night?'

'That is for Cenred to decide. All I conclude is that I was right: Gamelo was murdered by no one at the abbey.'

It was poor reasoning: just because the abbey did not have

its own stock of green hellebore did not mean no monk had committed the crime. Geoffrey wanted to point this out, but Roger was impatient.

'Never mind that,' he said, snatching the map from Burchard and holding it next to his own to compare them. 'We can discuss Gamelo in a tavern later, when we celebrate our success. But first we should concentrate on finding the treasure. Like you, Burchard, I do not want to spend the night here.'

He and the bursar tugged and pulled at the maps, each trying to see at the expense of the other. Geoffrey did not join in the tussle. He sat on the trunk of a fallen tree and tried to rub some warmth into his wet legs.

'There is the oak,' said Burchard, pointing to a great gnarled tree that stood on a rise. It was twisted and rugged with age, and at some point during its long life, lightning had struck, cleaving it in two. Miraculously, it had survived, and the winter-bare branches that reached towards the sky seemed healthy enough. Geoffrey imagined it would be there long after he was in his grave.

'And here are the streams and the path,' said Roger, pacing towards them. 'So, the treasure lies almost halfway between them, and slightly to the north.'

'Which way is north?' asked Burchard. 'And how do we tell what is halfway?'

'Geoff,' called Roger wheedlingly, after a period in which he and Burchard strode back and forth in ever more confused directions, bumping into each other and complaining that the other was more hindrance than help. 'Work this out, will you? And then me and Burchard will do the digging.'

Geoffrey took one map from Burchard's reluctant fingers, and compared it to Roger's chart. Needless to say they were different. Comparing them, he began to pace out distances, using small sticks as markers. Roger and Burchard grew impatient, but Geoffrey refused to be hurried, knowing that a mistake in his calculations would mean wasted time later. Eventually, he pointed to the stump of an ancient beech.

'I do not think it is buried at all. I think it is hidden in that.'

'Even better,' said Burchard eagerly. 'We will not have to spend the day wielding spades.'

He reached the tree and regarded it uncertainly. It had once been massive, perhaps the tallest in the area. Its great height may have been its downfall, because at some point its roots had proved inadequate and the whole thing had toppled. Over time, its branches had rotted away, so that only the trunk remained. It stood taller than a man, leaning precariously to one side, and was thick enough so that the arms of two people with joined hands would not have circled it. The trunk was split, and it was evident that the inside had rotted away to leave a hollow.

'If the treasure is inside, there will not be much of it,' said Roger, disappointed.

'You look,' said Burchard, turning to him. 'There are snakes in this area, and I have an aversion to things that slither.'

'You should not have become a Benedictine, then,' muttered Geoffrey, although he understood Burchard's reluctance to put his hand inside the wood. The hole was a sinister dark slit that oozed fungus. Even Roger, never fussy about where he put his hands, was not keen to thrust them through the slime.

'No, thank you,' said Roger with a shudder. 'The snakes around here are dangerous, and that trunk looks exactly like the kind of place one would use as a lair.'

'I thought knights were afraid of nothing,' jeered Burchard. 'Are you frightened of God's harmless creatures?'

'Snakes are not harmless,' Roger pointed out. 'And Finchale's are beasts from Hell, possessing venom that can strike a man dead in moments.' He jerked his thumb over his shoulder to indicate the opposite river bank. 'How do you think Durnais and his man met their ends? Both put their hands inside the tree and were bitten by snakes.'

'I will look,' said Geoffrey.

Roger caught his arm in alarm. 'These are no ordinary reptiles! If you put your arm in that hole you will be struck. Let Burchard do it. The gold is for *his* abbey, after all.'

'Go on, Geoffrey,' coaxed Burchard, with sly gentleness.

'Show us you are no coward. Put your hand in the trunk and see what you can feel.'

Roger bristled at the challenge, and looked set to ignore his own advice and search the tree, just because he objected to Burchard casting aspersions on the bravery of Holy Land knights, but Geoffrey merely smiled.

'I have no intention of putting my hand inside it. There are other ways to discover its contents.'

He took his sword in both hands, and brought it down as hard as he could on the ancient bole. The wood creaked and splintered. He struck it again, shuddering to think of what it was doing to the blade, and promising to spend the evening whetting it. It was not long before the old wood split completely, allowing them to peer inside.

There was a chest, a small black pouch, and an array of spikes to protect them, each one tipped with a dark substance that had a sharp, acrid smell, and that was undoubtedly poison.

Thirteen

Geoffrey, Roger, and Burchard stood silently around the shattered tree trunk. Anyone putting a hand inside it would certainly have cut himself, and Geoffrey suspected that the dark substance coating the spikes had been put there for the express purpose of repelling would-be thieves. He knew little of poisons, but the stench indicated this was a powerful one. Burchard crossed himself when he realized the danger they had been in. Roger, more curious than cautious, stretched out his hand as if he were going to poke one. Geoffrey slapped it away.

'Touch those and it will probably be the last thing you do.'

'But such a device means that anyone who puts their hand inside the trunk to retrieve the treasure would be killed,' said Roger, open-mouthed in horror.

'Quite. It seems your father did not want just anyone to take possession of his ill-gotten gains.'

'But the men most likely to come are his three chosen agents. Why would he harm them?'

Geoffrey sighed. 'He does not care. If all three men – prior, sheriff, and goldsmith – came together to collect the treasure as he instructed, then the first to put his hand inside the tree would die. The other two would be terrified into following his instructions – who would want to keep treasure that might prove fatal? Moreover, if one of the three disobeyed Flambard and came alone, then he would die without question. That, I imagine, is what happened to Durnais.'

He crouched down to inspect the spikes more closely, and pointed to a small thread that had caught on one of the barbs, then at several dark spots that had dripped on to the decaying wood.

'Here is blood, suggesting that someone has already injured himself, and the thread caught here is yellow. The sheriff's servant wore a yellow jerkin.'

'We found Pike on the other side of the river,' Roger explained to Burchard. 'He must have put his hand inside the tree and was poisoned for his pains. But what happened to the sheriff?'

'Perhaps he did not realize Pike had been poisoned,' suggested Geoffrey. 'Perhaps he thought he would not be harmed if he took more care. Doubtless Pike shoved his hand inside the tree very eagerly, wanting to see what it held.'

'That makes sense,' said Roger. 'While Pike crossed the river in a desperate bid for life, Durnais eased his own hand inside the tree. But the poison got him, too, because I saw the mark on his hand.'

'But it was not as deep as the one on Pike, and so less poison entered the wound,' said Geoffrey. 'He probably drowned when the toxin took effect and he found himself unable to struggle free of it.'

'Nasty!' said Burchard with a shudder. 'But enough chatter. Let us open this chest. This place makes me feel uneasy, and I want to be away from it as soon as possible.'

'Uneasy in what respect?' asked Geoffrey, looking around.

'Nothing specific,' said Burchard. 'But on my way here, I sensed I was being followed. I hid in bushes several times and heard nothing. I just put it down to excitement and nervousness – after all, I was about to confront you. Come on. Help me with this.'

Using his sword, Roger levered the box away from the treacherous spears, then hauled it a considerable distance, as if he imagined the poison might still affect him if he remained too close.

'It is heavy,' he said gleefully.

Burchard grinned at him. 'Then this will be a great day for the abbey – and the cathedral.'

While they discussed how to open the chest, Geoffrey concentrated on the black pouch. He donned his gauntlets to open it, and saw his precautions were not in vain. There were tiny pins at the neck of the bag, each one stained with black.

Whether it would prove fatal in such small amounts Geoffrey did not care to find out, but was glad he had been careful.

Inside the pouch were two pieces of parchment. One was yet another map, depicting not Finchale, but the cathedral: each flagstone in the Chapel of the Nine Altars was marked with great precision, and there was a cross on one of them. Another treasure trove? Geoffrey wondered. The second document was longer, with minute writing conveying a good deal of information. While Roger and Burchard argued about how best to break the two locks that protected the chest, Geoffrey went to a nearby rock and perched on it, smoothing out the parchment on his knee. He began to read.

It was divided into sections, each headed by the name of a local merchant or nobleman. The first on the list was Haymo Stanstede. The paragraph below his name described how he had been tried for murder in a court presided over by Sheriff Durnais. The account suggested there were witnesses to prove Stanstede had indeed committed the crime, but the verdict had been not guilty. The reason for this, the scroll stated, was the sum of twenty pounds, which had been paid by Stanstede to Durnais. Geoffrey's thoughts whirled. Was it true? Had a favourable verdict really been secured by a bribe?

Puzzled, he read on. Under the next name, the apothecary's, was a statement that the death of one Bertha Kepler three years before had been due to bad medicine, not a falling sickness as attested by the physician. There followed the names of three men who would swear under oath they had witnessed the apothecary pay the physician to hide the truth.

And so it went on. Several merchants were accused of having affairs with each others' wives, another was said to dabble in the black arts. The abbey sacristan was a felon, who had assumed a new identity to evade justice. Burchard's extortion activities were exposed, as was the fact that Hemming liked illegal cock fights, while Turgot had broken his vow of chastity with a nun called Sister Hilde. Minor noblemen were associated with misdemeanours that included cowardice in battle, treason, and a whole range of dishonest crimes. Each entry stated the case against the person, and concluded with a list of evidence or witnesses that would prove the validity of the accusation.

But what was such a document doing in the tree? Geoffrey continued to stare at it. The parchment was of high quality, and he was fairly certain it came from the same source as Flambard's maps. So, the list of accusations and the maps had probably been drawn up by the same person. Therefore, Geoffrey surmised that the author of the scroll was Flambard.

How had the bishop come by such information? Geoffrey knew the answer to that: he was notorious for hiring spies and informants, and these had apparently been working to build cases against many influential people in the county. Geoffrey could only assume he intended to use the information to accrue more power, and to force the people mentioned to support him when he demanded.

He rolled up the parchment when it occurred to him that speculating would be more pleasant in front of a fire than perched on a snow-covered rock at Finchale. He was about to put it inside his surcoat when he reconsidered. It had probably not been soaked in poison, but he did not want it too near him regardless. He shoved it down the scabbard of his sword.

'Was Stanstede ever tried for murder?' he asked, walking to where Roger and Burchard still wrestled with the chest. They had succeeded in forcing the first lock, and were busy with the second.

'Last summer,' said Burchard. 'But he was found innocent.'

'My sister's husband was a murderer?' asked Roger, horrified. 'No one has mentioned this before.'

'That is because folk are afraid of you,' said Burchard, which seemed reasonable to Geoffrey, given Roger's reputation as 'the Devil'. 'But Stanstede was acquitted.'

'Was it a good verdict?' asked Geoffrey. 'Or was there doubt?'

'There *was* doubt,' said Burchard. 'How he managed to convince Durnais is beyond me. He killed an apprentice who had been drinking and was pestering the brothel women. The boy would not leave, so Stanstede knifed him.'

291

'Perhaps he had a weapon, and Stanstede acted in self-defence,' suggested Roger.

'The brothel was busy that night. The lad was a nuisance and Stanstede did not want to waste time persuading him to leave. After he stabbed him, he ordered the body dumped in the woods.'

'You seem very sure about all this,' said Geoffrey. 'Can I assume you are an eyewitness?'

'No, you cannot!' declared Burchard, blushing so furiously Geoffrey was certain he was lying. 'I am a monk, who has sworn a vow of chastity.'

'I do not care why you were there,' said Geoffrey. 'But your account has a ring of authenticity. I think you saw it happen.'

'All right,' acknowledged Burchard irritably. 'I was there – but I was hunting errant novices, and was not there for personal pleasure. Why are you asking? The trial was months ago.'

'Was there a woman called Bertha Kepler, who died from a falling sickness?' asked Geoffrey, answering with another question.

'I remember her,' said Roger, looking up from where he was attacking the lock with a stone. 'The apothecary was accused of poisoning her by mistake, but the physician said no.'

'And Hemming?' asked Geoffrey finally. 'Is he the kind of man to frequent cock fights?'

Burchard nodded spitefully. 'The abbey does not approve of gambling, and Hemming has been warned on several occasions to take up a more godly pastime.'

Geoffrey rubbed the bridge of his nose. So, Flambard's accusations may have a basis in fact. Burchard's expression was questioning, but Geoffrey did not want to tell him about the list and let the man destroy lives in a frenzy of self-righteous bigotry. Then Roger issued a triumphant cry as the second lock shattered, and Burchard's attention snapped back to it. Breathless with excitement, Roger opened the lid, and all three men leaned forward to see what Flambard's chest contained.

'There is nothing here!' wailed Burchard, gazing down at

Flambard's treasure chest in dismay. 'At least, nothing but clipped silver pennies!'

'You are right; there cannot be more than five pounds here at the most,' said Roger, bitterly disappointed. 'When my father said he had treasure, I expected *treasure* – not a box of coin fragments that have been divided so many times for small change they are all but worthless.'

'These will not even pay for the flagstones in the new cloister,' bemoaned Burchard, taking a handful and letting them trickle through his fingers like sand. 'I have been exposed to evil, wickedness and murder for a box of coins so defaced that no sane builder will accept them as wages!'

'There are old dies in here, too,' said Roger glumly, picking up a weighty metal cast. 'From my father's own mint. No wonder the chest was heavy. What could he have been thinking of, making all that fuss over this?'

'Are you sure there is nothing underneath them?' asked Geoffrey, as startled as the others. Unlike them, however, he derived a degree of amusement from the fact that Flambard's fabled treasure did not exist. Roger might see the humour of the situation in time, but he suspected Burchard never would.

They dug their hands into the coins and felt around. Burchard even took Roger's dagger and poked in the lid, to see whether a false panel might yield something more profitable. But Flambard's chest was exactly what it appeared – a stout box half-filled with mutilated coins and out-of-date dies. When he said he had taken a percentage of the taxes raised from the people, he had done exactly that: most folk were poor, and the revenues they paid were minimal. Flambard had siphoned off a few clippings here and there, and that was his treasure.

'Nothing!' spat Burchard, giving the chest a solid kick. It hurt him more than it damaged the box, and he hobbled in a tight circle, swearing at the agony of stubbed toes.

'That is because Sir Geoffrey has the real treasure in his scabbard,' came a voice from behind them.

Geoffrey, Roger and Burchard wheeled around, the knights reaching for their weapons.

'No!' barked Hemming sharply. 'Leave your swords where they are. If you make any hostile movement, you will be shot.'

Flanking Hemming were three heavy-set men, all armed with bows. Unlike Brother Gamelo, these men handled their weapons with confidence, suggesting they knew how to use them. Geoffrey moved his hands away from his sword and raised them in the air. Roger did likewise.

'What are you doing here?' Burchard asked, gaping stupidly at his sub-prior.

'You mentioned what you were doing, so I decided to join you,' said Hemming. 'Where treasure is concerned, it is never wise to trust a Norman to do the right thing.'

'Well, you have wasted your time,' said Burchard. 'Flambard's loot contains nothing but mangled pennies. Look for yourself.'

'I have no need to look,' said Hemming, leaning against a tree and folding his arms. 'I have been watching you for some time now. I know exactly what the chest contains.'

'So, what do you want, then?' demanded Roger, angry at being held at bow-point. 'You have no need to threaten us: we have done nothing to warrant this sort of treatment.'

'Really?' asked Hemming softly. 'You come to Durham with Flambard's map, make a pretence at passing it to the prior, then spend the next few days making your own enquiries so you can claim the treasure for yourselves – and you think you have done nothing untoward?'

'It was not like that,' objected Roger. 'Turgot forced us into it. We do not want the treasure.'

'Really,' said Hemming coldly. 'Then why are you here?'

'So we can take what we find to Turgot,' said Roger, all the more indignant because his motives really had been honourable. 'We do not want these pennies.'

'As I have already told you,' said Hemming. 'I suspect the real treasure lies in the parchment Geoffrey hid in his scabbard.'

'What parchment?' demanded Burchard. He glanced back at the tree. 'Do you mean whatever was in that pouch? I wondered what he was doing so quiet and secretive while

Roger and I struggled here. He was stealing the real treasure, was he?'

'What makes you think it was treasure?' asked Geoffrey, wondering what Hemming thought he had found.

'I am not stupid,' said Hemming impatiently. 'I know why you asked about Stanstede's trial and Bertha Kepler's death. That parchment contains information about them – and other things.'

'What do you mean?' demanded Burchard. 'How could that be considered treasure?'

But Geoffrey understood, and the answers to various questions became clear. He forced himself to appear relaxed, hoping to draw Hemming into a conversation that would allow him to test his solutions, and at the same time lull the archers into feeling secure until he could act. His chain mail was no match for arrows, and there was no point in trying anything while they were alert and watchful.

'Flambard intends to blackmail the wealthiest people in the shire,' he said. 'Stanstede bought his favourable verdict from the sheriff: doubtless he would have paid handsomely to keep it from public knowledge.'

'And Durnais would have paid just as handsomely to prevent anyone knowing he had taken a bribe,' said Hemming. 'That document will provide ample funding for the abbey over time. When we run out, all we will need do is decide who to approach next.'

'That is clever,' said Burchard approvingly. 'I have personal experience in raising funds by this sort of means. I expect I shall be the one to implement Flambard's plan.'

'I do not think so,' said Hemming, as Burchard started to walk towards him, happily confident. 'You are not the sort of man I want in my abbey.'

'Your abbey?' echoed Burchard, stopping dead. 'Turgot will have something to say about that!'

'He will not,' said Hemming. 'Once Flambard learns how Turgot almost let the treasure slip through his fingers, he will be removed and the post given to a man of superior talents. I am better than him in all respects. I guessed what Flambard planned to do long before these knights arrived.'

'How?' asked Geoffrey curiously. 'Did he tell you?'

'He did not need to. He is determined to have the cathedral built, and a crafty man like him would not let prison stand in the way of his ambitions. I went with Turgot to visit him in the White Tower, and I guessed then he had something hidden away for us.'

Once Geoffrey learned that Hemming had suspected the existence of treasure before Flambard's escape, other things became clear. '*You* hired Brother Gamelo! You were shocked to see him dead – almost to the point of swooning – not because you have an aversion to violence, as you claimed, but because you were appalled by the death of a man so useful to you.'

'Hemming? An aversion to violence?' asked Burchard in disbelief. 'But he has a penchant for cock fights.' Geoffrey already knew this, because it had been written in Flambard's document.

'I was shocked to see Gamelo dead,' admitted Hemming. 'And he was useful.'

'But he was a Norman!' exclaimed Burchard. 'I thought you despised us all. And anyway, he was *my* man, my most assiduous rent collector.'

'Being Norman, he was not averse to dirtying his hands with theft and murder, too,' said Hemming. 'He sold his services to anyone who paid him. He even worked for Turgot on occasion, to carry messages to his lover. But I would like to know who killed him.'

'When Turgot ordered Algar to investigate Gamelo's death, you offered him advice,' said Geoffrey, recalling Hemming lingering to speak to the anxious secretary. 'You were not being kind to a man who had been given a task he did not know how to complete; you really wanted him to be successful.'

'Does this mean you hired Brother Gamelo to follow us in Southampton?' asked Roger, bewildered.

'He was ordered to watch anyone who visited Flambard in prison,' replied Hemming. 'When Flambard escaped, he followed him to Southampton. He overheard the three Hospitallers plotting, and knew about the maps. He killed the youngest in the hope that *he* himself would be appointed as the third courier, but then you arrived.'

'We witnessed the murder of Gilbert Courcy,' said Roger coldly. 'And Gamelo killed that witless lad – Peterkin – with his red-stained arrows.'

'That was Gamelo's attempt to make you refuse Flambard's quest,' said Hemming. 'He assumed you would be reluctant to go north when men were dying with unusual arrows embedded in them.'

But Gamelo had not anticipated Roger's willingness to serve his father, thought Geoffrey. The scarlet bolts had warned them to be alert, but had not made Roger think twice about helping Flambard.

'Gamelo was afraid of you,' continued Hemming. 'He said that coming with me to Jarveaux's house to make sure Burchard did not run off with the missing map was the last thing he would do for me. Unfortunately, someone ensured that was true.'

'But not you?' asked Geoffrey.

Hemming shook his head. 'Obedient men are hard to come by. I would not have harmed Gamelo.'

'Did you poison Jarveaux's oysters?'

Hemming raised his eyebrows. 'Is that what happened to him? Well, do not blame me for that. I am no poisoner.'

'But you strangle,' said Geoffrey quietly. 'You killed Xavier. And I know how and why.'

'Do you indeed?' asked Hemming harshly. 'Well, I am not interested in your nasty speculations. Give me that parchment. If you refuse, you will be shot and I will take it from your corpse. It is your choice.'

'You will kill us anyway,' said Geoffrey, making no move to comply. 'Why should we make matters easier for you?'

'We do not need to slay them,' said Burchard generously. 'We can take them back to the abbey and let Flambard decide what to do. After all, it was his treasure they tried to steal.'

'Now just a moment,' objected Roger, addressing Burchard angrily. 'We had an agreement. You are on our side, not his.'

'Circumstances have changed,' said Burchard archly. 'And I am trying to save your skin, so you will keep quiet if you have any sense.' He appealed to Hemming. 'There is no need for bloodshed.'

'Are you asking me to spare them?' asked Hemming, amused. 'You never fail to astonish me, Burchard. I thought you were just an insensitive oaf, and now I learn you are capable of compassion.'

Burchard glared at him. 'I cannot stand by and watch men slaughtered.'

Hemming laughed. 'You are deluded, my friend! Do you think we will shoot these men, then saunter back to the abbey together with Flambard's pennies? We will not, because you will die with them.'

'Me?' exclaimed Burchard, appalled. 'But we have known each other for years.'

'Quite,' said Hemming dryly.

So, Roger had been right after all, thought Geoffrey, watching Burchard gape at Hemming. He *had* seen Hemming move towards Burchard with murderous intent at Jarveaux's house. Hemming had lied when he said he was going to toss Burchard his knife to free his sleeve. And on reflection, Geoffrey saw he had been foolish to believe him. It had been dark. How could Hemming have seen Burchard's sleeve? Hemming had devised his excuse later, when he saw the rip in Burchard's habit.

'But I do not understand!' wailed Burchard. One of the archers raised his bow. 'Wait! Perhaps we can come to some arrangement.'

'I want nothing from you,' said Hemming in disdain. 'You Normans think you can buy anything with your filthy money. Well you cannot buy Saxon honour.'

'Is that what this is about?' asked Geoffrey. 'Saxon honour?'

'What else? The Normans marched into Durham, dissolved the ancient Church of St Cuthbert, and established their abbey in its place. We are the Haliwerfolc – Cuthbert's chosen. What right do you have to displace us?' Geoffrey's heart sank when he saw the fanaticism in the man's eyes. There was no reasoning with a zealot. 'I have plans for this money, and they do not involve Normans. I intend to build a new

298

shrine – a Saxon shrine – for Cuthbert on the Holy Island of Lindisfarne.'

'You plan to take him from Durham?' asked Roger, aghast. 'But he will not like it!'

'He does not want to stay here,' argued Hemming. 'Why do you think the foundations of the cathedral keep cracking?'

'Unstable bedrock?' suggested Geoffrey.

Hemming glared at him. 'That is a typical Norman response! You mock our Saxon saints and their wishes. Well, not for much longer. I will take this list, and use it to raise money for a beautiful Saxon shrine. Now, if you do not hand it to me by the time I count to three, Roger dies. One . . . two . . .'

Geoffrey moved his hand towards his scabbard. Two of the three archers had their bows trained on him, and he knew he would not be able to draw his weapon and rush them before they shot him down. Such an act would be futile in the extreme.

'. . . three,' said Hemming. 'Your time is up.'

'It has slipped,' said Geoffrey, shaking the scabbard. 'If you want it, I will have to draw my sword.'

Hemming smiled. 'Nice try. Put your hands in the air. One of my men will remove it.'

Obediently, an archer stepped forward, slinging his bow over his shoulder, while the remaining two kept their weapons trained on Geoffrey, Roger and Burchard. When the man reached for the sword, Geoffrey stepped behind him, so he formed a human shield. As the man extracted the weapon, the parchment caught on the blade and fluttered to the ground. All eyes were fixed on it.

Hemming shouted a warning to his archer at the same moment that Geoffrey dropped to one knee, reaching for the dagger that was tucked in his boot. He snatched it out and stabbed the man in one swift, decisive movement. Too late, the man tried to duck away, but his grimace of pain turned to shock when an arrow fired by one of his colleagues thudded into his back. Geoffrey hurled his dagger at the others. The

299

throw went wide, but it was enough to make one drop his weapon in alarm.

Roger acted quickly. Snatching up a handful of snow, he dashed it into Hemming's face, then raced at the surviving archers with a roar that reverberated around the desolate countryside. Both were too shocked by the speed of the attack to do more than turn to face him before they were bowled over. One snatched up a sword as he scrambled to his feet. With a diabolical smile, Roger drew his own and prepared to make a swift end to him. Geoffrey headed for his colleague.

'Please do not kill me!' the archer shrieked before Geoffrey had done no more than take a few steps in his direction.

'Do not blubber, John,' howled Hemming, rubbing the snow from his eyes. 'Fight him!'

'But I do not have a sword,' wailed John in terror.

'Shoot him, then,' yelled Hemming in furious desperation. 'Call yourself a Saxon? Use your—'

His words stopped abruptly as Burchard swung a hefty punch that connected with his chin and sent him reeling back on to the stump of the beech tree. Trusting the bursar to cope with Hemming, Geoffrey turned his attention to the frightened archer.

John, however, had taken the opportunity afforded by the distraction to grab a sword. An innate sense of preservation warned Geoffrey to duck, and the blow sailed clean over his head.

'Oh, no!' muttered John, seeing it would have been better had he just surrendered. The look in Geoffrey's eye told him his wild swing had not earned him any favours.

'Who are you?' Geoffrey asked, holding his own sword loosely in both hands. To anyone who did not know him, he appeared unready for an attack. 'Are you a monk?'

'A soldier from the castle. Brother Gamelo hired us.'

John misread Geoffrey's relaxed posture and lunged. Geoffrey parried the blow easily, sending him staggering back. John, it seemed, was better with a bow than a sword.

'You will die if you continue to fight,' warned Geoffrey. 'So, surrender.'

'If I disarm, you will kill me for certain,' said John, licking

300

dry lips. 'And anyway, Hemming told me I am too deeply involved now. The only way to escape will be if you all die. That is what he said.'

'He is preying on your fears,' said Geoffrey, side-stepping as John made another clumsy swipe and giving him a deft kick so he stumbled to his knees. Geoffrey could have killed him then, as he knelt on the ground, but he did not. 'What have you done that is so terrible?'

'Murder,' said John unsteadily, scrambling to his feet and turning to face Geoffrey. 'An old man.'

'Stanstede?' asked Geoffrey. 'You shot him, did you?'

John nodded, his face white and strained. 'Hemming should have let us kill you while we had you in our sights, and there would have been none of this messing around. The Littel brothers said we should not underestimate you. I told Hemming so, but he would not listen. He says all Crusaders are stupid, bloodlusting louts.'

'For the most part, he is right,' said Geoffrey. More facts clicked into place in his mind, now that he knew some of Gamelo's men came from the castle. 'Hemming came to Finchale a few days ago, did he not? He met Durnais here, but the sheriff and his servant both died from putting their hands inside the tree, and Hemming was left not knowing what to do.'

'A week ago,' acknowledged John, wiping sweat from his eyes. 'He paid me five shillings to find out where Durnais had gone. Pike's mother told me they had come here. They had been digging for buried treasure. You cannot see it now, with all the snow, but they made a terrible mess.'

'Then what?'

'Hemming had copied two maps owned by Turgot, and worked out that the treasure was in the tree. Durnais said we could all share it, but I do not think Hemming was interested in sharing. Durnais was not quite sane from his digging, and was ready to believe anything. We stood around the tree, and I told Pike that there might be a snake in it, but he was mazed, too. He shoved his hand in the trunk and screamed when something bit him. Durnais pushed him out of the way,

301

so he could try himself. He was more careful, but the snake had him, anyway.'

'And they both died.'

'Not immediately, but in hours. Durnais blundered off, and we found him drowned in the river. Hemming ordered *me* to look inside the tree, but I refused.'

'Very wise,' said Geoffrey. 'And since no one dared investigate further, you all decided to go home and try again later. As you reached the main road, thinking it would be empty so near dusk, you met others using it – Stanstede and his companions.'

John nodded again. 'He saw us. The women and the grooms were too engrossed in their singing to look into bushes at the side of the road. But Stanstede was not, and he saw us . . .'

'So you shot him,' said Geoffrey. 'Because he recognized you.'

John's hands were unsteady and his face was white. 'It was only a matter of time before Durnais was found, then Stanstede would have remembered who he had seen: he would have told everyone *I* had done it.'

'Did you kill the Knight Hospitaller and his squire, too?' asked Geoffrey.

'They came after us, and the knight recognized Hemming from the abbey. He said he had been to Chester-le-Street looking for Durnais, whom he believed was going to steal the treasure. Hemming hit him on the head with a stone. I shot the squire when he tried to run for help.'

'But Xavier was wearing a helmet,' said Geoffrey, recalling the dent in the man's bassinet. 'And the blow only stunned him.'

'Hemming strangled him as he lay on the ground,' John whispered. 'Then he ordered us to shoot the body, so it would look like outlaws had killed him, but we refused. He did it himself, but he had never fired an arrow before, and his shot was weak.'

And that explained why the arrow had barely penetrated Xavier's armour, Geoffrey thought. An experienced archer would have driven the shaft deep into the knight's chest, but Hemming's feeble attempts to master archery under pressure had resulted in the superficial wound that had alerted Geoffrey to the odd nature of Xavier's death in the first place.

'Geoffrey,' called Burchard. 'Stop dancing around with that Saxon peasant and come here.'

'Put down your weapon,' said Geoffrey to John, ignoring Burchard's peremptory command. 'I have had enough of this, and I do not want to kill you.'

John declined, so Geoffrey charged at him and sent the weapon skittering from his hand. Then he grabbed his arm and hauled him over to where Roger had made short work of his opponent, and hovered near the bursar.

'I have just heard Hemming's last confession,' said Burchard, glancing around at him. 'He fell on the poisoned barbs when we were fighting, and will die like the sheriff.'

Hemming was indeed dying. He lay on his back while the poison coursed through his veins, gradually depriving him of his senses. First he complained he could not feel his legs, then he lost all sensation in his hands, and gradually breathing became difficult. He said he could no longer see, and his mind began to wander between recent happenings and events from years ago. His ramblings became increasingly incoherent as time passed, although some of his mumbling confirmed John's story. Geoffrey and Roger moved away, so they could talk without being overheard by Burchard.

'What a waste,' Roger said to Geoffrey in disgust, as the sounds of Hemming's laboured breathing filled the clearing. 'The hoard was worthless, but it caused so many deaths. I cannot say I will grieve for the likes of Hemming and Weasel, but they should have died for treasure worth having.'

'As Hemming said, the real value of Flambard's "treasure" lies in the information contained in this document,' said Geoffrey, staring at the parchment in his hand. 'There is a fortune to be made in extortion money, and Flambard knew Turgot, Burchard and Hemming were the kind of men to know how to reel it in.'

'But they were on the blackmail list, too,' said Roger,

303

bemused. 'They would have been victims, just as much as the apothecary or Stanstede.'

Geoffrey rubbed his head, wondering whether it was his question about Hemming's liking for cock fights that had forced him to act. Perhaps if he had not been mentioned on Flambard's list, the sub-prior would have allowed them to go home, to tell Turgot that Flambard's treasure comprised clipped pennies and a scroll to blackmail local dignitaries. And then Hemming would still be alive and so would two of his men.

'So, who are the villains in this?' asked Roger tiredly. 'I am confused.'

So was Geoffrey, and it was good to go through what had happened, to clarify matters in his own mind. 'Jarveaux's map was delivered first, by Xavier. Instead of immediately visiting sheriff and prior, Jarveaux kept it in his house. I think Burchard was right: he was going to wait until he had seen and noted the information given to the others and then go to Finchale alone.'

'What makes you so sure?'

'He had ordered horses for the day Eleanor and I went to visit Alice,' said Geoffrey. 'She was angry because the groom forced her to pay, even though they were not going to be used.'

'But Jarveaux was dead by then. How could he have used horses if he were dead?'

'Because he expected to be alive – and to be in a position to look for the treasure himself.'

Roger sighed. 'All right. So much for Jarveaux. The second man to get his map was Durnais, delivered by Odard.'

Geoffrey nodded. 'Flambard chose his messengers well. You, Xavier and Odard all did exactly what you were instructed to do, and none of you tried to look for the treasure yourselves.'

'Aye,' agreed Roger. 'We are all honest men. It is a pity the recipients were not of like mind.'

'But Odard was not as trusting as Xavier. He suspected Durnais would look for the treasure – we know Durnais took bribes for the legal cases he heard, so Odard probably knew he was not an honest man. He decided to set up a test. He forged a map and waited to see what would happen. Durnais left at first light, according to Ida the Witch, while Odard was still sleeping. He probably did not anticipate the sheriff would snatch the opportunity quite so quickly.'

'So, why did Xavier go to Chester-le-Street when Odard's false map sent Durnais to Finchale?'

'Because Xavier and Odard travelled separately to Durham and did not meet once they arrived. Both knew what they were doing was dangerous, and neither loitered in the city once they had fulfilled their missions. Xavier would not have known that Odard had sent Durnais on a wild goose chase to Finchale, and would have listened to the story originating with the sheriff himself: that he had gone to Chester-le-Street.'

'Meanwhile, Durnais and Pike stayed here for a week, digging and driving themselves insane with dreams of gold.' Roger seemed oblivious to the fact that he also liked such visions.

'Durnais must have been desperate, thinking he would never find it. When Hemming arrived with the other two maps, he willingly agreed to share, and together they established that Flambard had hidden his hoard in the beech tree. Pike died first, and Durnais next, believing they had been bitten by snakes. Hemming lost heart, and returned to the Durham road with his men. There they encountered Stanstede and Xavier.'

'Knowing Xavier would later connect Durnais' corpse with Hemming's appearance nearby, Hemming killed him. What are you going to do with that?' Roger pointed to the scroll Geoffrey still held.

'I do not think the prior should have it,' said Geoffrey. 'We do not want to be held responsible for half the county being blackmailed by the abbey. We should destroy it.'

'Give it to me, then,' said Roger. He struck a tinder, and allowed the flame to devour the scroll. There was a strangled cry from the other side of the clearing, and Geoffrey saw that Hemming was still conscious enough to understand what they had done. Burchard did not object. He met Roger's eyes, nodded briefly, and turned his attention back to the dying man.

'Enough harm has been caused already,' he said. 'It is better this way.'

'Better for him,' muttered Roger, dropping the blazing text into the snow, where it twisted and blackened as the flames consumed it. 'He was on that list, too.'

Since they could not move Hemming, they were obliged to wait until he died before they could return to Durham. They carried his body across the river and buried it with Pike and the two archers in a snowdrift, marking the temporary grave so someone could come back for them later.

It took much longer to return to Durham than it had to reach Finchale. Thick clouds made the afternoon gloomy and brought an early dusk that rendered the way treacherous, and all of them were tired. Burchard was silent, and even Roger seemed to have run out of questions, his mind fixed on trying to find the best way to carry the chest of pennies with John.

When they rounded the bend in the river that brought the grey towers of Durham into sight, Geoffrey's legs ached from the effort of repeatedly planting one foot in knee-deep snow and trying to extricate the other. How Roger had managed to carry the chest, too, was beyond his imagination, and he could only assume the big knight possessed special reserves of strength and energy to be deployed specifically for the transportation of loot.

They reached the city, where walking became easier. Roger spotted the Littel brothers on their way to relieve Freyn and Tilloy from guarding Eleanor's house, and ordered them to carry the coins. Burchard, loath to let even a paltry trove out of his sight, stuck close to them.

'We found out about that pig,' said the younger brother to Geoffrey, as they walked awkwardly up the street, lugging the chest between them.

'What pig?' asked Geoffrey, too weary to be very interested.

Littel was offended that Geoffrey had forgotten the task he had set them. 'You told us to find out whether Simon's pig had been killed.'

'Oh, that,' said Geoffrey, recalling that he believed Simon and the pig were enjoying each other's company in a tavern where the landlord did not mind that sort of thing.

'It was slaughtered,' said the older Littel, pleased to see that his announcement took Geoffrey by surprise. 'The word is that one butcher was paid handsomely to do away with it in secret, and that it has been gracing someone's pantries for quite a while now.'

'Whose?' asked Geoffrey. Eleanor had been wrong. She claimed she would hear if someone had harmed the pig, but because the butcher had been paid for his silence, the pig's demise was not common knowledge. The fact was revealing, and Geoffrey supposed that whoever had slaughtered the animal would also know what had happened to Simon. Of course, Simon may have ordered it killed himself, believing that its disappearance might serve to protect him.

'The butcher is away at the moment,' came the disappointing reply. 'But he is due home soon, and we will ask him then.'

Geoffrey was about to reply, when he saw Cenred walking towards them, a group of soldiers at his heels. The under-sheriff stopped when he saw John, bedraggled and sullen next to Roger.

'Where have you been?' he demanded. 'I was told you had deserted. I hope that is not true.'

John hung his head.

'He has been serving two masters: you and Hemming,' said Roger. 'He has something to say about the attack on Stanstede that you may find interesting, too.'

'Escort him to my office,' said Cenred to his men. When they had gone, he regarded the knights coldly. 'I find it disconcerting that the moment you two arrive in my city people die. First there were Stanstede, Xavier, and the squire; then a bowman died on Eleanor's table; then Simon goes missing; Durnais and Pike disappear; Gamelo and two lay brothers were murdered—'

'It is nothing to do with us,' objected Roger. 'We are innocent—'

'—and finally, there is Mother Petra,' finished Cenred.

307

'My great-grandmother?' asked Roger, startled. 'She is dead? But she was alive the other day.'

'Well, she is not alive now,' said Cenred. 'Still, that is probably a blessing. I was on the verge of arresting her for murder.'

'Murder?' echoed Roger, aghast. 'But she was an old lady! How could she murder anyone?'

'With hellebore,' said Cenred. 'She sent Alice to the apothecary – twice – to purchase some. She was a witch, so she knew how to use powders to kill – and she used some in her son's oysters.'

'Jarveaux's house has rats,' said Geoffrey. 'The hellebore was supposed to be for them. How can you be sure *she* poisoned the oysters? It might have been Alice, who was delighted by his demise.'

Cenred gave a humourless smile. 'I heard you and Alice do not like each other. But I must disappoint you. Alice bought the hellebore, but she is innocent of her husband's death. I have sworn testaments from three cooks who saw Mother Petra doctoring the oysters with grey powder. And every servant in the house assures me that Alice never went near Jarveaux's food – ever.'

'And you believe them?' asked Geoffrey doubtfully.

Cenred nodded. 'Alice did not love her husband and refused to prepare foods he liked, so Mother Petra did it. I suspected the old lady from the start, although I had to bide my time to prove it. She was a witch, and her servants were afraid she would cast a spell on them if they betrayed her. Now she is dead they are ready to be honest.'

'How did Mother Petra die? She was not murdered, too, was she?'

'Thankfully not,' said Cenred. 'I have had my fill of those for now. She drank too much of that wine she keeps bubbling over the fire and fell asleep. The fire went out and there is a hole in the solar window. The room cooled down and she failed to wake up. That happens to old people.'

It seemed an extraordinarily banal way for the charismatic old woman to die, and not at all what Geoffrey would have expected from a witch. She was the kind of person to have been consumed by fire, or to have taken a dose of her own hellebore, not slipped away in a pleasantly drunken slumber.

'I examined her body carefully, and so did the abbey's physician,' said Cenred, as if reading his mind. 'There was no sign she had taken poison. Last night, she ordered more wine from the vintner, and was clearly intending to live to drink it. She did not kill herself.'

'Green hellebore killed Gamelo and his cronies,' said Geoffrey. 'Did she dispatch them too?'

Cenred nodded. 'I checked with the apothecary, and she was the only one in the city who possessed the stuff – he sold her all of it. She used the first lot to kill Jarveaux and the second to kill Gamelo.'

'Gamelo knew her,' said Geoffrey. 'She said she charmed his arrows for him.'

Had Geoffrey's questions led her to kill Gamelo? At first, he could not see why they should, then he thought about her relatives. She was Flambard's grandmother, and Gamelo was interfering with Flambard's plans. He suggested as much to Cenred.

'I agree,' he said, after a long pause during which Geoffrey thought he might dismiss the notion as improbable. 'But the question then becomes why would Gamelo accept poison from her in the first place? According to the physician, Gamelo died during the night. Why would he drink poison given to him by a witch at midnight?'

'Because he was a superstitious man, who believed in the power of witchcraft. His body was found on the Elvet side of the river, where Mother Petra lives. She must have met him and his cronies and offered them something to eat or drink that she claimed was good for them.'

'Good for her, more like,' said Cenred. 'Again, you are probably right. Alice told me Mother Petra had seen men struggling in the snow the night she was burgled. Doubtless she recognized Gamelo and exacted her own justice.'

Geoffrey nodded agreement. 'We have found Flambard's treasure,' he said, indicating the chest.

Cenred's eyebrows rose. 'That should please Turgot. It is a pity Durnais is not here to see it.'

Geoffrey knew Turgot would not have seen it at all had Durnais set eyes on it first, but said nothing. He told the Littel brothers to unlatch the lid and show Cenred the mess of silver fragments.

'Is that it?' asked Cenred, bemused. Gradually a grin split his porcine features, and then he broke into a genuine full-bellied laugh. 'I knew the cathedral's finances were shaky, but I did not realize they were that desperate.'

Geoffrey smiled. 'Every little will help.'

He led the way up the winding path towards the abbey. Turgot saw them coming, and hurried to escort them and the heavy box into his house, where he listened white-faced to the bursar's account of what had happened.

'So, there never was any treasure?' he asked. 'Just this chest of rubbish?'

Burchard nodded. 'And a worthless scrap of parchment containing scurrilous, unfounded gossip. We consigned that to the flames before it did any harm.'

'You burned a document Flambard intended for me?' asked the prior, aghast. 'What turned you squeamish all of a sudden? Hemming told me how *you* raise money yesterday. I was very shocked.'

'I am sure you were,' said Burchard sarcastically. 'But you have your informants, just as Hemming had his and I have mine. You knew the truth.'

'How dare you! And how dare you destroy property—'

'You would not want anyone to read what was written under your name,' interrupted Geoffrey, to prevent a row between the two men. 'Burchard's activities are common knowledge, so he had nothing to lose by burning the parchment. You, however, are a different matter.'

Turgot stared at him from under his bushy eyebrows. 'Me?'

'I did not know about that,' said Burchard, sounding annoyed with himself. 'What did it say? I heard what you said about Hemming and his cock fights.'

'Then it is better no more is said about it,' said Geoffrey.

'It was about a woman called Sister—' began Roger, before Geoffrey could stop him.

'Oh,' said Turgot, interrupting hastily. 'That.'

310

'There is one more thing,' said Geoffrey, standing to leave. He reached inside his surcoat. 'The pouch with the scroll also contained this. It is a plan of the cathedral with a cross marked on the Chapel of the Nine Altars.'

'Then the treasure will be there,' concluded Burchard eagerly. 'The pennies were just a ruse, to distract attention from the real stuff.'

'I do not think so,' said Turgot, sounding disappointed. 'The cathedral is a very public place, and no one could bury treasure in it without being observed. Oh, well. Perhaps Flambard will invent some other way to see his cathedral built.'

'I will see there is a steady flow of money,' offered Burchard helpfully. 'The city can—'

'No,' said Turgot. 'Your days of extortion are over. Perhaps *that* is why the foundations keep crumbling – not because St Cuthbert does not want women nearby, but because he does not want our cathedral built with immoral money. As from now, you are no longer bursar. I am putting you in charge of the guest house instead.'

'But that means I will have to welcome visitors,' cried Burchard, appalled. 'You know I do not have the kind of graces for that.'

'Then this is your opportunity to learn. You are not a truly bad man, although you are overly zealous. If you want to succeed in our order, you must learn to be subtle.'

Geoffrey wondered whether learning the art of subtlety would be enough, and was unimpressed that, after all Burchard had done, he might still be considered for high office in the Benedictine Order. Even Hemming, dead as a result of his own greed and lust for power, would be buried in the monks' graveyard and his evil deeds forgotten because it would reflect badly on the order. Geoffrey was tired of it all, and longed to be away from the abbey and its dark secrets.

'Come tomorrow,' said the prior as they took their leave. 'I will instruct a lay brother to prise up the appropriate stone in the Chapel of the Nine Altars, although I cannot imagine it will contain anything worth the effort. Still, you might want to see this business finally closed for ever.'

That was true: at that moment, there was nothing Geoffrey wanted more than to see Flambard's treasure finally exposed as a massive hoax, and to have done with the whole affair.

The next day dawned bright and clear. The sky was a flawless blue, and the sun began to melt the snow that had held the land in a stranglehold for the past week. Everywhere, small avalanches were sliding with soft plops from houses and trees, and icicles shed frigid showers on to the heads of the people who walked below.

'This is more like it,' said Roger, as he strolled with Geoffrey to witness the excavation of whatever lay in the chapel. He flexed his shoulders and turned his face to the sun. 'If you close your eyes, you might even imagine you were back in the Holy Land.'

'It smells different,' said Geoffrey.

Roger regarded him uncertainly.

'The Holy Land smells of dust, hot animal dung, and mud bricks,' elaborated Geoffrey. 'Durham smells of frozen sewage, dirty ice, and wet trees.'

'If you say so,' said Roger warily. 'Although you might think differently if you were to wash more often. Ellie was commenting on that only the other day.'

'On what?' demanded Geoffrey, affronted. 'My personal cleanliness?'

'Lack of it,' said Roger. 'She said she had never seen such a filthy pair as us, and that I never used to be so bad. I do not think I have changed. I think she just remembers what she wants to.'

'A lot of people do that around here. Yesterday, Turgot pretended he had no idea how Burchard raised money. He knew, but was prepared to turn a blind eye because it was good for the abbey.'

'That kind of thing will no longer be necessary,' said Roger, ever the optimist. 'We will witness a big treasure chest discovered this morning, then everyone's troubles will be over.'

They arrived at the abbey gates where Burchard, already relegated to his new post as guestmaster, came to escort them to the Chapel of the Nine Altars.

312

'This must be a blow for you,' remarked Roger bluntly. 'It must be galling to perform menial tasks, like taking visitors here and there, after what you have been used to.'

Burchard glowered and declined to reply. Geoffrey felt a mild sense of satisfaction in knowing that at least Burchard would be discontented with and resentful of his new duties, and felt perhaps he had been appropriately punished for his nasty treatment of the townsfolk after all.

Turgot was waiting for them in the cathedral. His secretary, Algar, was standing with him, holding a spade, while several townsmen and a few idle monks had gathered to watch the unusual spectacle of a newly laid floor being prised apart.

'Here,' said Turgot, pointing to a large flagstone with his toe. 'This is the one marked by the cross.' He offered the parchment to Geoffrey, so he could confirm the deductions. Geoffrey studied it for a moment, counted the stones from north to south, then nodded his agreement. With the help of two lay brothers, Burchard began to ease levers under the slab.

It took a long time. The stone was thick and heavy, and some of the watching monks were ordered to lend a hand. When it was finally out, a sweating Burchard took the spade and began to excavate the hard-packed dirt underneath. It was set hard, like mortar, and even Roger's great strength struggled with it. It was almost midday by the time the blade thumped against something hollow.

'Treasure!' crowed Roger in delight, peering into the hole. 'I told you so! There is a chest buried here that will be full of gold.'

'You were wrong,' said Burchard to Turgot spitefully, pleased to point out his superior's error. 'You said the chapel was too public to allow anything to be buried, but something is here.'

'I suppose it could have been left when the foundations cracked four years ago,' mused Turgot. 'We relaid the floor then. It is possible someone slipped a container in the earth at that point.'

Everyone watched Burchard excavate the hole. He uncovered a box, but it was much smaller than the one that had contained the pennies, perhaps two hand lengths long, and one across.

'Oh,' said Roger, crestfallen. 'Is that it?'

Burchard's energetic prodding revealed there was nothing more. He gave a heavy sigh. 'So Flambard cheats us yet again. I know this box. It is St Balthere's reliquary. I remember this crack in the lid. How did it end up here, after it was stolen from St Giles'?'

'Open it,' instructed Turgot. 'And then we shall see. Perhaps.'

'Be careful,' warned Geoffrey as Burchard tipped the chest this way and that. 'Remember the last treasure Flambard donated to your abbey was protected by poison.'

Burchard hastily donned a pair of gauntlets, although there was nothing to suggest that there was anything on the box that could be venomous. He levered open the lid. Inside was a smaller container, this one made of silver and covered in jewels.

'Here,' said Roger, confused. 'Burchard might know that wooden box, but I recognize this silver one. It is the reliquary where I found . . .' He faltered and gave a nervous wink. 'You know.'

'I do not know,' said Turgot. 'Found what?'

'St Oswald's skull,' said Roger in a whisper, casting a fearful glance around him, as if he imagined he might be struck down for mentioning it.

'This box?' asked Turgot, now confused as well. 'I do not think so! Oswald's head has always resided in St Cuthbert's coffin.'

Eilaf the priest had said as much, too, Geoffrey recalled.

'But this was the box I opened that night I . . . you know,' said Roger.

'No,' said Turgot irritably. 'I keep telling you that I do not know. What night?'

'I remember it clearly,' pressed Roger. 'It is the reliquary in which St Oswald's head—'

'It is not!' exclaimed Turgot, exasperated. 'How many more times must I say it? There is no reliquary for Oswald's head: that rests in Cuthbert's coffin. Always.'

'So, if Roger used the contents of this box for his candle holder, then it could not have been Oswald's skull?' asked Geoffrey. 'He is no desecrator of holy relics.'

Turgot gazed at him. 'Is that what he thought he did?'

'That is what my father *said* I did,' said Roger resentfully.

'Then he was not telling you the truth,' said Turgot. 'Or me. He told me you had opened St Cuthbert's coffin, and *that* was why you had to go on the Crusade.'

'I opened no coffin,' protested Roger indignantly. 'I looked inside this.'

'In that case,' said Turgot, 'it seems you did not have to leave after all. Still, knowing what you did to the Scots, I am sure it did your soul no harm.'

'And I did not have to look for your missing maps,' said Geoffrey. He started to laugh, his voice echoing around the hallowed silence of the chapel and drawing the curious looks of the onlookers.

Turgot pursed his lips. 'I do not see what is so funny.'

'Nor me,' added Roger.

'It was all for nothing,' said Geoffrey, still laughing. 'There is no treasure and Roger did not desecrate St Oswald's relics.'

'Who says there is no treasure?' asked Burchard. 'We do not know what this chest contains.'

'It will contain Balthere,' said Turgot. 'Everyone knows that cracked box is his reliquary, although I had no idea this beautiful silver piece was inside it. That will look nice in our new cathedral.'

'But it belongs to St Giles' Church,' objected Geoffrey. 'Balthere was stolen from Eilaf and his people, and should be returned there.'

'Perhaps we can come to some arrangement,' said Turgot thoughtfully. 'The abbey will keep the silver box, and Eilaf can have the wooden bit.'

'That sounds fair,' remarked Geoffrey facetiously.

Burchard pushed open the lid, jumping back with a cry of revulsion as he looked inside. Curious, Geoffrey peered over his shoulder. Inside the box was the shrivelled body of a snake.

Fourteen

'Horrible!' exclaimed the prior with a shudder, gazing at the coiled body of the serpent. 'Flambard is playing with us. You were right, Geoffrey. There is no treasure.'

Roger pushed Burchard out of the way so he could take a closer look, and pointed at a small bowl that rested in one corner of the box. 'There is St Oswald's skull.'

'That is not bone,' said Geoffrey, picking it up. 'It is wood.'

'Ha!' exclaimed Roger triumphantly. 'It *is* a candle holder!'

'And Balthere is still missing,' said Turgot. 'We have his reliquary, but no bones.'

'But how did Balthere's box end up in our chapel without its bones?' asked Burchard, bewildered.

'That is easy to answer – at least in part,' said Turgot. 'Poor Balthere was stolen a few nights after the foundations of the chapel cracked. Do you not recall people spreading the rumour that we had stolen them and that God had predicted we would do so, and had tried to warn the Saxons by damaging our cathedral?'

'I do indeed,' said Burchard. 'Seditious lies.'

'Right,' agreed Roger. 'It fell because Cuthbert did not want the Lady chapel near his shrine.'

Turgot nodded. 'That is a more likely explanation. But after the collapse, we had to re-pave the chapel floor. It seems someone took advantage of the upheaval to deposit Balthere's reliquary here. What was Flambard thinking to leave a trail that leads only to this?'

'He probably thinks that anyone who managed get his hands on all three maps, survived the poisoned barbs protecting his pennies, yet still lived to dig this up would be

316

a cunning old snake,' said Roger, his big shoulders quaking with laughter. 'It is a joke!'

'Not a very amusing one,' said Turgot stiffly. 'Because of it my sub-prior is dead, and I need to find a new bursar. I am too busy for Flambard's feeble attempts at humour.'

'Oh, come now,' said Roger, elbowing him in the ribs and all but knocking the breath from him. 'You must see it is a little funny.'

'It is not funny at all,' said Turgot sternly. 'But since you think it is, you can take that revolting object with you and bury it somewhere away from my abbey. Leave the silver casket, though,' he added, tipping snake and bowl into the wooden reliquary and tucking the valuable one under his arm.

With that he turned on his heel and stalked away, his worried secretary scurrying at his heels. Geoffrey heard the man offering his services for the posts of either bursar or sub-prior, immodestly reciting a list of his talents.

'Come on, Geoff, lad,' said Roger, picking up the box and its grisly contents. 'I have had enough of this place and its humourless monastics. Ellie asked me to see whether Simon has returned after we had finished here, and then we will throw this thing in the river. And after that, we will take her to her husband's funeral, which is due to take place this afternoon.'

'Well, it really is over now,' said Geoffrey, walking with him into the sunshine. 'Flambard's treasure turned out to be a hoax, and a number of people are dead because of it. But we have discharged our duties, and if the weather continues fine, I will be able to leave in a day or two.'

'I am coming with you,' said Roger firmly. 'I am not staying here.'

'What about Eleanor and her brothel? Will you abandon them?'

'They will be glad to see the back of me,' said Roger with uncharacteristic insight. 'And I long to feel the golden sun of Normandy on my back. But it is *you* who will be sorry to leave Ellie, not me.'

'Yes, I will,' said Geoffrey honestly.

'She likes you, too,' said Roger, giving him a clap on the

back with the hand that was not holding the box. 'And you could do a lot worse than old Ellie.'

'What are you suggesting?' asked Geoffrey warily.

Roger bawled with laughter. 'Do not be coy with me, lad! I have seen the way you leer at her when you think no one is watching. Stay a while, and try her out for size, or better still, tell her to come with us to the Holy Land. She will love it there.'

'I do not think she will appreciate being "told" anything, and I doubt she would like it, anyway. Most women do not. It is hot, dusty, and there are too many flies.'

'Do not stand for that sort of nonsense. Make her marry you. She is a widow after all.'

'Here is Simon's house,' said Geoffrey, not wanting to hear any more of Roger's recommendations for a life of marital bliss. 'You can climb over the wall yourself this time. The pig has gone.'

'No need for that,' said Roger with a grin. 'Ellie has a key and she gave it to me. Hold the snake, while I undo the lock.'

He swore and muttered under his breath while he fiddled. A mess of sloppy snow, half-melted from the sun, landed on Geoffrey's head, splattering him with cold water.

'Hurry up,' he grumbled, wiping drops from his eyes. 'This is useless. Simon will not have shut himself inside, and if the door is locked, then he is still out.'

The door swung open and Roger gave him a triumphant grin. 'Come on,' he said, leading the way inside. 'It will not take a moment, and Ellie will be pleased to know you did what she asked.' He gave a horrible, leering wink, and entered the smelly interior of Simon's house.

He had not taken more than a couple of steps before something dark swung toward him. He ducked, thus avoiding having his brains dashed out, but he still took a blow hard enough to knock him from his feet and send him sprawling to the floor.

Geoffrey had reached for his sword the instant he had detected a shadow moving behind the door. Part of his mind registered a sharp splintering as the box fell to the floor and cracked. He leapt into the room with his sword

318

raised to protect the fallen Roger, but froze when he heard the unmistakable click of a crossbow being readied.

'Do not fire!' cried a familiar voice in alarm. 'It is my son and his friend.'

'Flambard!' exclaimed Geoffrey in astonishment. He glanced to one side and saw that the man with the crossbow was Odard. Geoffrey looked from monk to bishop in confusion. 'Why are you here?'

'I want you to do something for me,' said Flambard, waving to tell Odard to lower his weapon.

'Oh, no,' said Geoffrey, backing away. 'Not again. Never again.'

'But it seems I do not need to bother you after all,' continued Flambard silkily, bending to inspect the objects that lay on the floor among the splintered wood. 'Really, gentlemen. This is no way to treat one of the kingdom's most sacred relics.'

'What do you mean?' asked Roger nervously. 'That is a candle holder. Turgot told me. You cannot send me off on another Crusade by telling me it is Oswald's head. I know it is not.'

'This is priceless,' said Flambard, holding the snake in his hat, careful not to touch it with his hands.

'It is some old serpent from Finchale,' said Roger, although his voiced lacked conviction.

'It is more than that,' said Flambard. 'This is the Holy Staff – Aaron's Rod.'

'It is a dried snake,' said Geoffrey, seeing Roger blanch. What dreadful price would Flambard try to extract from his son this time, to atone for his 'sin'? Geoffrey was determined the bishop would not take advantage of Roger's loyalty and gullibility a second time.

'Think of your scriptures, Geoffrey,' said Flambard smoothly. 'What happened to Aaron's Rod when God ordered him to lay it on the ground? It turned into a snake.' He held the withered body reverently in the air. 'And this is it.'

Geoffrey and Roger gazed at Flambard. Roger was fearful, concerned that he had treated another sacred object with disrespect. Geoffrey was unable to speak because he was too astounded by Flambard's claim. Meanwhile, Odard had not obeyed the order to dispense with his crossbow, and had it trained unwaveringly on the two knights. Roger climbed slowly to his feet. He deliberately avoided looking at the grisly object Flambard cradled so lovingly.

'What are you doing in Durham anyway?' he asked of his father. 'It is dangerous here. You should be in Normandy with the Duke.'

'I did not want to leave without this,' said Flambard, indicating the snake. 'It is worth more than all my other fortunes put together. I was beginning to despair that anyone would dig it up for me, and I could scarcely do it myself.'

'Why not?'

Flambard sighed and regarded Roger wearily. 'Fool! Because it would be impossible to excavate the Chapel of the Nine Altars with no one seeing me.'

That was certainly true, thought Geoffrey, recalling how many townspeople and monks had stopped to watch Burchard wield his spades and levers. It was a public place, and would not even be deserted at night, when monks would be saying their offices and private vigils might be kept.

'Put down the crossbow, Odard,' Flambard continued. 'Weapons make me nervous in confined places. You never know when they might go off and hurt someone. You have no need of it anyway. You can see it is only Roger and Geoffrey.'

Odard lowered the bow, although Geoffrey noticed it was still wound and that all Odard needed to do to fire it was to take aim.

'Turgot said you are a Knight Hospitaller,' said Geoffrey to the dark-haired man with his curiously bird-like features. 'Is that true?'

Odard nodded. 'But I occasionally wear a Benedictine habit for convenience, as did Xavier. Our order is young, and it is often easier to be thought of as a Black Monk than a Hospitaller.'

'Gilbert Courcy favoured civilian clothes, though,' added Flambard. 'He was murdered in Southampton. That Gamelo was a nuisance. He followed me from London, hoping to learn where I had hidden my treasure, chased poor Gilbert on to a roof, and killed him when he refused to tell. Gilbert was only a novice, and was an inexperienced fighter.'

'We noticed,' said Geoffrey, recalling the young man's tactical errors. 'And we know Gilbert's death left you short of a courier for your three maps, so you asked Roger instead.'

'Gamelo almost destroyed what was a very clever plan,' said Flambard. 'My Hospitallers are honourable men, and there are not many of those around these days.'

'Why do you serve a churchman from another order?' asked Geoffrey of Odard curiously.

'Our Grand Master knew Flambard would need loyal servants,' said Odard. 'So, four years ago, he ordered us to swear a sacred oath to Flambard. It is to be to our mutual advantage – we protect him and help him attain influence, and he will use that influence to favour our order.'

'I would have done that,' said Roger resentfully. 'I would have obeyed and not demanded anything in exchange. I delivered your map to the prior and did not try to steal anything for myself.'

'Was that because there was no treasure to steal, or because you really do honour your father?' asked Flambard. He studied Roger, as if meeting him for the first time. 'Yes, perhaps I should have used members of my family instead of my knights.'

Then he did not know Roger very well, thought Geoffrey, recalling how Roger had been more than willing to siphon off a little of Flambard's fabled wealth to compensate himself for his troubles. Roger was loyal in many things, but his Norman ancestry was strong in him, and wealth and riches were just as important as family ties.

'You *can* trust Roger,' came a voice from the hall. 'Although I cannot say the same for his friend.'

Geoffrey was not at all surprised to see Simon standing there, holding a sword.

'You rogue!' exclaimed Roger, springing across the room and giving his half-brother a clap on the shoulders that all but knocked the weapon from his hand. 'I was afraid someone had harmed you.'

Odard's sardonic features broke into a disgusted sneer. 'The likes of *him* would never come to harm – he is too quick to flee for that.'

'Burchard said he saw you in Durham recently,' said Roger to Simon, ignoring Odard.

Simon nodded. 'I've been in Chester-le-Street on business . . .'

'He fled there after Gamelo almost shot him in Eleanor's solar,' corrected Odard, unimpressed. 'He ran away because he was afraid.'

Simon shot him a withering glance. 'But then our father sent a message saying he needed a secure place to stay. My house is perfect – it can be reached easily from the river and my neighbours mind their own business, and do not prattle about what they see to the sheriff's men.'

'But it is not as pleasant as Eleanor's home,' said Flambard, wrinkling his nose fastidiously.

'Do not stay with Ellie,' said Roger quickly. 'It might be dangerous for her.'

'Dangerous?' asked Simon nervously. 'Why?'

'You are hiding England's most notorious escaped prisoner,' said Geoffrey dryly. 'Why do you think it might be dangerous?'

Simon was silent, gnawing on his lip, as though the thought had not occurred to him. Geoffrey saw that he was having second thoughts about his magnanimous hospitality. Odard merely sneered.

'Never mind all that,' said Flambard, raising the cracked box with the snake in it. He stroked it fondly. 'All has ended well, because I have brought Aaron's Rod to Durham, just as I promised.'

'I told you so,' said Roger gloatingly to Geoffrey. 'I told you it was real.'

'It is not Aaron's Rod,' insisted Geoffrey. 'It is a dead snake.'

'I have already explained that,' said Flambard impatiently. 'Aaron's Rod regularly turned itself into a serpent. Why do you think I drew a snake on one of my treasure maps? You are an intelligent man. I thought you would have guessed that.'

'Roger said there were snakes at Finchale, and so I thought your diagram, like the tree split by lightning, was to depict Finchale for the illiterate.'

'Well, you were wrong,' said Flambard. 'Can you imagine how many pilgrims will travel here to see this? King Henry will *have* to reinstate me and restore my fortunes when he learns I have it.'

'What about the candle holder?' asked Roger warily, pointing at the dish. 'Last time I saw that—'

'Last time you saw that, I had to send you on the Crusade,' said Flambard. 'I could not risk you telling anyone what you had seen rummaging through my personal effects four years ago.'

'You mean I am exonerated?' asked Roger hopefully.

'No,' said Flambard airily. 'Because you have done nothing to be exonerated from.'

'Four years ago,' mused Geoffrey. 'Four years ago you gave Balthere's bones to Eilaf, which were stolen the night Brother Wulfkill died; four years ago Odard, Xavier and Gilbert Courcy entered your service; four years ago the foundations collapsed in parts of the cathedral; and four years ago Roger was dispatched on the Crusade that might have ended his life.'

'But I am an excellent warrior . . .' objected Roger.

'I see the connection now,' continued Geoffrey. 'The wooden reliquary is the one Burchard recognized as containing St Balthere. The inner box, of silver—'

'Where is that?' interrupted Flambard, looking around as though it might suddenly materialize. 'I had it specially made to hold Aaron's Rod in its serpent form. It cost a fortune.'

'Turgot has it,' said Roger. 'He—'

'Balthere's relics never existed,' interrupted Geoffrey. 'You gave Eilaf a wooden box, claiming it contained bones. People were impressed by your uncharacteristic generosity at the time, and it was a safe place to store your snake. No one was likely to look inside the reliquary, especially superstitious Saxons, who believe it is dangerous to tamper with sacred things.'

'Is this true?' asked Odard of Flambard in astonishment. 'You stored Aaron's Rod in a mean little church? You never told me!'

'I told no one,' said Flambard smugly. 'I mentioned to one of the carpenters working on the cathedral that the Rod was in Durham, to ensure he kept a space for it when he built the shrine, but I gave him no details. It was safer that way. And Geoffrey is right: St Giles' was a perfect hiding place, among superstitious Saxons who would have protected their saint to the death. But, unfortunately, I did not anticipate the greed of a Norman abbey.'

'You were afraid Turgot would take it?' asked Geoffrey.

Flambard nodded. 'The abbey was collecting every other saint in the area – Cuthbert, Oswald, Aidan, the Venerable Bede, Billfrith, Ceolwulf, and so on. I was afraid Turgot would look inside St Balthere's box and claim the Rod for the abbey, when it is mine.'

Geoffrey stared at him. 'It is said Brother Wulfkill died protecting the relics. But he did not, did he? He was the one who stole them – for you. And then he was murdered so he could never reveal what had really happened.'

'You said nothing to me,' said Odard, regarding Flambard uncertainly. 'Your loyal servant.'

'I said nothing to anyone. I must have some secrets, Odard. I cannot tell you *everything* I do.'

Odard looked as if he strongly disagreed.

'And then you hid the box in a really safe place,' said Geoffrey. 'Part of the cathedral had just collapsed and that meant a new floor needed to be laid. What better place to store your snake until you were ready to collect it?'

'It was a perfect place,' agreed Flambard. 'Safe and holy. But then I was arrested, and I decided to take it to Normandy, so it can help change King Henry's mind about me.'

'But reclaiming it yourself was impossible, so you devised an elaborate plan involving Durnais, Jarveaux and Turgot.'

'Precisely. All three are greedy men, and I knew at least one of them would meet with success. I also knew he would think the snake was my idea of a joke and discard it. And then I planned to reclaim it – with no risk to myself. It worked better than even I hoped, although I anticipated it would be a little quicker. I have been forced to stay in this hovel for longer than I intended.'

'But why poison the tree?' asked Geoffrey. 'If you wanted the Chapel of the Nine Altars dug up, why risk the life of the man who might do it for you?'

'I wanted the finder to think he was about to discover something really worth protecting. Had I made it too easy, he might not have bothered, and then all my work would have been in vain.'

'What about that bowl?' asked Roger nervously. 'What is it doing with Aaron's Rod?'

'It is one of Aaron's priestly vessels,' said Flambard carelessly. 'It came with the Rod. I will sell it to some French monastery to keep me in funds while I wait for King Henry to invite me home.'

Flambard wiped the top of a stool with the hem of his cloak before lowering himself gingerly on to it. He gestured that the others were to sit also, and laid a proprietorial hand on his relic.

'There is no call for us to stand around as though we were all going to engage in some fist fight. Sit, and we will discuss the finer points of my plan in comfort.' He glanced around him disparagingly. 'Well, as comfortable as we can be, given the circumstances.'

'Surely there was an easier way to do this?' asked Geoffrey tiredly. 'Do you have any idea how many people died because of it? If you do not care about Jarveaux, Stanstede, Durnais, Hemming, and Gamelo and his various henchmen, then surely you must grieve for Gilbert and Xavier?'

Flambard nodded, but not with much sorrow. 'But I still have Odard, and he is the best of them.'

'You should not be here,' said Roger, casting an anxious glance toward the door. 'What happens if someone recognizes you? You are supposed to be in the White Tower.'

'I had fathomed that out, thank you, Roger,' said Flambard.

'But I have a ship waiting a few miles down the river. I will be on my way to Normandy – with Aaron's Rod – at dusk this evening.'

'How did *you* become involved?' Roger asked Simon. 'You are not a man for this kind of thing. You are plain and honest, like me.'

'Honest?' said Flambard with a sudden laugh. 'None of my children could ever be called honest, I hope. God spare me the indignity of having it said that I have sired *honest* brats!'

'Odard promised I would be rich if I helped Flambard,' said Simon. 'He asked me to hide his map until he was certain Durnais could be trusted not to steal the treasure for himself.'

'But you did not hide it very well,' said Geoffrey. 'It was found. You told Gamelo where to find us, too. You knew we would be at Eleanor's house that night, unarmed, and told him to attack us there.'

'I did not,' said Simon fervently. 'Do you think me mad? He would just have likely killed me by mistake. If I had wanted him to kill you, I would not have been around when he tried.'

'That I can believe,' said Geoffrey. 'But it was you who followed me into your house the next day, was it not? I saw your footprints in the yard, then you escaped through the window. You had come to collect Odard's map. It had to be you, because you were familiar with the layout of the house, and you knew that the window would open easily when you climbed through it.'

'I did not know that the timbers would break under my weight though,' said Simon ruefully. 'I could have broken my neck in that fall, and it would have been your fault. But I had nothing to do with Gamelo bursting into Eleanor's house. Horrible little man!'

'Gamelo was all right,' said Flambard. 'It was he who told me about Turgot's affair with Sister Hilde, and Hemming's unmonkish passion for cock fights. Both snippets of information were included in the document hidden in the beech tree. What happened to that?'

'It fell in the river yesterday,' said Geoffrey, before Roger could admit to burning it.

'Pity,' said Flambard. 'But it does not matter. I will be able to secure a lot more from the pilgrims who come to see the Rod. Mother Petra got rid of Gamelo for me. Did I tell you that?'

Geoffrey was not sure whether to believe him. 'Did you order her to do it?'

Flambard smiled. 'No one *orders* my grandmother to do anything. She is no man's servant.'

'Was,' corrected Roger. 'She is dead.'

Flambard nodded. 'Simon told me. Durham will miss its only real witch.'

'There is always Moon Mary,' said Geoffrey. 'She is a real witch. She told me to beware of the serpent. I thought she was speaking gibberish, but bearing in mind what we have just excavated from the cathedral, I think she probably has genuine powers of prediction.'

'Really?' asked Flambard, impressed. 'Perhaps I should take her to Normandy. Someone with that kind of talent could be very useful to a man like me.'

'Take her,' said Geoffrey, thinking it would serve Flambard right to be saddled with Moon Mary.

'You signed Gamelo's death warrant by telling Mother Petra what he had been doing with his red-stained arrows,' said Flambard, sounding amused. 'She was furious, and decided to kill him, so he could interfere with my careful plans no further.'

'What did she do?' asked Odard. 'Offer him wine to drive out the winter chill?'

Flambard nodded. 'He did not go far after the fight outside Jarveaux's house. Mother Petra beckoned him inside, and offered him and his cronies wine. They drank it and died in the woods a short while later.'

'Why did she kill Jarveaux?' said Geoffrey.

'He was going to steal my treasure, too. She knew about my plan, and that he was to receive one of my maps. When he hid it, instead of showing it to the others, she put hellebore on his oysters.'

Geoffrey sighed, weary of the misguided loyalties that led Flambard's relatives to commit murder for him. He stood.

327

'All this has been very interesting, but the day is wearing on. I want to ride out of the city today, to see whether the road is clear enough for us to leave tomorrow.'

'It will not be,' said Flambard confidently. 'It takes more than a morning of sun to clear Durham's highways. You can come with me on my boat, if you like.'

While a ride in Flambard's ship would certainly allow them to reach Normandy more quickly than riding south to find another, Geoffrey did not want to spend any more time in the company of the dangerous cleric. Not only would it mean certain death for him if he was caught, but he was afraid the bishop would use the opportunity to devise more nasty plans involving Roger.

'No,' he said, seeing Roger about to accept. 'We will leave from Southampton.'

'Very well,' said Flambard, disappointed. 'But do not go yet. I will be bored waiting for dusk, and would like your company.'

'But it is Stanstede's funeral this afternoon,' said Roger. 'I promised Ellie I would be there.'

'Then I will go with you,' announced Flambard. 'She will like that.'

'No!' cried Odard in alarm. 'You will be recognized and captured.'

'I shall wear your Benedictine habit,' said Flambard, rubbing his hands enthusiastically at the notion of an adventure. 'And I shall blacken my beard and eyebrows with soot from the chimney. It will prove an amusing diversion, and will help while away the hours.'

Idly, Geoffrey wondered whether Flambard thought all the funerals of the men he had helped to kill were fun. One look at the self-indulgent, crafty features suggested he might.

A short while later, Roger, Simon and Geoffrey, followed by a Benedictine with a curiously dark beard, dirty face, and a habit that was too small, made their way towards St Giles' Church. No one paid them any attention, although Odard, walking behind and scowling furiously, earned one or two curious glances from passers-by.

They were almost late. Eilaf had already lit the requiem candles and the nave was half full with people who had known the brothel-keeper-cum-spice-merchant. Geoffrey noted they comprised mainly men, while the women were limited to those who had worked for him. But Stanstede had a better turnout than the mean gathering that had assembled for Jarveaux, suggesting he had been a more popular figure.

Flambard chose a suitably shady corner, and watched the proceedings with bright-eyed curiosity. Eleanor glanced over at him, and Geoffrey saw her jaw start to drop in astonishment before she gained control of herself and her mouth set in a firm, hard line. Geoffrey did not blame her. Flambard showed a deplorable lack of tact in attending Stanstede's funeral, given that his treasure had brought about the man's death. Geoffrey admired the fact that Eleanor had managed to keep her calm.

The requiem was unremarkable and over quickly. The mourners followed the coffin and its pungent contents into the graveyard, where Eleanor had purchased a considerably deeper hole than Alice had bothered with. Geoffrey looked at the mound of soil that marked Jarveaux's resting place, and saw tell-tale scratches where dogs had already explored it. At least Stanstede's mortal remains would not suffer the indignity of being a mongrel's meal, as would Jarveaux's before the end of winter.

When it was over, Eilaf approached Geoffrey and shyly indicated the faded, but warm, winter cloak he wore. He also had boots, too big and with scuffed toes, but of a good enough quality to keep out the melting slush through which he waded.

'Prior Turgot sent these,' he said. 'And I am told there is work at the scriptorium whenever I need it, and a loaf of bread will be on my doorstep each morning from the abbey bakery. I cannot imagine what you said, but thank you.'

Geoffrey nodded acknowledgement, and only hoped Turgot would not forget the poor parish priest when more important issues took his attention. He was about to suggest Eilaf made himself indispensable around the scriptorium in case the deliveries of bread became unreliable, when he felt a sharp poke in the back. He turned, his hand resting on the hilt of his sword.

'You do not need to pull that thing out,' said Alice, eyeing him disdainfully. 'It is only me, not one of your rough Holy Land friends.'

'It seems condolences are in order,' he said, refraining from adding that the likes of Alice and her relatives were a good deal more dangerous than most knights he knew. 'I heard Mother Petra died.'

Unexpectedly, Alice's eyes filled with tears. 'I will miss her – a good deal more than that husband of mine. She was a good woman, always kind to me.'

'She was not kind to everyone though, was she?' said Geoffrey softly. 'Not to her son, whom she poisoned, or to Brother Gamelo and his cronies.'

'They deserved what they got,' said Alice, brushing away the tears and glancing around to make sure no one had seen her moment of weakness. 'My husband was going to steal from the cathedral, and Gamelo was responsible for the death of one of your own men in Southampton.'

'True,' said Geoffrey. 'But it was not for Mother Petra to dispense justice. Flambard is quite capable of doing that himself.'

'I know,' said Alice. 'When she told me what she had done to Gamelo, I was terrified for her.'

'I do hope it was not you who pulled the rags from the broken window,' said Geoffrey mildly. 'I heard she froze in a drunken slumber, because the fire went out and there was a hole in the glass.'

Alice laughed nervously. 'There you go again, making nasty accusations. What makes you think the rags had been pulled from the window?'

'They were conspicuous by their absence in Cenred's tale,' said Geoffrey, certain his suspicions were correct. 'I suppose she was too much of a liability for you, was she?'

'*You* were the liability,' snapped Alice. '*You* accused me of poisoning my husband in the market square and of changing the lock on my door for some sinister purpose. Mother Petra poisoned four people, but it was *me* you caught buying the damned hellebore. I knew it was only a matter of time before you accused me of killing Gamelo, too, so I decided I had better do something to save myself, since no one else would bother.'

'So, you allowed Mother Petra to die.'

'We sewed together by the fire, and she drank her wine. Then she fell asleep. She was old anyway, and banking a fire and pulling rags from broken windows are not acts of murder.'

'You should have been a lawyer,' said Geoffrey. 'Perhaps you *should* give your jewellery to the cathedral, so it can go towards expiating your sins.'

He gave a curt bow before she could reply, and left her, bringing up the rear of the procession that traipsed through the melting snow to the town. When they reached Eleanor's house, people began to disperse, although Flambard, Odard and Simon were asked inside, and Eleanor invited Geoffrey to join them for a modest meal. Spending more time in the company of the devious bishop and his ruthless henchman was not something that filled Geoffrey with much enthusiasm, but Eleanor looked tired and drawn, and he felt obliged to dine in her house if she wanted him there.

Outside, still keeping watch, were the Littel brothers, faces turned to the sun as they enjoyed the first warm day of the year. The older one saw Geoffrey and left his post to intercept him.

'I met that butcher,' he began without preamble. 'The one that killed Simon's pig.'

'Thank you,' said Geoffrey, not having the heart to say it no longer mattered, because Simon was alive and well and about to enjoy what would doubtless be a well-cooked repast in Eleanor's house.

Littel glanced uncomfortably at his brother, and shuffled his feet. 'It was . . .' He swallowed, and fiddled with his belt.

'Come on,' said Geoffrey impatiently. 'If you know who took it for slaughter, then tell me.'

Littel leaned towards Geoffrey, muttered a name in his ear, and darted away before Geoffrey could react. Geoffrey's first instinct was to think he was mistaken, but the final pieces of the puzzle snapped together in his mind and he saw he had been blind not to have seen them sooner. Thoughtfully, he walked inside Eleanor's house and climbed the stairs to the solar. The others were already there, helping themselves to food, although Odard was nervous and stood at the window. Geoffrey saw he had brought his crossbow with him, and had even managed to keep it wound under his cloak.

'This is delicious,' said Flambard, reaching out for more bread and smiling benignly at his daughter. 'Is there more meat? I have dined on nothing but biscuit these last few days, and it is a pleasure to taste flesh again.'

'I will fetch some,' said Eleanor quietly. Her face was pale, as if she had been crying, and Geoffrey thought Flambard was unkind to foist himself on her on such a day.

'It was worth my while attending Stanstede's funeral after all,' remarked the bishop happily, taking an apple from a plate and tossing it in the air before taking a bite out of it.

'I am glad he managed to be of use to you,' said Geoffrey, resentful of the way the man viewed everything in terms of his own interests.

He saw the bishop's eyes narrow in anger, but Geoffrey was tired of the whole business and wanted to spend time alone, away from Flambard and the people who would do anything for him. He did not want to hear any more gloating revelations that would show him how clever Flambard had been.

'I am going for a walk,' he said abruptly, starting to walk to the door.

'No,' said Odard quietly, and Geoffrey turned in surprise as he heard the crossbow click. 'You will remain in this room until the bishop is safely away.'

'Here!' exclaimed Roger, looking up from his food in astonishment when he saw the weapon pointed at Geoffrey. 'What are you doing, man? Let him go for a walk, if he wants to.'

'I have had enough of this foolery,' hissed Odard, stepping between Geoffrey and the door. 'I should have killed you in Simon's house, instead of allowing Flambard to endanger us all by romping all over a city that would dearly love to see him hang.'

'You will not harm my son,' said Flambard softly, but with steel in his voice. 'We agreed.'

'But I can kill Geoffrey Mappestone,' said Odard. 'He is too clever to set free.' He gestured with the bow that Geoffrey was to sit in the window. 'And you go with him, Roger. No sudden moves from either of you, or I will fire.'

Roger gaped at him. 'But—'

'Sit!' snapped Odard. 'Or I will shoot Geoffrey now.'

Roger sank on to the window seat. 'Will you stand by and let him do this?' he appealed to Simon.

Simon swallowed nervously. 'Just do as he says and nothing will happen to you. You will be well rid of Geoffrey anyway. A man who reads is no company for a brother of mine.'

'But this is Eleanor's house,' cried Roger. 'She does not like blood on her rugs.'

Flambard gave a sudden and inappropriate gulp of laughter. 'I have been asked to spare people's lives on many occasions, but never on the grounds that their deaths will spoil the carpets.'

'Did you plan this from the start?' asked Roger, turning on him accusingly. 'As soon as we arrived in Durham, you intended to be rid of us?'

'No,' said Flambard soothingly. 'You will come to Normandy, where you will enter my service.'

'But Geoffrey—' protested Roger.

'You can be moulded to suit our needs; he cannot,' said Flambard bluntly.

Geoffrey looked at the bishop's hard, cold eyes and at Odard's determined face, wondered how he could have been so foolish as to imagine they would let him go, given all he knew. And his naiveté had cost him his life, because Odard was a skilled fighter who would have a quarrel in Geoffrey before he could touch the hilt of his sword, let alone draw it.

'It is almost time to leave,' said Flambard, glancing out of the window. He gave Geoffrey a sad smile. 'Do not worry. You do not have long to wait.'

'Then answer some questions,' said Roger in a valiant attempt to prolong the occasion, doubtless anticipating that Geoffrey would be able to think of a way to escape if he bought them time. Geoffrey, however, could see no way out of his predicament: Odard would not be tricked by any ploy that would fool a lesser man into lowering his guard.

'I thought we had been through all that,' said Flambard tiredly. Geoffrey knew how he felt. He did not much want to review the plot, either. 'What else do you want to know?'

'I do not understand how Gamelo knew we were at Ellie's house the night he attacked,' said Roger. 'The only person who knew what we planned was Simon, and he said it was not him.'

But Simon had not been the only other person who knew, Geoffrey thought. Although he had already guessed the identity of their betrayer, the knowledge still sent a cold stab of dismay through him when he realized how blind he had been.

'Someone else knew,' he said. 'And this same person also knew that we would go to Simon's home today, to see whether he had returned, and thus meet Flambard.'

'Who?' asked Roger, puzzled.

'Who told you to go?' pressed Geoffrey. 'Who even gave you a key to Simon's house, for God's sake, so we could be caught inside it, where no one would see what was happening?'

'Oh, no,' whispered Roger, white-faced. 'Not Ellie!'

'Eleanor,' said Geoffrey bitterly. 'She has been keeping Flambard informed of every step of our investigation. It was she who told Flambard that Turgot had ordered us to find the third map.'

'Ellie would not harm us,' declared Roger unsteadily. 'Besides, she always says our father is a treacherous serpent, who cannot be trusted to tell the truth about anything.'

'Does she indeed?' asked Flambard coolly.

'An act, to disguise her true feelings,' said Geoffrey. 'She knows it is the wrong time to tell folk she loves a man who has been accused of treason by the King and who is hated by the people.'

'I confess there have been misunderstandings,' began Flambard smoothly. 'But—'

'It all makes sense now,' said Geoffrey, thinking fast. 'She did not trust me to hand the third map to Turgot. She thought I might try to cheat you – like Durnais and Jarveaux had already done.'

'We do not know you,' explained Flambard. 'Roger's recommendation of your virtues is hardly something to trust, and all men are potentially dishonest. It is because of the State of Original Sin. I know what I am talking about here, because I am a bishop.'

Geoffrey was sure Flambard knew a good deal more about dishonesty than the average man, but that it had nothing to do with his priestly office. 'Eleanor told Gamelo we would be with her that night, hoping I would be killed and thus never reveal details of the treasure maps. You need not have gone to such extremes: to have told anyone else about this would have been stupid and dangerous.'

'But it was not Ellie,' protested Roger reproachfully. 'Not her.'

'When Gamelo and his accomplice burst into her solar, she did not dive for cover as most people would have done,' said Geoffrey. 'She knew *she* was in no danger from them, so she stayed where she was. It was me who wrested her to the ground.'

'I do not believe you,' said Roger, his face an agonized mask of indecision.

'And when killers burst into folks' homes, their bodies are not usually treated with the kind of respect she showed Gamelo's friend,' Geoffrey continued remorselessly. 'Eleanor would not look at his face, and felt guilty about his death.'

And she had insisted that he and Roger dispensed with their armour, Geoffrey recalled. She said it was because she did not like weapons in her solar, but it was so the two knights would be helpless when Gamelo came. Geoffrey would be dead, the map would be gone, and Roger was malleable and would do what she demanded. Because she loved Roger, she would have ensured he was not harmed.

335

'She did not want us to investigate for Turgot,' acknowledged Roger. 'And she was angry I had agreed to carry the map in the first place. She did not want us involved.'

'So she did,' said Flambard. 'But I told her I stood a better chance of getting the Rod if you were helping, than if I had to rely on that dim-witted bursar.'

So, that explained why she had gone from dismay that her brother had allowed himself to become embroiled in Flambard's affairs to being helpful – accompanying Geoffrey to speak to Alice and the witches. She had cared deeply for Roger's welfare, but none for Geoffrey's. The realization stung.

With a sudden wrenching feeling, he remembered she had even tried to kill him with her own hands the night she had slipped up behind him with her noose. He had assumed it was to prove her point: that it was possible to sneak up behind a knight and throttle him. He saw that had she been able to tighten the rope, he would not have lived to acknowledge she had been correct.

'I was glad of Ellie,' said Flambard complacently. 'It was reassuring to hear about your progress, so I would know exactly when to step in and reveal myself with the least risk. *And* she said Turgot would be too ignorant to recognize Aaron's Rod for what it is and would throw it away.'

'I was right.' All heads turned as the door opened, and Eleanor stepped inside.

'Eleanor,' said Flambard, beaming fondly at her. 'The best of all my brats.'

She walked daintily across the room and set a tray containing more food on the table. 'It will be a long journey, and you should rest and eat now.'

'Ham pie,' drooled Flambard. 'And marchpanes. You are a good lass, Ellie.'

She smiled, and bent to kiss him on the top of the head. Geoffrey found he was unable to watch and wondered how Roger felt.

'Ellie,' said Roger hoarsely. 'What are you doing? I am your favourite brother.'

'You are, and no harm will come to you, I promise. We

will go to Normandy – you, Simon, father, and I, where I will not have to run a brothel.'

'But what about Geoff?' asked Roger wretchedly.

'Forget him,' said Eleanor, her eyes fixed on Roger so she did not have to look at Geoffrey. 'Forget the bloodshed and slaughter of the Crusade, too, and become what you once were: gentle and kind. I did not want you to go on that Crusade in the first place, and I was furious when I learned today – from our father – that Turgot had you sent on false pretences.'

Flambard gave Geoffrey a wink, and the knight knew there was no point in trying to convince Eleanor that it had been Flambard, not Turgot, who had insisted Roger was sent away. Eventually, even Roger would come to believe the pilgrimage to the Holy Land had been Turgot's idea, and Flambard's role would be forgotten.

'You desecrated nothing,' continued Eleanor. 'So that horrible expedition was quite unnecessary. You have returned rough and wicked, thanks to men like Geoffrey, but I will make you good again.'

Geoffrey almost laughed, thinking she would have a lot of work to do to turn Roger into the kind of man she wanted as her brother. It was desperately unfair that Geoffrey should be held responsible for Roger's proverbial decline into devilry, since he was nearly always the one to urge moderation. And as for wickedness, if Geoffrey lived to be a hundred years old, he could never attain the standards of deceit and greedy self-interest that drove Flambard and his offspring. How Eleanor had convinced herself that Geoffrey was a bad influence, but Flambard was not, was beyond his comprehension.

'This is good, Ellie,' said Simon, grabbing a thick slice of meat and cramming it into his mouth. 'You always were a good cook.'

'Do not enjoy it too much,' said Geoffrey. 'It is pork.'

Eleanor looked at him sharply.

'So?' asked Simon, eating more of it. 'I like pork.'

'Have you seen your pig recently?' asked Geoffrey. 'The one of which you are so fond?'

Simon stopped chewing. 'She is with Cenred. He always

looks after her when I am away. I will collect her tonight though, and she will sail to Normandy with us.'

'You will find Cenred does not have her,' said Geoffrey. 'And all traces of her are long gone – some of them via your stomach.'

Simon gazed at the chunk of meat in his hand. 'No,' he said, although he did not take another bite.

'I do not want to discuss pigs while I am eating,' said Eleanor quickly. 'It was bad enough having to listen to Roger's tales of slaughter, and I will not have talk of swine at my table.'

'Cenred does not have your pig,' Geoffrey continued, his attention fixed on Simon. 'Ask anyone at the castle. In fact, he is concerned because the pig has disappeared. He likes her, too.'

'He does,' agreed Simon. 'That is why I allow him to care for her while I am away.'

'Enough,' said Eleanor sharply. 'I said I do not want to talk about pigs.'

'I am sure you do not,' said Geoffrey, 'because all that is left of your brother's sow is what is lying on the table. The Littel brothers spoke to the butcher this morning: you paid him well to keep your secret, but not well enough.'

'What do you mean?' asked Eleanor coldly.

'When the issue of the missing pig first arose, you told me not to waste time looking into it. I should have realized sooner what had become of the thing – your larder was full of hams when I was looking for somewhere to leave my dog the other day, and we have eaten pork at every meal.'

'You are wrong when you say there is nothing left,' said Eleanor, turning on him suddenly, eyes flashing with anger. 'There is another ham in the larder and the trotters are waiting to be made into broth. Your dog made off with the snout, but I found it under your bed this morning.'

Simon backed away from her in horror. 'Why?' he whispered. 'You know what she meant to me.'

'Because you would have wanted to take it to Normandy with us,' said Eleanor harshly. 'Its squealing and grunting would have given us away. Now that will not be an issue.'

338

'Taking a pig would reduce our chances of escape,' agreed Flambard. 'It is better this way, Simon. Ellie was right to do what she did.'

'How could you?' Simon whispered to Eleanor, his face drained and white.

Geoffrey glanced from Simon to Odard, who was watching the scene with detached amusement. Meanwhile, Simon was clenching and unclenching his fists in mute fury, and Eleanor, fearful for her safety, had grabbed a knife from the table. While Odard's attention strayed to her, Geoffrey leapt from the bench and dived at him. Odard swung around with the crossbow, and Geoffrey winced as the mechanism fired close to his ear. Then he and Odard were rolling on the floor, grappling with and scrabbling at each other. Odard was a good fighter, and quickly abandoned the crossbow in favour of a dagger. With demonic strength, he thrust Geoffrey away from him and lunged with the knife. Geoffrey saw it glitter as it began to descend.

With a bellow of rage, Roger launched himself from the window seat and joined the affray. Geoffrey winced a second time as Odard's arm broke with a sharp snap, even as it was gathering strength for the downward plunge. Odard screamed in agony, and the fight was over. He held his wrist against his chest, his face contorted with pain, and the dagger clattered to the floor. Geoffrey scrambled away from him, backed up against the wall, and drew his sword.

But the danger was over. Odard sat cursing vilely, while Simon stood with his hands dangling uselessly at his sides. Flambard knelt on the floor, next to the prostrate Eleanor.

'Ellie!' cried Roger, rushing to her and elbowing his father out of the way. 'What happened?'

'A crossbow bolt,' said Flambard angrily. 'When Geoffrey leapt at Odard, the weapon went off. I have told him time and time again that crossbows are dangerous and should not be kept loaded in small rooms. And now look what has happened.'

'It was not my fault,' whispered Simon, horrified. 'She had a knife and was going to stab me.'

'Simon went for her at the same time as Geoffrey went for Odard,' explained Flambard. 'She defended herself with a knife. Then the crossbow went off. It should have hit Simon, but he twisted her around so the bolt hit her instead.'

Roger gave his half-brother a look of such hatred that Simon backed away.

'It was an accident,' Simon insisted. 'What I did was instinctive. I would not hurt her deliberately.'

Geoffrey, whose own instincts had saved his life on many occasions, did not know what to think. Even a strong sense of self-preservation had never induced him to use the body of a friend to take an arrow intended for him. He looked away from Simon to Eleanor. A small trickle of blood eased from her mouth and ran down her chin.

'Roger,' she whispered in a voice that was little more than a breath.

'All right, Ellie, lass,' said Roger, gruffly gentle. 'It is only a scratch.'

But Geoffrey could see it was not, and the crossbow bolt protruding from her chest meant she was going to die.

'She killed my pig,' said Simon in a choked voice. 'And then she gave her to me to eat!'

'Then let us hope it tasted good,' muttered Odard nastily. No one found his comment amusing. Still holding his shattered arm, he struggled to his feet. Geoffrey responded by stamping on the crossbow to destroy its firing mechanism, then removing the Hospitaller's other weapons. Seeing he was defeated, Odard became bitter. 'We almost succeeded in everything we wanted to achieve! We have Aaron's Rod, a ship is waiting, and I had Geoffrey in my sights. Then Simon had to start an argument over a pig! I should have killed *him*, and allowed Geoffrey to go free.'

'She was not "a pig",' shouted Simon furiously. 'She was *my* pig – my companion, my friend.'

'Please,' said Flambard. 'Keep your voices down. Your sister is dying. At least have the grace to allow her to do so in peace.'

'Why, Ellie?' asked Roger, his big face creased with hurt. 'Why did you betray us?'

'Not you,' she whispered weakly. 'Never you. We were to go to Normandy together. We would have been happy again, like we were when we were young.'

'But you were going to kill my friend!'

'No,' she whispered. 'I wanted to at first – I even considered strangling him, since it worked for whoever murdered Xavier. But I saw he was good to you, and I intended to help him escape.'

'Did you indeed?' demanded Odard unpleasantly. 'I would like to have seen you try.'

'I had his horse brought to my yard. I was going to pretend I had poisoned him, so you would not consider him a danger, and then I intended to help him leave. It was a pity he mentioned the pig.'

'Give her last rites,' Flambard ordered Odard. 'You are a priest, as well as a soldier, are you not?'

Odard hesitated, but the flash of anger in Flambard's eyes convinced him to crouch next to Eleanor and begin to mutter prayers for the dying, while Roger looked on, stricken.

Eleanor said nothing more, and her breathing became softer until it stopped altogether. For a moment, no one moved or spoke.

'I do not know who to kill for this,' said Roger brokenly. He looked at Flambard. 'You came here and led her into all this danger; Odard's crossbow bolt brought about her death; Geoffrey caused the thing to go off in the first place; and Simon pushed her into the quarrel's path.'

'I am sorry,' said Flambard softly. 'More sorry than you can know. Ellie was the best of all my brats. But standing here discussing who to kill will do no one any good. It is dark outside, and it is time I was on my way.'

'What about him?' asked Odard, gesturing to Geoffrey. 'We cannot leave him. He will have Cenred after us in an instant, and he knows more than enough to bring us a traitor's death.'

'He will not betray us, because he will not want to see Roger in trouble,' said Flambard. 'We will let him go, as Eleanor wanted.'

Odard's face was pale, and he was in too much pain to

argue. 'Very well. Then let's be on our way. Roger will have to help me, because I do not think I can walk far.'

'I am not going anywhere,' said Roger softly. 'I am off to the Holy Land, to kill honest Saracens.'

'In that case,' said Flambard, 'Odard must also remain, since he says he will not be able to keep up with us. I will not risk capture because of him.'

'What?' asked Odard in horror. 'But you cannot leave me here. I have served you faithfully and without question for four years. You cannot abandon me now, just because it suits you.'

'You have not served me as faithfully as you claim,' said Flambard frostily. He picked up the box containing the snake. 'Carry this, Simon.'

'What do you mean?' asked Odard nervously. 'I have done all you asked, even murder. I have been faithful to the sacred vow I swore to my Grand Master.'

'Quite,' said Flambard enigmatically.

'Come on, Roger,' said Geoffrey, who had heard enough accusations for one day. 'There is a full moon and the sky is clear. We can be twenty miles away by morning.'

'Yes, go,' said Flambard. 'You can be of no further use to me for the time being.'

'That implies we may be of use to you in the future,' said Geoffrey coldly. 'And I can assure you we will not. Your greed and games have cost the lives of too many people already.'

'What are those lives compared to what I plan to build?' demanded Flambard dismissively, gesturing towards the cathedral. 'They are nothing!'

He began to gather his belongings, including a thick slice of Simon's pig to eat on his journey, while Simon held the snake box in dazed immobility.

'But we have Aaron's Rod!' cried Odard desperately. 'You cannot leave me now!'

'You can go back to your Grand Master,' said Flambard, 'and tell him that your four years of "loyal" service to me have not brought him what he craves.'

'What do you mean?' asked Odard indignantly.

342

Flambard gave a cold, humourless smile. 'You must think I am stupid! Do you imagine I do not know why your Grand Master sent me three knights? He knew I had Aaron's Rod, and he also knew I had hidden it. *That* was the essence of your sacred oath, Odard – not to serve me, but to discover the location of the most sacred relic in Christendom!'

'No!' cried Odard. 'That is untrue!'

'You cannot fool me,' said Flambard. 'I am a good liar – better than anyone I know – and I always recognize untruths spoken by those less skilled. Your real objective was never to serve me: it was to find out where I had hidden Aaron's Rod and steal it for the Hospitallers.'

'It is a sacred thing,' said Odard softly, evidently seeing further denials were pointless. 'It should not be hidden in dirty peasant churches or buried in the cold ground. It should be somewhere safe, where it will be revered.'

Flambard pushed his way out of the solar and down the stairs. Simon followed in a daze, carrying the box. Still clutching his arm, Odard staggered after them.

'I cannot fail now!' he cried, distraught. 'Not after four years!'

Geoffrey took one last look at Eleanor, and then grabbed Roger's arm to lead him outside. If Odard and Flambard intended to shout at each other in the street, then it would not be wise for the two knights to be present when troops came to arrest the escaped bishop and his henchmen. And Geoffrey had no intention of answering Cenred's questions about how Eleanor came to be dead, either. The story was far too convoluted, and Geoffrey was not sure what Cenred would believe. He might even decide to play safe and hand everyone over to King Henry, and they would all be executed as traitors.

Outside, the sun had long since set, and the sky was dark blue. There was a warmth in the air that had been absent before, and Geoffrey sensed spring would soon come. Snow lay in melting piles, while roofs and leaves dripped constantly. A faint crack caused Geoffrey to glance upward, to where a line of huge icicles hung like pointed fangs from the eaves of Eleanor's house. With horror, he saw one detach itself and begin to plummet down. With a yell, he barrelled into Roger, pushing him out of harm's way. The icicle smashed on the ground. Startled, Odard also glanced up.

There was another crack and Odard crumpled. The broken end of the second icicle protruded oddly from his head. It had killed him instantly, the hard ice driving through his skull to pierce the brain inside. Flambard gazed down at him dispassionately.

'That is God's divine judgement,' he declared. 'For four years he has wormed his way into my confidence, pretending to be my friend. But all the time, his sole aim was to take Aaron's Rod and present it to his Grand Master. But he shall not have it. It is mine.'

'Then it is ironic that it is no more Aaron's Rod than that icicle,' said Geoffrey softly.

'What do you mean?' asked Roger, sounding more tired than Geoffrey had ever heard him. 'It is real.'

'Of course it is not real, Roger,' said Flambard scornfully. 'How do you think such a thing could have survived all these years? What Simon is holding is the corpse of a grass snake I had prepared four years ago.' He gave a sudden diabolical grin. 'But no one knows that except you and me, and you will never be able to prove what I have just told you.'

'But why?' cried Roger, appalled.

'Why do you think?' asked Flambard with a shrug. 'It will make me rich and powerful.'

'Moon Mary was right,' muttered Geoffrey in disgust. 'But when she told us to beware of the serpent, she did not mean your dried snake – she meant you.'

Flambard laughed. 'Perhaps she did. But when Turgot and Burchard learn what they allowed to slip through their fingers, they will spread my story for me. And the Saxons would love to imagine their St Balthere playing a role in this. Everyone will believe I possess the genuine article. After all, we all know that what people believe is far more important than what is actually true.'

He sketched a mocking benediction at them, and disappeared with Simon and the snake into the gathering gloom.

Historical Note

Holy relics – either items like splinters of the True Cross or the bones of saints – were important in medieval times. The bodies of famous saints, like Cuthbert, were especially revered, although lesser-known ones, like Balthere, would also have been worthy of worship. Cuthbert was a hermit who founded a monastery on the remote island of Lindisfarne in the seventh century. Viking attacks meant the monastery had to be abandoned in the ninth century, and the monks excavated Cuthbert to take with them. The body was discovered to be 'uncorrupted', perhaps because it had been preserved by sea salt, and this was declared a miracle. Cuthbert and his monks wandered for some years before finally settling on the rocky peninsula known as Dunholm, or Durham.

The monks built a shrine, which was later replaced by a Saxon chapel, and the Church of St Cuthbert was founded. By the time of the Norman Conquest in 1066, the Church of St Cuthbert was strong and highly respected by the local people, who regarded themselves as 'Haliwerfolc' – Cuthbert's chosen. Most information from this time comes from a monk called Symeon, who wrote an account of life at Durham in the early 1100s. Cuthbert's priests were married and had families.

In 1083, a Benedictine abbey was founded, and the Church of St Cuthbert was disbanded. Symeon says most of the married priests left, although some – including men named Eilaf, Hemming, and Wulfkill, said to be direct descendants of the monks who had brought Cuthbert to Durham – remained. Symeon suggests the Norman takeover was peaceful, but the north was a rebellious place, and it is difficult to imagine the proud Haliwerfolc giving up their sacred relics to an order dominated by Normans. However, Symeon was commissioned to write his history of Durham by Bishop Ranulf Flambard, and so was unlikely to make too much of any opposition encountered.

Durham was well off for relics. Although Cuthbert was the jewel in the crown, it also boasted St Oswald, parts of St Aidan, and the Venerable Bede, all of which are still thought to be in the cathedral today. Lesser saints included Billfrith, Ceolwulf, Eadfrith, Eithilwald, and Edbert. At one point, it also possessed the bones of a Saxon hermit called Balthere, although these probably disappeared during the Dissolution.

Just after the Benedictine abbey was founded, work began on a mighty new cathedral. By 1101, the foundations for the nave had been laid, and the chancel was completed. Several times, cracks appeared in the foundations of the Lady chapel that was to be at its eastern end, and it was said that Cuthbert did not want women near his shrine in the Chapel of the Nine Altars. However, it is more likely that the ground at the eastern end of the cathedral was too unstable for such a structure. The Lady chapel, called the Galilee Chapel, was built at the west end, rather than the more usual east.

The abbey was also beginning to rise. The prior's house, chapter house, frater, and dorter were all completed by 1100, as was a small prison. The abbey, like many others, suffered during the Dissolution, although parts of it still survive, including the splendid cloisters. The cathedral is essentially Norman, and most of it was raised between 1093 and about 1130, under the driving forces of three of its prince bishops, one of which was Flambard. Visitors to this magnificent cathedral today will see that the building has been changed very little, and it is one of the finest Norman buildings in the world.

Finchale (pronounced 'Finkle') was reputed to be a wild and boggy place, inhabited by snakes and waterfowl. It stood on the banks of the River Wear, a few miles north of Durham. Much later in the twelfth century, it was occupied by a hermit called Godric, who was eventually canonized. A shrine was erected on the site of his hermitage. Later still, it became a retreat for monks, and the evocatively serene ruins can still be visited today.

In terms of people, a man named Turgot was prior of Durham Abbey in 1101. He presided over a ceremony in 1104, where the bones of Cuthbert and other saints were translated from the Saxon church to the chancel of the new cathedral. He remained in Durham until 1107, when he became Bishop of St Andrew's in Scotland, and in 1109 Flambard petitioned for him to be made Archbishop of York. He died in 1115, and was buried in the chapter house of Durham Cathedral. He was succeeded as prior of Durham by a monk called Algar.

Flambard obtained – evidence suggests that he bought for a thousand pounds – the post of Bishop of Durham in 1099. Within a year, King William Rufus had been shot in a hunting accident, and Flambard lost his protector. Rufus' younger brother, Henry, was much less tolerant of Flambard's indolent and thieving ways, and Flambard found himself arrested and placed in the White Tower of London in the autumn of 1100.

Flambard was too cunning to rot in prison for long, although contemporary sources suggest he was well looked after. A rope was smuggled to him inside a barrel of wine that he shared with his guards. While they drowsed drunkenly, he climbed out of his window, to where horses and faithful followers were waiting below. The story goes that Flambard lost the skin from the palms of his hands when the rough rope grazed them. He then fled to Normandy, apparently in company with his mother, who was a one-eyed witch.

He made his way to the Duke of Normandy, where he offered advice as to how the Duke should invade England. However, he eventually managed to wheedle himself into King Henry's favour, and was restored to the see of Durham, where he continued to oversee the building of his cathedral. The last years of his life were devoted almost entirely to architectural projects; he built much of the cathedral's nave, raised the curtain walls of the castle, and destroyed the huddle of peasants' houses that occupied the land between cathedral and castle because he deemed them a fire hazard. He died in

1128, having been ill for two years, leaving behind a number of illegitimate children.

Flambard was a colourful figure, even by medieval standards. He was unquestionably intelligent, and almost certainly worked hard on his cathedral for his own personal aggrandizement. He was a political animal, and owed allegiance to the leader who could best fulfil his interests at the time.

It is difficult to judge how long the antipathy between Norman invaders and native Saxons lasted. Certainly, Norman domination would still have smarted in 1101, only thirty-five years after Hastings. The north, perhaps because of its geographical location away from the seat of power in the south, tended to be rebellious for longer. That Norman rule entailed Normans being appointed to the most prestigious, influential, and lucrative posts must have rankled, not just among the dispossessed Saxon nobility, but among the peasantry, too. The twelfth century was a violent and unsettled age, and there is no reason to suppose that rivalries and feuds like the ones in this book did not take place.